Also by Lucy Coleman

Finding Love in Positano
Christmas at the Highland Flower Shop
Summer at Green Valley Vineyard

Christmas at the Snow Covered Inn

LUCY COLEMAN

embla books

First published in Great Britain in 2023 by

 embla books

Bonnier Books UK Limited
4th Floor, Victoria House, Bloomsbury Square, London, WC1B 4DA
Owned by Bonnier Books
Sveavägen 56, Stockholm, Sweden

A CIP catalogue record for this book is available from the British Library.

ISBN: 9781471415654

This book is typeset using Atomik ePublisher

Embla Books is an imprint of Bonnier Books UK
www.bonnierbooks.co.uk

To MaryAnn, a truly wonderful host, who made a stay in Shelburne so memorable that it inspired this novel...

Monday, 28th November

Prologue

'Good morning, Ria. It's Hayden Reynolds.'

'Oh, hi, Hayden. Perfect timing – I have some good news to share.'

· Whenever I speak to Ria, I can't help trying to conjure up a picture of her in my head, but all I get is an intriguing question mark.

'Great, I was rather hoping you'd say that.' My fingers aren't actually crossed, but mentally that's exactly the situation I find myself in.

'I've just forwarded an email on to you. The painters have addressed those final items on your father's snagging list at The Inn on the River,' she confirms. 'I suggest you check with him yourself, of course, and let me know immediately if he still has any outstanding issues. However, it looks like it's all set up ready for our arrival next week.'

With no time at all to get involved with the day-to-day issues, I've had to put my trust in a woman I've never shaken hands with. Admittedly, she did come highly recommended via a lifelong friend, and so far I have no complaints.

'I've just received the company's invoice so that's what prompted my call. I'm sure if my parents weren't happy I'd have heard by now but I'll check in with them. Thank you for the regular updates, Ria, and for smoothing things over whenever necessary.'

'Oh, that's no problem at all,' she reassures me. 'I fully appreciate how unsettling it can be for the homeowners. Having a team of tradesmen on site for a couple of months, given the size of the job, is disruptive. From the video calls

I've had with the team leader, it's all looking good and the colour palette I pulled together works really well. There are always minor issues and niggling little things that need touching up, but there didn't seem to be anything major.'

'Passing on my father's string of emails without having time to digest them was purely down to time pressure, I'm afraid.' When I did get a moment to glance over them, it was all trivial stuff, which is totally out of character for him. 'He's more of a *stand back and see the bigger picture* type of man and it's usually my mother who believes that if you take care of the small things, the bigger things will take care of themselves. However, my father finds change a little unsettling at times and, unfortunately, this seems to be one of them.'

'Don't worry, I'll be casting my own eagle eye over the finishes when I get there and I won't miss a thing. I can't wait!'

At least one of us is excited about flying out to the States next Monday. Personally, I'm dreading what we're going to be walking into.

However, I'm looking forward to meeting Ria, to put a face to that name and bubbly personality. Nothing seems to faze her and that's a quality I admire in anyone. Sadly, the thought of getting to the bottom of why my father has been so nit-picking is another matter entirely.

Monday, 5th December

Hayden

1

Honesty is the Best Policy

My stress levels are through the roof as I anxiously check my watch for the umpteenth time in quick succession. Who in their right mind would cut it this fine to catch a plane? I ask myself. And what am I supposed to do if Ria doesn't make it in time?

The seconds tick around and my heart is racing in my chest as the tension builds. Then I notice a stylish pair of navy-blue shoes draw to a halt in the gangway next to me. The person lingers for a moment, and when I glance up, a pink-cheeked woman is checking her boarding pass. When our eyes meet, we exchange pleasant smiles.

'Hayden?' she enquires, hesitantly.

I stand, hoping she didn't hear my huge sigh of relief. Until she started speaking, I thought the person in front of me was flying standby and my interior designer was a no-show.

'Ria, it's lovely to meet you at long last.'

Her smile expands as I offer my hand and we shake. 'Same here, Hayden, and thank you so much for upgrading my ticket to business class. This looks extremely comfortable.'

'Considering the favour you're doing me, it was the least I could do.' She seems totally oblivious to the fact that her late arrival sent me into panic mode.

She's actually a little younger than I was expecting, probably late twenties. There's a graceful elegance to her demeanour and she exudes a real sense of energy. With a head of dark-brown tumbling curls falling a couple of inches below her shoulders, she's the sort of woman who turns heads. 'I was rather hoping to meet up with you in the business lounge beforehand. I do hope my PA sent through all the details as I instructed?'

'She did, thank you. In fact, I received a whole package of information. I was en route to join you but one of my clients had a problem that needed a quick fix. Well, not quite as quick as I would have liked, but we got there in the end. That's why I'm late boarding.'

Hmm. A text would have been thoughtful and saved me a lot of angst. 'Well, I'm simply relieved you made it in time. This makeover is a Christmas present to my parents.' I manage to make it sound light-hearted but it's way more than just a gift, it's a lifeline. 'Anyway, let me help you with that.'

I reach out to take the heavy-looking briefcase from Ria's hand, but she shakes her head. 'No, really, I'm fine. Um, where . . .'

Doing a half-turn, I reach across and flip up the lid of the storage facility beneath the window.

She grins at me. 'Sorry, I'm used to overhead lockers and jamming things under the seat. This is so civilised.' She laughs. 'I don't care if my suitcases go missing but not my mobile office.'

Well, I can't knock the fact that she's got her priorities right, which bodes well. 'I hope you don't mind, but I assumed you'd prefer the window seat.'

'That's most kind of you, thanks.'

I step back to allow Ria to pass and watch as she stows her hand luggage away. 'It's the first time I've been to New Hampshire,' she explains, glancing at me over her shoulder. 'I had to look up the White Mountains online. I've been to the west coast numerous times.'

'Well, I hope you like snow because there's going to be lots of it!'

I watch as Ria sinks back gratefully into her seat. 'Oh, this is bliss! I've been pacing up and down for the best part of two hours making call after call. Now, thankfully, I can finally relax and think about the second half of this exciting project.' She looks at me expectantly.

'You certainly seem to have made a good start. I will warn you, in case you haven't already sussed it out, that my parents are a bit of a law unto themselves.'

'It was certainly the most unusual brief I've ever been handed.'

'Yes, and I can't apologise enough for that because I've been rushed off my feet. I simply handed my PA a memory stick full of photos my mother sent me and a one-liner description of the job on my way out the door.'

Her look is full of empathy. 'It was enough for me to provide you with a breakdown of the costs and a visual presentation. And busy is good! I hear congratulations are in order. Stylish Homes is one of the top suppliers in the country. Opening your first store in Europe is a big deal,' Ria adds, sounding impressed.

'It's been a learning curve, I will admit, but hopefully the next one will be easier. However, this personal project is very important to me. It's unfortunate that I had to clear the decks first before turning my attention to it, so now I'm on catch-up. That's why I needed a professional on board who could take control and make sure it could be achieved within a rather tight timescale.'

'I will admit that I've never liaised with painters and decorators via video calls before, or pre-ordered such a long list of furnishings and fittings without having met the customer – sorry, *customers* – face to face.'

That's another thing I like about her; she isn't just out to make a good impression, she's honest.

Her face is animated as she talks. 'Being given an unlimited budget is also a dream, so I'm not complaining. I'm assuming that if I've over-ordered, the returns won't be a problem?'

Ria's comment makes me smile to myself. 'When we get to our destination, you'll understand it's not that easy to pop out and grab a few things if there's something you've forgotten. That's why I gave you carte blanche.'

Ria gives me a reaffirming nod. 'I figured that one out when I was doing my online research. I work with a lot of property developers styling show homes. I've lost count of the number of times I've turned up with my team to stage a property and the painters are still tackling the snagging list. But I'm used to working around the problems, it's what I do best. I had an inkling from the start that this project wasn't going to be a run-of-the-mill job. When the CEO of Bespoke Interiors sends me flowers and asks if I can do him a big favour, I know he has a very special client lined up. Naturally, I couldn't refuse when he said the job called for his top freelance consultant.' A smile tweaks at her lips.

'I'll hold my hands up and say that I did call in a rather big favour, and Peter came up trumps when he gave me your details. It was a big ask, Ria, and I can't tell you how grateful I am that you're prepared to work over the festive holidays. Planning a big party to mark the reopening of the inn on Christmas Eve was my mother's idea and it worked, as they're fully booked. It—'

When an announcement overhead informs us to fasten our seat belts and make sure our seats are in their full upright position, it halts the conversation. Both Ria and I immediately reach for our phones and set them to airplane mode.

On the surface, this probably isn't too dissimilar to other jobs Ria has tackled in the past, but with the added bonus of travel and snow thrown in. When my childhood friend Peter Faulkner launched Bespoke Interiors, he put in every penny he had, but funding was tight. I extended a line of credit to him so that he could have the stock he needed upfront and pay it off further down the line.

They say a good deed never goes unrewarded and he certainly pulled out all the stops for me. Any debt he feels he owes me is now well and truly repaid. When I asked him if he could recommend a good interior designer, he told me that in just a few years Ria has made quite a name for herself.

'You aren't a nervous flyer, are you?' Ria's voice interrupts my thoughts and I realise I'm frowning.

'No. I'm just . . . it takes a while for me to switch off and wind down for the holidays, that's all.'

The steward arrives with the bottle of champagne I pre-ordered and I can see Ria is impressed. It's time to sit back and enjoy a relaxing glass of bubbly, and a reasonably good meal.

Chill, Hayden, I tell myself firmly. *Ria's here now and together you're going to pull this off. She deserves a little wining and dining for getting this far*, my conscience nags at me for good reason.

Granddad hoped that I'd be the one to take over running the inn and not my parents. That's not an option with my own business expansion plans at a crucial stage, but if I don't do whatever I can to help, then I'll be letting him – and my parents – down.

I hate awkward silences. 'How about you, Ria?'

'It's not that I don't love Christmas,' she admits, 'but for me it's simply two days spent at home with the family. The whole thing has become far too commercialised for my liking, and I draw the line at eating my turkey off a plate with Santa's face on it.'

'Hmm . . . my sentiments exactly. It's all about family, friends and tradition. I'm afraid I'm robbing you of two fun, relaxing days, though.'

We pick up our glasses and chink, her eyes smiling as she continues.

'Fun is one word for it.'

'Ah, the joys of being quizzed over the dinner table.'

'Yep. I'm the second youngest of four and my siblings are all married, two with kids, so it's chaotic. A couple of days

13

is about my limit, I'm afraid, as I don't have the stamina. I like my own space and a little peace and quiet at times. But I wouldn't change them for the world.'

When the plane begins to taxi away from the terminal at Heathrow Airport my spirits lift. I was rather hoping we'd get on; it's a long flight if you find yourself sitting next to someone and having to pretend to be asleep just to avoid conversation. I did bring a book with me just in case, as that works equally as well, but I don't think I'm going to need it.

I watch with interest as Ria leans forward, pulling the amenity kit from the pocket of the seat in front of her. It's a navy-blue pouch with white snowflakes on it and an annoying little bell on the pull string keeps tinkling as she empties the contents on to her lap.

'They don't miss a trick when it comes to churning out the Christmas paraphernalia, do they?' Ria muses, holding up a pair of navy-blue socks with snowmen on them and a matching sleeping mask. Even the lip balm, toothbrush and toothpaste, headphone covers and a small packet of biscuits are all in a matching festive theme.

'No, they don't, and with three weeks still to go it's only going to get worse,' I reply, groaning. A whole lot worse in fact, because my father is at The Inn on the River anxiously awaiting our arrival. It's usually all trimmed up by now, but I told him that he can't unpack so much as a bauble until we get there. The decorations must reflect the new, upmarket look. Ria's vision is to turn a rustic inn into a boutique-style hotel and from a purely business point of view I think she's nailed it.

Ria gives me a warm smile. 'It would be extremely helpful to have a little background about the inn, your family connection and what triggered this makeover.'

If the tables were turned, I'd want the full picture too. I guess I'd better start at the beginning.

'When my granddad, Jackson, died, my father inherited everything, including his charming, family-run inn.'

I can see that Ria's interest is piqued.

'My grandma was British, but her family settled in New Hampshire, which is where my father was born many years later. The company he worked for offered him an overseas posting and he moved to the UK when he was twenty-eight years old. He met my mother, Evie, and they settled down in Surrey. It's where I was brought up.'

Her smile is engaging. 'I had no idea you had an actual American connection.'

'The inn is a home away from home for me. Granddad worked right up until the day he died, at the age of eighty-two. Losing Grandma ten years earlier hit him hard, but the inn gave him a reason to keep going. He took on a live-in housekeeper and together with a small team of local part-time helpers, he made it a welcoming and cosy place to stay. Many of his customers came back time and time again.' I pause to collect my thoughts. 'Every Christmas, and for three weeks in summer, we'd fly over. The holidays were always magical. Granddad would hand-pick his guests, and from Christmas Eve until the second of January, it was like one big party. My mother's parents would join us sometimes, and memories like that stick with you forever.'

'Even so, the move from Surrey to the White Mountains . . . that's quite a change in lifestyle for your parents.'

'Yes, and it's coming up to their third Christmas living in the White Mountains.'

'What did they do before?'

'After a career as a corporate training and team-building specialist, my father then went into consultancy, teaching martial arts and survival training. It took him off on adventures all around the world. Naturally, he loves spending time in the White Mountains, but he's also a surprisingly good cook. He was more than happy to take on the role of chef at the inn, although normally they only offer breakfast to fee-paying guests. My mother is . . . was . . . a yoga teacher and a well-being mentor; the change in her role has had the most impact. And given that they aren't used to working together twenty-four/seven, it's been quite a challenge for them both.'

Ria pulls a face. 'Oh dear.'

'Naturally, my father feels he's finally come home. And, following in Granddad's footsteps, he likes to go over the top at Christmas. My mother is very Zen inspired. Clean lines, no clutter. Back in the UK she was able to restrain my father most of the time. Given free rein, he'd have lit up the whole street. In the White Mountains things are very different. Americans love to celebrate the holidays in grand style and, like Granddad, he's in his element.'

'Interesting. Your mother is modern contemporary, and your father is . . .' Ria pauses, casting around for an appropriate description.

'A traditionalist and a Christmasaholic – unapologetically so.'

'I see. If you have guests staying during the holidays, trimming up a hotel is rather different to decorating one's own home though.'

Ria is starting to get the picture. 'The truth is that my parents inherited a property that was outdated and struggles to attract new visitors. At the moment they're losing money every day it's open.'

'Wow. That's a tricky situation to find themselves in.'

'Granddad attracted a regular clientele who have become old friends of the family but some can no longer travel or have passed on. It's time to focus on making the inn profitable again.'

'In effect, it's a rescue package then. I can assure you that it will look stunning when we've finished, Hayden.' She leans in a little closer and I watch as she absent-mindedly scoops a stray curl away from her cheek.

'Yes. It's not been an easy time,' I continue. 'However, your input directing the team of decorators and trades who went in to blitz the place while the inn has been shut, was more significant than you probably realise. Your presentation managed to sell my parents on the idea that it was time for a makeover, and that was a huge step, particularly for my father.'

'Oh – I assumed this was their idea. I thought you were joking when you said it was a Christmas present.' Ria eyes me suspiciously. 'They're happy with what we've achieved so far . . . aren't they?'

'According to my mother, yes. I think the nit-picking comments from my father were triggered by the general disruption to their daily lives, rather than a criticism of the standard of work. He often keeps his thoughts to himself, but when he does speak up, he's not averse to saying his piece without holding back.'

'I see. He couldn't exactly refuse a Christmas gift, could he?'

I give her a wry smile. 'I did rather spring it on them. I couldn't sit back and watch everything going downhill. My granddad did his best to keep it going because he wanted the inn to have a future. I'm hoping this will guarantee it for years to come.'

'I suppose it's only natural that your father is feeling unsettled with everything in a half-finished state. Normally, I have a small team I can direct when it comes to unpacking and setting everything up. It's a pity your parents weren't amenable to drafting in some extra help.'

All I can do now is be upfront with her. 'My mother said he's reached his limit when it comes to total strangers "invading the inn" as he put it. I'm afraid you're stuck with a team of three to assist you, as he fully intends to be a part of everything that happens from here on in. I know that's not ideal, but do you think it's still possible to get everything done in time?'

Ria's forehead is pinched, but she gives me a reassuring look. 'I appreciate your honesty and, given what you've just told me, I can totally understand that. We have, what, eighteen days to get the rooms set up again before the relaunch party on Christmas Eve. I'm assuming everything I pre-ordered from your company is there waiting for us?'

'Yes.'

'Then, as a team of four working together, it should be doable.'

My body sags back into the seat, so great is the relief.

'This Christmas is a big deal in the Reynolds' household. It's the start of a new era.'

'It's obvious you're doing everything you can to make it work for them, Hayden, but it's not exactly going to be a holiday to kick back and recharge your batteries,' she warns.

'It doesn't matter. The White Mountains is the only place I could ever imagine myself celebrating Christmas, anyway.'

Ria drains her glass and I immediately grab the bottle to top it up.

'My parents have everything it takes to make The Inn on the River a special place to visit. Once the work is completed, I'm sure they'll soon get back into their stride.'

Ria frowns as my words sink in. Fortunately, the steward appears with our starter and it gives me time to gather my thoughts together.

'If I'm capable of buying up a small company on the verge of bankruptcy and turning it into a thriving business, then I'm sure that – with your help – I can find the right strategy to turn The Inn on the River into a money-maker and my parents' forever home. A place they can enjoy doing the things that come naturally to them, which is being wonderful hosts and socialising.'

'And Christmas is a time when people are usually in good spirits, so that's a big plus,' Ria replies, encouragingly.

Bringing a professional like Ria into the equation is a game-changer. My parents are polite people and having a stranger in their midst while we complete the transformation will make all the difference. Instead of the petty squabbles, which appear to have been going on while the inn has been shut and crawling with tradesmen, hopefully we'll have a blending of ideas to resolve any little issues that crop up, as the vision is brought to life. Well, that's the general idea.

2

It's a Whiteout

'I'm afraid that due to the heavy snowfall we don't have a Cadillac Escalade available. We have several that were due back to the depot, but we don't appear to have revised ETAs for them. I'm desperately trying to find a suitable replacement as all we have at the moment are seven-seater MPVs or sedans,' the guy behind the car rental desk explains, apologetically.

It's not his fault we've arrived during a snowstorm, but this is really bad news.

'We're heading for Gorham and with a three-hour-plus drive in the dark, I'm afraid a sedan won't cut it and I'd rather not be driving a seven-seater in such hazardous conditions.'

'I understand that, sir, and I can assure you that I'll do my utmost best to find you something as quickly as possible. If you'd like to take a seat, I'll make some calls.'

Ria is sitting on a bench seat over by the window, our suitcases piled up next to her.

'Bad news, I'm afraid. Due to the weather, it's going to be a waiting game. Alternatively, I can try to sort out somewhere close for us to stay overnight and we could set off in the morning.'

Ria glances down at her phone. 'It's almost eight-thirty. How long a drive is it?'

'At least three hours. Depending on how long it takes for them to find a replacement vehicle, we'd get to the inn around midnight. What would you like to do?'

'Sir?' I turn and the guy at the desk waves me over. 'There's a Ford Escape SUV being valeted as we speak. It's the best we can do unless you're prepared to wait and see what else comes in.'

Ria appears next to me, and I turn to look at her.

'What do you think?'

'If you're happy to drive, Hayden, it's fine by me. The last thing we want is to end up getting stranded here if it gets any worse. Every day counts.'

It would have been wrong of me not to ask the question, but it's heartening that she's as eager as I am to get on our way.

I sort the paperwork while Ria walks over to begin rummaging through one of her cases. By the time I'm done at the desk she's wearing thick fur-lined snow boots and a long, padded coat with a hood.

'That's better,' I muse. 'It's good to see you've come prepared.'

'I have thermals, too!' Her eyes light up and I can see she's excited about the prospect of what's to come. Let's hope it turns out to be a good experience all round.

I've driven this route every Christmas since my father decided he could trust my driving, but tonight it's difficult to get a grip in places. Ria is extremely quiet and I can sense how nervous she is; at times it's hard to see out of the windscreen. In places I slow to a crawl, as there's little on the road other than the huge snow ploughs. Sometimes even they have a tough time keeping up and it must feel relentless on a night like this.

'We're about forty-five minutes from the inn now, so the worst is behind us,' I confirm.

'I bet your parents will be worried as we're running later than expected. It's going to be almost one o'clock by the time we get there.'

'They know in conditions like this the journey takes as

long as it takes if you want to get there in one piece. Is this your first experience of a whiteout?'

Ria laughs. 'Yes, although I flew out on Boxing Day last year to Lake Tahoe with a friend to give skiing a go. It was all blue skies and gloriously sunny the whole time we were there, but even so, it was freezing. We had a great time, though.'

'Ah . . . and this year I've blown all your festive plans out the window. Now I feel bad.'

'There wasn't anything I wasn't happy to duck out of,' she states matter-of-factly. 'After being engaged for four years, I've been on my own for eighteen months now. My one regret is that friends and family assume that means I'm lonely, so all I'm missing is an endless round of parties. And well-meaning introductions to friends of friends who also happen to be single.'

'That's awkward.'

'Tell me about it. Why are people so afraid of spending time on their own? When you have a busy job, it's a luxury.'

Now that's a bit of a surprise, although I had noticed Ria doesn't wear any rings.

'I couldn't have put it any better myself. I married young and divorced a year later. It's not something I'd jump into so easily next time. To be honest, I'm too busy juggling work and coping with family matters to find time to be a considerate partner to someone. Maybe when the inn is sorted out, now that the new store in Lisbon is up and running I might be able to ease back a little. That's what I've promised my mother, anyway.'

Ria chuckles. 'Until the next opportunity rears its head.'

'I know . . . there's always something new to grab my attention. Would you mind passing me another bottle of water off the back seat, please? I'd love a coffee and I'm hungry. You must be too.'

'Starving, actually. It's all this nervous energy. I had no idea how bad the drive was going to be. I have to say, kudos to you because I wouldn't have had the courage to attempt this.'

'It's fine if you keep your eyes firmly on the road and take it real slow. Jumping on the brakes is a no-no. Can you crack the top for me? I can't risk pulling over as it's impossible to tell how deep the snow is on the verges.'

'Of course! Here you go.'

'Thanks.' I down half the bottle in one, handing it back to her to stow away. 'How long have you been running your own business?' I ask.

'Three years. It was a huge risk going out on my own but I like to pick and choose my jobs. Favours aside.'

I glance at her momentarily and see that she's sporting a broad smile.

'It's not just about the money; designing interiors gives me a buzz. I've done a few projects in France and one in Spain, but this is a real adventure.'

Ria is easy to talk to and that's a plus when it comes to working with my parents.

'For me it's all about the challenge. My granddad was a stubborn man, my father is too. It's not an easy trait to inherit. I can be a little too focused at times, but it's a problem I'm working on.'

'Any tips you'd care to share with me?' Ria asks, sounding intrigued.

'A childhood friend of mine, Izzie, is a personal trainer, and my mother talked her into putting together a fitness programme for me. As her goddaughter, Izzie didn't really like to refuse. It's supposed to help me work towards leading a more rounded lifestyle, which it probably would if I could get into a proper routine.' I feel a tad guilty because it's only three sessions a week and I can't even manage that.

Ria sighs. 'I know that feeling only too well. I'm thirty next year and you can imagine the conversation around the dining table when I'm at home. It's like you can't possibly be happy if the main focus of your life is work.'

'If the opportunities are there, you have to grab them because you might not get a second chance,' I point out.

'When I split up with my ex I don't know who was more relieved – him, or me. The pressure on us to settle down and start thinking about having a family was ridiculous. We were best friends, but in hindsight it was only really peer pressure that forced us together in the first place. I figure that with two brothers and a sister all happily married, statistically the odds of making it four out of four are slim.'

I burst out laughing. 'I'm not sure that's a good way to look at it, Ria, but you might have a point there. I'm an only child and I'm really close with my mother, but I don't call her as often as I should. I know she has her subtle little ways of keeping tabs on me.'

'That's what mums do. And it's obvious you keep an eye on your parents' well-being, too.'

'Yes, but I've spent years putting work first and it's time to redress the balance to make her happy. Regrettably, I keep falling back into my old ways.'

'Perhaps that's because you're doing it for the wrong reason.'

'Old habits die hard, I'm afraid. It's as simple as that.'

Ria gives a little laugh. 'Whatever advice I'm given, I make up my own mind. We're all so busy these days and who can blame us if we go in search of a quick fix, but it only works if it's sound advice and we stick to it.'

'Hmm . . . it's probably six weeks, maybe seven, since I last got to the gym. Just thinking about it puts me on a guilt trip.'

Ria gives me a rueful smile. 'My point exactly! The timing isn't right for you, but one day it will be.'

The rapport between us is both interesting and somewhat amusing.

'You sound like you know what you're doing anyway. I'm definitely one of the quick fixers. I'm not sure I'm quite so in tune with the inner me. To be honest, I'm happy with my life exactly as it is for now, but I make an effort to keep the peace.'

Ria nods in agreement. 'I do exactly the same thing. Even though, ironically, I have a younger sister with a two-year-old who would willingly change places with me for twenty-four hours just to get a good night's sleep. Out of the two of us, I think I'm the least of my mother's worries. Even though building a business takes time, at least I wake up each morning excited about the new day ahead of me.'

'That certainly comes across. You mentioned having a small team of helpers; are they employees?'

'No, it's not skilled work as such. It's mainly unpacking boxes and packets, ironing bedding, steaming curtains – that sort of thing. I do have a guy who is handy with a drill for putting up blinds and curtains rails. I usually pay casual staff by the hour. I have a list of reliable people; most are self-employed and work from home doing a whole range of different jobs. They're all in the creative field and working their way up the ladder.'

Hand-picking her team means details matter to her at every level.

'Learning to delegate as I built the business was the toughest challenge for me. Even now, if something goes wrong, the first thing that comes to mind is that if you want a job done properly it's best to do it yourself. Which is ridiculous, because there aren't enough hours in the day as it is, but I've succeeded in building a good management team and that's the key to success.'

Ria's eyes light up. 'That's something I've yet to experience, but it's the ultimate dream. My mother says I try too hard, but it's all or nothing, isn't it?'

'I'm afraid it is, Ria, but not everyone has the drive or determination to see it through. The problem is that I've taken my eye off the ball when it comes to my parents' difficulties. I feel like I've left them to it, when the reality is that we all have some sort of responsibility for my granddad's legacy. It's not just a case of throwing money at it, it's time for me to put that right and get hands on.'

Ria gives me an affirming nod. 'Don't worry, it's going to be just fine.'

'I, um . . . just like to keep everyone happy whenever possible. Hopefully, it will all go smoothly and tempers won't get frayed.'

'It's not easy handling differing points of view when it comes to friends and family. I can totally understand your concern. My role is to find the middle ground if there are any disagreements,' Ria points out. 'Trust me – I, too, like an easy life and that means encouraging all parties to have their say.'

I burst out laughing. 'Spoken like a true diplomat.'

'Whatever I can do to help you achieve your goal this Christmas, Hayden, I'm up for it,' she continues. 'Who doesn't want to see the people they love enjoying their lives? As much as I complain about my family, we're there for each other. It's just that at times it all gets a little claustrophobic for me, but my life wouldn't be as wonderful as it is without them.'

'Good things are best enjoyed in moderation,' I declare resolutely and out of the corner of my eye I can see her nodding her head.

'I couldn't have put it any better myself!'

'My poor dears. I've been pacing up and down for the last hour. Come in, come in!'

Ria raises her eyebrows at me and she's right; I should at least have texted to update them on our arrival time.

'Sorry, Mum. It was quite a drive and I was one hundred per cent focused on getting here.' She stands on tiptoe, throwing her arms around me and her lack of height belies her strength.

As she steps back, I do the introductions.

'This is Ria Porter.'

'Oh, Ria, it's lovely to finally meet you,' Mum says, sounding a little emotional as she gives her a hug.

'It's so good to be here, Mrs Reynolds. I feel I know the inn so well and yet in real life it's a lot bigger than I imagined.'

My mother smiles at Ria. 'Please call me Evie. Thank you for coming all this way and for giving up the comforts of Christmas with your family. Let's head into the kitchen and get you both warmed up. You must be exhausted and, I bet, rather hungry after what must have been a nightmare of a journey.'

'At last!' My father appears at the end of the hallway, hurrying forward to greet us. 'It's so good to have you home again, Hayden. And this is Ria? If it's not, we're in serious trouble.'

'Yes. Ria – this is my father, Mason.'

He holds out his hand and they shake, before turning around and giving me a firm pat on the back.

'Mason, can you take their coats please before you fire up the grill?' my mother calls out. 'I'll turn the coffee machine on. These two will sleep a lot better on a full stomach.'

My father helps Ria out of hers while I shrug mine off, then he strides away to hang them in the hallway closet.

I lean into Ria, keeping my voice low. 'You'll be plied with food. If you're not that hungry, just say. They won't be offended but Dad's franks are unforgettable.'

She gives me a grateful smile. 'I could eat a horse. Well, you know what I mean. This place is incredible!'

Mum swings open the door to the kitchen to check where we are. 'Coffee? Tea? Hot chocolate?'

'Coffee would be wonderful, thank you,' Ria replies, happily.

'Make that two, Mum. It's good to be back.'

We follow her through to the enormous kitchen and Ria is taking in every little detail. My father is a few paces behind us, and as soon as he steps through the door, he reaches out to grab his apron.

'Right. We have my signature The Inn on the River franks, hot roast beef rolls, or I can do a vegan or a vegetarian option if meat isn't your thing, Ria.'

'Oh, I love hot dogs,' she immediately replies and my father smiles broadly. 'And, Hayden?'

'I'll go for the roast beef, Dad. Maybe cut it into two as Ria might like to try it.'

Our body clocks are all over the place, but Mum is right, we'll sleep a lot better on a full stomach.

It's strange being at the inn knowing that we're the only ones here. It's a first for me, now I come to think of it. But as I gaze around the kitchen, I can picture Granddad walking back and forth, fussing over us just like my father is doing now.

Family and close friends tend to eat in here when they're visiting, rather than using the formal dining room. This table has seen a lot of celebrations and, sadly, heartache too. Especially after we lost Grandma. But its history is etched in every little dent, ding and scratch of the well-scrubbed surface. I run my hand over it, then realise I'm being silly. It's just an old farmhouse table and memories relate to people, not things.

'Ria, what do you want on your frank? My speciality is caramelised onions with a hint of garlic, a touch of French mustard and a home-made tomato salsa.'

'Yes, to everything, please, Mason.'

My father stops what he's doing to look at her, clearly delighted she isn't a fussy eater. Then he turns to face me.

'And, Hayden, what about you? A three-way?'

I nod my head enthusiastically, as my mother places two mugs of steaming hot coffee on the table. 'Please. It's a chef's special, Ria. Thinly sliced roast beef piled high on a butter-griddled onion roll with American cheese, barbecue sauce and mayonnaise. You have to try it to believe how good it is.'

'Help yourself to milk and sugar,' Mum says, as she walks back again to place another two mugs opposite us.

'I presume you cross paths with Hayden frequently, being in the business, Ria.'

'If my brain wasn't so foggy due to tiredness, I could probably work it out in terms of hours, but my watch is still on UK time,' Ria jests, casting me a sideways glance.

'We met in person for the first time on the plane, Mum.'

'I'm a devoted customer though,' Ria declares. 'I spend hours in Hayden's stores around the country, choosing items.'

'I didn't know that. I do hope he wasn't head down working during the flight, Ria. Hayden has this habit of getting caught up in something and tuning out.'

. 'Not at all. The flight was fine, we talked for most of the journey although, thankfully, we did manage to get a couple of hours' sleep.'

My father hums to himself softly while he moves between the grill and the frying pan, where onions, garlic and a handful of herbs are filling the air with the most appetising smell. It's making my stomach rumble.

'Honey, can you set up the plates and grab some napkins, please?' my father calls out and my mother is on it.

'Are you pleased with the work on the inn so far?' Ria ventures, hesitantly. 'The photos certainly looked amazing.'

My mother is busy lining plates up on the stainless-steel counter next to the grilling station, but my father stops and does a half-turn to look directly at her. His light-hearted mood instantly changes. He furrows his brow and, if I'm not mistaken, that was a glare he just flashed my mother. It's becoming clear that there have been some more serious disagreements between the two of them over the work that's been done and, for whatever reason, they've chosen to keep me in the dark about it.

'It's such a huge transformation that, to be honest, Ria, we haven't had a chance to stop and take it all in since the painters and the plumbers left.' My mother's words come tumbling out and she sounds a little flustered. 'We've been working flat out cleaning and packing things up ready to put into storage, isn't that right, Mason?'

The ensuing silence is ominous.

'I said, isn't that right, Mason?' She presses my father for a reply. It's not at all like him to be rude in company.

'Well, you've been directing me, Evie, and I've been doing exactly as I'm told.'

My mother looks mortified but quickly recovers her composure. 'We've had a few disagreements deciding what had to go and what can stay,' she explains. 'I'm really looking forward to the next bit.'

'There's so much character in the fabric of a building like this, that the less-is-more approach often accentuates those wonderful features and really brings them to life.' Cleverly, Ria picks up the conversation, choosing to take it in a slightly different direction.

'That's the point I made, Mason, wasn't it?' My mother tries to draw my father back into the conversation again, but he simply shrugs his shoulders and carries on with what he's doing.

Unfazed, she continues. 'I think the whole place was badly in need of a refresh and I can't wait to see each room brought to life again.'

This time my father makes a disparaging 'harrumph' as he passes my mother a platter piled high, before lightly buttering the onion rolls for the steak and then browning them on the griddle.

'Mason isn't one for change but he's coming around, aren't you, darling?' The question goes unanswered.

My father clearly has the hump over something, but it's my mother's body language that is worrying me. She looks anxious.

'I can't wait to make a start,' Ria continues, sounding full of enthusiasm, even though she must be equally as tired as I am. Ria is making an effort to be upbeat. Me, I'm sitting here wondering what's going on.

As my mother slices the hot dog buns and places a frankfurter in each one, she passes them back to my father to put on the toppings. When he lays a plate in front of

Ria, her eyes light up and he stands there eagerly waiting for her to take that first bite. Give the woman her due, she plays the game and even before she swallows, she lets out a satisfied groan.

'Now that hits the spot and some. I've had a lot of these on my visits to the west coast, but this is by far the best I've ever tasted, Mason. Thank you for cooking for us at this unearthly hour.'

Judging by the look of satisfaction on my father's face, she's cracked it. If that's an act, then it's deserving of an award, but judging by the way Ria is wolfing it down, I can't wait to see her reaction to the beef roll. I'm a foodie myself; it's one of life's little pleasures and suddenly I'm looking forward to introducing Ria to some gastronomic firsts. New Hampshire has so much to offer, and food is high up on the list.

For now, I'm choosing to sidestep the invisible, albeit obvious, elephant in the room. There's an uncharacteristic sense of disparity between my parents that I wasn't expecting. It's something I hope I can quickly get a handle on, so we can deal with it. No doubt a part of the tension is due to my mother being on edge, knowing how bad the driving conditions are out there, but I fear it goes even deeper than that. Saying everything is fine when it clearly isn't, doesn't exactly fill me with a sense of optimism.

Ria

3

Divide and Conquer

'Hi, Mum. We're at the inn and I'm just about to take a shower before I collapse into bed.'

'Ah . . . I've been dozing off and on since you texted to say the plane had landed. You sound exhausted, but it's wonderful to hear your voice. And a relief for your dad and me to know you've arrived at your destination safe and sound.'

'I probably won't surface for another seven hours so I didn't want to just text. You're such a worrier!'

'It's what mums do. What time is it there?'

'Two in the morning, which means it's what . . . seven in the morning in the UK?'

'Yes, we're just having breakfast. How was the flight?' Mum's questions usually skirt around what she really wants to know, which is *what do I think about my client now that I've met him in person?* Nothing about this job has been normal so far and Hayden himself is a bit of a surprise.

'Great. Although flying won't ever be the same for me again after going business class.'

'And the inn?'

'It was pitch black and snowing heavily when we arrived about an hour ago, so I can't wait to see it all in daylight.'

'Your dad and I have been following the weather updates for the White Mountains. We thought that maybe you'd find a hotel near the airport to stay overnight.'

'Oh, my client is used to driving in the snow. Hayden spends Christmas here every year.'

'I bet his family really love having him home. It must be even better when you can accommodate everyone under one roof!'

While my parents would never put me on a guilt trip, it's obvious they're disappointed I won't be a part of this year's celebrations. When I broke the news, they both plastered on a smile, doing that proud parent moment because they understood that this project is a bit of a coup for me. What interior designer wouldn't jump at the chance of doing a job for the CEO of Stylish Homes? Let alone staying at his family's home in the White Mountains.

'It's also a business, remember. Anyway, I'm struggling to keep my eyes open. The welcome was amazing and I've just eaten the best hot dog ever.'

Mum chuckles. 'As long as they keep you well fed, you'll soon sort them out. Is there a . . . um . . . a chance you might make it back before Christmas Day if things go smoothly?'

Aww. The tinge of hope in her voice is poignant. 'I doubt it. There's a lot to do, and part of my remit is to make sure that when the inn is reopened I'm here to remedy any little snags. Besides, the chance of changing my flight at the last minute is highly unlikely.' There's no point in giving them false hope, but who knows?

'Oh well, we'll make New Year's Eve a bumper celebration instead. Actually, I'm thinking of doing a rerun of Christmas dinner before the party kicks off in the evening, what do you think?'

I shake my head, thinking only Mum would come up with that suggestion to make sure I don't feel left out this year.

'It sounds perfect . . .' I trail off, unable to suppress a huge yawn.

'Thanks for calling, lovely. The worst bit is over. Sleep well. I know you're going to be busy, so just call or text if, and when, you can. Love you!'

'Love you all, too.'

When I open my eyes, it takes a few moments for my brain to kick in. I slept like a log, and as I come to, I glance around the room feeling a little disorientated. The two long sash windows to my right are bare, and aside from the sturdy four-poster bed, there's only one bedside table and a single chair in the far corner of what is a well-proportioned room. What excites me is that, lying here, I can see tall trees heavily laden with snow. It's a winter wonderland setting and I jump out of bed, eager to get a closer look.

Oh, my goodness! Aside from the fact that a shiver runs down my spine because it's a little chilly, this is incredible. My phone pings and I scurry over to grab it before diving beneath the covers once more. It's just after seven and yet I feel refreshed and raring to go as I read Hayden's text.

Let me know when you're awake and I'll bring you up a coffee. Don't rush, it was a late one and my parents won't surface for a while.

My fingers get busy.

Give me twenty minutes and I'll join you in the kitchen.

Seconds later, there's another ping.

I hope you're hungry.

Finally experiencing the inn for myself, when we make the change over to duvets they're going to thank me. I mean . . . sheets, several blankets and a handmade patchwork quilt, and still I woke up feeling chilly. It's also a lot of bedding to launder and I was delighted when Hayden gave me the go-ahead. I bet his mother breathed a sigh of relief!

The bare bones of the room are fine now that the old

dark wood panelling has been painted a soft grey, with the walls and ceiling a pristine white. But it was clear from the awkwardness between them last night that Hayden's parents are divided, and that's something I need to address with him before we make a start.

'Morning!' I call out, breezily as I step into the kitchen. The smell of bacon frying makes my mouth water.

Hayden has a spatula in his hand and is tossing a pancake. 'A bit of a chilly one, too,' he replies over his shoulder. 'I hope I didn't wake you, Ria, as that wasn't my intention.'

'Oh, you didn't. I was looking out the window and marvelling at the view.' I loiter uneasily.

'Take a seat.'

'Um . . . can I make myself useful?'

'OK. The coffee machine is switched on, there's a touch pad. I'll have an Americano, please.'

Approaching the machine with a little trepidation, I grab one of the mugs off a warming plate on top of it and place it on a small metal grille beneath the spout. Here goes. One press and within twenty seconds the beans are ground and that comforting, slightly bitter aroma fills the air. It dispenses a single espresso with a wonderful tan-coloured crema on the top, and then fills it two-thirds full with hot water. Any restaurant that doesn't serve a good cup of coffee isn't worth visiting in my opinion, and I'm impressed, given this is really a B & B. We're about to turn it into a countrified boutique hotel, and once Mason and Evie adjust to the changes, I hope it will inspire them in ways they can't quite see yet.

'Milk . . . sugar?' I enquire and Hayden turns to smile at me.

'No. As it comes, thanks. Do you want bacon or fruit with your pancakes?'

'Oh, bacon would be great.'

I walk over to the table and place the mugs down, feeling

a tad awkward that my client is cooking for me. Hayden looks at home standing in front of the cooker, which is a bit of a surprise. He's obviously a man of many talents.

'Take a seat, Ria, it's almost ready. I was hoping we'd be able to catch up before my parents surfaced.'

I take a tentative sip of coffee, letting out a satisfying sigh. 'Me, too, actually. Oh, this is just what I needed.' I'm in danger of burning my tongue, so I stop to blow on it.

'Right. Help yourself to maple syrup. It's from a local supplier here in the White Mountains. Fuller's Sugarhouse is a small, family-owned-and-operated business that specialises in gourmet coffee beans and locally produced maple syrup. My grandfather has dealt with them for years.'

'He has?' I query, a little confused.

'Sorry *had*. But he's not gone, he'll always be here with Grandma in spirit.'

Aww . . . what a lovely thought! 'I can't wait to do the tour both inside and out.'

Hayden hands me a plate with a stack of three fluffy-looking pancakes and some strips of golden brown, crispy bacon.

'I feel really spoilt.' I give him a warm smile and wait for him to take the seat opposite me.

Hayden passes me a small jug of maple syrup. 'It's my pleasure. I don't know how long we have, so if you don't mind talking over breakfast, I think we need to hatch a plan.'

At least he realises we have a bit of a problem. 'Most definitely.'

We begin eating and I figure he's waiting for me to set the scene.

'Your mother seems to be on board with the overall changes. However, I'm sure she'd love a little time to catch up with you this morning. It might be a good idea if you could offer to cast your eye over the furniture they've decided not to use. Just in case there's anything you feel attached to, or maybe even something you feel your father might have . . .' Hmm, I'm not sure how to put this.

Hayden's face brightens and, as I pop a loaded fork into my mouth, I wait for his reaction.

'. . . given up on, when they were bickering back and forth about it? That's good thinking. He tends to withdraw, rather than risk getting into a full-blown argument, if he can see that my mother's patience is wearing thin.'

'I did notice. Ideally, I'd like to spend some one-to-one time with him this morning.'

'To get him on your side?'

I point at the pancakes on my plate. 'These are really good,' I commend him. 'No, it's really more about listening to what his expectations are for the final look. It's his home too and I don't want him to feel his voice isn't being heard.'

Hayden puts down his fork and picks up his coffee, cradling it in his hands. 'Right, I get it. Maybe he can take you on a tour of the outside while I spend an hour or two with Mum.'

'That works for me. Then we'll swap over, and your mother can give me a tour of the inside. By then, hopefully, I'll have a better understanding of what the real issues are before we make a start. It's vital they feel you and I are taking time out to listen to what they have to say, but preferably when they aren't in the same room together.' I hope he doesn't think I'm being rude, but there isn't time to waste with endless back and forth that gets us nowhere.

'Your people skills are exemplary,' Hayden replies, a look of relief flashing over his face.

'I deal with this sort of thing almost every single day of my working life. Believe me when I say that it's rare to find a couple who agree on everything, or even a developer and his team, for that matter. Sometimes people can't quite see the vision until it's done. But if there's more than one person calling the shots, things can become a little fraught at times.'

As Hayden is about to reply, the door opens and his father appears.

'Mornin', guys! I thought I could smell bacon, but Evie

insisted it was my imagination. I'll just take her up a coffee so she can have a bit of a lie-in, then I'll come and join you.'

Hayden gives me a knowing look as his father walks over to the coffee machine.

'I'll do that, Dad. Why don't you grab some breakfast from the warming plate? Afterwards, Ria is keen to have a tour of the grounds and get her first proper view of the inn. I was wondering whether you'd do the honours?'

'Of course I will. It would be my pleasure.'

I struggle to suppress a little smile. Well done Hayden for tackling that first thing, especially as Evie isn't here. It would have been difficult if she'd suggested she join me and Mason.

'It's really cold again this morning,' I remark to Mason, as we trudge across a path of compacted snow. We're heading for a picket fence beneath the sign advertising the inn. 'What temperature is it today?'

'Thirty-three degrees Fahrenheit. It always warms up a little when there's a heavy snowfall.'

'What's that in Celsius?'

'Probably minus one. Here you go, let's stop here. And this, as they say, is the money shot.'

As I turn, he's right. The Inn on the River is simply stunning. It sits on a flat plain and I should imagine that beneath the snow there's probably a wide swathe of grass that sweeps around a sprawling collection of buildings. A variety of trees frame the picture, an interesting mix of leafless skeletons intermingled with firs.

'Wow. A Christmas tree doesn't need baubles and a star on the top, all it needs is a generous coating of snow!' I exclaim. 'It's breathtaking, Mason. Aside from the incredible scenery, I'm guessing the inn itself dates back a good couple of hundred years?'

'Yes. It was built in the early eighteen hundreds.'

The main buildings are set towards the rear of this large parcel of land and there's a collection of smaller wooden huts or cabins at the far end which abut a sprawling forest. The inn itself, with its offset gables, has a magnificent and imposing three-storey facade. Either side of it, two-storey wings extend in both directions and in the far right-hand corner there's a quirky turreted addition.

Cladded with pine boards and with a shingle roof to the charming wrap-around raised porch, it's picture perfect. The windows, with their cute shutters, dominate from every angle and, aside from the two chimney stacks standing proud on the A-line roof, three dormer windows grace both sides at the third-floor level.

'It's Federal style, with the farmer's porch and a backyard that would originally have housed the animals but is now filled with raised beds. My father liked to grow as much as he could, so everything was fresh to the table, and he was also passionate about trees.'

'It was a farmhouse originally, then?'

'Yes. My grandparents turned it into an inn. It was the only home my father ever knew.'

'My goodness, that's quite something, Mason.'

He seems perfectly happy to chatter away and I'm pleasantly surprised; maybe last night he was too tired to talk. 'I think so, too. We're on the northern side of Mount Washington, in the north-east corner of New Hampshire. In the spring you can see Giant Falls from here as it tumbles over the Mahoosuc Range in Shelburne.'

'It certainly has that Old England charm, but it's way more beautiful in person; the photographs don't do it justice in my opinion. The grounds look extensive.'

'Oh, they go quite a way back. Beyond that range of trees behind the main building. Let's have a wander.'

I can't take my eyes off the beauty of the place as we trample fresh snow, making a crisp, crunching sound as we walk. The trees that loom up all around us seem to add an echo to our footsteps. It feels cosy and private, and yet the reality is that we appear to be in the middle of nowhere.

Mason leads me over to some ranch fencing to the rear of the plot where the trees are much denser. There's a wide swathe beyond where the snow is pristine as far as the eye can see.

'I want to jump over the fencing and throw myself down to make a snow angel,' I blurt out.

'Please don't,' Mason begins laughing. 'We're on the banks of the Androscoggin River, and while the ice is mighty thick, it's not advisable.'

My jaw drops. 'Oh my . . . I had no idea!'

'You're perfectly fine this side of the fence, and a little further along there is a trail that's safe to walk. It's been well trodden by four generations of our family now.'

Mason's voice wavers a little. His connections to this place run deep and rightly so.

'It's tranquil here,' I reply, softly.

'Evie complains about the isolation sometimes, but that's what I love about the area. Little changes, only the seasons. Over the years we've lost a few trees, but for every single one my father planted another two in its place.'

'Are they all indigenous to the area?'

'Mostly. We have quite a few sugar maples here. New Hampshire produces around ninety thousand gallons of maple syrup every sugaring season. Then there are some American beech and eastern white pine. Mountain holly, too, which looks glorious at this time of the year. And black walnut. The latter was one of my granddad's favourite woods, apparently. It has a fine straight grain, and traditionally it was used for gunstocks; it also made hard-wearing pieces of furniture built to stand the test of time.'

'I've never seen a walnut tree before,' I declare and Mason grins at me.

'It's always a case of being quick to harvest the nuts before the crafty squirrels get 'em, of course. My old man made a wonderful apple walnut ice cream. It was one of the highlights of my Christmas when I was a kid. It was my job to keep an eye out and chase the little critters off.'

I'm touched that Mason is happy to take the time to share some of his precious memories with me. But on a practical level, a huge place like this requires constant maintenance, and to ensure that, the inn requires a healthy income stream. Closing it for a period to carry out the work will have added extra pressure on top of everything else.

'And Christmas is your favourite time of the year?'

His smile grows exponentially as we make eye contact. 'Ah, Hayden has been filling you in. Go big or don't bother, is my motto when it comes to putting up the lights. It drives my dear wife mad. She says it isn't tasteful.' His eyes widen. 'A little sparkle brightens up the dark winter days; where does tasteful come into it?'

I make a mental note to tackle that topic first when we all get together.

'Can I get a tour of the outbuildings? One of them is a lodge, isn't it?'

'Yep. We don't use it in the winter, as it only has a log burner to warm it, but we sometimes let it out in the summer. Come and have a look.'

It's quite slow going given the depth of the snow, but when we step up onto the porch and I wait as Mason pulls out a bunch of keys, I turn around to take in the view from yet another angle. At this end of the plot the height of the trees obscures the mountains in the distance. The air is full of a variety of scents, the strongest of which is very distinct. It's fresh but almost medicinal.

'The firs here are lovely and that smell reminds me of Christmas morning, peeking over the banisters to peer through the sitting-room door to see if Santa had been.' I think back fondly to some of my earliest childhood memories.

'Balsam firs, mostly. My mother said it was sweet like a rich balsamic vinegar with a grounding woody fragrance. To me it just smelt like camphor and reminded me of a rub she'd use on my chest if I caught a cold. Right, come on inside.'

Mason unlocks the door to the log cabin and we step onto a colourful rug, stopping to slip off our wet boots. The air is chilly, but as I wander around the open-plan area I notice there's a free-standing heater with a timer on it to ensure the cabin doesn't get damp. It's everything you'd expect from a traditional cabin in the woods. Heavy dust sheets encase what are obviously two large sofas, but it's surprisingly minimalist in here. A solid oak table doubles up as an island and, in the far corner, the kitchen is made up of free-standing units.

'I store most of the Christmas decorations upstairs. There's a large bedroom and a bathroom up there. As a kid, I had a few birthday parties in here and many a sleepover with a gang of friends. Didn't end up getting much sleep, but we sure had some fun times.'

'I bet. This is delightful, Mason.'

He tugs at the sleeve of his ski jacket, checking his watch. 'We'd better head back. Evie will be wondering where we are.'

There's no edge to his voice when he says that and I'm curious now about what exactly the problem is between them.

4

The Work Begins in Earnest

When Mason and I join Hayden and Evie in the kitchen, the mood is quite jolly. Given the amount of sleep we've had, I was a little worried whether tempers would be short. However, after another strong cup of coffee and a delicious, freshly baked apple and pumpkin muffin, everyone seems eager to make a start.

'Right, it's day one and with eleven bedrooms and suites, the hallway, landings and the three main communal rooms on the ground floor to stage, it's going to be tight.' There's no point sugar-coating it because that's what we're facing.

'Tell us what you want done and we'll get to work,' Hayden confirms, glancing at his mother first and then his father. They nod their heads in agreement.

'Evie, it would help to have a quick look around the inn just to get my bearings and we can decide on which room to tackle first. Maybe one of the smaller ones. While we're doing that, perhaps you two guys can start sorting out the Christmas dec—'

Evie interrupts, glancing nervously at Hayden. 'I'd like to be a part of that, too.'

Hayden flashes me a look of concern.

'Naturally, but it would really help us to quickly finalise the overall style if we can see what we have to work with. I'm sure we'll be able to accommodate everyone's preferences and still achieve that festive ambience without detracting from the new, upmarket feel we're aiming for.' I smile at Evie and to my relief she seems content with that. Mason isn't.

'Folk are wondering why the inn isn't all lit up already, so we're running way behind. What sort of message does that send out to the community when we're supposed to be building up to the big relaunch? Besides, I don't see what all the fuss is about. Now Hayden's here, the two of us should be allowed to get on with it. You can't control everything, Evie, and you've more than had your say when it comes to what's been done so far.'

'You're missing the point,' she replies firmly.

I glance in Hayden's direction. It's time he spoke up.

'Perhaps we can unpack everything and lay it all out on the floor of the cabin,' Hayden suggests. 'The lights will all need checking anyway, won't they, Dad?'

Mason replies with a disparaging, 'Hrmph. It seems I don't have a choice in the matter.'

'Stop making a fuss, Mason,' Evie retorts, her tone clipped.

If this is typical of what's been going on for the last two months, no wonder they're both on edge.

'Naturally, we'll have a session together to discuss ideas about the placement of the decorations. I've put together some visuals that I hope you'll find inspiring. Something similar will make the inn feel festive and welcoming ready for the party. I'll just grab my notebook, Evie, and meet you on the top landing, in say, five minutes?'

I think Mason and Hayden need a little time alone together to talk. There are three people's views to consider and it won't work if Hayden is going to sit back and say nothing every time his parents disagree over something. In fact, that might be the root of the problem. Was Mason disappointed Hayden didn't jump in and take his side when he had the opportunity? I ponder. If that's been his typical response to everything his father has raised since the project began, Mason might have reason to feel a tiny bit resentful. To be honest, I was a little shocked when Hayden revealed on the flight over that he'd simply been forwarding his father's emails to me without really taking the content on board. Now that's called burying your head in the sand, and no good can come of that.

It's a bewildering array of rooms and each of them is unique in some way or another. Often, it's the view.

'I love the dual aspect rooms, Evie. And with the three-storey turret, the unusual en-suite bathrooms add a touch of quirkiness to the bigger suites. But even the smaller bedrooms are charming with the half-height wall panelling.'

'Your colour palette was spot on, Ria. I would never have gotten Mason to agree to painting the panelling, but even he begrudgingly admits that it makes everything seem a lot lighter and brighter. And it's not bland; we don't have the same colour throughout. Just soft, subtle shades that are calming.'

It seems that Evie's vision of perfection and Mason's are poles apart. To her mind, the aesthetics and ambience are everything. From his viewpoint, I fear that we're paring down and stripping out the very things that remind him of the past; our nostalgic little chat this morning hinted at that. Reading between the lines, I think he wanted me to understand what it all means to him.

'Where would you like us to start today?' I ask.

Her eyes light up. 'Room number seven.'

'Oh, the one on the top floor that looks out across the river to the rear. I had no idea the river was there!' I laugh. 'I thought it was a field with snow on it, until Mason mentioned it.'

Her face lights up. 'Just stay this side of the fence if you go wandering and you'll be fine.'

'Is there any reason the rooms don't have individual names?'

'They've always had numbers. Why?'

This is a chance to build bridges. The idea came to me when Mason and I were looking around the grounds. I'm hoping he'll see it as a way of acknowledging his father's love of nature. And, more importantly, a meaningful gesture if it comes from his wife.

'With so many marvellous trees around I just thought . . . maybe next time we're all around the table together, it might be worth you raising the subject, Evie.'

'Oh, what a lovely idea, Ria. I will.'

'Good. Let's make our way back to room seven and work out what we need. Then we'd better start unpacking those boxes. Hayden was most accommodating and they should all be numbered.'

'He's a thoughtful son and a good businessman. I just wish . . . well, who knows where the future will lead us? I know for a fact that life's little complications are par for the course. Still, we have a solution to make the inn profitable again, and fingers crossed it'll save the day.'

If this truly is a make-or-break situation then perhaps it isn't about egos or differences of opinion; it could be panic because Christmas is looming.

On first sight what we have now is a blank canvas and I'm confident things will soon start coming together in a cohesive way. At the moment it looks like a shell. However, when I suggested they strip out anything surplus to requirements, I can appreciate now why Mason might have been upset. In the before photos there was an abundance of furniture; Evie's desire to declutter – and streamline the look – has been a tad heavy handed.

'Let me see . . . room seven . . .' I check through my notebook. 'It has its own bathroom, but it's across the hallway.'

'Yes. Oh, we have some wonderful soft furnishings for this room and I think you're going to adore the pattern. Let's get busy.'

The guests' dining room is stacked full of boxes. I wasn't kidding when I said to Hayden that I hope returns won't be a problem. I wanted to give Mason and Evie options if my vision for each room didn't quite meet with their expectations. An hour and a half later, the new bedding is ironed and we're finally able to make up the two single beds.

'This was one of the biggest issues for Mason,' Evie reveals as I place two pillows on each bed and then search around for the bolster cushions as a finishing touch.

'It was?'

'Yes. The idea of moving to duvets and covers is a huge deal for him. Sheets, blankets and handmade quilts remind him of his childhood.'

I stop what I'm doing and straighten to look at her. 'I fully understand that, but when you're dealing with eleven rooms it's more practical, Evie.'

Having read the reviews for the hotel, this topic cropped up time and time again. Even adding extra blankets doesn't always keep out the chill, and in December the temperatures are going to plummet. Some overseas visitors actually stated that they would have preferred to have had the option of a duvet.

'Mason finds it hard to accept the need to modernise the inn, but he isn't the one who changes the beds or does the dusting. It was filled with items his parents collected over a lifetime and while I understand his nostalgia, this is a business and now it's our home, too. I just feel there's hardly anything of *us* here. It's all back in the UK.'

I can only hope that once this room is put back together, it's enough to convince him it was the right decision. At the moment it seems he has a real problem visualising it, and who can blame him?

'Evie, I'm happy with the soft furnishings and the bedding, but it's lacking something. I don't suppose you and Hayden found any items of furniture you had second thoughts about, this morning, did you?'

She hesitates for a moment or two. 'There were a few things he said it would be a real shame to get rid of.'

That's all I need to hear. 'Maybe we could go and have a quick look?'

50

'Of course.' She stops to look around. 'It does look lovely now. I hated all that dark wood everywhere. I can't believe the difference it's made.'

'If you can find an interesting little table, I have the perfect ornament inspired by the pattern on the duvet, and a sidelight I think you'll love.'

Evie's eyes light up. 'I have just the thing. Mason will be delighted, as it was one of his mother's favourite pieces of furniture. I thought that maybe you'd think it was a little too old-fashioned to fit in.'

That makes me feel as if I haven't done my job properly. With the brief I was given, and with no direct contact with Hayden's parents, I was working blind.

'If there's anything at all either you, or Mason, want included then we'll find a place for it. I design interiors for property developers, hotels and corporate venues, as well as for homeowners. Each project is different and unique. The inn offers its guests a more authentic feel and that's important.'

Evie's brow furrows. 'How do you get the balance right?'

'The first thing I did was to jump online and check out your competitors' websites. Then I trawled through the online reviews for The Inn on the River. Things like that carry a lot of weight and it's important that the inn stands out when people are looking for a place to stay in the area.'

'Goodness, I had no idea how much work went into getting to this stage in the process. Hayden didn't mention that to me, I mean us.'

I'd assumed he would have passed on a copy of the overview I attached to the presentation I sent him, but it seems not and that's puzzling. Yes, there were quite a few negatives, but I rather hoped that would be a bit of a wake-up call.

'Your guests love the ambience of the building and the feedback on the hosting, cleanliness and awesome breakfasts was glowing. They also loved the small touches . . . the home-made cookies and cakes left in the rooms each afternoon. But it's important to meet all your guests' expectations and with the changes we're making we'll be addressing the main issues. Mostly, that centred around the inn looking a little tired, the decor being rather busy and problems with the hot water supply to some of the showers.'

'There were a couple of major plumbing issues that were on our to-do list. Hayden was right suggesting we shut the inn to allow us to get everything done in one go.'

'And I understand that must have been quite stressful for you both, but the end is in sight. What we don't want to do is to strip out the things that enhance the character and the history of the place.'

'Perhaps we have been a little hasty in clearing some things out.' Evie leans forward to smooth out the duvet cover, avoiding eye contact. 'Right, it's almost one o'clock and lunch will be ready soon. Afterwards, we'll check out that table and maybe find a chair or two.'

'That sounds good to me.' I certainly don't want Mason to see the room until it's perfect, because naturally he's more emotionally attached to what's here than Evie. It's important to gain his trust. I have an idea that I'm going to put forward when we get together later this afternoon before we do the reveal.

'Thank you for lunch, Mason, that was amazing. It's the first time I've had New England clam chowder and I hope it won't be the last.'

Mason is noticeably subdued but he gives me an engaging smile. 'New Hampshire has plenty of wonderful seafood recipes. Hayden must take you out to Shelley's Bar and Grill one night, to try their lobster rolls. Then I'll make you one from a recipe my father inherited from his mother. My great-grandma's version wins hands down!'

Hayden chuckles. 'It's a battle of the recipes between Dad and Shelley, but it goes back a long way.'

'Right,' Evie pronounces, suddenly pushing back on her chair. It scrapes the floor, noisily. 'I'll just get these plates washed while you clean up, Mason.' Her tone is unnecessarily sharp, which is puzzling.

I glance across at Hayden and he tilts his head discreetly in the direction of the door.

'Ria, would you like a hand shifting some of the boxes in the dining room before we all start work again?'

'Um . . . well, yes, but can I lend a hand in here first?' I feel awkward being treated like a guest when I'm not, but Mason immediately replies.

'No, we're fine. You've a mountain to tackle in there. We'll uh . . . have dessert and coffee a bit later?'

Hayden and I both nod in agreement as we head for the door. Evie is making quite a clatter as she swills off the pans before loading them into the dishwasher. It's time to make a hasty exit.

Once we're out in the hallway, Hayden looks at me, pulling a face. 'Sorry about that. And I will take you into Shelley's, it's just that she's not one of Mum's favourite people.'

'I'll try to remember that,' I acknowledge, keeping my voice low. 'Thanks for the heads-up.' Whatever the issue is, it looked like a playful, off-the-cuff remark turned out to be a bit of a mistake.

However, when we open the double doors into the spacious dining room, Mason wasn't joking about this. The stack does rather resemble a mountain. It obscures at least half of the room.

'What are we searching for?' Hayden enquires, standing with his hands on his hips.

'The boxes marked Z.'

'Z for . . . ?'

'Miscellaneous items that haven't been allocated to a specific room. There are various ornaments and sidelights I thought might work. I'm glad I added them as an afterthought, as Evie tells me that few of the existing ones were worth keeping and they've already been disposed of.'

'Yes, she had a really good sort-out.' Even Hayden sounds miffed about it.

'I will be reclaiming some of the furniture they set aside, but sometimes just switching things around makes an item more useable, if you know what I mean.'

'The right piece in the right place. I think my father will appreciate it.'

'I think so too.'

'Right, I'll trawl through the boxes and pass them to you until we find what you're looking for. You seemed to get on well with my father this morning. He's been quite cheerful as we've been unravelling the lights. He loves to talk about the old days but he can go on a bit at times.' It's obvious that Hayden is curious about what was discussed.

'He was telling me about the river. I had no idea how close it was to the inn. And about the trees, which got him talking about his own father.'

'It was a smart move letting him natter away,' Hayden confirms.

That comment doesn't sit well with me. 'It wasn't a "move"; it's great to learn more about New Hampshire and the White Mountains in general. And the history of the inn.'

'But you did your research before you came.'

I look at Hayden, narrowing my eyes a little. 'Yes, but Mason is an interesting man and it's anecdotal stories that help people to really connect with their surroundings.'

'Oh, right.' Well, that remark went straight over Hayden's head. 'Ah . . . I've found a whole stack of your miscellaneous boxes. I'll put them over by the china cabinet. At least that made the cut.'

I continue searching, while trying to fathom out whether that last comment came from the heart, or whether he was being facetious. Hayden must have his own attachment to some of the things here. 'This makeover is the end of an era your father remembers with great fondness, Hayden. Maybe he didn't appreciate that the inn will look totally different afterwards and he's struggling with the reality of it.'

'But that's the general idea, Ria,' he replies, sounding rather blasé to my ears. 'If the bills don't get paid, this could drain their bank account of every penny they have.'

'I understand that all right, it just sounded like you, too, were getting nostalgic there for a moment.'

He stops what he's doing to glance in my direction. 'That's a luxury I don't think my parents, or I, can afford at this stage.'

That was a prickly response.

'Now I understand a little better what the inn means to Mason, it's simply a case of treading carefully.' It's a well-meant warning which I hope Hayden will take on board.

'The reality is that the inn needs a small team to keep everything ticking over. They've managed with just a groundsman, the occasional help from a cleaning company owned by a lovely lady named Kendall, and a local woman who comes in at breakfast time to help wait on the tables if required. No wonder they're both tetchy, the pair of them haven't stopped since the day they took over.'

'You're convinced this will work, aren't you?'

Hayden shrugs his shoulders. 'In business you have to put your feelings to one side, that's why I've stepped in. I love this place too, but if my parents can't make it work, I honestly don't know how my father will handle it.'

I can't help wondering whether Hayden is talking about himself, too, and not just Mason. He did say he couldn't imagine spending Christmas anywhere else.

'And how about your mother?'

His arms are wrapped around a box and he turns his head to give me a quizzical look. 'She's the one who keeps it real. Without her, he'd flounder.' Hayden says it with conviction and I hope I haven't just put my foot in it. 'They differ on a lot of things, but when it comes down to it they've always had each other's backs.'

Well, it's my job to bring the inn up to spec and give them

a real chance of succeeding. I'm sure I can make this work and, hopefully, leave Mason with a few more memories intact. I know I couldn't walk away from a place like this, but now I'm thinking a little less stylish boutique and a little more of the New England charm is called for. I seriously doubt whether anyone will even notice the little changes I'm going to be making, but I hope the outcome will be more acceptable to Mason.

Hayden

5

A Sea of Baubles and Tangled Tinsel

The day my mother called, and unexpectedly burst into tears when I simply asked how she was, sent me into a panic. I'd never heard her sound so distressed before and it was shocking. She'd just had two cancellations within an hour of each other and told me she was waiting to pick the right moment to tell my father.

My mother admitted that she was at her wits' end struggling to cope with what felt like an endless list of domestic tasks with hardly any help at all. With so few bookings, her and my father had to count every single dollar they spent. It was then, way back in August, that I realised I had to do something but I didn't know what. Offering them money wasn't an option. As the weeks passed, I eventually came up with an idea they couldn't really refuse. I said it wasn't just for their sakes, but for mine too. It was the Christmas present to beat all Christmas presents in honour of Granddad.

Before I arrived, I felt pretty confident that with Ria directing us, we could quickly complete the project. What I hadn't realised was that exhaustion and worry has taken them both to the edge.

It turns out that being a dutiful son is much harder than I thought. I mean . . . Ria and I have clearly walked into a situation that's been brewing for a while. In fact, although this is costing me a small fortune, I don't think I'm paying Ria enough. But she did say that she deals with this sort of thing all the time, although I'm not sure when she said that whether either of us really appreciated the complexity of the situation.

Glancing at my watch, there's just time to make a quick call.

'Hey, Izzie, it's only me.'

'About time, too. Out of sight, out of mind. Not that I'm offended of course, because your mother sent me a lovely text to say you'd arrived safely.'

'Did she now?'

'Don't get defensive. My godmother is allowed to keep in touch. You are her beloved son and she's excited to have you there for Christmas. She mentioned you landed just as a blizzard hit.'

'Sorry, Izzie. Mum asked me about you, too.'

'Oh, really. And what did you say?'

'That you don't change.'

A loud 'What?' is followed by a gentle laugh.

'You bossed me around when we were growing up and you're still doing it now.'

'Yes, but admit it – when we don't see each other for a while you miss me.'

'Only because I'm not used to having a quiet life. Anyway, Mum rolled her eyes at me and said she can sleep at night knowing you're keeping an eye on me back in the UK.'

'Hmm . . . so why are you calling me now?'

Where do I start? 'I've never known my parents to be so edgy, it's like something is simmering away in the background ready to erupt. They've always been so mutually supportive. Now my father blows hot and cold, and my mother is struggling not to be constantly on his case. Seriously, if it wasn't for Ria's presence, I'm pretty sure they wouldn't even be speaking to each other. Goodness knows what she thinks of it all.'

'This is a huge deal for Evie and Mason, Hayden. Your mum did mention there was a bit of friction between the two of them, but surely that's to be expected. They've had an army of men crawling all over the place. You never do things by halves, do you? As for your interior designer, she's doing what you're paying her quite handsomely to do, so don't feel guilty about that. It's in her own interests to keep you all happy as it isn't just about signing off on a job. She'll no doubt be looking to capitalise on your name and will probably ask if she can use some of the photos of the end result on her website. As for your parents, you knew it was going to make waves, but things will get back to normal once you're out of their hair.'

That wasn't quite what I was expecting Izzie to say. 'Hmm. I hope you're right, but even I'm feeling awkward at times and that's hardly fair on her.'

Izzie sighs. 'There you go again. Delegation means letting go and accepting that someone else is in charge of whatever task you've given them. Let the woman do her job.'

Inwardly, I groan; Izzie thinks I'm exaggerating because she knows this is way outside of my comfort zone.

'I thought . . . hoped . . . that running the inn would bring them even closer together. Later this afternoon my father and I will get to see the first room Ria, with Mum's assistance, has taken several hours to stage. Either he'll nod his head politely and agree just to please my mother, or this could be the moment he says exactly what he thinks.'

'You mean you're having *everything* replaced?'

'New soft furnishings, bedding, cushions, lamps . . . the whole works.'

'Are you sure this is what they wanted, Hayden? I mean, they've been running the inn since the Christmas before last and I got the gist that there were a few problems but this seems a—'

'Oh, she's mentioned it to you, then.'

'No, of course not. I overhead a snippet of conversation one evening when Evie called my mum. As soon as I realised they were having a heart to heart, I made myself scarce. It sounded serious though.'

'The cost isn't important, Izzie. I just need this to work.' Of course my mother was fed up; not being able to employ anyone to help with the general housekeeping because the inn was rarely more than 20 per cent full, was hard all round. My father, too, must have felt that there weren't enough hours in the day for him to keep on top of everything.

'You can't control the people around you, even to avoid them making what you feel might turn out to be a huge mistake. Life doesn't work that way. You're doing everything you can to help, but the outcome is entirely up to your parents, Hayden.'

Every single word of what Izzie's saying is true, although it's cold comfort.

'I think I made it even worse by starting the ball rolling and leaving them to it. Now I'm coming in late in the day and I'm banking on Ria being able to regain control of the situation to steer things in the right direction. It's beginning to sink in that if I can't sort this out, it could be the last Christmas we spend at the inn.' Giving the inn a future won't count for anything if the process ends up driving them apart, and that's something that hadn't occurred to me.

'Don't assume the worst, Hayden. Your parents aren't quitters; everyone knows that. They'll find a way to fix what's wrong. Step back and see how it all unfolds.'

'You're probably right.' I'm in panic mode because I don't have a handle on the situation. I'm used to sitting in the driving seat, not being a passenger. 'Thanks, as always, for being my listening ear and a voice of reason.'

'That's what I'm here for, Hayden. You've helped me out numerous times in the past. It's what we do for each other, isn't it? It's just a pity you're so far away and I can't pop in to give you some moral support.'

'Your mother would never let me hear the end of it if you spent Christmas in the White Mountains,' I point out. 'Where do you think you get your tenacity from?'

'It's a pity,' she muses, 'because I love skiing.'

'There won't be time for anything as indulgent as that, I'm afraid. The way it looks, we'll be working right up to the wire to get everything straight, and after that it'll be focusing on our guests.'

'I'm sure the tension will ease once the makeover is complete, so there'll be no excuse this time next year.'

'Actually, I can't think of anything worse than spending the entire festive season with you and my mother both fussing over me!' I laugh.

'You call it fussing, we call it looking out for you. Right, um . . . I'd best go. We'll speak soon. Have a nice day!' The last thing I hear as I click *end call* is the sound of Izzie laughing at my best American drawl.

As we all gather inside the log cabin, it looks like a Christmas shop that is so tightly packed with stock, it's difficult to move around. We're going to have a quick look at the decorations my father and I have been busy sorting out, albeit reluctantly on his part.

'You put all of this up every year?' Ria gasps, as she steps over the threshold. Her expression instantly changes and I can see she's annoyed with herself for blurting out what was obviously a gut reaction. In truth, I feel sorry for her, because it's a lot to take in.

Unfortunately, it immediately puts my father on the defensive. 'Half of it goes outside,' he retorts. 'The inn is a big place and being set back from the road it requires a lot of lights and decorations to make it stand out.' He's not happy.

'There's a life-size handmade sleigh in one of the other outbuildings too, Ria, with four reindeers,' my mother adds.

It's like adding fuel to the fire and my father scowls.

Gazing around, I'm not sure it's going to be possible to get all of this put up given the deadline we're working to anyway – normally, the process begins on the first of November – but that could work in our favour. I'm no designer, but even I can appreciate that this is an overload of absolutely everything – colour, styles and the whimsical. That was mainly down to Granddad and I'm not sure my father gives it any thought, it's simply tradition.

'We managed to get all but one set of lights working, didn't we, Dad?' I confirm. When it comes to this topic I don't intend to have a voice as I think it's important I remain neutral. Especially after my chat with Izzie.

Ria wanders around in a bit of a daze and I can see she's reeling a little but keen to get a feel for what's here. How on earth she's going to come up with a plan that will satisfy both of my parents, I don't know.

'There are some fabulous things here,' she remarks. 'Classics that stand the test of time. And a few things that haven't weathered quite so well. Let's head back and I'll show you some ideas I've come up with.'

'Hayden, why don't you show Ria the storage area in the barn and your dad and I will head back and get afternoon tea ready.' My mother gives me a pointed look. She wants Ria to see everything.

'No problem. We'll catch up with you in a bit.'

When they're out of earshot, Ria turns to give me an apologetic look. 'I'm so sorry those words just slipped out of my mouth before I had time to think. It was a bit of a shock, that's all. I knew there would be a lot of stuff but—'

'If it's any consolation, I've got a feeling you'll approve of the sleigh and the reindeers. It was the last thing Granddad bought and he had it specially commissioned. I remember helping him to assemble it on what turned out to be his last Christmas. Unfortunately, there's also a giant inflatable snowman that bends in the wind, and it's a bit much for my liking, but they're popular around here.'

As I start to push on the sliding door to the barn, it gets stuck.

'It won't shift. I'll grab a shovel to move some of the snow that's drifted up against the runners.'

Ria's brow wrinkles and I wonder what she's thinking. 'Do you mind if I pop back into the cabin and take a few photos of some of the trimmings?'

She's a woman who thinks on her feet, that's for sure. 'Feel free. It'll take me ten minutes to sort this out, anyway.'

We walk off in different directions and I'm simply relieved that she's taking all this in her stride. I text my mother to warn her we'll be a little while and then begin shovelling. It's hot work, but by the time Ria returns I'm about done.

'I feel guilty for not giving you a hand. I didn't realise how deep that snowdrift was!' she exclaims.

'It's fine. I get a kick out of it, actually, as I've always loved snow. Anyway, come and take a look.'

As I pull off the tarpaulin, Ria starts smiling.

'Now that's something that will fit in with the new style perfectly. It's lovely and I have no doubt at all that it will look even better when it's all lit up. It's all about shape and colour; it's definitely something to help advertise Christmas at the inn in a stylish rather than a gaudy way.'

'At last!' I grin at her. 'Something you can work with.'

She gives me a knowing look. 'I think there's quite a bit we can work into the plan. I don't think I need to see the blow-up snowman, though. Perhaps that could quietly disappear.'

I laugh as I cover up the sleigh and Ria reaches across to give me a hand. Mum tried to make a few things disappear last Christmas, thinking my father wouldn't notice, but he did. I stayed well out of it.

'Perfect timing. Your dad has made a batch of apple cider doughnuts. Sit down, they're best eaten warm.'

My mother seems in good spirits although my father hasn't said a word, but then he's busy turning doughnuts to make sure they don't burn.

'The smell is amazing, Mason.' Ria reaches out to him to get him talking.

He does a half-turn to glance at her. 'I figured you deserve something sweet after the shock of walking into the log cabin.'

My father gives her a knowing look and a big grin appears on Ria's face. I could hug her for the way she's trying so hard to be a peacemaker as I can see that he appreciates it.

'With the number of times I've been up and down those stairs today, you won't get any complaints from me. I've burnt off way more calories than I'm likely to consume.'

It's good to hear the two of them bantering, while my mother is fussing over making the tea. 'Earl Grey or English breakfast tea, Ria?'

'Ooh . . . the breakfast tea for me, please.'

'And me,' I chime in.

My mother carries a tray over and begins laying the table. 'I'm excited about the big reveal of our first room, Ria.' She sounds upbeat. 'I think Mason will be pleasantly surprised.'

When my father doesn't respond the silence is heavy.

'It's not quite ready,' Ria interjects. 'If Hayden doesn't mind giving me a hand, I think it needs a little festive decoration to finish it off.'

My father carries a plate of freshly baked doughnuts over to the table and his expression is giving nothing away.

'Please help yourselves.'

Even though he's not happy, he still manages to be the perfect host. The wonderful thing is that, as we sit here eating, the mood does begin to lift. Good food and good company bring people together, and it isn't until after Ria refuses a third doughnut, stating she's so full she couldn't eat another mouthful, that we get back down to business. She reaches into her bag to pull out an iPad.

'I have a collection of photos for you to look at. Some examples of jobs I've done over the last few years, showing the before and after look but focusing on the Christmas theme. Most are hotels or B & Bs, although there's also a manor house and a sprawling cottage in the Cotswolds. It'll give you a feel for the direction I think we should go in when it comes to decorating The Inn on the River. Simple, colour-coordinated touches that enhance what you have here but won't swamp a building that is already full of character and wonderful features.'

Ria's presentational skills are impressive. She understands the old quote that a picture tells a thousand words . . . and it's true. Rather cleverly, she ends with a section entitled 'Do's and Don'ts'.

'There's a reason why the big shops and hotels spend an extraordinary amount of money each year getting professionals in to create their Christmas look.'

She flips through a couple of dozen photos of the sort of festive displays you find in country living magazines.

'When I say less is more,' she continues, 'that doesn't always mean less decorations. Sometimes it simply means a lesser combination of colours. I know you're used to trimming up every single room at the inn, but time isn't on our side this year, I'm afraid. So, if you can give Hayden and me half an hour, I'd like to use the first completed bedroom as an example.'

'This is right up Evie's street; our home in the UK was, in her words, very *tasteful*. The agreement was that I could have as many lights outside as I wanted, as long as they were white.' Unusually for my father, there's a distinctly sarcastic edge to his tone.

My mother is clearly annoyed. 'What about the ones that looked like red berries? You wrapped them around the fir tree next to the patio,' she reminds him. 'And one of the wooden skeleton trees you made had more than two thousand lights on it alone, so I don't think you can justify sounding hard done by!'

'OK . . . so I admit that I can get a little carried away.' Now he's embarrassed and he lowers his eyes. 'I'm open to suggestions, which is a start, isn't it?'

This is so unlike their old banter; it was never personal, it simply reflected their differing points of view. Now they seem to be constantly winding each other up.

Ria begins packing away her things and I stand.

'What do you want me to do?'

'While you were shovelling snow I gathered together a few decorations and popped them into two jute sacks. I left them just inside the door to the log cabin. If you'd like to collect one while I pop up to the room to rearrange a couple of items of furniture, it won't take long to get it sorted.'

'Right, I'll fetch that now and I'll meet you upstairs.'

As I hurry out into the hallway to don my snow gear and boots, I'm relieved that went reasonably smoothly. However, my father's going to be even more vocal when it comes to the ground floor and the exterior, so Ria was right starting on the smallest guest room to test their reaction. That was an inspired move.

6

Ho . . . Hum!

When my father follows my mother through the door of the revamped room his jaw drops.

'Isn't it lovely, Mason?' My mother turns to look at him and then spots Ria's final finishing touches. 'Oh, Ria. Simple *is* best!'

Instead of a tree covered in baubles packed tightly into the corner and tinsel scattered liberally on every available surface, the room is like something out of a magazine. Even my father seems impressed, and why shouldn't he be?

'And those decorations were in the log cabin?' my father queries, pointing to the festive display on the window seat.

'They were, Mason,' Ria replies. 'I'm suggesting that in the bedrooms we keep it simple and the festive touch frames the window and the views. With the backdrop of that glorious snow, you really don't need anything else.'

'And that was your grandmother's favourite side table, Hayden,' he confirms. 'It's made of black walnut and it's a lovely piece. I thought it was earmarked to go.' My father runs his fingers lovingly across the top of it, lingering to look at the lamp. 'This is new. The bird theme is great.'

'It's a tiny house sparrow and it's a part of the same range as the soft furnishings.'

'Ah . . . we call them song sparrows in the States,' he informs Ria.

The new decor has taken what was quite a dark room and

really brought it to life. Ria kept the old hardwood flooring throughout but had everything stained a dark walnut to keep it uniform. I questioned her decision at the time. She said that once the wooden wall panelling, which is a feature in most of the rooms, was painted a lighter colour, the floor would complement it perfectly. And it most certainly does.

'I really can't remember seeing anything as lovely as this in the cabin.' My mother wanders over to the window seat.

'It was a festive garland that I cut in half and deconstructed. Let me show you.' Ria leads my parents into the adjacent bedroom and swings open the door. 'That's the other half of it without the changes.'

'Oh, that used to go at the back of the buffet table.' My mother laughs. 'Those bunches of plastic flowers have yellowed with age and it looks tired when you compare the two. I like the way you've stripped it back in the other room. The white silk leaves have a sparkle I hadn't noticed before.'

'I also attached a few tiny bunches of red berries to give it a pop of colour.'

Ria turns to look at my father and I can see she's keen to get his approval.

'Hmm . . . I see what you mean. Some things don't quite work, do they?' My father pulls a long face. 'I like the pared-down version.'

'With less ornaments and decorations, it's going to be so much easier keeping the rooms clean,' Ria explains.

'I think that's a resounding thumbs-up,' I confirm, as it seems we're all in agreement.

My father's eyes light up. 'Great. Does that mean I can now make a start on putting up the lights outside while you all focus in here? I'll need to get on to that a bit sharpish. Once we start looking at the ground floor, what with cutting down the trees and getting them all trimmed up, it will be a team effort.'

My mother bites her lip and glances at Ria. He's implying that he intends to do the same old thing and that's not part of the agenda.

'It will, Mason. I thought maybe you and I could have a little chat first thing tomorrow morning before you make a start?' Ria suggests.

My father's brow wrinkles. 'Oh. Right. OK.'

Ria continues, 'And Evie had a great idea, didn't you?'

My mother seems puzzled for a moment and then her eyes widen. 'Oh, yes! Instead of room numbers, it might be nice to give them names. Jackson loved his trees, didn't he, Mason? What if we rename room number seven The River Birch?'

'That's a wonderful idea, Evie. Let's get our heads together and come up with a list. I like the sound of The White Pine Suite for the corner room overlooking the forest to the east.'

And just like that, a potentially awkward moment passes. Albeit, Ria has her work cut out first thing tomorrow when she tries to steer my father in the right direction.

Considering the day we've had, it seemed the right thing to do to bring Ria to Shelley's Bar and Grill to eat tonight, as her first full day in the White Mountains draws to a close.

'I feel bad that Mason dropped us off but wouldn't stay for a drink. It's been quite a day, hasn't it?'

Ria obviously thinks I should have talked him into it, but when my father said he had a few errands to run, I knew it was just an excuse.

'It certainly has. I've no doubt at all he'll be stopping off at The Logger's Rest for a chat and a beer on his way back, though.'

'This bad feeling between Evie and Shelley is serious enough to make him avoid the place?'

I grimace. 'To keep the peace, yes.'

'That's a real shame. It's nice in here. The red-and-white check tablecloths are charming, they suit the exposed wooden walls and beams. And they're clearly rushed off their feet tonight.'

I watch as Ria scans around. Every table is full. The background music is soft and can barely be heard above the general hubbub of chatter and laughter.

'It's always like this. It's not just their reputation for some of the best classic New England fare around here that draws the diners in, but it's the relaxed atmosphere. What you see is what you get.'

Ria gazes down at the menu in front of her, which displays a photograph of each of the dozen or so dishes on the limited, but mouth-watering, menu.

'I see what you mean!' She laughs, pointing to the picture of a stuffed and overflowing lobster roll. 'That's what we've come to try, isn't it?'

'Yep. You get to sample Shelley's first, then my father will make you his version at some point and ask for your opinion.' I roll my eyes, and she smiles back at me.

All credit to her, she's wearing a Christmas jumper in a soft blue with white snowflakes on it and she fits right in. In contrast, I look a little reserved in a dark-blue plaid shirt and a plain navy-blue fleece. I regretted my decision the moment she took off her coat, but I was playing it safe.

'Sorry for the delay, guys. I'm Sal. What can I get you to drink?' I don't recognise the waitress. I swear they get younger with every passing year. She places two large tumblers of water in front of us and stands back ready to take our orders.

Ria studies the drinks menu before glancing up at me. 'Why don't you order for us both?'

'No problem. Let's go for two beer sliders and I think we've settled on two number eights please.'

Ria nods her head in agreement.

'Old style, or newfangled?'

A smile twitches around the corners of my mouth, as obviously our waitress thinks we're holidaymakers. 'Old style, please. With the works.'

'You got it!' She tilts her head in approval and scurries off to place our order.

'Beer sliders?' Ria questions. 'I must admit that I'm not a huge drinker and my experience with beer is minimal.'

I raise my eyebrows. 'It's not quite the beer fest you're probably imagining. Besides, Shelley wouldn't allow drunks in here anyway.'

Ria has no idea why I'm laughing, but when two barmen arrive with the wooden paddles and place them on the table between us, she relaxes.

'I wasn't expecting shot glasses,' she muses.

Each slider has six glasses and each one bears the name of the beer. They're a little bigger than a single shot, but in total it's probably no more than a pint at most.

'It's a great way to find something you like. I'm easy, as I'll drink more or less anything.'

'OK . . .' Ria picks up the first glass. 'Trail Angel.' She holds it up to her nose. 'It looks dark and heavy.'

'It tastes smoother than it looks,' I encourage her. 'It's an oatmeal and vanilla stout. It's rich, sweet and malty.'

She takes a sip then instantly puts it back on the paddle.

'Dam Delight. I like the lighter colour. I'll try this one.'

While she gingerly takes a slurp, I down my shot of Trail Angel and to me it smacks of Christmases past. 'Now that hit the spot!'

Ria, I notice, is quite content to empty her glass in a couple of gulps. 'That was very pleasant. Citrusy, with a bit of a grapefruity tang.'

'It's a lager. What's called an American Light and it's also low calorie.'

'Is that Hayden Reynolds, or am I seeing things?' Shelley's voice reaches my ears even before I spot her. I stand as she rushes over to the table.

'You snuck in when I wasn't around, and you've got company.' She throws her arms around my shoulders and I stoop to kiss her cheek.

'I swear you don't look a day older than when I was in here this time last year.'

'Get on with you, you charmer, but there's something about that British accent that's irresistible. So, are you going to introduce me to your lady friend, or what?'

Ria doesn't quite know how to react and I do the honours.

'Shelley, this is Ria Porter. She's an interior designer who has flown over from the UK to get The Inn on the River ready for the big relaunch.'

Shelley sticks out her hand and Ria stands, leaning across to shake it. 'You have a lovely place, here. It's very cosy and welcoming.'

'I guess you haven't eaten yet then, 'cause if you had, you'd be talking about the food,' Shelley quips.

'Hayden is just introducing me to your wonderful range of beers. We do dessert taster plates in the UK, but this is a first for me and I think it's a great idea,' Ria replies, as she retakes her seat.

'We aim to please. Are the two of you staying at the inn for the entire holiday through to New Year, or only hanging around to make sure the relaunch party is a success?' Shelley checks, curiosity getting the better of her.

I sink back down into my seat, but before I can answer, Ria responds.

'If everything goes well, I'll be flying home in plenty of time to celebrate New Year with my family in the UK.'

'By the way, Hayden, tell your dad I'm still awaiting my invite.' Shelley turns to look directly at me. 'Considering I'm doing the catering, I'm trying my best not to take it personally.'

I clear my throat, awkwardly. 'Oh, right . . . I wasn't aware of that . . .' Words fail me and, thankfully, Ria comes to my rescue.

'It's difficult being in the restaurant business, as no doubt you're fully booked here for Christmas Eve. I'm so looking forward to the lobster rolls. Hayden's parents suggested he bring me here as a special treat.'

'They did, did they? Well, that's progress, I suppose. It's been a while since I bumped into Evie and it's time we shut the door on the past.' Shelley sounds adamant and worryingly optimistic.

'Well, I've been informed you do the best lobster rolls in New Hampshire,' Ria states.

This woman knows how to calm troubled waters.

'You can tell Mason that sweet-talking about me doesn't forgive him for going newfangled. I'm all about tradition and my recipe wins every time. It's nice to see you here, Hayden, and I hope you guys have a great time this evening. Lovely to meet you, Ria. Dessert and coffee are on me tonight.'

As Shelley walks away, I let out a huge sigh.

Ria stares at me. 'I don't even know what's going on, but I hope I said the right thing.'

I pick up one of the shot glasses in front of me and down it in one. 'Back in the day, my father dated Shelley and they had quite a thing going. When he was offered a promotion and a job in the UK, she decided it wasn't for her. She eventually married a local man, but she's been a widow for more than ten years now.'

Ria's face pales. 'Your father asked her to go with him?'

'Yes. When I was here helping my parents move in, at one of the local gatherings someone happened to mention it to my mother when they were talking about the past. For whatever reason, it was something my father had never talked about. Shelley was standing close by and tried to laugh it off, mumbling something about the one who got away. Unfortunately, that made it even worse as I don't think Mum realised she was joking.'

Thankfully, Sal is heading for our table and begins to decant the large platter onto the rather limited space.

'This looks amazing but it's a lot of food,' Ria remarks, lowering her voice.

'I asked for *the works* as I wanted you to sample everything. No one does potatoes like Shelley's.'

'Right – I'll just go for it then!'

I watch, amused, as Ria picks up her knife and fork, unsure where to start. I do my best to hide my grin as I grab the fluffy white roll with both hands. It's overflowing with succulent lobster meat, tossed in home-made lemon mayonnaise and coleslaw. She watches as I stuff the end into my mouth, taking a generous bite.

'Ah. I get it.' She lays the cutlery back down on the table and follows suit.

'The bed of crisp lettuce at the bottom of the roll helps keep it together,' I explain. She nods her head, her mouth full. I indicate to the row of side dishes between us. 'Here we have home fries – chunky potatoes with onions and red peppers. Then Parmesan fries with a garlic dip and last, but my personal favourites, truffle fries.'

Ria grins at me. 'This would be a nightmare to eat if the lobster was hot. It would all fall out.'

I quickly gaze around, checking that Shelley isn't within earshot. 'You wait until you try my father's version. Shelley says there's a secret ingredient she can't fathom out. It's a great annoyance for her, because my father knows he wins hands down.'

Ria relinquishes her roll to try the fries. 'It's only your mother who doesn't really speak to Shelley, then?'

I sit back in my chair, swiping my mouth with a napkin before responding. 'In a small community like this, ignoring someone doesn't really work. Not least because you never know when you're going to need a helping hand. Winters here can be brutal and even enemies come together in times of dire need. Besides, Shelley does the catering for most of the parties around here. Not only is it the best eatery, it's also the closest.'

'Your mother did seem a little upset when your father suggested we come here, but she didn't make a huge fuss.'

I raise an eyebrow. 'She took it out on the pots and pans instead.'

'Ah!' Ria frowns and I simply shrug my shoulders.

'Most of our guests eat at Shelley's. Providing a substantial breakfast menu is one thing, but going full-on restaurant wouldn't be viable at the inn. It would push my father to breaking point unless they could employ more staff. Besides, my mother would never speak out against Shelley, that's not her style.'

'You obviously get on well with her yourself,' Ria points out.

'She's a character and I've known her all my life. My grandparents always brought us here to eat over the Christmas holidays. Mum was fine around her until that fateful day and I could see by the look on Shelley's face when the subject was raised that it was the last thing she wanted raked up. Dad would never come here without Mum, and she'll only come if it's Shelley's night off. It's a real shame, because we had some good times here in the past.'

It's pleasant chatting with Ria and I'm glad to see she has a healthy appetite. The beers seem to be going down well, too, I notice.

'This is on me tonight,' she informs me and I can tell by the look in her eyes there's no point in arguing.

I pick up one of the shot glasses and raise it in the air. 'That's really not necessary, Ria, but thank you. Here's to what has been a successful first day on the job, if an extremely long one. I don't know about you, but I'm flagging.'

Her eyes light up. 'You took the words out of my mouth. And I'm totally stuffed – I can't eat another bite.'

We clink glasses.

'I'll tell Shelley we'll take a rain check on dessert, as I'm sure we'll find our way back here again. I can get us a lift home with Frank, an old mate of mine, if you give me a couple of minutes.'

'Right. No problem. I'll pay the bill while you sort out our transport. When my head hits the pillow tonight I doubt I'll even get to the count of three before I pass out,' Ria declares. 'I'd hate to do that head lolling thing on the trip back to the inn, and if I do, dig me in the ribs or something!'

Well, considering I wasn't too impressed at Ria's tardiness in boarding the plane, she's blown any concerns I have right out the water.

Tonight has been fun, more fun than I've had in a long time, and it wasn't even a date. Either I'm choosing the wrong women to take out, or it's easier to relax when there isn't that awful pressure to make a good impression. She's getting to see a side of me – and my family – no one else has been privy to. Admittedly, I'm not entirely comfortable about that given the situation, but there's nothing at all I can do about it. To her credit, Ria seems to be taking it in her stride.

Ria

7

Peace and Goodwill to All

'Judging by the look on your face this morning, you don't approve of the inflatable snowman, Ria, do you?' Mason glances at me, his shoulders slumped.

To my dismay, it was the first thing I spotted when I walked out the front door and realised that was the reason why Mason was up and about exceptionally early this morning.

'Sorry. On its own it's fun and it does put a huge smile on my face,' I declare, with enthusiasm. 'But we should take a step back and consider the overall picture. Let's head for the log cabin and have a chat.'

We walk in single file where the snow is compacted. Today it's a good couple of degrees warmer and my toes are toasty but trudging through the undisturbed snow is hard work and there's no sign of it melting. Once we're inside the cabin, Mason insists on lighting the log burner and after slipping off my boots, even though I'm wearing thermal hiking socks, the chill immediately begins to kick in.

'Come on, Ria, make yourself comfortable. Ten minutes and I'll have this fire roaring. Then I'll put on a pot of coffee. I think I'm going to need a big shot of caffeine to see me through this conversation,' he replies, solemnly.

'Mason, this isn't about taking sides and I'd be gutted if you thought that. The focus is on what's best for the business – isn't it?' I check.

He nods his head, as I watch him place a bed of firelighters, then kindling, carefully constructed in a criss-cross pattern on top to allow air to flow through. Next, he strategically balances a couple of sturdy logs, big enough to wedge in.

'While I get the coffee on, can you keep an eye on this? I'll leave the door ajar to create a draught, but once it starts roaring if it begins spitting ram it shut.'

'Oh, right. No problem.'

Mason stands and I settle myself down on a floor cushion in front of the hearth. Rather thoughtfully, he offers me a small, handmade quilt.

'My mother sewed this; pop it over your legs until the fire warms up. She was a part of the River Ladies Quilting Guild. Each of the members made patches with their initials on them and then they did a swap. Sewing occupied her time during some long, cold winters here at the inn, I can tell you.'

In one fell swoop I replaced those wonderful quilts with duvets, because that's what holidaymakers expect. Who could blame Mason for thinking his voice doesn't count? It matters to me and I want him to know that I'm listening. If I'd realised how delicate the situation was, I would have insisted on talking to both Evie and Mason separately, before I drew up the plans. That's down to a total lack of communication on Hayden's part. Now I understand why he was so nervous on the flight over. He wasn't joking when he said that now he'd cleared the decks he was *on catch-up*. That's utterly ridiculous, as from what I've seen so far this isn't just a case of rescuing an ailing business, and if Hayden didn't realise that before, he does now.

'Is it roaring yet?' Mason calls out to me.

'No, but the flames are beginning to lick up around the sides of the kindling. That's a good sign, right?'

Mason gives me a wink. 'Yep. Nothing beats a real fire in my book. It takes me back to my childhood. We toasted bread, marshmallows and chestnuts in here. And even franks; best hot dogs ever! Who needs barbecue sauce when you can get that real smoky flavour from a blazing log?'

He walks over, carrying two mugs. 'Here you go. Not quite as good as the machine in the kitchen, as the beans aren't freshly ground, but I like to think the ambience in here makes up for it.'

My chin wavers a little at Mason's words; he's feeling nostalgic as he plonks himself down on the cushion next to me.

'I'm sorry if you think I'm being uncooperative, Ria. It's just that . . . uh . . . well, life can get really complicated at times.'

I turn to look at him questioningly. 'I need a little more than that, Mason. You have a voice in what's happening here, so use it in a constructive way. Help me to help you.'

He raises his eyebrows as he considers my words and if ever there was a time to talk frankly, it's now.

'My son means well, but he's so like his mother. He gets an idea in his head and, come hell or high water, he turns it into reality. Hayden thinks that saving the business is the best gift he can give us this Christmas. He thinks it will put his mother and me back on track.'

I didn't realise things were that bad, but I think I do a good job of hiding my surprise. 'Will it?'

Mason bows his head, staring down into his mug. 'I don't know. It seems that there isn't much Evie and I agree on these days. I have to keep biting my tongue for fear of causing yet another ruckus. My mother referred to it as those darned little ankle-biters, the annoying things that add up if you let them. And, one day, something insignificant turns out to be the final straw.'

Mason lapses into silence.

'And all these little decisions being made about the inn are ankle-biters?'

'Yes, noise. Distraction.'

'But, for you, disturbing?'

'Evie is the love of my life and I thought that agreeing to this idea of Hayden's would make her happy, but, for whatever reason, it hasn't. And, at this rate, I won't even recognise the inn anymore. If I disagree with her, she makes a big deal out of it, like I'm being unreasonable. So, I give up. Then something trivial sets me off and I end up being snappy. I know it's not been an easy time for either of us since we took over the inn. The worries and the pressure just kept building, but closing down and having guys everywhere turning everything upside down, I haven't been easy to live with and I know that.'

The sorrowful tone in his voice pulls on my heartstrings. He sounds regretful, as if he wishes he could turn back the clock.

'Oh, Mason. I'm so sorry. I had no idea how tough this was for you.'

I sip my coffee as Mason closes the door on the log burner. The flames are now dancing around the logs and a glorious red glow is comforting to see. We sit for a few minutes staring into the fire and basking in the warmth radiating from it.

Mason turns to look at me, frowning. 'This is going to sound awful, as both Evie and I look forward to having Hayden here, but it's another pressure on top of everything else. We can't let him down, not when he's gone to such great lengths. He thinks it's simple. Fix the inn, fix the business and job done. And yet, for whatever reason, all it's doing is pushing Evie and me further apart.'

What can I say? I can't just steamroll through with the grand plan because Hayden is paying me. Besides, the inn doesn't belong to Hayden, it's Mason's inheritance for the foreseeable future.

'This is awkward, Mason, I can't deny that. I have three clients to satisfy on this project and I could tell Hayden that there's no point going any further until everyone is in full agreement. We don't have time to delay, though, so it will certainly bring things to a head quickly.'

'When the three of us can't agree, Hayden will simply reiterate that the inn won't be viable if we don't move with the times. Evie will sit there nodding her head in agreement. I'm the only one standing back and wondering why it's making things worse and not better.'

From what I've seen, I think he has a valid point.

'There are no guarantees that, even with Hayden's generous rescue package, we'll get through the next financial year without going into debt,' he adds, dejectedly. 'And there I'll be, griping about losing some of the intrinsic history of the place. But most of the improvements are just that, so I'll end up sounding like a fool when I'm reduced to digging my heels in over an inflatable snowman simply to make a point.'

'Which is?'

'If Evie's heart isn't in it, there's no way we'll succeed. We knew it was going to be tough, but it's like the stuffing has been knocked out of her.'

'Have you talked to her about the future?'

'If you think my moods are up and down, Evie's no different – but she won't admit that. She'll do anything not to worry Hayden, but I see a change in her. Personally, I think it's because she isn't sure this is going to work and she's worried how he'll take it.'

'Why?'

'Because he's not one to accept failure, even if the fault lies with his mother and me.'

I take a deep breath in. 'Mason, the inn has been totally pulled apart and we've only just begun to put it back together again. All three of you are putting too much pressure on yourselves. Emotions are running high and it's no wonder there's tension in the air. Once we've finished the job, the inn will be a serious contender to attract those holidaymakers. With a brighter future on the horizon that could turn everything around for you and Evie. You're in the process of building something together that you're both a part of, so just give it a little time.'

'That's what I keep telling myself, Ria – every morning when I wake up and every night before I fall asleep.'

I sigh, my eyes wandering around the log cabin and taking in the piles of decorations heaped up behind us, rather than looking directly at Mason while I think.

'I'm just being honest here, Mason, but in my opinion the silent treatment you sometimes employ to avoid upsetting Evie is actually making things worse.'

'Ah.' He glances at me, pulling a face. 'You're probably right there but I'm tired of arguing.'

'You've already admitted the inflatable snowman isn't really an issue so let's use that and a more laid-back approach to the decorations as confirmation that you're not opting out or being . . .'

'Obtuse for the sake of it?' Mason starts laughing.

I gaze at him, narrowing my eyes. 'Why does that amuse you?'

'The snowman is one of the things that drives Evie mad. I'm just trying to get her to stop and think for a second about how ridiculous this all is. I don't mean the fact the business isn't doing well, I'm as worried about that as she is. But I'm beginning to wonder if there's another reason Evie is pushing me away little by little. It's the same with this nonsense over Shelley. Why would I ever look at another woman when I have Evie by my side?'

'I'm sorry, I don't understand what you mean.'

'I'll always love Evie, no matter what. The problem is that I don't know if she's still in love with me.'

'Oh, Mason.' That hadn't even occurred to me.

'I think Evie is just as confused as I am, to be honest, and maybe you're right. It's been a trying time. But, while I might – actually – be a bit of an old fool, I don't like making myself look foolish. They're two very different things and I rather think that's what I've been doing lately.'

'Let's remedy that, shall we?'

'I promise to be on my best behaviour, and with you there to jump in if you think I'm not doing myself any favours, maybe all is not lost.' He chuckles to himself and I start laughing too.

There's a wicked sense of humour lurking beneath that often charming exterior but there's also a man who's afraid he's about to lose everything that's important to him. As we mull over the next steps, I'm getting a much clearer picture of what matters to Mason and where he's prepared to compromise. One thing I can say is that he's not an unreasonable man, he's just at the end of his tether.

As for Evie, still waters run deep, but what I see is a woman who is trying hard to please both her husband and her son. Personally, I think she's putting herself last and that's the real danger here. It could be a seemingly insignificant little thing that tips her over the edge. If that happens, from Mason's point of view, his life will fall apart.

Late morning, when all four of us convene in the kitchen for today's meeting, Mason immediately dons his apron and heads straight for the refrigerator.

'We could eat later, Dad. Why don't you come and sit down while we discuss this morning's progress.' Hayden glances at his mother briefly, a look of concern passing between them.

'I'm happy to work and listen at the same time until I can get this in the oven,' Mason responds, genially.

I don't know quite what Hayden and Evie were expecting, but it wasn't that sort of reaction.

'Perhaps you guys could give us a bit of an update first?' I suggest.

'Oh, right. Mum, it's over to you.'

Evie opens the notebook lying on the table in front of her. 'As agreed, we tackled room number nine – which Mason suggested we now call The White Pine Suite.' She pauses, but he doesn't turn around as he's busy spooning something into individual pots. 'We've made a good start. Now that the bed's made up, I'm not sure the layout is quite right but let's wait until you've all seen it.'

'Everything has been unpacked,' Hayden confirms. 'It's looking good.'

'We just need to hang the curtains,' Evie continues. 'You'll love the soft furnishings, Mason. It's a raised diamond-shaped lattice design and in the middle of each is a little motif. If you glance at it quickly it could almost be a pinecone – how coincidental is that?'

Finally, Mason turns around to look at his wife, giving her a pleasant smile. 'I can't wait to see it.'

The general mood around the table instantly brightens, but I can see Hayden is still a little tense. 'How was your morning?' he enquires.

'Good. Productive, wasn't it, Mason?'

Our chef is in the process of sliding a tray into the oven, but he gives a slight turn of his head to talk over his shoulder. 'Ria's a tough negotiator but we got somewhere in the end. Evie will be glad to hear that the inflatable snowman has to go. He won't be homeless; I've a friend who'll be more than happy to find a space for him this Christmas.'

I almost burst out laughing at the seriousness in Mason's tone. It's so effective that I watch as Hayden's eyes widen and Evie opens her mouth to say something, then seconds later changes her mind.

Mason undoes his apron and walks over to join us, taking the seat opposite his wife.

'Right. We have thirty minutes before the lobster mac 'n' cheese is ready to dish up. You now have my full attention.'

Evie clears her throat as she gazes across at him. 'You're happy with the changes to the external decorating plan?'

'I am. After a little back and forth, Ria and I agreed that the sleigh ride would be better located alongside the inn's signpost. It'll attract more attention as people drive by. She said that keeping it simple and hanging the white lights around the porch will welcome visitors without making it look too cluttered.'

Both Hayden and Evie are genuinely surprised.

'And you're OK with that, Mason?' Evie checks.

Mason purses his lips and tilts his head from side to side. 'I can live with it, I—'

Hayden interrupts. 'So, all the flashing, multicoloured bulbs are going where, exactly?'

Mason shrugs his shoulders. 'Into storage, unless I can find someone to take them off my hands, but who wants second-hand lights?'

I can see that Hayden is now panicking a little, thinking I might have gone too far.

'It would be a shame not to use them, Mason,' I interrupt. 'How about giving the log cabin a really festive feel? You have so many vintage decorations, and if they're displayed in the right way, it could turn the cabin into a cosy place where your guests could have afternoon tea. Or maybe hot chocolate in front of the log fire as an extra. What do you think?'

'It's a wonderful idea! I'm in,' Mason agrees, feigning a look of surprise.

Perhaps he was a tad too quick off the mark, as this was most certainly not what Hayden and Evie were expecting. But Mason takes the prize for the most enthusiastic response as Evie and Hayden simply look relieved.

'How on earth did you manage that? I mean . . .' Hayden is lost for words as he follows me upstairs to The White Pine Suite, after yet another amazing lunch.

'A bit of clever negotiation.'

'Yes, but it's little short of a miracle getting my father to rein it in when it comes to creating a festive spectacle.'

'Your father is a reasonable man when he's confronted with the facts. I gave it to him straight. We're trying to save a business here.' I labour the point.

'I know, but . . .' Hayden seems confused. 'He loves that giant snowman and those over-the-top gaudy lights.'

Seriously? Now is the time Hayden chooses to have a crisis of conscience? I have no idea what exactly he does or doesn't know, but if none of them are talking openly to each other, we could be heading for a disaster.

'Your mother didn't seem to have a problem with it, are you saying you do?'

'No, of course not. But I don't want my father to feel that he's been pressed into doing something he'll regret later.'

'Mason is just fine with it, Hayden. And now he seems excited about turning the log cabin into a Christmas cave. What harm can it do?'

I stand back, waiting for Hayden to open the door with a flourish to proudly reveal his hard work. Instead of the 'ta-da' moment I was expecting, though, he's rather subdued. I step past him and my smile grows exponentially.

'Mason won't be disappointed, but Evie is right, the bed needs shifting. And it's a queen-size, so we'll need a hand. Luckily, in one of the boxes I have some packs of felt pads which should make it a lot easier if we can slide it over.'

'I'm glad to hear it,' Hayden mutters. It's obvious his mind is elsewhere. 'It's a bit of a ritual for him . . . you know, the trimming up.'

'Your father is over it, so there's no need to worry. But I think it's a good idea if the two of you work together for the next couple of days to make it happen. It'll reassure Evie we're on the right track, ready for when we turn our attention to the communal areas on the ground floor.'

'Of course. That's a great idea.'

'While we wait for your parents to join us, let's get those curtains hung and make up a festive display for the window seat. Once that's done, if everyone is happy from here on in, hopefully we can spend less time talking and more time doing.' I give Hayden a reassuring smile. 'Do you know where the ladder is?'

'It's in the cupboard on the landing. I'll fetch it.'

I momentarily turn away to stare out the window, which looks out over an endless stretch of forest with that mountainous backdrop. A snap of this scene would make an amazing Christmas card. 'Great. I'm hoping there's enough leftover items in the sack of trimmings you brought in yesterday so that a trip back to the log cabin won't be necessary. Although, I think we can be a little more opulent with the Christmas display in here, given that it's a suite.'

But when I turn back around to get his approval, Hayden has already left the room. He's obviously eager to press on and, I think, a little surprised at how smoothly this morning has gone. Fingers crossed this afternoon, too, will herald another success.

8

Full Steam Ahead

When I suggest we unmake the bed and lift off the mattress to make it easier to move, Hayden and Mason laugh. Standing either side of it, they lift the end up a good two feet off the floor as I scrabble to peel the backing off the felt pads and get them in place. Evie is already following my lead, and give the lady her due, as the two men lift the headboard end, she sinks to her knees and does the business.

'Right. If we're all ready, let's push this over to the wall facing the window, hopefully without scratching the newly varnished floor. Let's go on three . . . one, two, three!'

When we stand back, the difference it makes to the feel of the room is worth the effort. I leave Evie to fuss with straightening out the duvet cover and replacing the pillows and scatter cushions, while I engage Mason in conversation.

'Is this little display festive enough?' I ask and he wanders over to the window seat. The seconds tick by.

'It'll do!'

We walk through into the bathroom and with the Roman blind at the window matching the fabrics used in the bedroom, and the plush towels picking up the soft green on the motif, it has a genuine country feel.

'I love the turret en-suites. The unusual shape adds a sense of decadence.'

'It's a folly,' Mason informs me, 'but I agree. What's life without a bit of fun in it?'

Heading back into the bedroom and gazing across at the sitting area on the far side of the room, he frowns. 'That doesn't look right, it's like something is missing.'

Both Hayden and Evie immediately look up.

'Do you think it's worth putting Grandma's old rocking chair back in that corner?' Hayden asks.

Well done that man!

Evie straightens, placing her hands on her hips. 'Hmm . . . I think it would finish it off quite nicely. Great idea. Mason, it'll mean a trip up to the attic.'

'It's fine by me.'

I suggest that Hayden and I leave them to it in order to start bringing up another batch of boxes.

'What room shall we start on next, Evie?' I enquire.

'How about number one, the twin single? Mason, any ideas for the new name?' Evie turns to her husband, and he presses his lips together for a brief moment.

'The Cherry Tree,' he replies. 'In honour of the beautiful specimens that grow just outside the window.'

'That's perfect!' Evie agrees.

If the two of them can start working together in a more positive way, it will begin to heal the rift. And, hopefully, before too long they'll start opening up to each other again. No one's to blame here and I'm beginning to see there are three very different sides to this story. Evie's, Mason's and Hayden's.

My least favourite part of the job is traipsing up and down the seemingly endless number of stairs but at least the next room we're about to tackle is on the first floor. Some of the boxes are quite heavy, the bedding in particular, but I notice that, as Hayden rummages around and I stand ticking them off the master list, he places the lighter ones to the left.

'I think that's everything. Let the carrying commence.' Hayden comes to stand next to me. 'That stack is for you,' he indicates.

'You don't have to always take the heaviest ones, you know, but it's thoughtful of you.'

Hayden seems a little embarrassed that I'd sussed it out. 'I'm not doubting you have the strength,' he instantly responds. 'It's more of a health and safety thing. Besides, you're more than pulling your weight in ways I can't even begin to thank you for. Peter said you were good, but you've exceeded my expectations and some.'

He looks a little shamefaced. The problem with opening a proverbial Pandora's box is that you don't know what you're going to uncover; from what I can tell, none of them are ready for that conversation. While I'm doing what I can to get them all on the same page, I don't intend to get pulled into it.

'Peter's a really good friend of mine. You do know that his admiration for you goes a little deeper, don't you?'

My smile fades. 'I do.'

'He's a great guy,' Hayden remarks, trying to sound casual.

'Was that part of the bargain, putting in a good word for him?' I demand.

What I get in return is a distinctly sheepish look. 'Err . . . no. I just wondered, I mean . . . he's—'

'—recently divorced for the second time. Anyway, I don't mix business and pleasure.' After refusing Peter's string of offers to take me out to dinner, I thought I'd made myself very clear. When it comes to work, he's my top client and I admire his business acumen. He *is* a great guy, but for me it stops there.

'Right. I get it. Let's shift this lot upstairs then. At this rate we'll soon be running ahead of schedule.'

It seems I have three happy clients for now; long may that continue. If it doesn't, I might find myself flying home ahead of time.

Early evening, after insisting on helping to clear the dishes, I make my apologies and head back to my room as I have paperwork to attend to. It's not just that keeping track of everything is crucial at this stage but I'm in need of a little alone time to clear my head.

When my phone kicks into life, I'm delighted to see it's my sister, Kate.

'The speed with which you answered means I probably worked out the time difference correctly.' She laughs. 'How's it going there?'

'Better today than yesterday,' I admit. 'It's been a bit tricky, but we seem to be getting into the swing of things. It's very different not having my team here to do the setting up.'

'It must be slowing you down. Mum said the flight went well and no surprises with your client. What's he like?'

'Professional, but a real gentleman.'

'How I envy you the snow. We've had three days of non-stop rain here and it's miserable.'

'It is a real winter wonderland in the White Mountains. The inn itself is incredible and the food, well, it's a good job I'm on the go all day to work off those calories. Is everything going well at your end?' I can usually tell when there's something up and I hold my breath, wondering if Mum has asked her to check on me.

'Actually, I'm ringing to share some news and it's hot off the press.' Her voice is upbeat. 'I'm pregnant again!'

'OMG! And I'm not there to give you a hug in person. I'm so thrilled for you and Scott. How far along are you?'

'Twelve weeks, maybe thirteen, we're not sure. We'll know exactly next Monday as we're going back to that private clinic we used before, to have a scan. We weren't going to tell anyone until after Christmas, you know because of the miscarriage I had before Alex, but Scott let it slip in front of Mum. We then had to pop in to tell his parents and, naturally, you're next on my list.'

I wonder what my nephew, Alex, will make of having a little brother or sister. 'Goodness, you're going to have your hands full, Kate.'

'I know. It wasn't planned but we're both delighted. I've told Scott two is it, though.'

'What if it's twins?' I muse.

'Don't even joke about it, I'd have a total meltdown! By the time the new baby is here, Alex will be almost two and they don't call it the *terrible* twos for nothing. Wish me luck on Monday, as it's likely they'll both have the same star sign, so that's a good omen.'

That's my sister. Never mind about the fact that she'll need to have eyes in the back of her head, astrologically her offspring will be in tune.

'I'll be waiting for your call. I bet Mum and Dad were over the moon. It's the best Christmas gift you could give them – my present can't compete with that.'

'If it's something for their house, Mum will adore it because you have such good taste.'

'Yes, but it'll just serve to remind her that one of her daughters is still single and unloved.'

Kate bursts out laughing and I join in. 'Ria, the right man is out there for you somewhere. Just don't chance upon him while you're in the White Mountains, that would really upset Mum. It's going to take her a while to get over you not being with us all on Christmas Day. You aren't going to make a habit of this, are you? It's not some sort of avoidance tactic because we're such a noisy bunch when we get together?'

'Of course not. This is a pretty unusual project and it was too good an opportunity to turn down. Having this on my CV is going to really boost my business in the coming year.'

'Well, Alex and the new baby are lucky to have an aunt who is such a great example. You work hard and you deserve every little bit of success that comes your way.'

'And the bonus is that, thanks to you, I get to enjoy all the baby and toddler cuddles but escape the sleepless nights and the angst of parenting.'

Kate lets out a groan. 'Oh, don't get me started on lack of sleep. Alex has a chesty cough and last night I doubt either of us had more than three hours' sleep in total. Scott, of course, didn't hear a thing. That man would sleep through an earthquake.'

'Yes, but you love him to bits and he's good at DIY, so he's handy to have around.'

'True. Oh, I'm going to miss you when we're at Mum and Dad's. You will make it home in time to see the new year in, won't you? We'd all be gutted if you don't.'

'I'll be back several days beforehand, all going well. Take it easy and put your feet up whenever you can. Let Scott fuss over you because it's what he does and give Alex a big hug from me. I hope he feels better really soon. Thanks for ringing and love to you all!'

When the line goes dead I suddenly feel a little homesick. Being here is like being in a bubble. It almost feels unreal at times. *It's one Christmas, that's all*, I tell myself, as I get up and turn off the sidelight before wandering over to the window. Gazing out at the dark velvety-looking sky, the sheer number of stars to be seen with the naked eye is unbelievable. With hardly any light pollution other than the lights from the inn, it's almost impossible to find a part of the sky that isn't full of tiny twinkles. The longer you look, the more you see.

I undo the window latch and slide the frame upwards, kneeling down to lean on the window seat and draw in a few deep breaths. It's bracing, as the temperature is dropping fast, but the air is invigorating. There's a sweetness to it, and a sense of stillness washes over me before I start shivering and reluctantly slide it shut.

I make my way back to the bed, and as I'm about to turn on the sidelight again, I hear a loud creak over by the door to the en-suite as if someone has trodden on a floorboard. My pulse begins to race and I spin back around, my eyes scanning the room, but there's no movement to be seen. Quickly reaching out to flick the switch, I take a deep breath as my eyes adjust to the light when a sudden tap on the door makes me jump.

'Ria? It's Hayden.'

I swing it open, surprised to see him.

'I know you're busy, but you remember Frank who kindly gave us a lift back to the inn the other night?'

'I do . . . don't stand in the hallway, come inside.'

'Ooh, it's a bit chilly in here. Is the heating working?'

I pull a face. 'Sorry, I spent a few minutes sitting next to the window with it open. I wanted to get some fresh air and look at the stars. It's all still quite a novelty to me.'

'Oh, no problem at all. I often do the same thing. When I'm not here I miss it. But it's good you enjoy the fresh air, because Frank has offered us the use of his cabin up in the woods for an overnight stay. You must have made quite an impression on him, because he thought you'd get a kick out of it.'

Hayden closes the door and I indicate for him to take a seat on the only chair in the room, while I plonk myself back down on the bed.

'That's very kind of him, if you think there's time to fit it in.'

'I'll send you some photos before I take him up on the offer. It's rustic and rather basic. There is a queen-size bed up in the eaves and a pull-out day bed downstairs that extends out into a double. The cabin is in a beautiful spot, with no one else around for miles and there's both an indoor and an outdoor kitchen. We could eat under the stars, but you will need as many layers of clothing as you can fit in a backpack.'

'It sounds awesome,' I confirm. 'Frank was a real laugh. Was he serious about his bear-wrestling story?'

'Yep. He lived to tell the tale and that's precisely what he does. Mind you, since that episode I don't think his hunting rifle is ever out of reach. Anyway, I'll email that over to you shortly and let me know what you think. The way things are going I reckon we'll be able to press ahead a bit quicker now, so I'm sure we can carve out some time. The cabin is small but equipped for short stays. If you're looking for an experience you'll never forget, this is your chance, but it wouldn't suit everyone. Anyway, I'll leave you to it. And um . . . don't work too late.'

Hayden hesitates for a couple of seconds with his hand on the doorknob. When he turns his head and our eyes meet, his smile is warm and engaging. 'Sleep well, Ria. See you in the morning.'

As I get back to my spreadsheet, it occurs to me how difficult this must be for Hayden. Would I have the courage to bring in a total stranger to carry out a task like this, given what's going on with his parents? Talk about getting up close and personal; I've been pulled into their situation whether I like it or not. Mason is now opening up to me as if I'm a friend of the family, not someone being paid to do a job and even the rapport between Hayden and me is beginning to blur the lines a little.

I force myself to focus on the task in hand, when several minutes later, an email notification comes through. When I open it, Hayden has sent me a link to a folder of photographs and curiosity gets me clicking. He's keen.

Oh. When he said basic, he wasn't joking. And small. The outdoor kitchen is three times as big as the inside one but I instantly break out into a smile. It's one night of living off-grid and getting back to nature. I can hack that and I doubt I'll ever get the chance again. My fingers get typing.

It's amazing! If the next couple of days go well, and we can get ahead, I'm totally up for a night in the wilds as long as it isn't putting anyone out.

As I get back to work, I can't help wondering whether taking me to Shelley's, and now this cabin experience, is down to Hayden being on a bit of a guilt trip. The job has turned out to be way more demanding than I was led to believe. Managing expectations is one thing, treading on eggshells around an explosive domestic situation is something else entirely. His response is almost instant.

Great. Let's make it happen, one way or another. I'll tell Frank we're free Saturday night and organise some supplies to be taken up ahead of our arrival. I'm excited – he's never offered a stay there before and it's all down to you.

Mmm . . . I guess he's not feeling that guilty, after all. Still, how lucky am I, and at least Hayden is good company. I'm guessing that as his father is an expert in survival training, he'll be pretty clued up himself. Which, given that we're spending the night in such an isolated location, is a comforting thought even if, on another level, it's a little unsettling. I mean, Hayden is an attractive guy, but I'm not one to get cosy with the boss.

I guess this is a little different, though. Maybe what happens in the White Mountains, stays in the White Mountains. Would that really be so bad? Especially as I'm feeling rather excited about this unexpected little trip. *Is that the only reason?* my inner voice pipes up. *Or are you also looking forward to spending some alone time with a man you're finding more intriguing by the day?*

Hayden

9

A Little Give and Take

Day four and when I unlock the log cabin, my heart sinks. How on earth we're going to make this presentable I have no idea.

'Where on earth do we start sorting this lot out?'

My father joins me, as we slip off our boots. 'I thought after putting up the lights around the inn yesterday, it would make a bigger dent in it than it has. Still, your mum was happy and Ria was right, the sleigh looks perfect underneath the sign up by the road.'

'You'd better enlighten me on what the plan is in here. It was a bit vague. I was surprised Mum didn't pick up on that.'

He hangs his head a little. 'She did, actually. We had a brief chat, late last night. I'm prepared to be reasonable and make sacrifices, but Ria thinks we're missing a trick not utilising this space for our guests.'

That might have been a clever move on Ria's part, because my parents will need to be on the same page when it comes to trimming up the communal areas of the inn. At least my mother will be less inclined to get upset if the log cabin ends up looking like it's Christmas in Aladdin's cave, rather than the inn.

'That's fine, but how do we turn these piles into some sort of cohesive look? Has Ria given you any visuals?'

My father frowns. 'Not exactly, but she said she'll be popping in.'

'When?'

'I don't know, just when she can. They're hoping to finish off the room they started late yesterday and move on to The White Spruce Suite.'

Great. Surely by now Ria realises giving my father free rein isn't the best idea.

'OK, what do you want me to do?'

'Ria likes everything to be coordinated, so let's start by sorting out the piles into colours. She suggested that we look out for anything that is damaged, or past its sell-by date. Which I think means she wants me to have a good clear-out.'

It's good to hear that Ria has given him a little direction, which is a start. Instinctively, I reach out to detangle one of Grandma's favourite decorations: a bell which, when you pull the round weight attached to a cord, plays 'Frosty the Snowman'.

'Are we separating out the stuff for the inn?' I check and my father shrugs his shoulders.

'I guess so. Nothing's been said about that.'

'The bell has to stay, though,' I state, adamantly. 'And what about the village snow scenes?'

Another shrug of the shoulders. 'Don't ask me.'

'And the *Arctic Express*?' Everyone loves a train layout and I can't remember a Christmas it didn't take pride of place in the hallway.

'I'm sure Ria will tackle that in good time. I have no idea what will be deemed suitable.'

'Oh, come on, Dad. Some of these things are classics, stuff you rarely see elsewhere.' Now I'm the one wallowing in nostalgia. 'What I meant to say is that you can stand your ground you know, if you feel strongly about something.' I can't believe I just said that.

My father doesn't look up, as his hands are busy trying to untangle two coils of lights shaped like icicles. 'Ria made me see sense and, when all is said and done, it's not just about me, is it? We can't keep everything now that the inn is coming together. I approve of the new look having seen the results and your mother is letting me sneak some of the items of furniture back in that we originally argued over. It was overcrowded in the first place, I get that now. We're definitely heading in the right direction, my son.'

'That's good to hear, Dad.' I grab a bundle of tinsel and begin separating the strands. To say I'm surprised at his reaction is an understatement. He was feisty to begin with and now Ria has him firmly in check. I mean, that's a good thing on one hand as my mother seems a lot happier, but he's not the only one who has childhood memories buried in among this glittery lot.

'Can we just decide that when it comes to packing the trimmings back up, we do a better job in future?' I offer.

My father starts laughing as he glances up at me from his seated position on the floor. 'Ah, Christmas is a test of one's patience, my son. All this is usually sorted by the time you arrive. Sadly, it's not Santa who makes it happen. Since your granddad's passing, it's been down to me and I don't mind telling you that it's flippin' hard work! Now stop complaining and let's get this into some sort of order before the boss arrives.'

I stare at him, wondering whether he's referring to my mother, or Ria. Either way, he's right.

Actually, once we get into the swing of it, it's not quite as bad as it looks and before long we have gold, silver, red, white and green areas spread out around us. And a huge pile that we both agree is only fit for the trash can.

'I don't know about you, Hayden, but the chill's getting to me. Why don't I get the fire going while you make us a coffee?'

As I stand, I stretch my arms in the air and my back cracks. 'Great idea. Remind me not to keep bending over; I'm used to sitting at a desk in an ergonomically designed chair and I'm not sure how much of this my spine can take.'

He chuckles as he grabs some kindling from a basket in the corner and kneels down in front of the wood burner.

'It's all in a day's work here at the inn. I meant to ask, what did Ria think of Shelley's place?'

I switch on the coffee machine and wait for it to do its little cycle while I grab two mugs. 'I told her to hold off on judging the food until she's tasted your equivalent. They still scoff at the newfangled version, although it's on the menu.'

'Ha!' He laughs. 'What Shelley would give for our family recipe; it annoys the heck out of her. I was tempted though.'

In surprise, I spin around a bit faster than expected and suddenly the machine is dispensing coffee and there's nothing to catch it. 'Darn it.' The only thing at hand is a tea towel and it takes quite a bit of mopping before I can stem the flow. 'Tempted to do what?' I enquire, cagily.

When I walk over to my father with a mug in hand, he sits back on his heels and his expression is dour.

'Look, this is just between us, although your mother will find out in good time. I'm hoping by then she'll be so over the moon with this place, she'll forgive me.'

My jaw drops. 'You haven't told her Shelley is doing the catering for the Christmas Eve relaunch party?'

My father rolls his eyes. 'Oh, Shelley mentioned it to you, then.'

'She did. And she was a bit upset that she hasn't had an invite to the party itself.'

'Hmm. Well, that's unlikely to happen.'

'Dad, why go to Shelley?'

He takes the mug from me. 'Because it's the closest eatery and who else could I get at such short notice? When your mother suddenly decided that treating our guests to a big Christmas Eve party would soon fill the rooms, she was right. She suggested Ralph's Country Kitchen, but he looked at me as if I was mad.'

It was a big mistake leaving my father to organise anything. It's not his strong point, even at the best of times.

'I can't cook and host, and I don't want mediocre – we're doing this properly. It's worth the price I had to pay.'

Oh no . . . this is going to be bad news, I can feel it in the pit of my stomach.

'OK, she took it on as a favour. It was either let Shelley in on the secret family recipe or cover a shift some time in January. Her chef's about to become a father for the third time and his assistant will need backup when they get the call.'

'I can't believe what I'm hearing. Mum will go ballistic when she finds out.'

The guilty look on his face tells me he's already regretting his decision. 'It's done now. And I don't know why your mother needs to make a thing of it anyway. There's nothing going on between me and Shelley, that's all water under the bridge. If it hadn't come up, they'd still be on speaking terms. You don't think Shelley meant it . . . about an invite, do you?'

I shake my head at him, unable to hide my disappointment at the mess he's got himself into.

'I'm guessing it was real. Shelley thinks it's time to *close the door on the past* and why wouldn't she, when there's nothing to hide? But, Dad, seriously – what were you thinking?'

'Make yourself a coffee, my son. Let's focus on keeping Ria happy when she turns up to check on us. I'll sort the other issue. Promise.'

There's nothing as tragic as a man who has dug himself into a hole and doesn't even realise it. The only thing that I find encouraging is that if he had anything at all to hide, he'd stay a million miles away from Shelley. Unfortunately, I fear my mother might not see it that way.

'Sorry, guys. I lost track of time.' Ria bursts through the door and by now we're down to T-shirts, as the wood burner is pumping out the heat.

'Wow – what a difference!' she exclaims.

'See, I do listen!' My father is quick to respond.

Ria turns to look at me. 'You've both worked really hard to get it to this stage. Where is everything?'

My father winks at me. 'That's our little secret, isn't it, Hayden? The thing is, do you approve of the new look?'

Ria claps her hands together. 'It's beautiful, guys. Really beautiful.'

Thank goodness for that! My father was adamant that Ria doesn't like multicoloured, so anything that wasn't white, or silver, had to go. That meant, after untangling everything, boxing a lot of it up again. Admittedly, upstairs is jam-packed, but it's out of sight.

'I love the simplicity of it and it's so . . . so . . . oh, it's like taking a trip to the North Pole and walking into Santa's cabin. All that's missing—'

It's my turn to step up. 'Is a real Christmas tree.'

Ria spins around on sock-clad feet to grin at me.

'That would make it perfect. Honestly, if you offer your guests afternoon tea here, sitting by the log fire, they'll be enthralled. And imagine it at night.' Her face lights up. 'Hot chocolate, gingerbread men. This is precisely the sort of experience they'll remember forever.'

'I . . . um . . . had an idea. We weren't sure whether it would meet with your approval.' I glance across at my father, hoping he'll back me up.

'Hayden's granddad had a train layout that usually sits in the hallway in the inn, Ria, but there's more than enough space to set it up in here. What do you think? It's a snow scene my grandfather built for my father when he was a boy, and the locomotive is named the *Arctic Express*. As a boy, it was one of the highlights of Hayden's Christmas.'

Oh, Dad! Now she's going to think I'm encouraging him to hang on to things, instead of letting them go. I was rather hoping I wouldn't have to prompt him, but I can't stand back and see an important piece of our tradition banished like a tattered old decoration. It's a vintage piece, a collectable.

My father breaks out into a huge smile and Ria nods her head in total agreement.

'Who isn't fascinated watching a train going around a

track? It's a wonderful idea that will no doubt bring back memories for adults and delight the children who are seeing something like that for the first time. You really do need to give the log cabin a name, though. I'm sure you'll come up with something suitable. Now, I hate to dip in and then head straight out, but Evie and I are on a mission. I promised I wouldn't be gone long. She asked if we could delay lunch today, if that's all right with you? One o'clock?'

'Sure, no problem, Ria. I'll start unpacking the train set.'

'Santa's Retreat!' My father calls out as Ria's about to step out the door.

'Fabulous!'

'You do know I've been anxiously waiting for an update from you,' Izzie levels at me, as her voice filters around the room. I place the phone down on my bedside table and laze back against the headboard. 'You can't leave me hanging, wondering what's going on at your end.'

'I'm literally exhausted. All those stairs; up and down, and in and out, traipsing back and forth to Santa's Retreat. When the snow is two feet deep it's a pain; snow gear on, snow gear off . . . ugh. You have no idea!'

'Santa's Retreat?'

'That's the old cabin you might have spotted in some of the outside photos I sent you yesterday.'

'Oh, just to rub it in when I said you were exaggerating about how deep the snow was. You're enjoying yourself, aren't you?'

'Well, it's festive and I've never actually been involved in trimming up the inn before. My father pointed that out to me and he was right. I usually fly in at the last minute, to see the parcels I sent neatly stacked beneath the tree, and the only person I have to organise is . . . me. Now we're gearing up to welcome at least nineteen guests and, at the last count, an additional twenty locals for the Christmas Eve party. It's all go.'

'How are you coping with the pressure?'

'Hmm. It varies.' I pause for thought. 'Moment to moment, if I'm being honest.'

'Why?'

I let out a low groan. 'Ria had no idea what she was taking on, but she's risen to the challenge. My father is like a different man. He's stopped digging in his heels and he's cooperating.'

Izzie giggles. 'Isn't that a good thing? Your mother certainly sounded cheerful enough when we spoke just now.'

'Oh, so that's why you called. She wanted you to check up on me.'

'Not at all. I still haven't received my Christmas Eve party invite, that's all.'

My mother has a lot to answer for, because I bet she's the one who prompted this. 'I know, but there's literally no room left at the inn I'm afraid.' I say it tongue-in-cheek, but when my mother and Izzie get together they're a force to reckon with. Listening to subtle hints about high-flying executives reaching burnout and the need to take more time out for relaxation, is wearing. I can cope with them individually, but not in tandem.

'You seem to find it amusing, Hayden, but I was being serious. You're well aware that I haven't seen your parents since they left the UK. I'd happily swap the rain for snow. I might even be able to ease things along, you know, with Mason and Evie.'

I'm not falling for that. Izzie just hasn't had any better offers to keep her occupied this Christmas and she's at a loose end. 'Aren't you accompanying your parents on the obligatory trip to some luxurious skiing resort this year?'

'My mother says she wants to go somewhere hot so I'm tempted to give it a miss. What's Christmas without snow?' Izzie replies, sounding miffed.

'You'd only get bored here. I won't have any free time at all because it's going to be all about the guests. I'll be fetching and carrying, and generally at everyone's beck and call trying to keep the peace. Then Christmas Day I'm wearing my chef's apron and Boxing Day I'm organising some party games. On the twenty-seventh, I'll be driving Ria to the airport and then rushing back to help take the pressure off at the inn.'

I sincerely hope it won't be quite as boring as I make it sound; however, Izzie is the sort of woman who commands your full attention. I need to be fully charged to keep up with her. Yes, we do enjoy some fun times together back in the UK, but it usually takes me a day or two to recover afterwards. Izzie never stops talking, she's a real live wire, and mostly she loves to talk about the need for me to step outside my comfort zone.

'I know you're under pressure and you've sacrificed what should have been a well-earned break, Hayden, to make it all happen. Still, it must be working because Evie was singing Ria's praises.'

It was worth taking the call just to hear that. 'Mum does seem a lot happier, but there's still a lot to do and the pressure is on. I only hope we can keep the momentum, and the goodwill, going.'

'Whatever the outcome, you've more than done your bit.' Izzie's voice is gentle, comforting. 'Just remember that there are no guarantees. The move was harder on your mother than it was on your father and there's no denying that. It's not solely about making the place viable, it's about her missing what she left behind.'

Izzie has a knack of saying something to stop me in my tracks and I remember why she'll always be on speed dial. The truth is hard to hear, but I needed reminding of that and, as a close friend, she doesn't hold back.

'Thanks. You know what I'm like, I panic if I don't have a handle on things. How's life at your end? Any promising dates on the horizon? Have you been out and about Christmas shopping yet?'

'Goodness, no – on both scores! I've written a list and I'm

about to order everything online. The shops are manic at this time of the year and I can't stand queuing to pay for things.'

'Ah . . . of course not. It is annoying. But the ambience is rather nice, you know, all that cheesy Christmas music playing in the background.'

She laughs, disparagingly. 'That's so not my style and you know it. And my love life is in the doldrums, but I'm hoping it'll pick up at Christmas when I get into party mode. Anyway, I'm probably stopping you from doing something useful. I wanted to check in, say thanks for the photos, and let you know I'm here if you need me.'

'It's appreciated, Izzie. I'm sorry I left you hanging when I know you're concerned, but it's been non-stop.'

This time her laughter is different, teasing. 'If you want something doing, give it to a busy person. In your case, Hayden, it's time to start putting yourself first. We must arrange a day out together when you get back, it's been a while since we let loose.'

'As long as it's not abseiling, like the last time. Never again. You know I don't like heights!'

'Yes, that was a bit of a mistake.' She belly-laughs at the memory of me freaking out when I got the rope stuck and couldn't move. 'Take care of you and we'll speak soon. Give my love to your father and stop worrying about your parents – that's an order.'

She always puts a smile on my face. I make a mental note to think of a way to get Izzie over here for a week next year when the summer season is over. I'll take her trekking; she'll adore the colours as autumn begins to transform the scenery, and you see a lot more before the snow hits.

10

Mixing Business and Pleasure

'It doesn't feel like a Saturday to me, does it to you, Hayden?' Ria asks, as she plumps up the scatter cushions before laying them out on the sofa in Santa's Retreat.

'Not really. I tend to lose all sense of time whenever I'm here. My routine at home is pretty much the same every day but this is an enforced digital detox. Which isn't a bad thing, and Izzie is always berating me for not factoring more time for that into my schedule. I also forgot to put on my watch this morning, which doesn't help.'

'That's got to be a good sign, though, as Izzie is right. You know, stepping off the daily treadmill helps you to get a better perspective on life.'

'I suppose so. She'll give me advice whether I want it or not. She was a nightmare when we were growing up. It's more like having a bossy sister and my mother is partly to blame for that. It's a comfort to her knowing that Izzie keeps an eye out for me and vice versa. How are we doing for time?'

'We've got about another thirty minutes before your father brings your mother over to get her reaction. I hope you didn't mind me asking for your help to get those boxes stowed away upstairs. Your parents were just so chatty over elevenses and when your father offered to give your mother a hand putting up the curtains in The Mountain Maple Suite, I thought they were best left to it.'

'It's fine by me. I'll shift that last box and then I'll get the fire going. The electric heater is all right, but it doesn't have the same ambience, does it?'

'Not really. It's that evocative smell of woodsmoke that adds the charm. And the beautiful tree you and Mason cut down first thing this morning, of course.'

The clock is ticking, so I race upstairs and when I return, Ria is wiping down the table-cum-island, fussing over the little details. It's time to get those flames roaring as it always takes longer than I think it will. I don't get as much practice as my father does. When Ria gives me the nod that they're on their way, I glance around with a growing sense of satisfaction.

'Keep your eyes covered, honey,' my father insists, as he carefully guides my mother through the door. 'Now stand still while I slip off your boots. That's it, then if Ria will be kind enough to flick that switch' – he tilts his head in the direction of the railway set – 'you can open your eyes.'

My mother pans around. *Toot-toot*, goes the *Arctic Express* as it slowly rumbles around the track. Her hands fly up to her face.

'That looks absolutely delightful in here! Much better than in the hallway of the inn. It was in the way and I was always scared someone was going to walk into one of the sharp corners. I love it, Ria.'

'It wasn't down to me,' Ria insists. 'Mason chose the colour scheme and did the decorating. Setting up the train set was Hayden's idea and it really does feel like Santa's Retreat now.'

My mother continues wandering around, seemingly enthralled and homing in on every little detail. She may even be a little glassy-eyed. I will admit that the sparkling Christmas tree does look and smell amazing. As I glance over at Ria, I can see how thrilled she is with the response.

My father's broad smile is tinged with pride, but it's the way his eyes follow my mother as she wanders over to stare down at the train set that brings a lump to my throat. He wants her to be happy and that stands out a mile.

'It wouldn't be Christmas without the *Arctic Express*, would it, Mum?' I stride forward to stand next to her.

She turns to look at me. 'No, Hayden, you're right. It wouldn't.'

I never thought I'd hear her say that. Last year she hit a low point, saying how on earth was she supposed to keep the inn clean when every available bit of space was covered with something. My father was immediately on the defensive, of course, because everything has meaning to him. My mother called it clutter, and Christmas Eve was frosty, both inside and out. But some of this stuff is important to my father, and – to my surprise, if I'm being totally honest – to me, too.

'What do you think of the display of Grandma's collection of handmade quilts?' my father asks, rather gingerly. 'Ria said it was a pity to store them somewhere out of sight.'

We all watch with bated breath as my mother walks over to what was once a floor-to-ceiling pine shelving unit next to the kitchen area. It was formerly used to display a random collection of crockery which, as far as I'm aware, didn't have any special meaning or value attached to it.

'I did a little research online and they're collectables,' Ria adds. 'I admit I had no idea they aren't all simply decorative patterns for what was a very practical thing back in the day. Some of the designs actually tell a story.'

Ria has a knack of saying exactly the right thing, at the right time.

'I remember coming in here when Grandma and her quilting friends were sitting, gossiping away as they sewed. They were a noisy bunch,' I remember, fondly.

'Brave lad. I always gave them a wide berth.' My father chuckles.

'She'd have approved of this.' My mother runs her fingers lightly over the carefully folded quilts, stowed neatly away on the shelves. 'Time marches on, but it's a part of the history of the place.'

It was clever of Ria to factor in a way to display them in

here. It certainly adds to the homely, authentic feel. While they're out of kilter with the colour-coordinated rooms inside the inn, they look perfectly at home in Santa's Retreat.

'It'll be a lovely place for our guests to sit on a cold evening with the fire going and a quilt draped over their legs. They were meant to be used. And what fun to sit and enjoy playing cards, or a game of chess maybe. We could reclaim that little wooden chest from the attic and put some board games in it. It would tuck into that space next to the rocking chair over there.' My mother indicates with her hand.

'That's a great idea, honey,' my father replies, walking over to catch her hand in his. Glancing across at Ria, I can see even she's feeling emotional.

Who would have thought that what was a clever plan to appease my father, would also mean something to my mother.

My father clears his throat, feeling a tad uncomfortable. 'I'd best get off, as I've arranged to meet Frank up by the ridge and these two need to think about getting themselves ready.'

'The supplies are all packed up,' I confirm.

'Don't forget to pull out the fresh stuff in the fridge, Mason,' my mother adds. 'The cool box is in the utility room. Are you and Ria all packed and ready for your overnight stay? You have no idea how delighted Hayden is, Ria. He's been itching to get himself invited up to Frank's little getaway in the woods.'

'I packed my bag yesterday,' I confirm, unable to hide my enthusiasm.

Ria starts laughing. 'It probably took me longer to decide what to pack for twenty-four hours, than it did to fill my two suitcases for the entire trip. But I had some expert advice.' She grins at me.

My mother walks over to place her arm around Ria's shoulders. 'You're in very good hands, my dear. I remember the first time Mason took me on a day-long trek. We didn't stay overnight, but – as tiring as it was – I was captivated.

It's an experience that will stay with you forever; nature at its best.'

I'm pretty sure this whole thing is a trip that Ria will never forget, but not necessarily for the intended reason. She's no longer just an interior designer here to bail out a failing business, she's become instrumental in helping a family to heal. The biggest shock for me is that while I thought I was doing this solely for my parents' sake, I'm also getting a buzz out of it. If I ever settle down and have kids, I'll delight in telling them stories about playing with the *Arctic Express* and now it seems that tradition is going to live on. That's quite a thought.

We're forty minutes out from Frank's farm, where we parked the car. Ria still hasn't quite found her stride, but she's not a complainer.

'Is that backpack more manageable?' I check. When I saw what she'd tried to cram in, it wasn't easy to convince her that she'd thank me for lightening her load. I reiterated that basic means just what it says. Essentials only. When it comes to her snow gear, Ria came well prepared. Fast-wicking long johns and the all-important non-cotton item next to the skin can be the difference between a miserable hike and an enjoyable one.

Ria nods her head, only the lower half of her face visible due to the furry hood on her jacket and the mirrored sunglasses. 'Definitely. What was I thinking? I'm warm and have everything I need to survive overnight. The truth is, I'd already be struggling if it weren't for you doing a double-check.'

Something tells me that she's a little outside of her comfort zone, perhaps daunted by the cabin's isolated location, but that didn't deter her. I admire Ria for that and for putting her trust in me. For some absurd reason it means a lot.

'There's an impressive waterfall off to the right-hand side of the trail if you're up for a little detour. We can take a break once we get there.'

Ria's cheeks are glowing, but she's doing just fine and has a lot more stamina than I figured. There's a huge difference between just being on the go all the time and physical endurance. Snowshoeing is way more strenuous than it looks and I'm beginning to feel the burn, so I know I'm out of shape.

'I'm game,' she replies, trying her best to keep her breathing even.

'Keep digging in your toes to get a good grip as the incline steepens. Use the trekking poles to take your weight and give you leverage; it saves energy once you know how to use them properly.'

'This is nothing at all like skiing,' she confirms. 'Snowshoeing isn't exactly easy.'

Ria draws to a halt in front of a sturdy pine tree that towers high above us. Leaning back against the sparse lower trunk for a moment, she stops to take in the scenery.

'You haven't quite got the knack of using the flexible pivot bar when you lift your foot,' I explain. 'The sharp crampons dig into the snow and the aim is to let the snowshoe cope with the angle. It's a bit like rock climbing. Try to keep your foot level and let the equipment do its job. Believe me it'll be a whole a lot easier.' Goodness, just listen to me. It could be my father talking.

It reminds me of the way he instructed me whenever we went on one of what I called our expeditions, when I was a boy and then on into my teens. Ria takes it on board as we press on and ten minutes later I clear the snow off a fallen tree trunk for a welcome rest. With the gentle sounds of the waterfall now audible in the background, this is a pleasant place to rest up.

'Coffee?' I offer and Ria gives me a grateful look.

'If you're not joking, then you are a total star!' she exclaims.

Lowering myself down next to her, I pull the small Thermos flask from my backpack. 'I usually just pack water, but my father made this. You have a real fan there, and he thought you'd appreciate it.'

As I slip off my gloves Ria already has her hands out ready to hold the two metal mugs while I pour. She draws in a deep breath as a little white cloud escapes into the air, savouring the aroma as it reaches her nose.

'That was kind of him, and it smells so good. Seriously, if this doesn't revive me, nothing will.'

'We're halfway there and you've done well tackling that climb. It levels out a little now and the slope will be less noticeable from here onwards.'

'It's so beautiful and pristine. I hate trampled snow and the only tracks here are ours, and an animal or two,' she comments, passing me the small metal mug. I watch as she wraps her hands around the other one, looking content.

'That's why it's such a bonus to be able to get out here. Did you catch the sound of a snowmobile off in the distance shortly after we set off?'

'I did. It sounded like it was struggling a little.'

'It took the shortest route, which is a fair bit steeper. That was Frank, taking our provisions up to the camp and checking everything there is in working order. Sometimes the snow needs clearing from the solar panels. It's not fun to shower in icy cold water.'

Ria gives a little laugh. 'I'm just delighted to hear there's going to be some heated water.'

'Frank's what they call a ghostwriter for sports personalities when they want to write their memoirs. He often spends a couple of weeks at a time up there, so while the cabin is small, it's liveable. Back in the day, he was a champion alpine skier; he even won a silver medal at the Winter Olympics one year.'

'That doesn't surprise me at all. The night he gave us a lift back to the inn it was obvious he wasn't just your average farmer,' she reflects. 'This is probably the most exciting thing I've ever done and it's very generous of Frank to offer us the use of his cabin.'

'He can't resist a British accent. He's a widower now, but his late wife was born and brought up in the Lake District. You struck a chord with him; she had a bubbly personality too.'

'You think I'm bubbly?'

Have I offended her? Maybe that wasn't the best word to use, even though I think it sums her up perfectly.

'You know, full of energy and proactive. I will admit that few people surprise me these days, but you did from day one.'

Ria turns to face me. 'How?'

'I set my goals high for myself but have found that it pays to be more realistic when it comes to my expectations of others. Few exceed them, but you have, and I admire that. Some people have that innate sense of drive and determination, others don't.'

Ria frowns. 'I agree with you there. Sometimes, when the going gets tough, you just have to grit your teeth and power through it.'

'Exactly! Izzie thinks I push myself too hard. She says that having a balanced life is the ultimate fulfilment, but I guess I haven't got to that point yet. I've worked hard to get to this stage and I'm not about to take my foot off the proverbial pedal. Izzie doesn't intend to give up on me, though, and in some ways she is my voice of reason.'

'It must be nice to have someone like that in your life.'

'Yes, and when Izzie needs someone to lean on for the more practical stuff, she knows exactly where to come. The two of us seem to ground each other in different ways.'

Ria and I lapse into silence for a while.

'Is it possible to get a little closer to the waterfall?' she asks, a few minutes later. 'I thought it would be a raging torrent considering it comes from way up there' – she points to the mountain range in the background – 'and yet it's rather tame.'

'If we're done, I'll show you why.'

She's eager to set off again, which is a good sign. The next bit involves navigating the result of several landslides over the years. 'You'll need to sling your snowshoes over your shoulders. Use the quick release on the ratchet, like this.' I demonstrate the one-finger action.

'Great. I'm looking forward to this.'

'It's such a pity about the cloud cover today, Ria. Everything has that white haze to it. I prefer it when the sky is blue and you can see the tops of the snow-capped mountains. Anyway, follow me. Just take care and don't rush it.'

Once we've skirted around the bottom of the pile of boulders, it's a lot easier underfoot. The dense fir trees are snow-covered but the ground beneath them is mostly powdery stuff as the rocky mountainside provides protection. The roar gets louder and when we step out onto an elevated platform Ria is stunned and her jaw drops. 'That's not what I was expecting at all!'

'Finger Falls is worth a little detour, isn't it?'

'It's not one waterfall, it's a whole collection of little waterfalls, but hardly any of them are flowing, only that section in the middle.'

'It got its name because the water seeps through the striations that were gouged out of the bedrock as a glacier moved downstream. Coarse gravel gets trapped, and builds up over time, blocking the flow, so for the most part water only seeps through in places. As you can see, it freezes solid like a row of fingers, but the icicles are crystal clear and to me it looks like glass, reflecting how beautifully clean the water is.'

'Extremely large fingers,' Ria points out, tilting her head back as far as she dares without toppling over.

'The pressure of the flow of the water once the snow does start to melt is what causes the landslides and it's now gouged out that central part, which is pretty much free-flowing all year round.'

'It's magnificent.' Ria lets out a deep breath, the warmth of it hitting the cold air around her and instantly vaporising.

As I watch her reaction, I remember the first time my

father brought me up here. That was just before Christmas one year, too, and I was equally as stunned and in awe of nature's creation.

'OK, I know you said the selfie stick was optional, but it's time to pose with my intrepid tour guide.'

I roll my eyes. 'Really?'

'You are joking – this is the photo opportunity of a lifetime for me!'

If this impresses her, then I can't wait until she sees the cabin. I've visited it so many times to hang out with Frank and my father, but never stayed overnight before. This is one little excursion we're likely to remember for a long time to come. I'm looking forward to it and Ria more than deserves a little time away from the inn.

In fact, on reflection, I can't think of anyone else I'd rather share this experience with. Not only do I find that thought rather surprising, it's actually a bit of a shock to the system.

Ria

11

A Real Adrenaline Rush

In my head I'd wistfully pictured something about the same size as Santa's Retreat back at the inn, but in a more isolated setting. What I see before me looks like a larger version of a kiddie's tree house on stilts, with a large outbuilding a few feet away.

'What do you think?' Hayden asks, enthusiastically.

'It's delightful. It just . . . um . . . looked a bit bigger in the photos.'

Hayden yanks the largest key fob I've ever seen in my life from his backpack, unaware of my misgivings. This is really going to get up close and personal.

'Is that a piece of a branch?' I ask him.

'Yep. Out here you don't want a couple of keys on a tiny metal ring.'

Goodness, it's big enough to be classed as an offensive weapon, I muse. We're standing on the cute raised porch, which is set back a little, almost like an extension. The main part of the cabin is obviously one room with a sort of mezzanine above. Judging by how close the two slightly offset windows are, it's going to redefine my interpretation of the word *cosy*. What I saw as a rustic, wonky little cabin is more of a hobbit house up close. Given the steep slope of the roof, only a hobbit could stand up in the upstairs bedroom.

Having placed our snowshoes in a convenient store cupboard recessed into the wall, Hayden swings open the door and immediately reaches out to flick on a switch. Several strings of lights suddenly add a rosy hue to the outdoor space. We quickly step over the threshold and immediately slip off our boots. There's a tray just inside for the footwear, to catch the melting snow.

The cabin is surprisingly warm and I glance around, entranced. It's easy to take it all in because, quite frankly, there isn't much to it. Hayden told me there's a queen-size bed and a pull-out sofa, but he didn't say we'd be more or less sleeping in the same room. The ladder to what is an open loft space doesn't come as a surprise but climbing up isn't going to be easy as it's almost vertical. You certainly wouldn't want to be rushing down it in the dark.

'It's the perfect getaway, isn't it?' Hayden is clearly excited as we slip off our backpacks and heavy jackets to hang them up. In fairness, everything is both well ordered and practical.

'Give me the tour.' I say that tongue-in-cheek and Hayden grins at me. The tour consists of simply pivoting around on one's heels.

As if he's an experienced estate agent – or realtor, as they say in the States – he does the honours. 'Pegs for snow gear and storage here to the left, then in front of us is the compact kitchen which extends along the full length of the rear wall.'

It's all I can do not to burst out laughing. That's a great way to describe a couple of units, a worktop housing the tiniest sink I've ever seen and a table-top camping stove.

'Notice how the open treads of the stairs allow for additional storage, which includes a bookcase,' he continues, grandly. 'In the far corner is the ladder to the bedroom. Then opposite that is the L-shaped bench-cum-day bed, for relaxing. Bedding is stored in the cupboard beneath it. At night, one side pulls out to turn it into a small double. Last, but not least, the table has a lovely view out over the front and down to the creek.'

The table is barely three-foot square, but everything is rather charming and the longer I stand here the more it's growing on me. It's like staying in a big doll's house. But it's the small design features that have been cleverly thought through. Every wall has a window and a stunning view; above each one is a shelf with various baskets for additional storage. As I follow Hayden over to the ladder, I notice there's a hinged flap on the table and when it's extended and butted up to the day bed, it could possibly accommodate a family of four.

'I'll leave you to discover the delights of the magnificent queen-size bed,' Hayden finishes, extending his hand and breaking out into a huge smile. 'Just mind your head when you get near the top as you'll need to duck.'

I tentatively make my way up one step at a time and the bed does look extremely comfortable. However, the rafters are on such a steep pitch that they taper off to no more than a few inches above the tail end of it. If you kicked out your legs, you'd hit them. Thankfully, at the headboard end there's probably five feet of clearance. The joy of it is that as I lie in bed I'll be able to turn my head to the right and gaze out of the huge window. Bending double, all I can see is forest and mountains. It's magical, truly magical.

'I love it!' I declare, as I sit on the edge of the opening and stare down at Hayden. He's lying out on the day bed, his arms stretched back behind his head. I burst out laughing, as it's short by at least a foot, and he wriggles his sock-covered feet in the air.

There's only one teeny-tiny little issue that I can see and that's a total lack of privacy. Still, he's been here before, so if it doesn't bother him, then it shouldn't bother me, I suppose, but it's not quite what I expected.

'Great, I'll get the kettle on while you unpack your things,' Hayden suggests. 'We'll take a gander at the bathroom facilities and the outdoor kitchen after we've warmed up a bit.'

It's certainly not going to take me long to unpack, that's for sure.

* * *

'That cloud is clearing up nicely now. There's even a patch of blue sky coming through,' Hayden points out as we traipse over to the outbuilding. 'This is, rather unglamorously, referred to as the bathhouse.'

We enter a smaller wooden cabin, a stone's throw from the main building.

'The water remains hot for several minutes if you're taking a shower, but if it starts to run cold, you have to wait for it to heat up again. But, as you can see, the facilities aren't bad. Frank invested quite a bit of money in making off-grid living as comfortable as possible.'

'Is it safe walking over here at night?' I query.

'There's a hunting knife and a hurricane lantern in the log cabin. You'll find it in the cupboard underneath the kitchen . . . the kitchen . . . sink.' Hayden is already laughing before he can finish his sentence. 'Don't worry. It's well lit up and I wouldn't let you wander around outside on your own, anyway.'

I raise my eyes to the heavens, not appreciating him joking around. When I tilt my head back to try to get a glimpse of the top of the skeleton trees, it makes me dizzy. There are a few fir trees scattered around too and the general scenery is exactly how I hoped it would be.

Attached to the bathhouse is a separate storage area where the logs and kindling for the fire are stacked, and there's a large, vented metal cabinet where the solar batteries are kept. Hayden leads me back outside and I wander over to a covered, raised deck. It's an outdoor kitchen with a solid wooden worktop. There's even a sink, albeit there isn't any running water by the look of it.

'This unlocks.' Hayden indicates to a double cupboard next to the sink. 'There's a barbecue, a portable water dispenser, which is obviously empty as everything freezes at this time of the year. It's the business, though, because nothing beats throwing a steak on the grill – that's the plan for this evening.'

I look at him aghast. 'Doesn't that encourage bears to come in search of food?'

Hayden's eyes sparkle with a sense of amusement. 'I think we'll be all right. I understand the importance of keeping a clean camp. All rubbish will be tied up in sacks and put in the shed. It's best to keep strong cooking smells outside of the main cabin, where they can't linger.'

I narrow my eyes as I stare at him. 'Oh . . . they hibernate at this time of the year, don't they?'

He nods his head, still keeping a straight face, but turns away to point a finger in the direction of a swathe of fir trees. 'I hope you have your phone, because you'll want to take some pictures of this. It's about all it's good for as you won't get a signal.'

The snow is powdery in places, and at one point as I'm following in Hayden's tracks, he lifts his foot and ends up leaving one of his snowshoes behind. He's already had a few laughs at my expense, so I simply smile as I overtake him, finally getting into a comfortable stride I can maintain. Overhead, it's wonderful to see the clouds retreating to reveal a pastel blue sky, but the light is already beginning to go and I'm glad that we're almost there. From here, it appears that the ground beyond the trees falls away, and with nothing to shield them, their branches bow under the weight of the snow.

'You seem to have discovered the knack.' Hayden is slightly breathless as he appears alongside me.

'I'm getting tired though,' I confess. 'I'm glad tomorrow it'll be all downhill.'

'You're doing great. I'm out of practice and I'm feeling it, too. We're heading for that small gap in the trees. I'll go first. There are a few low-hanging branches and I'll knock some of the snow off with my walking poles as we go through. Just keep a watchful eye.'

This isn't a place anyone should come without a guide who knows what they're doing. Even the trail wasn't as obvious in places as I'd expected. There were forks where it veered off at an angle and it was hard to know whether it was a split in the path, or just circumventing rocky outcrops.

When we eventually find ourselves back out in the open again, the view is singularly spectacular. As the land slopes down quite sharply, the snow is untouched and perfect. Not even an animal print, as far as I can see. On the horizon, the sky is darkening now and it's like a filter has been overlaid. The expansive river at the bottom of the valley is a mirror reflection of the contours of the mountain range. Between the two, a band of fading light illuminates it.

'Breathtaking, isn't it?' Hayden asks, his voice low.

It's a place where you feel inclined to whisper, afraid to shatter that sense of total peace and tranquillity. The light catches here and there on the water below, tiny little glints that indicate it's still flowing in places. The contrast with the backdrop of the dark mountains, some with seemingly little snow on them, indicates how far away they are.

I take over a dozen photos but I can tell that Hayden is keen to return to the cabin.

'Thank you for bringing me here. What a contrast to the falls, earlier on. The irony is that from the cabin no one would even know this was here.'

'Only gold miners.' He chuckles.

'Really?'

'Yep. The glaciers carried with it gold-bearing gravel. They do say that there's still a fortune to be found in the stony deposits on the huge bends in the riverbed below.'

'I can't even begin to imagine how you could get mining equipment down there, or even supplies.'

'It's not for the faint-hearted, but many have tried over the years. Right – let's set off. I don't know about you but I'm starving.'

As we begin the trek back, I feel a sense of exhilaration. I can't remember ever feeling so . . . alive. It's like all my senses have kicked in simultaneously. It's exciting but also a little bit scary, but then it's the most adventurous thing I've ever done. I've stepped outside of my life and discovered a whole new world about which I knew nothing at all. From time to time, I've glanced over articles about people who live off-grid, but the reality of it is eye-opening. And as the darkness begins to descend rather quickly, I'm suddenly very aware of the fact that, as far as I can tell, Hayden and I are the only people for miles around. Just the two of us in a wilderness of snow and trees. It doesn't get any more real than this.

'There's no chance we could get stuck up here, is there?' I call out to him. 'I mean, if there was a heavy snowfall overnight.'

Hayden stops for a moment to allow me to catch up. 'There's no snow forecast and I'm hoping for a clear sky, as the stars here are phenomenal. If there's unexpected snowfall, or we aren't back at Frank's by noon tomorrow, he'll take a trip up on his snowmobile to check on us, anyway. Don't worry, Ria – if I couldn't guarantee your safety, I wouldn't have brought you here.'

I do feel safe . . . just nervous. But I'm also a little confused about some of the other feelings that are beginning to stir inside of me. Is it because I've never really been in a situation where I've felt this vulnerable before? I wonder. I'm used to looking after myself, but I'm enjoying . . . *Hang on there, Ria*, that inner voice pipes up. *You can stop right there. Business brought you together and this is just an unexpected perk of the job.* I knew that, of course. I'm simply feeling a little distracted and for good reason. I mean . . . snowshoeing in the gloom in the White Mountains – never in my wildest dreams did I ever imagine I'd be doing this.

The table is laid and I stare at the outline of Hayden's back as the lights from the outdoor kitchen frame his body. On the barbecue grill the flames are leaping, and it isn't long before he hurries back inside. I take the covered casserole dish from him while he peels off his snow gear and kicks off his boots.

'I said it wouldn't take long. There's a nice bit of caramelisation on the outside. My father would be proud of me.'

The buttery boiled potatoes and baked beans are ready, the saucepans covered in a double layer of foil on the lowest heat, so it doesn't take long to serve. I carry the plates across to the table and Hayden pours the wine.

'This feels rather decadent,' I remark as I lay the plates down. 'With the cabin all aglow, the food smelling amazing – it's hard to take it all in.'

We raise our glasses and chink. 'Here's to what has been a really enjoyable day, Ria. I'm sure we're both going to sleep like logs tonight. I'm certainly feeling the effects of that hike now. What about you?'

'Cheers, Hayden. Yes, and it's certainly been a day I'll never forget. Thank you for taking such good care of me. I'm simply relieved I managed to make it up here without getting myself into trouble.' I giggle. *Giggle?* I'm not the sort of woman who giggles, I reflect, as Hayden stares at me.

'You had a bit of a slow start, but once you got used to the equipment there was no stopping you. Remember, I've been hiking the trails every year since I was a kid. I learnt from the best.'

As we tuck into our steaks, we lapse into silence for a little while. My thoughts are in a whirl because this feels so surreal. In fact, I can't even imagine a scenario where I would have cause to cross paths with Hayden Reynolds, the CEO of Stylish Homes, back in the UK. We hardly mix in the same circles.

'I have an admission to make.' He stops eating, resting his knife and fork on the plate in front of him, looking a little uncomfortable.

What have I missed? I wonder.

'I didn't really appreciate just how much planning goes

into pulling a design project together. Having to pre-order everything so far in advance, I'm in awe of the way you've even catered for the unknown. You seem to have pre-empted every little whim my parents have, when you didn't really have much information to go on.'

It's good of him to acknowledge that. 'It was a bit of a challenge, but your new designer range made it easy. I wanted fabrics and accessories that would enhance some of the beautiful features of the building and complement the traditional furniture that embodies the New England style. It's popular everywhere, not just in New Hampshire.'

'Do you ever tire of addressing the issue of decluttering?' Hayden picks his knife and fork up again, a look of amusement on his face.

That's a tricky question. 'Let's just say that it's easier to stage show homes as I'm starting from scratch. Most developers – although not all – focus on how much it's going to cost, and once that's agreed, I have free rein. When it comes to homes, or smaller businesses, it is more work, but so much more satisfying when you can meet, or exceed, a customer's expectations.'

He looks up, smiling. 'I'm delighted, and – I will admit – a little relieved, at how well it's going at the inn.'

I can feel my cheeks heating up and I hope he doesn't think I was sitting here waiting for a compliment. Oh gosh. Is he going to start quizzing me about his parents? It's important that not only do I remain neutral, but each of them feels they can talk to me openly and in confidence.

'It's been a team effort from day one, Hayden. Nothing is fixed, I simply listen and hopefully steer things in the right direction.'

He stops for a moment, his eyes scanning my face. 'You've successfully managed to get my father to toe the line.'

'No,' I state, quite firmly. 'I simply asked what was important to him. The answer was very little, as it turns out, and I think he's being very accommodating.' It's the truth and worth pointing out, but the moment I stop talking I wonder if I've gone too far. My tone was a tad accusatory.

Hayden instantly looks up and I can see he's feeling a little put out. 'Sorry, that sounded rather dismissive on my part. Naturally, I'm beyond grateful to you for the way you've skilfully managed a delicate situation. Even Izzie thinks I've crossed the line this time and should back off.'

The sadness I see reflected in his eyes is touching, but this isn't a conversation I want to get pulled into. Izzie obviously has a lot more influence over Hayden than I thought and, as far as I can tell, he's happy with that. Instead, I busy myself clearing the plates, hoping he'll change the subject.

'Coffee?' I ask, sounding bright and cheerful and he nods his head.

'I'll do the dishes.'

'No. You cooked the food. Just sit and relax.'

Hayden expels an agonisingly deep breath, and my heart goes out to him. He's doing everything he can to fix something that might not be fixable and the reality of that is finally beginning to dawn on him.

He stands to open a small box on the shelf above the table area.

'Um . . . there's only chess. Do you play?' he calls out, as I run a bowl of hot water.

'Yes, but not very well.'

It doesn't take long to get everything cleared up and when I return to the table with the coffees, Hayden has set up the board. As it turns out, he's not much of a better player than I am and it's kind of fun. We pretend to be overly competitive, but we're both aware that it could go either way. On the last game he makes a silly mistake and I end up winning. I glance over my shoulder, as if I heard a noise, and when I turn back around, I have my thumb and first finger of my right hand held up to my forehead. He gives a belly laugh.

'Loser? That's rich, you're calling me a loser when it's three–two to me – I'm in the lead!'

'But I won the final game. My nephew does that whenever we play together. He's eight and he can beat me every time. I knew you'd find it funny.' I laugh. It seems that the two glasses of wine I drank earlier are beginning to relax me a little too much.

'Before we turn in for the night, why don't we tog up and step outside. It's an awe-inspiring sky out there and you'll see twice as many stars as you do even at the inn. I promise you it'll be worth the effort. What do you think?'

I'm not about to say no. I haven't had as much fun as this ever. I just need to remember where I am, and who I'm with, so I don't wake up in the cold light of day regretting something I've said or done.

12

A Truly Unforgettable Night

As I'm about to step out the door, Hayden slaps his hand to his forehead.

'Oh, I nearly forgot. Frank left us a little present. A bottle of his infamous apple brandy. It'll make a nice nightcap; you can compliment him on it tomorrow, when we collect the car. If nothing, it will generate a little internal heat to get us through the night. However, I will be stoking up the log burner as a backup.' Hayden raises an eyebrow, making me laugh. 'I'll just grab two glasses and I'll be right out.'

Holding on tightly to the handrail as I descend the five wooden steps leading down from the cabin's porch, everything underfoot crunches, shattering the eerie silence. There's a crispness in the air that makes me fasten the toggle on my hood to keep out the chilly night air. It's enchanting until I hear a loud cracking sound among the trees which makes me gaze around in terror.

My instinct is to turn and run back inside, but Hayden is hastening down the steps to join me.

'Did you hear that?' I ask, nervously.

'No. What was it?'

'Splintering wood then a thud and it was close by.'

Hayden holds out a glass to me and I do a double-take. Even in the soft exterior lighting that bathes the cabin in a whimsical glow, I can see that it's in the shape of some sort of animal's head. It looks a bit weird with the dark amber liquid inside.

'Don't worry, branches break off all the time. Here you go.'

'This is a little bizarre.'

'Oh, that's Frank to a tee. It's a shot glass sitting in a moose's head with antlers. I was tempted to use the tumblers but when it comes to his home-made liqueur, a little goes a long way. Cheers!'

We air-toast and I very gingerly take a sniff. It makes my eyes water, and as I'm about to take a sip, there's another loud thud. I quickly turn around, slopping some of the liqueur over the edge of the glass.

'Hey, don't be so nervous. It's going to be like this all night long.' Hayden seems quite relaxed, but I'm on edge. 'It's just snow falling off the trees. Sometimes it makes the ground shake a little if the snow is compacted.'

I guess the sound of a hungry bear disturbed from a deep sleep would be a lot scarier and the noise it would make would tell us exactly what was coming. It seems falling branches, or a cascade of snow being dumped on my head from a great height, presents an even greater danger. Which is a real surprise.

'As long as you avoid standing under the trees you'll be fine,' Hayden assures me. 'Anyway, what do you think of the apple brandy?'

I take a cautious sip. 'Should my tongue be tingling?'

'That's a good sign, it means you're alive and kicking,' he jests. 'I'd be concerned if it didn't. This is definitely one to drink slowly, but it's not bad.'

Even though I'm not one for brandy, the taste is rather nice and it certainly accounts for that warm glow suddenly rising up inside of me. 'It's surprisingly sweet, very apple-y and I'm getting a hit of cinnamon which gives it a nice kick.'

We tramp past the outdoor kitchen to stand in the large open space.

Hayden passes me his glass. 'Hang on to this for a moment and I'll grab us a couple of seats.'

I do as I'm bid, wondering how long we'll be content to sit outside. While my face is feeling chilled, the rest of me isn't exactly cold, just not toasty.

'There's no point getting a stiff neck, is there?' Hayden busies himself setting the chairs on an angle. He takes the glasses from me as I settle myself down.

Supported by the headrest, I lie back and then sit here cupping the moose's head in my gloved hands.

'Have you ever seen a sky like that?' Hayden asks, as he stretches out. 'It's as if the heavens are made up of an endless succession of infinite layers. The longer you stare up at it, the deeper it extends.'

Taking a sip of Frank's warming brandy, I have to agree with him. 'With light pollution maybe what most people are used to seeing are simply the biggest stars because the tiny ones aren't bright enough to catch the eye. I was wowed by the night sky at the inn, but this has a hidden depth to it.'

We're both entranced, but every little sound has me casting around, nervously.

'The noises in the background are more obvious at night,' Hayden explains. 'During the day you don't notice them as much. I remember one particular year when my father and I were camping. I was probably about thirteen years old at the time. It was the summer holidays and that's when we spent the most time together. In the early hours of the morning there was an almighty crash and, boy, as I scrambled to undo the zip on my tent, my heart felt like it was going to jump out of my chest. My fingers were literally shaking as adrenaline flooded through my veins. It turned out to be a dead tree toppling over but it must have been a good thirty-foot tall. It wasn't that close to us, as checking that the trees around your camp site are sound is the first rule up here. But I didn't get much sleep after that, I can tell you.'

'It's nice to have memories like that to look back on, even if it was a sharp reminder of the hidden dangers.'

'Hmm. It is. It's been probably three years since my father and I even ventured out on a hike together and I miss it.'

That would be the year before Mason and Evie took over the inn, then. I can't help wondering what effect the loss of his granddad had on Hayden at the time. He doesn't talk about it. The first Christmas after his passing must have been a tough one for them all.

'Look!' I squeal, pointing excitedly. 'Is that what I think it is?'

A brilliant light travels in an arc across the heavens at such a speed that it looks like it has a tail. Then, just as suddenly as it appeared, it's gone.

'I caught it! Wow – a shooting star. In all the years I've been coming to the White Mountains I've only ever seen two before. Granddad believed it was a sign that a life-changing event was coming.'

'I saw it first though, does that mean it only applies to me?'

Hayden shakes his head. 'It's funny, I never thought to ask him that, but it's a good point. My father doesn't believe in old wives' tales, or superstitions, but my mother might know. She's into the spiritual stuff.'

I take another tiny sip of the apple brandy, filtering it around my mouth before I swallow, whilst contemplating what event I could be facing. Maybe this coming year will see my business grow exponentially. To the extent that I'll be able to afford to employ a small team of core people. Then another thought strikes me and I let out a gasp.

'What is it?' Hayden turns to look at me, wondering what's going on.

'I just found out that my sister, Kate, is expecting her second child. What if it turns out to be twins? I joked with her about it and she wasn't amused. Maybe it was a premonition. She's having a scan on Monday.'

'Stranger things have happened.'

'Goodness, I hope that's not the case. It's a bit like when they wish actors luck they say break a leg. It wasn't really a joking matter and now I feel bad.'

Hayden laughs, dismissively. 'She can hardly blame that on you if that's what the scan shows.'

'Oh, she'll find a way. We've always fought and made up, all our lives. She's two years younger than me and I still haven't forgiven her for all the toys of mine that she broke by standing on them.' I'm aware that I'm wittering on, but I'm feeling a little homesick.

'Well, the closest I came to a sibling is having Izzie in my life. Our mothers were best friends and we grew up together,' Hayden confesses. 'I was a shy kid way back then and, in hindsight, I've a lot to thank Izzie for. She drew me out of myself and made me join in whether I wanted to or not.'

He smiles to himself, no doubt some little memory coming to the forefront of his mind.

'I guess Kate wasn't that bad and we've had some great times together. We don't get to see each other quite as often as I'd like. I've been working six days a week and evenings aren't good for her. Little Alex is only eighteen months' old and a nightmare to get off to sleep. She also works part-time, so when she does manage to finally get him to bed, she isn't far behind him. Kate's husband is a paramedic, and he works shifts, which doesn't help the situation.' The chill is beginning to make me feel uncomfortable. 'I don't know about you but I'm ready to go back inside to warm up.'

Hayden jumps to his feet and offers his hand to help me up. 'Come on. You take the glasses while I stow the chairs away.'

He pulls me towards him, and suddenly he's looking down into my eyes. The next thing I know we're kissing each other as if it's the most natural thing in the world. As we pull away, there's a stunned silence and then the next thing out of both of our mouths is an apology.

'Sorry, Ria . . .'

'Sorry, Hayden . . .'

'It's the . . . uh . . . apple brandy,' Hayden suggests, sheepishly. 'I think it rather went to our heads, don't you?'

I'm mortified. For a moment there we let the magic of this setting get to us and now Hayden is doing the gentlemanly thing.

'Something to . . . um . . . to avoid in the future. The brandy, I mean.' I try to make light of it, but all I can think about is how natural it felt, the warmth of Hayden's lips on mine.

As I turn to head back to the cabin, Hayden light-heartedly calls out, 'Don't forget to keep an eye out for the bears, Ria.'

'I will! And you mind out for falling trees.' I'm so glad he can't see my face as I'm grinning like a monkey.

The surface of the snow beneath my feet glistens as I walk, head down, towards the cabin. I'm desperately trying to ignore a knot of emotion lying heavily in my stomach. The temperature is dropping fast and yet this little hobbit-style domain glows in the darkness, a golden sanctuary to see us through the night. However, I'm gutted. *What on earth were you thinking, Ria?* I berate myself. What was already going to be a little awkward with the two of us in such close proximity is now disconcerting. Yes, I wanted to kiss Hayden and, in that moment, he obviously wanted to kiss me. The fact that he was equally as quick to apologise indicates that he's as bewildered as I am. There's only so much you can blame on one small shot of brandy, I acknowledge, as I mount the steps to the porch. But this is highly unprofessional and I'm angry with myself for dropping my guard.

'Here, pass me the glasses.' Hayden suddenly appears at my side.

'Thanks. Even with gloves on, my fingers are feeling the cold.'

'Same here.' Thankfully, his tone is even.

I hurry inside, slipping off my boots and snow gear, then I take the glasses from Hayden and walk over to the sink unit.

'Would you like a hot drink?' I call over my shoulder, as if nothing at all out of the ordinary just happened.

'Please. I think there are sachets of hot chocolate in the basket on that shelf above you.'

I hear the sound of the key turning in the lock and metal on metal as he hangs the unwieldy key fob on one of the coat hooks.

'Just to put you at ease,' he confirms. 'I double-bagged the rubbish and it's stored in an airtight bin in the shed. All the windows are locked, I checked them earlier, so we're totally safe from marauding animals.'

Funny! I let out a hugely exaggerated sigh of relief. 'Well, that's good to know.' I laugh before I get a little more serious. 'Actually, it does strike me that people really have to know what they're doing out in the wilds; I have total faith in your abilities though.'

As Hayden walks past me, I turn to glance at him and we exchange somewhat timid smiles.

'That caught me unawares just now,' he confesses.

'Me, too. There's something about this place, isn't there?'

'Yep. Nature has a way of helping us to declutter our minds. Under different circumstances this would be a wonderfully romantic break for any couple, wouldn't it?'

Hayden's words confuse me a little and I stare at him blankly, until he breaks out into a huge grin. He's such a joker at times that he's hard to read.

'I can think of more romantic places,' I state. But it's enough to ease the tension between us as he attends to the wood burner and I carry two mugs of hot chocolate over to the day bed.

Watching Hayden sitting cross-legged on the floor in his thermal tracksuit, beavering away to resurrect the flames, he's an attractive and quite commanding man to look at. He carries himself with an air of determination and confidence, but I've already come to see that some of it is just a veneer. It might be pure coincidence, but whenever he's outside of his comfort zone he mentions Izzie. Is there some sort of dependency going on there? I can't help wondering whether the nature of their relationship is even more complicated than that. She's his mother's goddaughter, and a family and childhood friend too. Could it be that she's patiently waiting in the background until he's ready to see her as a love interest?

'Success!' Hayden eases himself to his feet, groaning a little. 'Now if this were a hotel I'd be heading straight to the spa for a massage. How about you?'

'Don't! That's downright mean. There isn't a single muscle in my body that I'm not aware of at this moment.'

When he joins me, we sit back, grateful to stretch out our legs.

'This is quite comfortable,' I acknowledge. At least it makes me feel less guilty about the sumptuous memory foam mattress upstairs.

'And it's next to the fire,' he points out. 'But you'll be directly above it and heat rises, so as long I keep it going all night we'll be fine. Ignore any noises you hear, OK? I've got your back, don't you worry.'

'I was rather hoping to have a shower before I turn in, if you don't mind escorting me over to the bathhouse after we've finished our drinks. I promise I won't hang around long.' Like it, or not, there's no way I'd venture outside alone late at night and I know Hayden wouldn't let me, anyway.

'Hey, it's not a problem. I can do a couple of trips to fill the log basket while I wait and then it'll be my turn.'

'And I'll keep watch for you,' I insist. When he gives me a frown, I continue. 'There's safety in numbers.'

Hayden simply shrugs his shoulders and we continue to laze around, sipping our drinks and taking in the awesome simplicity and cosiness of the cabin. He was right when he said Frank made sure he had everything here you need for small home living. How freeing it must feel to spend a couple of weeks here, detoxing from lives that have become impossibly busy and stressful. Or would I go stir-crazy? I don't know . . . but at this moment it feels like a little piece of heaven.

Crash!

In the dead of night, the sound of something metal hitting the floor is like an explosion and I sit bolt upright in bed. My heart is racing so fast that my chest feels tight.

'Hayden?'

'Sorry, Ria! I'm so sorry. I woke up freezing and noticed that the fire is almost out. I dropped the tongs, that's all. It'll take me a few minutes to get it blazing again, but I'll be as quiet as I can. It's only three in the morning, so go back to sleep.'

I snuggle back under the duck-down duvet, goosebumps already breaking out on my arms. As I turn my head to the right to gaze out the window, I watch my breath form a cloud when I breathe out. In the darkness beyond, all I can see are eery-looking shapes with no definition. Despite the gentle noises filtering up from below, there is a stillness in the air that is heavy. In the silent moments there's a hollow ringing sound in my ears, which aren't used to total silence. It's like a constant hum and it's disconcerting. The moment there's a noise it seems to disappear.

I have no idea how much time has passed, but it's been quiet in the cabin for a while.

'Are you asleep?' a soft voice enquires.

'No. Wide awake actually, why?'

'I jumped back in bed, but I can't see any glow from the log burner. I think I need to rake out the ashes and start over again but it'll involve a bit of noise.'

'It's not a problem. Would you mind if I wrap up and put the kettle on?'

'Go for it. I'll happily join you.'

I leap out of bed and immediately grab the hand-crocheted blanket ruckled up at the far end. As I throw it around my shoulders, I glance down at my not so glamorous raspberry-pink thermal PJs and black woollen hiking socks. This is definitely not a fashion statement that sits well with me but the chill is already taking my breath away and my teeth begin to chatter.

'I'm on my way down,' I warn, as I negotiate the dreaded ladder.

Hayden is wearing a dark grey top and jogger bottoms, but as he vigorously rakes out the fire I doubt he's feeling the cold quite as much as I am. When I glance over at the day bed, I see it probably is a double but he only has an assortment of blankets on top. No wonder the chill woke him.

We work in silence and I carry the mugs of coffee over to the table, to sit looking out of the window. I can see the reflection in the glass of the tiny flames that are now beginning to lick up around the logs.

'That's better,' Hayden murmurs to himself. 'Almost there.'

I pull the blanket around me like an overcoat and when Hayden straightens I suggest he grab something to wrap around him until the cabin warms up.

'What do we look like?' He grins across the table at me. 'Thanks for the coffee, it's very welcome.'

'I'm only sorry I slept so soundly. You must have been freezing for it to wake you.'

'It's my fault. Frank suggested I set the clock on my phone but I thought it might disturb you. If I'd woken an hour earlier it would have taken seconds to throw on a few logs.'

'Sorry I've been rather jumpy. What other animals might be lurking out there?' I ask, out of interest.

'Not much in the early hours of the morning. But, at this elevation . . . moose, who forage for willow. If necessary, during a harsh winter, they will fill their stomachs with tree bark at a push. Deer and elk, sometimes raccoons, when the sun decides to put in an appearance. My father is the expert on that. Most animals get spooked by humans and turn tail, running for cover. I know you have a thing about bears, but don't believe everything you read. In all the time I've spent over here I've seen maybe half a dozen black bears and none of them saw me as a threat. We headed off in opposite directions, but it all depends on whether they're hungry or not. That's not to say that they aren't dangerous, of course, and if they have cubs then it's best to stay well away.'

Wrapping my hands around the mug, I stare over at the fire and it's already taking the edge off the chill in the air. 'You're good at making fires.'

'I'm a bit rusty but rule number one when it comes to survival is knowing how to keep a fire going. It could be the difference between life and death.'

That's a sobering thought. While this is a truly awesome experience, I have no interest whatsoever in becoming an intrepid adventurer. I like my home comforts way too much.

The seconds tick by and the sound of silence is disconcerting because it's obvious neither of us are sleepy.

'Could you imagine stripping your life back and living simply, like this?' I'm curious to hear his answer.

Hayden chews his lip, a frown creasing his forehead. Then he takes a sip of coffee before placing the mug back down on the table. 'Not really. A couple of days at a time, maybe. However, I needed this little interlude. I'm hoping it'll be like a reset. Between you and me, there are moments when I feel everything is slipping through my fingers.' Hayden sits quietly, drinking the last dregs of coffee.

I'm shocked to hear him sounding so despondent. I have this troubling feeling that won't go away. A man like Hayden has enough real-life experience to build what is fast becoming an empire. Every day he'll have problems and battles to work through and he navigates them with skill, or he wouldn't be as successful as he is. And yet there's an underlying vulnerability in him when it comes to his personal life.

'What?' Hayden prompts me.

'Nothing. I was just . . . you know, thoughts running through my head.'

He studies my face. 'I value your opinion, Ria. You're

what my granddad would have referred to as a level-headed person. I freely admit that I can't cope when it comes to the emotional stuff. It clouds my judgement and, quite frankly, sends me into a panic.'

Oh dear. I'm feeling torn but I can see how conflicted he's feeling.

'You're thoughtful and kind, and not just to family,' I say. 'You've gone out of your way to assist me. And not simply to ensure you achieve your goal, but to make me feel comfortable and well, we're sitting here in a log cabin in our PJs. When someone goes the extra mile for you, you're happy to repay them in ways that money can't.'

He seems a little surprised by my honesty.

'There are plenty of people out there who would disagree with you. I have a bit of a reputation for driving a hard bargain.'

'There's nothing wrong with being firm but fair. I like to think that I live by the same principles. I care about my clients. Admittedly, I don't usually get as up close as I have on this project, but even so, it matters to me that I can walk away from a job feeling the best possible outcome has been achieved.'

'What exactly are you saying, Ria? My mother says I'll worry her into an early grave and I hate that expression. But maybe she's right and I need someone to enlighten me.' Hayden has now perked up a little and he gives me an artful smile.

I reply with a little laugh. 'I'm good at designing interiors but I'm hardly a life guru.'

'No?'

I stare at him, blankly. 'Hello? According to my mum, she fears I'll miss out by focusing on my career. She says in this day and age you can have both. It's never quite as simple as that, is it?'

'But you're in the process of building a young business. Things are going in the right direction and I've been impressed by your problem-solving skills. You focus on the customer and it's the one thing I go on about all the time when I'm at work. If we deliver what the customer wants, they'll keep coming back.'

That's easy to say when you own a massive company, but when you're out there on your own it's tough. Even when I'm not feeling my best, I have to be on my A-game. The responsibility is firmly on my shoulders to keep a roof over my head while I drive the business forward. If I make one single mistake, it could be costly.

'Everything in life is a gamble, Hayden. It's important to know your limits and recognise your weaknesses. We all have them. I thought I'd have the life my sister Kate has, but it hasn't turned out quite as I expected. The irony is that in some ways she envies me, and in others I envy her.' I shrug my shoulders. 'I simply believe that you have to make the best of the opportunities that come your way. If Will and I had got married, I wouldn't have considered setting up on my own. I love what I do, but I'm also aware that there's so much more I want out of life. Wanting is one thing, getting it requires hard work and dedication.'

Hayden purses his lips, clearly impressed. 'You're good at this life analysis thing, Ria.'

'Hardly. My no-nonsense approach could be viewed another way. Mum says I spend too much time standing back and looking at the bigger picture, when I should just go with my gut feelings. I see a problem and I have to fix it. When it comes to designing rooms, I know what I'm doing. Designing people's lives is another thing entirely.' Now I'm mocking myself for good reason. This is just my opinion and speaking my truth to Hayden might be something I regret in the morning. But as he looks at me, what I see is someone who understands exactly where I'm coming from.

'One thing you have in spadefuls, Ria,' he replies, with sincerity, 'is common sense.'

I put my head back and laugh out loud. 'But we live in a world where there's an expert at every turn, most trying to convince us that our gut instincts are suspect, Hayden. Common sense is now old hat.'

'Ha!' He chuckles, his eyes sparkling. 'OK . . . so, let's say I have a cold and I raid my bathroom cabinet – taking this, that and the other. A few days later, I'm feeling much better. Is it a modern-day miracle?'

'Who knows?' I reply.

'But what do you do in that situation?'

'I'd fill a large mug with hot water, add a spoonful of organic honey, a good squeeze of lemon and add a few slices of ginger, then I'd take it to bed with me. I'd repeat that several times over the next twelve hours and get up the next day and go to work.'

Hayden smiles at me, clearly amused. 'I rest my case. It seems to me that we're all too hard on ourselves. When life becomes a little too much, it feels defeatist to have a duvet day.'

'I love that expression and maybe sometimes it's precisely what we do need, a little rest and recuperation. Sadly, I think we've become lazy, always looking for a quick fix. Or worse, looking for something, or someone, to save us when we hit a stumbling block. When it starts to sink in that we're responsible for saving ourselves, it's a game-changer. It can be empowering.'

'Really?'

'If we're getting sick, then it's time to take better care of ourselves. If a plan goes pear-shaped, it's time to get stuck in and find another way forward. At work I'm sure you do it routinely without even having to think about it, Hayden. It's not exactly rocket science, is it?'

He bursts out laughing. 'No, it isn't. And thank you, Ria. I like your take on life, but I've had a sharp reminder that business problems are much easier to handle.'

'I like simple, and I hate labels. They confine you, often creating problems when that's not the case. We're all unique.'

'I kinda got that,' he replies.

We stand and Hayden carries the mugs over to the sink. I slip off my cosy blanket and place it on the end of his bed.

'I'll put this here just in case you need it.'

'That's very thoughtful of you, but I'm sure I'll be fine. I'm an early riser anyway and that fire should last a few hours.'

'Well, you never know. I need you well rested to get me back down to Frank's farm tomorrow in one piece,' I remind him.

'Ever the practical. I hope you manage to drift off quickly, Ria.'

I yawn, stretching my arms in the air. 'Oh, I don't think that's going to be a problem now.' I grin at him. 'Stay warm.'

When our eyes meet, a little tingle runs down my spine and I find myself wondering what it would feel like standing here with Hayden's arms wrapped around me. It's enough to have me racing up the rungs of the ladder at double speed. What on earth is wrong with me? Hayden and I have been thrown together under unusual circumstances and I'd be a fool to let my emotions get the better of me. I did that once before and I won't fall for it again.

Hayden

13

Some Sterling Advice

Frank is in the open barn, chopping wood, and as we walk towards him he stops. 'Hey, guys, you made it back in one piece! How did it go?'

Before I get a chance to speak, Ria answers for us both. 'It was amazing, Frank. We had a great time and it was so kind of you to let us use the cabin. The views are mind-blowing. And the apple brandy is the perfect nightcap, isn't it, Hayden?' She flashes me a mirthful grin.

'It went down really well,' I confirm. Perhaps a little too well, given what happened afterwards.

'I'm glad to hear you enjoyed yourselves,' Frank replies, smiling from ear to ear. 'Get yourselves inside and warm up. My brother Denny is in the kitchen. Say hello and tell him he can get on making the breakfast now.'

'Hot food . . . sounds wonderful. You go on inside, Ria, I'll be in shortly.' I turn to face Frank. 'One of the chains of lights is on the blink. I fiddled with the bulbs and got them working again but they might need replacing.' I half turn to check whether Ria is still within earshot, but she's tapping on the farmhouse door and about to step inside. 'Argh . . . I think I made a bit of a fool of myself last night.'

Frank's smile fades. 'What happened?'

'I kissed her.'

He smirks at me. 'Did she slap you?'

'No. She kissed me back.'

'I'd say that's a good result. What's the problem?'

'It was too soon. She wasn't ready and we ended up agreeing it was down to your goodness-knows-what-proof brandy.'

He shakes his head at me, sadly. 'You should have owned it; told her that you find her attractive . . . not make an excuse. It's time to man up, Hayden, and get back into your stride when it comes to courting a woman.'

'I don't think I ever did find my stride, Frank, and no one uses the word "courting" these days. I'll never understand women. I gave Georgina everything she wanted and a year after we tied the knot it was over. I don't exactly have a good track record, do I? The thing is, what do I do now? This is awkward. I mean . . . I made such a mess of it and things were going so well up to that point.'

'Was she angry afterwards?'

'No. In fact, we spent part of the night chatting, as the fire went out and the noise I made woke her.'

'Then there's no damage done. She's not going to sue you for harassment.' With that, he starts laughing, noisily.

'Shh . . .' I caution him. 'It's not funny. I find myself doing and saying the weirdest things when I'm around her.'

He frowns. 'Like what?'

'I'm clumsy and . . . she gets me talking about things I wouldn't normally discuss.'

Frank raises an eyebrow, questioningly.

'Like my feelings!' I blurt out.

'Oh . . . that's definitely out of character for you. Makes you feel vulnerable, does it? I'm with you there, brother.' Now he's making fun of me.

'Ria's here because I've employed her to do a job, and now I discover I'm attracted to her, big time.'

Frank tuts. 'Hayden, I'm no expert on this sort of thing, but the best advice I can give you is to tell Ria the truth. Say that's why you're acting like a weirdo before you scare her away.'

His laughter follows me all the way to the farmhouse. Some friend he is.

'Do you want a hand with that, Dad?' I call out, as I stomp over to Santa's Retreat. My father is anchoring a ladder against the side wall, ready to mount another set of lights.

'You're back then! How was the hike?'

'Good, really good.'

'And how was it for Ria?' he checks.

'She did well. I took her to Finger Falls and we managed to take in the views over the ravine, too.'

'That's great, my son. It's been a long while since I ventured up there. What did Ria think of the cabin?'

'She was fine with it once we settled in. How have things been here?'

'Your mum and I had dinner at Shelley's last night.'

'You did?' Unfortunately, I sound as shocked as I feel.

'I checked first that it was Shelley's night off, of course. Your mother insisted on that. It's still her favourite place to eat, but if Shelley had been there, we'd have driven all the way to the Wayside Diner instead.'

It's sheer madness but it's not for me to point that out.

'There's still no chance of Shelley getting an invite on Christmas Eve, then?'

'Goodness no . . . not yet, anyway, but I'm hoping your mother will come to see that Shelley isn't a threat.'

'You still haven't told Mum she's doing the catering?'

'I'll get around to it, don't you worry. I . . . um . . . just don't want anything to upset the mood between us as it seems to me that she's a lot perkier now. Anyway, you've arrived just in time to give me a hand putting these up.'

'I thought you were done with the outside lights.'

'I thought so, too. It was your mum's idea – she said it was festive inside, but outside it was lacking something. Imagine that! It was getting out of hand, I will admit, and we did need a good sort-out.'

I'm flabbergasted. Not only is my father embracing the changes, he seems to have conveniently forgotten that he was the one clinging on to everything in the first place. It's unbelievable.

'Anyway, I'm trying to get myself into her good books.' He raises his eyebrows to the heavens.

I'm not sure a few lights will count for much and I sincerely hope I'm out of earshot when they finally have that conversation about Shelley.

'I can only give you half an hour. Mum and Ria are having a cup of tea, and after that Ria wants me to give her a hand.'

'She doesn't stop, that young woman. I'm starting to look forward to this party you know. It's been a long time since your granddad's last big do, here at the inn. Your mum might have a funny five minutes over the catering but she'll thank me afterwards. The food has to be up to par.'

Crikey, my father seems to have done a complete three-sixty when it comes to the revamp. My mother was already on board, so maybe there is – finally – some light at the end of the tunnel.

'I'll climb up, you feed me the string of lights as I work my way along the ridge.'

'Hey, I'm not so old that I can't be trusted on a roof!'

I pull a face, but he's laughing and it's good to hear him joking around. Maybe I can talk him into taking a hike with me after Christmas. I think he'd enjoy that. Just like the old days.

'Ria, it's Sunday afternoon and we don't have to be working, you know. You said yourself that we're running ahead of schedule.'

She glances across at me rather dismissively.

'Why waste time, Hayden? We had a break and I've come back a little achy in places, but raring to go. It was all that fresh air. Your mother offered to join us but I said we could manage.'

Ria is glowing. She looks refreshed and there's a pinkish hue to her cheeks.

'Sunday afternoons my mother likes to batch bake. It saves her getting in my father's way in the kitchen during the week.'

'Mason really enjoys cooking, fixing things and jumping in the truck to fetch stuff, but your mother doesn't seem to have anything much to distract her. She spends her time dusting, sweeping, doing laundry and clearing up, but from what I've seen she never goes far, unless your father is with her.'

I'm kneeling on the floor in room four, which has now been named The Cedars Suite, unpacking one of the stack of boxes Ria and I just carried upstairs. I take a moment to sit back on my heels, thinking that's a good point.

'Mum doesn't enjoy driving when the weather's bad, that's why they only have the one vehicle. She had an accident on black ice the first winter they moved here and her car ended up in a ditch; understandably, it made her nervous. She meets up every now and again with some of the wives of my father's old friends they connected with every time we flew over.'

'It must have been a wrench for her, leaving her closest friends and family behind.'

'Yes, but she's flown back to the UK twice without my father in tow and it means she can catch up face to face.'

'It's not quite the same, though, is it? Oh.' Ria walks over to me, staring down into the box. 'That print won't suit this room. It's a little darker in here, despite the soft-taupe colour on the panelling. It needs a little pop of something brighter to lift the room and preferably with a white background to match the walls. Sorry to be a pain, but let's swap it over.' She scans down her spreadsheet, tapping the pen in her hand against her lower lip.

Suddenly, I'm feeling hot and bothered, remembering the feel of my lips on hers. She didn't complain at the time, but as it came out of nowhere I guess I took her by surprise.

That could be a good sign, or it might mean I caught her off guard, and when she said sorry, she meant it. On the other hand, I wasn't sorry at all, I was just mortified I'd acted without thinking.

'If you pack that back up, we'll move these boxes into room three, next door, and go in search of boxes H1 to H6, I think. Fingers crossed the swap will work.'

I give a little chuckle.

'What?' Ria glances down at me, a frown creasing her brow.

'If you ever tire of being self-employed, there's a job waiting for you at Stylish Homes.'

She pulls a face. 'Are you trying to tell me something?'

'No – I'm more than happy to do as I'm told. But anyone who can manage people the way you do is a valuable asset. You have my father convinced now that a lot of this was his idea, so I take my hat off to you. And I meant it . . . about the job, although it's clear you've got a good future ahead of you. Right, I'll start shifting this little lot into the next room.'

As I'm hanging the new curtains in The Cedars Suite, my mother steps into the room.

'Oh – my!' she exclaims. 'That's so pretty.'

She heads straight over to help Ria, who is putting a cover on the king-size duvet.

'I'm glad you approve. The trees outside cast a bit of a shadow in here and I wasn't expecting that. I swapped the designs around with the room next door.'

'I love the soft green fern print and the fabric is so bright and cheerful,' Evie replies. 'I'll help Ria with the finishing touches if you like, Hayden.'

'OK. I'll start carrying this stack of cardboard downstairs.'

'Could you ask your father to pop up? There's a bookcase we took up to the attic and I think he might like to have it in here now.'

'Will do.'

I think my mother is enjoying having another woman around. Once the inn is up and running again she'll have some company on a regular basis. It could make all the difference. With two waitresses keen to join the team and the cleaners on standby, hopefully the place will start to feel more lively again. They're going to have to hit the ground running, though, but I'm sure she already has them primed.

As I walk backwards into the kitchen, my arms full of flat-packed boxes, the phone in my pocket rings. By the time I dump it all in the utility room, I'm surprised to see two missed calls from my best friend, and general manager, Liam.

I quickly redial. 'Hey, buddy. How're you doing? Overworked and underpaid as usual?' I chuckle.

'Always. It's even worse when the CEO decides to take a few weeks off. Did I pull you away from something?'

'No. My two bosses are upstairs, while I'm in charge of the recycling.'

'Ha! That I'd like to see. Anyway, give my best to your parents, won't you? I bet they love having you there for an extended stay. I'd like to say it's all falling down around my ears at this end and we can't manage without you, but I'm calling with good news.'

'On a Sunday afternoon?' Liam's a family man with three young kids, and his weekends are sacrosanct.

'Our last quarter's return has just arrived in my inbox from the accountant. Sales are up over eighteen per cent to the end of November. And although it's only the eleventh of the month, early indications are that we're going to smash our December sales target.'

I close my eyes for a few seconds, tempted to punch the air. Opening that store in Lisbon was a stretch, but knowing sales are buoyant and we're beating our targets is a huge relief.

'That's brilliant news, Liam. I'm grateful to you for letting me know. Perhaps I should take more trips away.'

'I thought it would set your mind at rest. Things are ticking over here, so just get on with the job in hand. How's it going at your end?'

'Really well.'

'Will it solve the problems?'

I pause for a moment. 'I'm not sure, Liam. I'm starting to think that it's time I backed off a little and left my parents to it. We'll have this place looking really smart for the party, which is what we're all focusing on.'

'I heard Ria Porter was good. She's got a reputation for her attention to detail and she isn't afraid to complain if the quality of something isn't up to par.'

'When I jokingly said I left my two bosses upstairs, I was actually referring to Ria and my mother. She's happy with everything we've unpacked so far. Kudos to our buyers.'

'That's good to hear. She's one tough cookie, as the Americans would say, isn't she? A bit of a ball buster.'

We both laugh.

'Let's just say she has a way of getting what she wants but without upsetting people. That's an enviable skill and useful in this case. Miraculously, it seems she's managed to get my parents on the same page at last.'

A dismissive hrmph echoes down the line. 'Putting everyone in their place, is she? This isn't Georgina mark two, is it?'

'No, it's not like that.'

'But she also has *you* working on a Sunday afternoon. You're paying her, not the other way around. Am I missing something here?'

'You're reading this all wrong. Do you recall me mentioning Frank? He's a long-time friend of the family. Frank lent us his cabin in the woods and Ria and I spent last night up there. It's quite a hike but she's not a complainer. It was a welcome break, but the minute we returned it was straight back to work.'

There's a sharp intake of breath. 'OK . . . now you're worrying me.'

'I'm enjoying getting hands-on and taking a bit of a back seat, that's all.'

'What is it with you and bossy women?'

'Ria isn't bossy,' I blurt out.

'You were the one that used the word "boss", not me. You've been together what . . . five days?'

'Six, but who's counting,' I reply, soberly.

'Hayden, listen to me. You fell in love with Georgina on your first date and look how that ended. She tore you to pieces, mate. Pieces. Let that sink in. What did you say to me afterwards?'

I'm glad he can't see my expression. 'If you see me doing the same thing all over again, put me out of my misery.'

'That's what friends do. Seriously, my Tricia is always trying to set you up with someone suitable and you should heed her advice. I'm a happy man because I have the right woman in my life. You're a sensitive guy and you don't even know it, Hayden. You don't want a boss-woman, you want a nurturer, someone who will give as much as they take. You're a very eligible bachelor, as my marvellous wife keeps pointing out. She worries on your behalf and will blame me if you get yourself into trouble again.'

I adore Tricia. She's a strong woman who would do anything for her kids and her husband, and yet she takes time out of her busy life for lost causes like me. She's a great listener and has a heart of gold, but I do everything I can to avoid her well-meaning blind-date dinner parties. She once told me that I'm the brother she never had. Which means she isn't going to give up on me until I've found the one. But maybe I'm someone who is destined to mess up when it comes to relationships, because it's rare for me to follow up on a first date. If I do, the third one usually kills it anyway.

'This is different, I promise you.'

'All I'm saying, in the nicest possible way, is watch yourself. There's a lot riding on the outcome of this trip and you need to keep your wits about you.'

'I'll take that on board, Liam,' I assure him. 'And it's a real load off my mind to know we're beating those targets. If you need anything, anything at all, just let me know. Give Tricia and the kids a hug from me!'

14

An Emergency Meeting

Yesterday ended on a high, with Ria charging my parents with the task of assembling the festive decorations to complete The Cedars Suite. Afterwards, my father cooked dinner and there was a lot of laughter around the table. Which is why this morning I'm shocked to see my mother looking worryingly pale and edgy. Ria notices it too and suggests we begin with a round-table session after a subdued breakfast.

Diplomatic as ever, Ria eases into it. 'I thought it might be helpful to talk through where we are in the overall plan. With seven bedrooms, Santa's Retreat and the exterior decorations all complete, that's quite an achievement.'

My mother is clasping and unclasping her hands nervously in her lap. Something has happened, but what exactly? As I glance across at my father, his eyes dart in my direction. I notice a momentary look of panic reflected in his eyes, which indicates that he's as clueless as I am about what triggered this sudden change.

'It's the twelfth already, Ria,' my mother points out. 'Time is slipping away from us.'

Ria maintains an air of calm, glancing down at the printed copy of the spreadsheet on the table in front of her, before replying. 'We have four more bedrooms, the three main rooms on the ground floor and the communal areas, like the landings, left to tackle. Even if we factor in a couple of days downtime, that gives us seven full working days to hit our target. By close of play on the twenty-third I'm confident that everything will be ready.'

My father joins in. 'Kendall has arranged for three of her cleaners to be here on the twenty-second and the twenty-third, to go from top to bottom. Everything will be spotless. Frank has offered to come in mid-afternoon on the twenty-fourth to help me set up the dining room ready for the party.'

My mother's frown hasn't eased off at all.

'A few people are arriving on the twenty-third,' I confirm, 'but on relaunch day I'll be on hand to meet the bulk of our guests.'

Ria looks puzzled. 'Evie, it was slow going at first, but now we're all working together we're motoring along. Are you able to pinpoint your biggest concerns and maybe we could focus on those first.' Ria to the rescue.

The seconds tick by uncomfortably. 'I haven't even had time to look at my to-do lists. I was supposed to place the order for the drinks last week. Let alone stocking up the cupboards. If something gets forgotten, or we run out of time, it will all turn into a shambles!'

My father leans into her, placing his arms firmly around my mother's shoulders. 'Hey, come on, Evie. It's not like you to panic. Hayden can get the drinks sorted, can't you, my son?' I nod my head. 'And I'll run through the grocery and cleaning materials lists and get those orders off. We're a team, remember?'

My mother takes in a huge, albeit troubling, breath and makes a concerted effort to give him a watery smile. 'Thank you, Mason. I feel as if I'm losing control of the basics. There are things that need to be sorted before the guests arrive. The dining room is still a storage area and I have piles and piles of new bedding to put somewhere.'

Ria is listening intently.

'The idea of working from the top down seemed the right way to go, Evie, but maybe we should rethink that decision. Let's blitz the ground floor and get it all set up. That way, no matter what happens, the inn will look wonderful for the party. It wouldn't be the end of the world if we're still tinkering with bedrooms on the twenty-fourth, as we'll have extra helpers around if needed. I'm sure it won't come to that, but it's a fallback option.' Ria stops to let her words sink in for a few moments. 'Are we all agreed on the revised schedule – could I have a show of hands?'

My father and I raise our hands but my mother simply shrugs her shoulders.

'If you need some time to get a handle on things, Evie,' my father adds, 'it's not a problem. Frank said he's happy to help out in any way he can.'

My mother gives a half-hearted smile by way of apology as she stands.

Ria gives me a pointed look before the two of them disappear upstairs – hopefully for a chat to get to the bottom of what's really going on.

An hour later, Ria sets my father and me the task of getting three decent-sized Christmas trees. With roots. When I tried to explain that the ground is frozen and that was an almost impossible task, she looked at me apologetically, but she wasn't about to change her mind.

'I'll explain later,' she half-whispered as she leant into me, placing her hand on my arm. It was then that I knew there was some sort of significance to this – goodness knows what, though.

We jump into my father's pickup truck and drive to Frank's, as he's the only one with the necessary equipment to do the job.

'Do you know what's going on?' my father enquires.

'I'm as puzzled as you are, Dad. But if Ria says it's important, then it is. This isn't a whim, it's something to do with Mum.'

He lets out a subtle groan. 'Well, I can't fathom this sudden stipulation to have rooted trees in tubs in the house instead of cut ones. I was a bit concerned, as your mother spent a long time on the phone to Izzie, and then Izzie's mother, Claire, late yesterday. I'm not saying that's a bad thing; she obviously needed someone to talk to. I appreciate that it's tough for her, not having any long-time friends close by that she can open up to. But, when we turned in for the night, I could sense something was brewing. Honestly, sometimes I feel your mother talks to Claire more than she does to me. It's not right that I don't know what's going on inside her head, Hayden,' he states, sounding cross.

'It's my fault, Dad. I sort of sprung all this on you guys. I thought I was doing the right thing.'

He dismisses that with a shake of his head. 'It's a lifeline and your mother and I both know it, Hayden. You can't make a cake without breaking a few eggs, as she often reminds me, and we'll get there, but something has upset her.'

'She's probably tired; it's been a long haul for you both. Is there anything specific I can do, or say, to help?'

As I turn my head to glance at him, a frown creases his forehead but it's the sadness emanating from him that sends a chill to my core.

'I think you've pulled off a minor miracle, Hayden, but maybe even that won't be enough. Who knows? Just be wary of what you say to Izzie. Beware of using her as a crutch, my son. There's a chance your mother could pick up on it.'

He turns to face me and in that split second, when we lock eyes, his concern is troubling. 'Izzie adores Mum and no doubt spends her time reassuring Mum I'm just fine.'

His jaw tightens. 'Izzie and Claire might think they're doing right by your mother, but what if they're making it worse?'

'What do you mean?'

'When someone is upset they often say things they don't really mean. We all do it, then realise it's a way of venting and just get on with it. Giving advice to someone when you don't know both sides of the story can be a dangerous thing, Hayden, that's all I'm saying.'

My father seems to have a growing problem with Claire, and probably Izzie as well. If Mum is confiding in them instead of him, it's only human nature that he'll feel hurt and maybe even that he's being kept at arm's length.

'Fir trees with roots?' Frank looks at my father as if he's mad.

'We're just following orders. We need three fine specimens to keep the peace. Is it doable?' I ask.

Frank scratches his head. 'Considering the ground is frozen that's a pretty tall order.'

'You're the man when it comes to having the equipment to tackle it,' I acknowledge and he breaks out into a wicked smile.

'I most certainly am. I doubt there's a tool or a piece of equipment worth having that isn't in my old hangar. One day, maybe, I'll get the two-seater plane it was supposed to house, but for now I'll enjoy my big boys' toys.'

'It's a lot to ask, but I'll owe you big time, Frank.' My father was there for Frank when he lost his wife and it's a bond that doesn't have a tally. The two of them pump fists.

'OK, boys, we're gonna have some fun with this. It's time to break out the mini tractor and clamp on the snow blade. I'll let the two of you fight over who's going to clear me a path up to those trees. I think this calls for the backhoe loader. I reckon if I fix on the ripper attachment it could, if I'm careful, carve out a reasonably sized root ball. With the stabilisers in place, chances are it'll have enough power to lift the fir trees straight onto your pickup, Mason. At the other end you can roll them off the back. It'll probably need all three of us to get them in situ, so I'll follow you back to the inn.'

Three hours later, we're all sitting around the table at the inn, tucking into one of my father's traditional, slow-cooked Yankee pot roasts. The beef literally falls apart and it's real comfort food.

'This,' Frank states, stabbing his fork in the direction of

his plate, 'is what I call a great, home-style dinner. It reminds me of my grandma's cooking. Rib-sticking, honest food.'

'There's apple pie for dessert, Frank, and I've boxed one up for you to take home.' My mother is sitting next to him and he gives her a wink.

'Thanks, Evie.'

'No thanks necessary. I know it's a silly thing, but it means a lot to me the effort you've gone to getting those trees in place.'

Frank lays his knife and fork down on his plate, leaning back contentedly.

'As long as you keep them well watered, they'll pop back into the ground quite nicely. Maybe out back, ready to bring them in again next year.'

'I know everyone thinks I'm crazy.' My mother is clearly touched that we took her idea on board. 'Trees are a living thing and cutting them down just to brighten our spirits at Christmas feels wrong. I'd rather have a fake tree, than shorten the life of a healthy one.'

Why didn't she share that with us before? Now I feel bad about the one we chopped down for Santa's Retreat.

'Oh, Evie, why didn't you say something?' My father sounds disappointed.

My mother stares at him for a brief moment before turning to look at Frank. 'Well, we're in your debt, Frank. Was it a real nightmare of a job?' she enquires.

Frank reaches out to touch my mother's hand. 'Are you kidding me? We were in our element. Hayden drove the snow plough, and Mason and I took turns with the backhoe, ripping up the ground. In fact, I dug up an extra one for the farmhouse. As you know, I haven't bothered too much since I lost Cassie, but this year I thought I'd make a bit of an effort. Even when he's not doing a job for me, my younger brother keeps turning up on the doorstep to check on me. There are times when he gets on my nerves a bit, but he means well and it's high time I got my act together.'

I suspect everyone can say that about a member of their family, at times. Or a concerned friend. Izzie and Tricia instantly come to mind.

'I don't know why I didn't think of it myself, Evie. It could be a nice little sideline for me next Christmas if I get the word out. I've got a virtual forest and the necessary equipment. I can deliver decent-size trees with a good root ball, not those tiny ones they dig up with a spade and it's five years until it turns from a few branches into a proper tree.'

'That's a great idea, Frank. I'd be up for giving you a hand with deliveries. We could put out some fliers a couple of months in advance and get people to put in their orders,' my father joins in.

It's good to hear Frank showing an interest in something new; it's a small start but a big deal. Money isn't an issue for him, the struggle is that all he has is the farm to keep him occupied and not much else.

We wave Frank off and Ria, my father and I spend the afternoon upstairs. With a little encouragement, my mother takes the opportunity to catch up on some paperwork. No wonder she was frazzled, feeling she was falling behind on everything. At one point, my father disappears to make us all a hot drink and I waylay Ria as we pass on the second-floor landing.

'Thanks for calming Mum down this morning.'

Ria smiles at me with her eyes. 'We all get moments when we hit a wall.'

'I know and I guess my father and I should have seen it coming. What . . . uh . . . exactly did she say to you?'

Ria hesitates. 'I simply asked if she was OK. She just blurted out that no one worries about cutting down a good tree in its prime and how wrong it was. She mentioned it was bad luck to have a dying tree in the house and that this Christmas is really important for more reasons than one.'

'She always said she loved the scent of a real fir tree and

this is the first time she's made a fuss about cutting them down. I wonder what triggered that?'

'Evie did have tears in her eyes when the tree in Santa's Retreat was revealed, but I thought that was because it looked so wonderful.' Ria too is struggling to make sense of it.

I bend my head and let out a little groan. 'Back in the UK, every year on the first of December, Dad dragged in the potted fir tree from the patio to the rear of their property. Mum would get the neighbour in to water it while they were away. She would take down the decorations on the fifth of January, a couple of days after they'd fly back. I thought it was just for convenience, maybe it's a thing with her.' It could explain the look she gave my father before she turned to talk to Frank. Clearly Dad has forgotten why they had that ritual.

'I guess so. I'm glad we got to the bottom of it. She seems happy enough now.'

'I'll have a word with my father and make him aware. Next year I'm sure he'll have them all lined up in barrels on the back porch ready to wheel up the ramp before the first heavy snowfall hits.' He'll be cross with himself for forgetting that.

We fall silent as I wrack my brains for something engaging to say.

'Stay positive, Hayden.' Ria reaches out to touch my arm, encouragingly. 'The ground floor will soon be looking pristine and festive and maybe that's just the boost your mother needs. We're on target, so there's no need to worry – we've got this.' The look of reassurance Ria gives me takes my breath away for a second. This isn't just a job to her now, she cares about the overall outcome. Something changed while we were up at the cabin and we both know it.

As we look at each other, I so desperately want to say something, anything to connect on another level, but my mind is a total blank. Besides, now is hardly the time, or the place.

'Thanks, Ria.' It sounds lame and I wish I could find the courage to tell her how I feel.

She continues along the landing, and I turn to watch her walk away from me. Ria's phone rings and she pulls it from her pocket, her voice animated as she answers before disappearing out of sight.

I'm never going to be able to say anything to her while we're under my parents' roof, so I'll have to plan another little excursion. It's not going to be easy to get Ria to down tools and take a few hours off, but I'll think of something. I must, or I risk making an utter fool of myself if I'm reading the vibe between us all wrong. I'm so out of practice when it comes to flirty small talk, it's a joke.

Ria

15

A Day Full of Surprises

'Kate! I wasn't expecting you to call until later.'

'It this a difficult time to chat?'

'No, we're moving some things around that's all. I'll find somewhere quiet.'

When I glance over the banisters, I spot Mason mopping the hallway, so I descend to the first-floor landing and wander into The Mountain Maple Suite, quietly closing the door behind me.

'I'm all ears.'

'Everything is fine and I'm thirteen and a half weeks. It looks like Alex is going to have a little sister. At this stage it's a ninety-five per cent rate of accuracy, so fingers crossed!' Her excitement levels are through the roof and I break out into a huge smile. 'I've been a little concerned, to be honest. I feel nauseous from the moment I first open my eyes until mid-morning. I didn't have that with Alex. Now I can breathe a sigh of relief – I'm so happy!'

'That's wonderful news, Kate. I'm thrilled for you and Scott, and I'm sure Alex is going to enjoy having someone to play and fight with as he grows up.' I laugh.

'Just like us?' she quips.

'Not really. It was boys against girls in our house, wasn't it? We gave as good as we got, though.'

'We certainly did,' she replies, nostalgically. 'Anyway, how are you doing?'

'Things are going well but the pressure is beginning to tell.' I wander over to gaze out of the window, wishing Kate could be here too.

'You must be shattered.'

'Not really. We had a little trip out on Saturday and stayed overnight in a friend of the family's cabin up in the mountains.'

'You did? That's awesome.'

'It was quite a trek, and it took a while for me to get used to snowshoeing. I'd rather ski any day, even though I'm a relative newbie. But it was incredible. I took lots of photos to show you when I get back.'

'You must be getting on well with the family for them to arrange something like that. I did wonder if you'd find it a little awkward living on site, but I guess not.'

'Oh, um . . . it was just Hayden and me. The cabin was tiny, I mean one room up and one down, and a standalone bathhouse. Admittedly, it did have heated water.'

'That was rather cosy, considering you hardly know each other,' Kate replies, sounding a little surprised. 'And you were all right with that?'

I take a deep breath. 'Sort of, and it was nice to have a change of scenery.'

'That's not like you, it's normally head down until the job is done.'

'Things have been a little tense at times. Some of the changes have caused a few disagreements that have required smoothing over.'

Kate makes a loud tutting sound. 'Ria, you need to focus on what you're there to do and get yourself back home as soon as you're done.'

'How I wish it were as simple as that. We're working as a team remember. While I'm used to handling my clients' expectations they aren't usually working alongside me. I'm simply trying to make sure we achieve an outcome they can all live with.'

'You've turned into some sort of mediator? That's not fair on you and it's way more than you bargained for.' Now Kate is puzzled and I realise it was a mistake saying anything at all. 'So, you've been doing what, exactly?' she quizzes me.

'Trying my best to find the middle ground and we're getting there.'

She lets out a long, slow breath. 'That sounds like a result to me. All credit to you because most people in your position wouldn't have the patience and would probably have walked out. Anyway, I take it that means it'll get easier from here on in?'

'Yes . . . hopefully,' I answer, cagily.

'But?'

Do I tell her and ask her advice? Or do I keep it to myself?

'When we were at the cabin, which – in my defence – was a break that I felt Hayden needed, he . . . uh . . . kissed me. And I kissed him back.'

'Oh no,' she groans. 'You slept with him?'

'No! Technically, he's my boss; he's also a real gentleman and give me some credit, please – I'm a professional. He apologised afterwards, and I did the same, because it just came out of nowhere. Now I'm seriously conflicted, though. Considering he's such an astute businessman, outside of that he's a bit of a mess, if I'm being honest. For some bizarre reason I find that odd mix so darned attractive.' There, I've said it.

'Then you're in serious trouble, Ria.'

'I was hoping for some advice.'

'Get yourself on the next plane back because it sounds to me like you're in way over your head. I'd hate to see you get hurt.'

'I can't walk off the job. It's cost Hayden a lot of money and we're over halfway through.'

'Listen to me, Ria. Your trouble is that you might be a woman with a steely determination to succeed in everything you do, but when you see something that's broken you have this compelling need to fix it. And that includes people. This is different and you know it. Don't mistake sympathy for something more meaningful. You're caught in the middle of a bit of a mess there, by the sound of it. Just remember that you'll probably never see Hayden again after you fly home.'

My sister is right. 'I'm not looking at the bigger picture, am I?'

'No. And it pains me to remind you of this, but you were badly hurt once before, Ria. Don't make the same mistake again. Some people can't be fixed. Will was happy to put that engagement ring on your finger to please you; he had all the perks without making a long-term commitment. People change themselves, or they don't change at all.'

It's time to square my shoulders and face facts. 'I'm hearing you. At least this place is going to look spectacular when I leave,' I declare, positively. 'Anything beyond that is outside of my control. Right?'

'Correct. I understand that it's a big endorsement for your business, Ria but don't be tempted to lose your head – or your heart – for the wrong reason.'

'I won't. Thanks for the pep talk, I know you only want what's best for me and will always give it to me straight. Anyway, everyone will be wondering where I am. And congratulations, Kate – I can't wait to go shopping for baby clothes early in the new year!'

As I reach the last stair, the front door swings open.

'Perfect timing!' Mason greets me, stomping his boots on the mat.

He's carrying a jute sack in his arms and one slung over his back. I instantly step forward to help.

Hayden is a couple of paces behind him and he grins at me as our eyes make contact.

'One more run to do and then that's it for the gold trimmings,' he confirms.

'Drop the sacks here' – I indicate – 'and I'll carry them through.'

There's no sign of Evie, but the guys seem quite content to head straight out again, and if they're not worried, then neither am I. The next couple of days are the fun bit and I think it will lift everyone's spirits. Mason has obviously cleaned through, and the dining room sparkles.

'Oh, the sacks are here!' Evie calls out, as her head appears around the side of the kitchen door. 'I'll just clear away my paperwork and I'll come and give you a hand.'

When she returns, I've already stacked the sacks next to the tree in the sitting room.

'Oh, that tree is just perfect. Look at the shape!' Evie comes to join me and we stand side by side. 'It looks really happy there, doesn't it?'

All of the branches are pert, the smell is quite powerful and it's far enough away from the open fire and the radiators not to be overwhelmed by the heat.

'It does look happy, Evie.' When I think about the tree in Santa's Retreat, even though Hayden waters it every single day, the tips of the branches are already drooping a little. It is sad to see. I've had trees myself that literally shed everywhere as I'm taking off the decorations to pack them away. I've always appeased my conscience by telling myself that the bare bones of the trees end up getting turned into mulch, but it's not much of a consolation, is it?

'Where do we begin?' she asks, turning to face me.

'Let's sort the trimmings and decorations into piles. It will take Mason and Hayden a while to hang the lights anyway. I hope you have a tall stepladder,' I comment, as I untie the first sack.

'I think the gold is going to look lovely in here, don't you? You haven't seen the garlands that hang over the mantel shelves. Each one fills a sack. I bought them the first Christmas we were here. Mason's granddad always had fresh greenery, but with the log fire it dries out so quickly and the berries wither, losing their lustre. We can put out a few fresh displays for the party, of course, to add to the ambience.'

'Gold and green it is, then. How about the library?'

'There are some rather lovely vintage, burgundy-coloured glass baubles. Even though the tree in there is smaller, there won't be enough of them, but I have a basket of pinecones I gathered towards the end of the autumn. They'll look rather lovely if we spray them with a little fake snow. I thought silver would be nice for the dining room. I think Mason will approve. I do want him to be happy, Ria.'

The eye contact between us tells me there's a *but* coming.

'This is all my fault, you see, Ria. I'm trying to do what's best for everyone. Mason and Hayden think the problem is solely about the business not making any money. I can't lie, it has been tough doing everything ourselves. With the declining number of bookings it's been hard to see our savings eroded by the day. Then I did something silly. I was on a call with Hayden and I broke down. As if he didn't have enough on his plate at the time, there I was adding to his worries. And because of that momentary lapse, a few weeks later Hayden surprised us with his rescue plan.'

Hardly a lapse, more a surfacing of the truth.

'Timing is everything, Evie. Maybe, on reflection, it would have been better not to tackle everything in one go.' In this case I'm beginning to think that Hayden came in too heavy-handedly and without due consideration. He should have taken time out to fly over, sit down with his parents and draw up a plan of action they felt more comfortable with.

'Winter feels like it drags on forever here,' Evie says. There's a faraway look in her eyes and a sadness in her voice that's difficult to hear. 'There are times I feel hemmed in. I miss my old life; I had a freedom I don't have here because it's so isolated and often difficult to get around in the ice and the snow. It's not what I'm used to.'

'I can understand that, Evie.'

'Please don't mention a word of this to Hayden, Ria. I haven't the heart to tell him this was never something I really wanted to take on in the first place. I did it because I love my husband and the inn means so much to us all. What choice did I have?'

I'm in shock. Thankfully, all Evie needs is a listening ear, because what I can say? She's a woman who is doing what she sees as the right thing for her family, but it's not right for her. No wonder she's unhappy.

'Mason doesn't want to give up on the inn. I'm not trying to ignore the fact that it's been an emotional journey for him accepting the changes; but not as much as he made out at first when the decorators were here. All those emails to Hayden with trifling gripes . . . that was a little show for me, to prove that he'll put up with anything to make me happy. But I don't have the heart to sit him down and explain how I feel. Yes, I was upset about the trees, but the truth is—'

'We're back!' Mason and Hayden call out from the hallway and Evie places a finger against her lips before she turns around to acknowledge them.

'Did you bring the two special sacks from the wardrobe in the bedroom?' Evie checks.

'Um . . . I'm just on my way back to get them,' Mason replies. 'I won't be long.'

'And the tall ladders?' Evie glances at me rather anxiously.

'I mean, *we* won't be long.' With that the front door clicks and it all goes silent.

Suddenly, Evie breathes a weary sigh and I can tell something is wrong, very wrong. 'I'm not sure how much longer I can keep up this pretence that I'm fine, Ria, and this is going to solve all our problems.'

She's becoming agitated and I remain silent as Evie gathers her thoughts.

'You see, it's all coming to a head. I had a video call with my dear friend Claire yesterday and suddenly I just told her the truth. This isn't what I want day in, day out for the rest of my life. It was a huge relief, even though it brought me to tears when I realised how much I long to go home. That's why I suddenly felt overwhelmed by it all.'

'Oh, Evie.' Now I understand and I wish I didn't.

'Claire is the only person I can talk to without holding back. She also brings me up to date with everyone's news back home; the problem is that it makes me miss it even more.'

'That must be hard on you, Evie.'

'It is. Really hard and it isn't getting any easier. Deep down Mason knows I haven't settled here, he just doesn't know what to do about it. It's a heartbreaking conversation that's long overdue, Ria. Given everything that's going on here, it's one I can't face until after the Christmas and New Year celebrations are over.'

'It's not a joint decision?'

Evie's expression is pained and it's understandable why she's been avoiding the issue.

'It's easier for me to walk away from this place than it is for Mason. Truthfully, it would have been better if Hayden hadn't got involved in the first place. We were losing money and I hoped that would give Mason a good enough reason to want to return to the UK. And to do so with a clear conscience, knowing we'd done all we could. Now that the business has been given a second chance, Mason is doing everything he can in the belief that it will make me feel at home here.'

'But it won't?'

'The inn is a wonderful place, but to me it will never be home – that's back in the UK, close to lifelong friends and family. For Mason, it's not just a business, it's about keeping the legacy alive for our son and I understand that, really I do. Hayden has gone to great lengths to make it all happen and he was right, this refurbishment is exactly what the inn needed. I'm afraid that he, too, won't understand why it's not enough to keep me here because the inn means as much to him, as it does to his father.'

I feel sad for Evie; it's a horrible situation she finds herself in because she doesn't want to hurt the two people she loves the most.

'Where does that leave us . . . I mean, I don't want to add to what is already a stressful situation for you, Evie.'

'We continue on with the plan, not least because if this is my last Christmas here I'd like it to be a happy one for us all. I thought it was only fair to explain that the tension between me and Mason is nothing at all to do with the renovation of the inn.'

That's a conclusion I'd already reached for myself.

'I'm so sorry you find yourself in such an impossible situation, Evie. If there's anything I can do to ease things, just say.'

'Thank you, Ria. One thing guaranteed to put a smile on Mason's face is the village snow scene.' She leans into me, conspiratorially but there's no one around to overhear us.

'A village?'

'There are more than twenty little buildings that light up. They are pretty but accommodating a trestle table in here on top of everything else made it feel really cluttered. And then with the model railway in the hallway, if we had little ones running around it was a constant worry they'd hurt themselves.'

I can't even begin to imagine what it was like; at the very least, a housekeeper's worst nightmare, I should imagine.

'As you can see, Mason flatly refused to consider moving anything around in here, let alone even discussing paring it down. He's more amenable now, so together we'll get it sorted, but it would be nice if you could find somewhere to display those models. If I do walk away, I want to do so knowing he has meaningful things around him.'

My thoughts turn to Mason and Hayden, but Evie said 'if'. They're going to be devastated if she can't bring herself to stay. And what if she does? Will she end up sacrificing her future happiness for theirs?

I give Evie a look of empathy that comes straight from my heart. 'If you, Mason and Hayden focus on putting up the trimmings, I'll push on upstairs. You need time together as a family, doing something fun. It's a chance to let the memories flow and I think that's important this year, don't you?'

Evie's been through a lot; she's understandably emotional and probably feeling drained by it all. But I'm not giving up. She might have second thoughts when everything is looking amazing and the inn is full of chatter and laughter again. It's time to press on regardless and hope for a change of heart. Love's supposed to conquer all, so anything could happen. And I truly believe that Mason and Evie have an enduring love.

'It is, Ria, and it'll be the first time Hayden's been here to lend a hand,' she reflects. 'The last two Christmases, Mason and I just got on each other's nerves. I'd make suggestions and he'd still end up putting the same old trimmings in exactly the same place. You made him see sense.'

'I think he was struggling with it all and it's only now that he's starting to enjoy the process,' I reply, softly.

'You could be right, Ria. The other thing is that Hayden spends way too much time worrying about us. I have no intention of ruining the holidays for him. It's bad enough that we're all working flat out, but he's sorely in need of a rest himself. He's such a wonderful and thoughtful son. And thank you for what you've done, Ria. I'm sorry it's been so difficult but the inn will have a new lease of life. Of that, I'm totally convinced.'

With everything she's juggling, Hayden is always on her mind and that puts me on a guilt trip of my own. I make a mental note to give Mum a call a bit later on just to let her know how things are going.

After dinner, I excuse myself and when I come back downstairs, all togged up and ready for a walk, I bump into Hayden in the hallway. I'd hoped they'd all assume I was in my room and I thought I'd have a wander around outside while I chat to Mum.

'I was just coming to find you to ask if you fancied some fresh air. Do you mind if I tag along, or were you going in search of some peace and quiet?'

Best laid plans and all that . . . 'Of course.' At least there'll be no danger of falling into the river if I stray in the wrong direction. But Kate's words are still resounding in my head and maybe this is a mistake. The less time I spend alone with Hayden, the better – especially after my potentially heartbreaking talk with Evie.

I hang around in the hallway waiting for him, when I hear the sound of tinkling laughter coming from the kitchen. It's heartening to hear and a part of me wonders whether, when it comes to the crunch, Evie really is capable of walking away.

'Sorry to keep you waiting.' Hayden descends the stairs two at a time, making a clatter. 'Mum – Ria and I are going for a walk,' he calls out at the top of his voice and she steps out into the hallway.

'Enjoy the fresh air. See you in a bit.'

Once outside, I take in a deep breath and it's invigorating.

'I suspect you're a little like me. I swear I eat twice as much while I'm here than I do at home. It's always a mistake turning in early rather than walking off a big meal.'

'Your father's newfangled lobster rolls were so good. The sweetness of the warm lobster bathed in that buttery sauce was an unforgettable experience. He's the hands-down winner.'

Hayden breaks out into a smile. 'Just don't mention that if you cross paths with Shelley. Talking of paths . . . given that there's a full moon tonight, let's head over to the stile the other side of Santa's Retreat and we can take the trail along the riverbank. It's light enough to make for a great walk.'

It's slow going on the crisp snow in places, although at one point I follow in the trail Mason and Hayden made earlier on, going back and forth with the sacks. There's a stillness all around us only interrupted by the occasional vehicle driving past, but even that noise is muted. Hayden climbs the wooden step first, extending his hand to help me over.

'We're forecast to get a flurry of snow tonight,' he informs me.

'That's bad news for anyone having to travel but it'll make it all pristine again.'

'Spoken like someone for whom snow is still a novelty.' He laughs.

'I know. But it's magical and so Christmassy. My nephews would love this, heck – the adults too. The number of times I can recall getting a chance to build a decent snowman in the UK I could probably count on two hands and have a couple of fingers left over.'

'I feel much the same way, but if we get a few inches, everything seems to grind to a halt back home, doesn't it?'

I so want to talk to him about his parents but it would be very wrong of me to interfere. Nothing is cast in stone, and in all honesty I think if Hayden got involved it could bring the situation to a head at a very inopportune time. If his parents fall apart before the big relaunch party, everyone would be devastated. It's time for me to stop dwelling on something that is none of my business. If I don't and Hayden picks up on my concerns, everything could begin to unravel and tempers will flare.

'Talking of kids, my sister is having a little girl. She rang me earlier on.'

'That's exciting news. What a Christmas present. And you're off the hook – it isn't twins.'

He has been listening to me when I chatter away then. What else did I say, I wonder, because I can't quite remember.

'Ria, I wanted to tell you that . . . this is so awkward. No, it's not, it's just that I'm messing it up. I wasn't being truthful the other night, up at the cabin.'

We're approaching some low overhanging branches and Hayden sprints in front of me, snapping a sizeable twig off a fallen branch and using it to clear the snow over our heads.

'There you go.'

I pass underneath and he keeps hold of the twig, falling in alongside me.

'I made an excuse for kissing you because I was embarrassed as I wasn't sure it was in order. We were out there alone together and I didn't want you to feel I was taking advantage of you. The thing is, I wasn't sorry about it at all, only the realisation that you weren't expecting it.'

He steers us off to the right and beckons to me. 'Here, reach over and dig the stick into the snow. Bang it a couple of times.'

I'm so astonished by his unexpected admission that I simply do as he says. When I finally find my voice, I turn to look at him.

'That's not snow, it's ice, isn't it?'

'It's the edge of the Androscoggin River. You could probably walk out a good few feet before you'd hear a crack, but it thins in the middle where the water still flows until the big thaw. They used to float the logs to the sawmills along here.'

I have to say something now, as he's feeling uncomfortable.

'It was mutual, Hayden. I think you sort of know that, but this is just such a weird situation we find ourselves in, isn't it?'

His eyes search mine. 'I wasn't imagining it then?'

'You were right when you said it was the perfect place for a romantic break. Maybe that didn't really help either of us in the moment.' I hear Kate's voice loud and clear in my head. *Don't make the same mistake again.* If I don't encourage him, this can't go anywhere.

We stand, staring out across the river. For the most part

it's covered in snow, and the moon overhead highlights silver glints, I presume where the water is still flowing.

'Now who's making excuses?' he teases.

'I'm being honest here. If we were back in the UK and we saw each other across a bar in a pub, would you walk over and ask me out?'

Give him his due, he takes a moment to consider it. 'I'd saunter over and offer to buy you a drink. Then I'd engage you in conversation. If I didn't have your number at the end of the evening, I'd be gutted.'

His honesty is disarming and catches me off guard, but I say nothing as I peer up at the trees overhead.

'And would I have succeeded?' he prompts.

My voice is hardly audible but I can't lie. 'Yes.' Hayden is so . . . nice, so gentlemanly that he doesn't even have a glib chat-up line.

'Maybe it was the ambience at the cabin that night.' He looks at me, frowning. 'You know, we had an exciting day, all that adrenaline and the potent apple brandy.'

I know exactly where this is leading, as I turn my gaze towards Hayden.

'It might have been a moment of madness. What do you think?' he asks.

'Perhaps we should check, just to make sure?' I offer and seconds later Hayden's mouth is on mine and I'm in his arms for a second time. I can hear Kate saying, *What on earth are you doing, Ria? Have you totally lost your mind?*

The problem is that I don't want to hold back because my heart is telling me this could be one of those *what if* moments. I don't want to look back and wonder about what might have been. When I step away from him and our eyes meet, we both know it isn't a mistake. It's one of those moments in time that marks a turning point from which there is no going back.

Instinctively, you feel it deep down inside of you. Acknowledging you have feelings for someone brings with it a wonderfully uplifting surge of tingly excitement. It's also accompanied by a sense of vulnerability, when you realise you're about to lay your heart on the line. The trouble is, there are no guarantees that it won't get broken.

16

A Wasted Trip Into Town or a Clever Move?

The following morning, Hayden agrees to drive me into town when the consensus of opinion is that the central light fittings in the sitting room are looking a little tired. The minute we're in the car I can tell he's feeling conflicted.

'Are you sure it's a good idea to leave them alone together? Can't this wait until tomorrow?'

This is tough. My chat with Evie didn't fall on deaf ears. Encouraging Mason and Evie to work side by side might be all they need to make them both think about what really matters, and that's their marriage. To do that it means distracting Hayden, even if it is a little bit devious of me. If you do something with good intent, that doesn't make it wrong, does it? I throw the question out there, but if I was expecting some sort of divine guidance, it's a good job I'm not holding my breath.

'I think we've reached the point where they're in control and you and I are just two extra pairs of hands. Having some time alone together while they can, ahead of having an inn full of people, might be exactly what they need.'

I glance at his side profile and his jawline is firm; he's tense. 'I sincerely hope you're right and this doesn't undo the good that's been done.'

'Relax, Hayden. It's a key room and in my opinion, from a design point of view, at least a third of the furniture needs to go.'

'You're letting them duke it out?' He's joking, but I notice that his shoulders have relaxed a little.

'Oh, I think they'll come up with a workable solution,' I reply. I'm not expecting any problems, but I can't say that in so many words.

Evie's focus will be on keeping the peace. Mason will probably see that as a good sign, wanting to believe that they're finally turning the inn into a place she'll regard as home.

The fact that Evie is going to see this project through demonstrates how much she cares for her husband. Perhaps they can come up with a solution that works for them both, but that will only come to pass if they can be totally honest with each other.

'You sound hopeful.'

'Even when they're cross with each other, your parents still care about what the other one thinks, and that says a lot, Hayden.'

'Wise words.' He lapses into silence for a while. 'You do know that the choices are going to be limited at the store I'm taking you to?'

I smile, cagily. 'We might get lucky and find something that will work. If not, then we'll have a go at updating what's there.'

He turns to grin at me.

'Don't take your eyes off the road!' I stress, anxiously. 'That sprinkling of snow overnight has frozen, see how it shimmers.'

'Don't worry, I can handle it. You don't intend buying new lights, do you? Be honest with me.'

'No. By the time we get back, your parents will have come to an amicable agreement and we'll be able to move swiftly on. Well, it will probably involve a little task for you and Mason out in the barn, but by the end of the day the sitting room will look absolutely charming.'

'Yes, ma'am.' Hayden sounds amused by my tactics. 'And, uh, how are you doing this morning?'

191

'Having had a catch-up chat with my mum last night, I'm feeling like a dutiful daughter. We're really close, but I'm coming to realise that I talk to my sister way more than her. Just to save her worrying about trivial stuff, of course, but that's remiss of me. She likes to know what's going on in my life.'

'Bit of a wake-up call there for you. Parents always worry, though, no matter how often you keep in touch. And . . . our walk last night?'

I try my best not to grin to myself but I fail miserably, so I turn my head to gaze out the window at the scenery flashing by.

'Fine. As you already have my number, I guess it's a case of waiting to see what happens after we get back to the UK.' Despite the calmness in my voice, my heart is beating so fast it makes my pulse race.

'That's a start, anyway. Spending so much time together has been a bit intense. In a way I feel like I've known you for a while.'

'Hmm. I feel the same way.'

'Unexpected, too, the way things have turned out.'

He's desperate for me to say something meaningful.

'I admit it's something I wasn't expecting, Hayden. Who knows what sparks that initial attraction? It's either there, or it isn't. When it is, you can choose to lose your head and risk disappointment if it fizzles out, or you can proceed slowly and see how it goes.'

He nods in agreement. 'Taking it one day at a time works for me, Ria. But I'm really looking forward to next year. That's unusual for me, as I often find January a tough month.'

'You do?'

'The festive holidays are just a memory and I get withdrawal symptoms thinking about the White Mountains. The days are still short and the weather isn't the best, so it's nice to know there's something a bit different to look forward to.'

That's quite a telling admission for Hayden. If you miss

a place it's because it means something to you, but it's not my place to say that, so instead I pull his leg.

'And I'm *a bit different*?' I tease him.

'Sorry, that sounded much better in my head. What I meant is that I've got a first date to plan, and after a creaky start I intend to make a good impression.'

'When we get back we're starting from scratch?'

'Yep. Pretend you don't know about my family troubles and ignore the fact that we've slept under the same roof, or even – more or less – in the same room.'

'I think I can do that. I might not be able to forget that first kiss, though.'

'Last night's wasn't as good?' he challenges me.

'It was even better, as no apologies were needed afterwards, but there's something special about a first kiss.'

'I know,' he groans. 'I immediately knew my timing was off but I couldn't stop myself.'

I rather like that thought and I'm going to hang on to it, because I felt the same way.

'Wow!' I'm wide-eyed when, back at the inn, Hayden and I walk into the sitting room. We didn't make a purchase, but after walking hand in hand around the store in a decidedly flirtatious and light-hearted mood, our spirits are high. 'What a difference!'

'There's even enough room now to accommodate the sofa from the library. What do you think?' Evie asks.

Hayden is quick to reply. 'Come on, Dad, let's give it a try.'

I flash Hayden a look of caution, as he sounds like he's high on caffeine, or something. We both need to bring it down a notch. I'd be horrified if his parents picked up on the buzz between us, as that would make things awkward.

'There wasn't anything that I felt was quite right, Evie, so Hayden has offered to take the lights down. I have some spray paint that will tidy up the tarnished metal frames and I'll have a look at the light shades to see what I can do.' Hayden and Mason are now out of earshot. 'What a result in here!'

'Isn't it?' She hastens over to stand next to me, keeping her voice low. 'After taking the spare trimmings into the dining room, I swept up and mopped the floor while Mason drew up a plan. I was shocked, I can tell you. We moved the spare items into the library for now, but once the other sofa is in here we can start rearranging things in there.'

'Mind your backs,' Mason calls out.

'I didn't realise they're matching sofas,' I remark.

'Yes, although they're a slightly different design, but we had them re-covered in the same taupe-coloured fabric. It goes so well with the wall colour now.'

I walk around, taking in the room from every conceivable angle.

'Right, guys, if you don't mind taking down the light fittings, I'll see what I've got in my little stash of paint. I believe I have a soft, Grecian ivory that will work. I'm thinking it's best to spray the metal frames and those two side tables in the same colour. Are you content to tackle that, too, guys? If not, I'm happy to do it.'

'No problem, eh, Dad?' Hayden really needs to get himself under control. His mother is studying his face and I can only hope that she thinks this burst of energetic enthusiasm is inspired solely by the task in hand.

'Let's get to it, then. Evie, we'll head upstairs and dig out the new table lamps and the soft furnishings. I think there's a good chance we'll have this room finished by the end of the day.'

Mason looks happy, believing that Evie is over her little wobble. If only that were true.

By late afternoon, we're all beginning to flag a little, but Evie stands back, looking content.

'You can actually move around in here now without fear of bumping into anything or knocking over an ornament.'

She does a half-turn, glancing over at me as I gather up the rubbish. 'When you showed us the photographs from those glossy magazines, Ria, I couldn't imagine this room looking anywhere near as elegant. Or decluttered. On entering the room now, the pieces we decided to keep take pride of place, don't you think, Mason?'

'I do, and the curve of the drapes doesn't block the light.'

'This is the contemporary New England style that I'm sure will delight your guests,' I add. 'The oversized tasselled tie-backs have that vintage look and add a touch of opulence. The pale-green fern leaf print against the off-white background draws your eye towards the windows and the trees beyond. They'll block some of the draught in winter and at night they'll act as a frame when the Roman blinds are down.'

'It's a total transformation.' Evie turns to gaze at her husband, checking his reaction.

'Yes, honey. I'm sold so you can relax.'

'You're not just saying that to please me, Mason? The inn is your legacy, darling.'

I find myself unwittingly holding my breath, and Hayden hasn't moved a muscle. I'm concerned it could be taken two very different ways. Hayden hopes they're finally in agreement, but is Evie now intent on making sure she can walk away knowing her husband is happy?

Mason takes Evie's hand in his. 'You wanted changes made and I didn't listen because . . . because I can be stubborn at times. You were right, Ria.' He turns to face me. 'The inn was stuck in the past and, miraculously, you've managed to incorporate most of the things that have meaning for me, while delivering on Evie's dream of what this place could be. I just didn't have a vision; I feared I wouldn't recognise it anymore.'

From the look on Hayden's face, he's hopeful this is a meaningful moment.

'It's beginning to feel like our home, isn't it?' Mason mutters, softly. He raises his wife's hand to his mouth and kisses it tenderly, but Evie merely smiles back at him. Ironically, everything he's saying bodes well and it obviously comes from the heart. What he, and Hayden, seem oblivious to is Evie's silence.

This evening, Mason and Evie insist the four of us eat dinner in the formal dining room. Even though it's not fully extended still, the main table seats at least fourteen people easily. Sitting at one end, the cavernous room is still a blank canvas, with most of the furniture lined up against one wall, but it's a nice change.

I can't help comparing the atmosphere this evening to what it was like when I first arrived. The tension between Hayden's parents had built up to a point where they were both overwhelmed by it. Tonight, however, the two of them are working in perfect harmony, and it's wonderful to see.

When we suddenly find ourselves alone, Hayden looks at me ruefully.

'This is agony, isn't it? I want to ask you so many questions.'

I peer at him, widening my eyes. 'Like what, exactly?'

'Everything and anything. I don't know—'

The kitchen door swings open and Mason hurries over to the table, carrying a wine cooler.

'This is Evie's favourite wine, Ria. It's from Flag Hill Winery, New Hampshire's oldest distillery. It's a Cayuga White.'

I reward him with a grateful smile but I've never even heard of it before. Hayden comes to my rescue.

'I bet you'll like this one, Ria. Eh, Dad?' He turns to face me. 'I'll pour a little so you can try it. There's a bit of a fizz to it; it's rather like a Riesling. Orange, pear and green apple add a sweetness to balance the acidity.'

As soon as Mason is out of sight, Hayden pours some wine into my glass. 'He's going all out to impress you tonight. He's grateful for what you're doing to please Mum, and this is his way of saying thanks.'

'Ah, that's so lovely, but I hope it pleases him too and he's not just paying lip service. That's not what this is about.'

Hayden pulls a frown. 'It's funny, you came here a total stranger and yet my parents are as comfortable around you as I am.'

I take a leisurely sip of the wine, savouring it. 'I'm definitely getting the fruit and the fizz – it's quite refreshing. OK, you can ask me one question.'

Did I just bat my eyelashes at him? Come on, Ria, you can do better than that.

'You mentioned you were engaged for what was it . . . four years? That's a long time. Do you still talk to him?'

It's a fair enough question, as I'm curious to know more about Hayden's failed marriage. It only lasted a year, which means things went downhill quickly. Hayden doesn't strike me as the sort of man who, once he's committed, quits easily.

'No. It didn't end well. Will couldn't see why our relationship couldn't continue as it was.'

'And you felt differently about it?'

I fiddle nervously with my wine glass, absent-mindedly moving it in circles on the tabletop. 'If two people spend as much time apart as they do together, something isn't quite right. Oh, he was attentive, if rather predictable. Flowers . . . chocolates, that sort of thing. I can't quite explain it other than to say that he never swept me off my feet. It all sounds rather pathetic now.'

'What a fool he was,' Hayden reflects, soberly.

'It wasn't an open relationship. Well, it wasn't for me and I assumed he felt the same way.' That's something I've given thought to numerous times since the break-up and I ended up realising it was better not to ask the question. As my sister pointed out, Will liked time to himself. The trouble is, I was equally as guilty. I've never turned down a job I wanted to do, although Will never once complained about the long hours I worked. In hindsight, I realised that was because he wasn't around to notice it.

'Here it comes!' Evie announces, holding the door open for Mason to carry in an oversized tray.

Hayden looks up at his father. 'It certainly smells good. What's on the menu tonight, Dad?'

'Three pulled-pork sliders, topped with beer cheese and crispy onions. On the side, my special skin-on fries with a lemon and pepper crumb coating. Enjoy!'

'It looks amazing, Mason. I've never heard of beer cheese before,' I comment.

'It's a combination of several cheeses with a blend of spices. I use cayenne pepper, mustard powder and garlic, to give it that kick. It's spreadable, so a little flat beer adds to the flavour and gives it that smooth texture.'

After several bites, I think this is my second favourite dish so far. Mason really could be a full-on chef. The beer cheese goes so well with the melt-in-your-mouth pork. As for the fries, he has the knack of combining flavours that lift even the humble potato to a whole new level.

The conversation tonight is both fun and engaging, as Mason trots out some stories about the past, with both Evie and Hayden joining in. It's a real insight into what life was like before Hayden's granddad passed. Evie obviously loved visiting the inn, she just never saw her and Mason running it. It's heart-warming to hear them talking with such fondness about the past but also poignant if Evie doesn't have a change of heart.

While we're waiting for dessert to arrive, it's my turn to ask Hayden a question.

'What's your idea of a perfect first date?'

'I take that to mean the one after that initial introduction. Which, in my case, has usually been engineered by well-meaning friends or colleagues. Actually, more often than not by Tricia, my best friend Liam's wife.'

'That's rather telling.' I'm surprised Izzie's name didn't come up.

'Yes. Well, there haven't even been that many, to be honest.'

'Why?'

'Small talk isn't my thing. That getting-to-know someone phase is so . . .'

'Repetitive?' I throw out there.

'Precisely! I usually end up thinking that's another couple of hours of my life I'll never get back.'

I burst out laughing just as Mason and Evie step back into the dining room, a plate in each of their hands.

'Did we miss out on a joke?' Mason enquires.

The seconds pass and Hayden, ever the gentleman, comes to my rescue. 'Why can't you trust snowmen?'

Evie and Mason exchange a quizzical glance, shrugging their shoulders as they place dessert in front of us and take their seats.

'Because they're a bunch of flakes.'

They both smile indulgently, Mason shaking his head as he stares at his son. 'Every year it's Hayden who can't wait to pull the crackers. He insists we all wear those silly hats and everyone has to read out the joke.'

Hayden gives a beaming smile. 'It's the kid in me,' he replies.

For some reason that touches my heart. I've no doubt he's done that every year since he was old enough to read – I know I have – and I swallow a small lump that is suddenly blocking my throat. It's hard for me to keep my feelings out of it when I think about where this could all be leading.

'My favourite dessert!' Hayden declares.

Evie points to the plate in front of me. 'It's a deconstructed layering of cannoli shell with ricotta crème, topped with powdered sugar and almond chips, Ria. Usually, cannoli is served as a tube with a whole variety of different fillings piped inside. It's an Italian creation with a limitless array of options. Sometimes they're dipped in chocolate, but some of my favourite flavours are raspberry, pistachio, amaretto and strawberry – the list is endless. This is my version of it.'

Mason smiles across at Evie. 'All credit to you, it's a refined way of eating it, honey.'

'It sounds a bit like a ginger snap filled with cream,' I reply.

Hayden leans into me. 'This is Mum's signature dish, so heap on the praise.'

His smile as our eyes lock momentarily makes me freeze. Suddenly, his parents are staring at us intently. Hayden has to stop doing that. I can feel my cheeks colouring up and I feel awkward now.

'Ah. Well, it . . . um . . . tastes wonderful and I'll—'

'Oh,' Mason interrupts. 'Before I forget. How do the two of you feel about a little trip out tomorrow.'

'Tomorrow? Where?' Hayden seems genuinely surprised, so this isn't a ruse.

I keep my head down, wondering what's coming next.

'Frank did a favour for a friend and he gave him two tickets to Santa Town. They're for tomorrow though. It's some sort of special event. Frank thought maybe Ria might enjoy going.'

Mason fixes his gaze on me.

'It sounds like fun but I'm not sure it's wise to . . .' My words tail off, rather pathetically.

'Oh, it's not a problem! This is something you simply can't pass up. Tickets are hard to come by,' Evie insists. 'Mason and I can up the pace a little, can't we? We'll get the study sorted.'

Hayden's father agrees. 'You can't let them go to waste,' he adds.

'That's settled, then,' Evie confirms. She makes eye contact with me, and although it's not really my thing, it would be impolite of me to refuse.

'Oh, and Frank's invited us all to a little drinks party at the farm on Wednesday the twenty-first,' Evie continues. 'It's an informal affair, Ria, and I'm sure he'll have everyone up dancing at some point during the evening.'

When I glance in Hayden's direction, he's tucking into his dessert, seemingly happy with the arrangements. A drinks party is fine, but I'm not sure it's wise to spend the day together when we should be working.

Kate's advice is still rattling around inside my head. What if Hayden turns out to be another Will? A man who likes the idea of having a special someone in his life, but doesn't realise that inviting a person in means making compromises. It's a two-way thing and I'm not sure now is the best time for me to be diverting attention away from the job in hand. And yet, every time I look at Hayden my heart begins to race, and it's exhilarating.

Hayden

17

Reindeers and Sleigh Rides

'You know, this could be regarded as our first real date.' I raise my eyebrows at Ria, but she shakes her head dismissively as we get out of the car. When I walk around to join her, she gives me a questioning look.

'A day out, courtesy of Frank having some tickets he can't use and your parents graciously allowing me time off because I'll enjoy a day out? I don't think any of them would want to be a party to you turning it into an actual date,' I declare.

'I see what you mean, but they won't know that, will they? Besides, you have no idea how lucky you are. Tickets sell out quickly and Santa Town usually only opens at weekends. This year it also opened on the last Friday in November, so a mid-week opening is a special event. In this case it's a charity fund-raiser.'

'It's not that I'm unappreciative,' I remark, stamping my feet on the ground to warm my toes. 'I just feel I'm skiving off, and it is freezing!'

'That makes two of us skiving off then, but there was no arguing with my parents, was there?'

'I thought the same thing. It's nice for them to have a day to themselves.'

'You'll warm up once we're walking around. Trust me, it's going to be worth it as it will bring out your inner child. The entrance is over there.' I point to the far side of the car park.

Nestled among the pine trees is a collection of quaint-looking log cabins that extend way back. In front of us, the main building sports a huge welcome sign above it. Decked in lights, Santa is holding up a sign saying: YO-HO-HO AND WELCOME!

'The massive A-framed roof reminds me of the gingerbread house my siblings and I made every year when we were small. Mum always had to intervene to stop us arguing over who was going to do what. We'd end up with blobs of sticky icing sugar on our hands, the floor, the table, and – more often, than not – in our hair, too.'

'It sounds like great fun, regardless.' It's also good to hear Ria talking about her childhood.

'With the backdrop of snow-laden trees, through the eyes of a child this would be like going to visit Santa at the North Pole.' Her eyes are shining and my heart skips a beat.

I catch Ria's hand, steering her towards the entrance and we up the pace a little.

'What do you want to do first?' I enquire. 'My two personal favourites are feeding time at the Reindeer Rendezvous – see, it's the barn over there with the magnificent golden reindeer gracing the roof. Or we could take a trip on the Skyway Sleigh monorail.'

Toot, toot! We turn to watch, as a train with open carriages filled with people rattles along on a track that weaves between the tall trees. Most of them wave as they pass by and Ria and I join in with the people around us to wave back.

It's impossible not to walk around with a smile on your face, as Santa's helpers are everywhere and it's obvious they all genuinely enjoy what they do.

'Let's try the Skyway Sleigh,' Ria declares, as I pull her into my arms.

'On our first unofficial date I took you to a cabin in the woods; on our first official date I took you to see Santa. It doesn't get any more romantic than that, does it?'

As I look down at her, what I see are those glowing pink cheeks, a slightly red-tipped nose, and a fetching pale blue bobble hat in which she looks really cute.

'I told you; this doesn't count as a date. I will admit it's going to be hard to beat though.' With that, she joins in as a troop of strolling carollers start singing that wonderful old classic 'Joy to the World'. She yanks on my hand and I do my best, but my voice is nowhere near as good as hers. When it finishes, I drag her away and I can see she's torn but there's a lot to see.

'I knew you wouldn't be able to resist.'

'You mean getting in the festive mood, I presume?' she muses.

I give her a cheeky wink as we join the queue for the ride.

'There are more lights here than I think I've ever seen in one place before. It's like living in a pop-up Christmas book, where every page you turn heralds a new surprise.'

Ria's right, how am I going to beat this back in the UK? But, for the next couple of hours, I have her all to myself and I intend to make the most of it.

'That was incredible!' Ria's eyes gleam. 'Chilly, but wonderful. When I closed my eyes I really felt like I was riding along in a sleigh. With the jingling of the bells, the view of Santa Town, the forest and the mountains, that was awesome!'

It feels good knowing she's enjoying herself. 'It's a ride to remember but there's lots more fun to come.'

Clasping her hand, I lead her away – it's time to warm ourselves up.

'It's strange,' Ria muses, as she wraps her hands appreciatively around a mug of hot chocolate and gazes around The Jingle Bells Café.

'What is?'

She turns to face me, looking wistful.

'As much as I complain about my family and the chaos of Christmas Day, I will miss them this year.'

That throws me a little. 'I thought you were having fun?'

'I am, but watching the little kids and their parents enjoying themselves—' She comes to an abrupt halt.

It's obvious Ria is feeling homesick and the guilt starts to set in. 'Look, if you want me to try to rearrange your flight, Ria, you only have to say.'

'No, no . . . it's fine, really. It's just a fleeting thing and I've never once quit early on a job when it wasn't finished.'

Now she's embarrassed for voicing her thoughts and is switching back into professional mode, darn it. Just when we were beginning to break down that invisible barrier.

'I mean it. We'll be done by Christmas Eve; I have no doubt of that.' *But please don't take me up on the offer*, my inner voice pleads. I've been increasingly looking forward to the upcoming festivities, knowing that Ria will be there. The thought of spending time around her when the job is finished is what's keeping me going.

She pauses for the briefest of moments, before laughing it off. 'What, and miss out on a once-in-a-lifetime chance to experience a real American-style Christmas? I'm the envy of my sister and my friends. Can we see the reindeers next?'

Ria was tempted, but a part of her also wants to stay. I can't assume that's because of me, of course, but I can live in hope.

'Rudolph awaits us. How's the hot chocolate?'

'Utterly divine. What I love about this place, I mean the whole area in general, is seeing the lengths people go to when decorating the outside of their homes. As we drive along it's one display after another. We're a little more reserved in the UK, aren't we? I've often taken my nephews out for a ride around the neighbourhood to check out the special outdoor displays. Funnily enough, even I don't put up outside lights.'

'I guess as I've spent every Christmas here, I hadn't really taken much notice, but come to think of it, you're right.'

'Do you trim up back in the UK before you fly out?'

I shake my head, emphatically. 'I don't get the time. If I

entertain in the run-up to the festive period, I usually take people out to a restaurant to get their festive kick,' I chuckle.

'Out of interest, where are you based?'

'My head office is located on the outskirts of Oxford. I had the top floor converted into an apartment.'

Her eyes widen in surprise. 'Ah, the M4 corridor is a central hub for businesses, isn't it? Handy, too, given the number of outlets you have around the UK and the travelling involved. How does that work out for you, living above the office? Is it hard to switch off?'

I shrug my shoulders. 'It beats having to sit in traffic to get to and from work. I do have a home away from work . . . well, a house in the village of Wheatley. It's about six miles away but I rarely spend time there. In fact it's been rented out for almost two years.'

Ria looks a little uneasy. 'Sorry, I didn't mean to pry. I was just—'

She thinks it's my former marital home. 'It's not a problem. I bought it after the divorce, fully intending to settle there. After about a year of mainly spending only weekends at the house, I realised the apartment was more convenient. Especially as it has a gym and a cinema room. It also has the added benefit of some spectacular views out over the countryside.' I grin at her, haplessly, realising that sounds like I don't have much of a social life. Which, I guess, has been true for longer than I care to admit.

She grins back at me. 'The apartment sounds perfect. What more could you possibly need?'

Now she's simply being polite. It's a convenient place that suits my needs. 'Where do you live?'

'I have a little terraced cottage in the Cotswolds, a place called Bourton-on-the-Water.'

'Ah, very picturesque. I bet it's quaint and full of charm.'

She dismisses that, pulling a long face. 'If charm means draughty old windows and walls that have never seen a plumb line then yes, it is.'

'You're not happy there?' It's an honest question and her body language is telling as she shifts uneasily in her seat.

'I moved in shortly before I met Will. He had a four-bed house that was only a couple of years old. After we became engaged, I didn't think it was worth continuing to update the cottage as I sort of assumed we'd end up buying something together. Now I'm trying to play catch-up. However, with my business taking off, it's going nowhere fast as I'm away from home a lot. It's a place to lay my head at night and spend my Sundays stripping back layers of paint from the woodwork.'

'It sounds delightful.' I grin at her ruefully.

'I know you always spend Christmas over here, but do you ever bring anyone with you?'

'Only my ex for two consecutive years. It wasn't much fun to be honest. She isn't one for rolling up her sleeves and helping out. Georgina's the sort of women who likes to be waited on, not the other way around. It was all a little too rough around the edges for her.'

I think we're both done talking about the past, it's time to get moving. 'Are you ready to set off again?'

'I am.'

'OK, let's head outside.'

For the life of me, I can't imagine what the guy was thinking letting Ria get away. Why be with someone if you don't intend to carry it through? Either you enjoy the freedom that being on your own brings with it, or you want to commit and build a life with someone by your side. That thought passes through my mind increasingly these days, but it's not something you can engineer. Finding the right person is only the first step, the second is discovering whether you want the same things out of life.

Business-wise I think Ria is at a stage where it's now, or never. Sometimes timing sucks. I know it's a long shot, but I wonder if I can convince her to take a risk – on me. I'd certainly never want to hold her back, but I'd regret it forever if I let this opportunity pass me by.

* * *

'Oh, they're so adorable!'

Ria and I stand watching a group of small children feeding the two reindeers with rather bland-looking biscuits, handed to them by one of Santa's helpers.

She leans into me. 'That's lovely, but are all those snacks good for the animals?'

I give her a reassuring look. 'They're special and they rotate the reindeers. They have a whole herd of them behind the scenes. They get to roam free in between doing their little stints.'

'Ah, that's good to know.'

When it's our turn, I let Ria step forward. As she holds out a small sausage-shaped treat, the reindeer is straight on it and Ria is startled. She lets out a little squeak of a sound and the animal backs away. Ria immediately puts out her hand to smooth his head, apologetically.

'Sorry, Rupert. You made me jump but I didn't mean to scare you!' She turns to me. 'Can you grab me another one, please, Hayden?'

When I return she's still patting him but there's a little boy standing next to her now.

'This is Noah, Hayden.'

'Hi, Noah. I see you've met Rupert. Would you like to feed him?'

Ria gives me a beaming smile as I kneel down to hand two biscuits to the lad.

'Thanks!' He calls out, 'Mom, can I feed the reindeer?'

A woman hurries over, looking hot and bothered. 'Noah! I told you not to keep running off like that. Thank you for looking after him and of course you can.' She flashes us a grateful smile.

We leave them to it, but before we exit the barn Ria pauses to take a few snaps. 'Can we stop by the shop? The kids will love hearing about Santa Town and it'll be even better if I take a few mementoes back with me.'

211

'Sure. Are you feeling hungry yet?'

'Hmm . . . not really. Your father makes a hearty breakfast, doesn't he? How about you?'

'I'm good, actually. I think it's time for a little shopping, then a ride on Santa's Express. After that maybe the Penguin Spin Out coaster and we could pop into the Olde Book Shoppe on our way back to the car. I reckon it'll be two, maybe half past, by the time we're done. We could head to Shelley's afterwards for a late lunch. What do you think?'

'I'd like that. By then, no doubt I'll be more than grateful to get warm and cosy.'

We walk off arm in arm and I realise that I haven't given thought to anything at all other than what we've been doing. It's like life is on hold and nothing matters except for talking, laughing and living in the moment. I can't remember the last time that happened. Even up at Frank's cabin, in quiet moments I found myself thinking about the potential turmoil a new year might bring. Now I'm more relaxed about that. I suppose it's time to get my life back on track, and what a promising start.

'The two of you look very cosy sitting here in the corner. Are you thawing out?' Shelley gives me a little wink as she puts two steaming mugs of coffee in front of us.

'We are now the fire's been stoked up,' I reply, gratefully.

'I was frozen to the core!' Ria exclaims, bright-eyed.

'You'll feel even better after some hot food. It won't be long. If there's anything else you want in the meantime, just holler.'

I don't want to spoil the ambience but now's my chance to do a little digging.

'How are the catering arrangements coming along for the relaunch party, Shelley?'

'Fine. I have the final headcount and, after a bit of back and forth, we've thrashed out the menu. The party is the talk of the town and I'd have been sorely disappointed not to have been involved.'

I grin at her. 'That's wonderful news!' And it's a mega relief.

Shelley turns to look at Ria. 'How are things shaping up at the inn?'

'The transformation is really coming together and everyone seems pleased with it.'

'That's a complete understatement, Shelley,' I jump in. 'Ria is underselling her skills. It looks incredible. You won't know the place when you see it.'

'I won't? Oh, I can't wait. Now I'm counting down the days!' Shelley smiles to herself as she turns to walk away from the table.

Ria leans in, lowering her voice. 'Your father has talked your mother around?'

'So it seems. Perhaps it wasn't as much of an issue as I'd feared. People don't always mean what they say in the heat of the moment, and Mum isn't usually one to hold grudges.'

Ria reaches out to touch my hand, as it languishes on the table.

'I hope things work out for your parents' sakes, and for yours, Hayden.' Her words sound heartfelt and for a moment I'm taken aback.

'Me, too, Ria. The White Mountains is a very special place and it leaves a lasting impression. Living here isn't for the faint-hearted, but those who appreciate it wouldn't want to be anywhere else.'

Ria frowns. 'I will come clean and say that at one point I wondered whether—' She cuts herself short.

'Say whatever it is that's on your mind. You don't have to hold back.'

'I wondered whether you were getting the inn ready to sell.'

'You did? Whatever gave you that impression?'

'Well . . . you're a businessman, Hayden, and an astute one at that. Shortly after we arrived, I recall you telling me that in business you have to put your feelings to one side, and that was why you were here.'

It sounds like something I'd say, but when it comes to the inn it's personal. 'I meant because my parents were getting bogged down with the minute details and couldn't grasp the bigger picture, that's all.'

Ria looks down at her hand, still covering mine. As she glances up at me from beneath those dark, tantalising eyelashes, my pulse begins to race. 'The inn represents a lifetime's worth of precious memories for you, too, so it's much more than a rescue package, isn't it?'

Before I get a chance to reply, our food arrives and it's a welcome reprieve as that's a question I don't quite know how to answer. What stops me in my tracks is that Ria is talking from the heart because she cares, she understands what this means to me. I'm not imagining this . . . whatever I'm feeling. It's not one-sided. But on the relationship front I'm a walking disaster. What man wants to admit that?

I'm desperately in need of some advice. If I talk to Izzie, she'll probably jump on a plane, thinking I need saving from myself because this has come out of the blue. Which, I freely admit that it has. The only person I feel comfortable talking to about it is my best mate's wife, Tricia. But where would I even begin to explain how I feel about Ria? Will she think I'm throwing caution to the wind for the second time, as I'm pretty sure Izzie will? But this is different. Way different and I'd be gutted if I messed it up.

18

It's Time to Relax and Be Myself

Ria and I arrive back at the inn on a high. Shelley fussed over us as if we were her personal guests. Our stomachs are full and it's been a great day.

'You look like you've enjoyed yourselves,' my father comments, as we walk into the library.

'We've had a wonderful time and we stopped off to eat on the way back,' Ria replies, happily. 'My, you two have been busy! It's much cosier being able to draw the chairs up closer to the fire.'

'We thought it would make it more useable for our guests. It works now both as a snug and a library. Somewhere people can sit and enjoy the peace and quiet.'

'Moving the sofa into the main sitting room encourages couples and families to lounge around in there. It was a great idea,' Ria responds, enthusiastically.

'You'll have noticed that we moved the heavy bits of furniture stored in here, out into the dining room,' my father informs us.

'I did. We'll soon get those shifted, Dad.'

'You did a great job decorating the tree,' Ria comments and I wander over to stand next to her.

'It does look lovely,' Ria continues. 'You were right, Evie, the burgundy-coloured glass baubles and the pinecones work well together on the smaller tree.'

My mother gives a satisfied nod. She's unusually quiet as if she has something on her mind.

My father walks over to join us. 'I suggested we leave it at that. What do you think, Ria?'

I can't believe this is my father talking. Usually, my mother is the one constantly trying to restrain him when it comes to trimming up. But in a room this size, and with hundreds of books lining the shelves, the tree now takes centre stage in the far corner. It's spot on to my eye, but we all turn to look at Ria.

'I think it's perfect. Absolutely perfect!'

While my father prepares dinner for him and my mother, Ria and I head off in different directions. When I return to my room, the first thing I do is call Liam, conscious that it's probably coming up to ten o'clock in the UK.

'Hi, Liam. How're you doing?'

'Hayden – we were talking about you earlier. Mainly snow envy. It's been cold here but dry. We've had a few sharp frosts but not a single snowflake.'

I laugh, scornfully. 'Be careful what you wish for, Liam. Any more than six inches and people start to panic in the UK.'

'We do, don't we?' he replies, good-naturedly. 'How're things at the inn?'

'Shaping up nicely. I'm . . . I wondered if Tricia was free for a quick chat?'

'Oh, so you don't want to talk to me at all. Thanks, mate. Out of sight, out of mind, is it?' He's joking and I can tell he's walking as we talk. 'She's just here. I'll pass over the phone. Take care, Hayden. I'm looking forward to seeing you back at work. Boy, do I need this upcoming holiday!'

'I bet and thanks, mate.'

'Hayden?' Tricia's voice echoes down the line.

'Hey, how are you?'

'Sitting in front of the fire toasting my toes.'

'Try going into minus double-digits and spending the day walking around Santa Town,' I moan.

'Oh . . . please, that would be heaven!' She chuckles. 'Snow is so romantic!'

'Ah, talking about romance.' This is tough. Where do I start? 'You know what I'm like when it comes to dates—'

'Tongue-tied and looking so far outside of your comfort zone that the women run in the opposite direction? You either say very little, or it turns into a job interview.'

I emit a long, drawn out, 'Hmmmmm . . .' It makes her laugh. 'OK, there's no fooling you, is there?' And she's right, I've already offered Ria a job – even if it was a bit tongue in cheek. It's just the way my mind works.

'Hayden, I've seen it up close and every time it makes me cringe. You simply need to relax and understand one thing.'

I pause. Tricia won't hold back, she's all about tough love.

'And what's that?'

'You're a catch, you just don't know it.'

Like that helps.

'You're too nice, Tricia. You see what the others clearly don't.'

'What, that soft side of your nature?'

'There is someone who has caught my eye. We have a few things in common and she's easy to talk to.'

'You're dating her?'

That's a tough one. 'Not really. Not yet.'

'What's she like?'

I stop to consider how best to describe Ria.

'She's where I was maybe ten years ago. Keen to grow her business and preferring to focus on that because someone broke her heart. That's why this has come out of the blue. Neither of us was expecting it.'

Tricia lets out a gentle sigh. 'Really?' She pauses for a moment. 'It's in our nature to want to love and be loved. Your problem is that you gravitate towards the wrong type of women.'

I give a somewhat embarrassed laugh. 'I do?'

'Yes, the sort of woman who wants to take charge of you. Like the rather intimidating Georgina, or Izzie, your go-to friend. You're an intelligent man, you don't need someone to tell you how you're feeling or what's right when it comes to affairs of the heart, Hayden. I hope this woman you're interested in is a little more sensitive.'

'I believe she is, Tricia. Liam is a lucky man; he found a woman who enriches his life in ways he couldn't even comprehend. You do know that I envy him?'

She gives a little giggle. 'He's not quite as soft as you, but he's a teddy bear in his own way. The point I'm trying to make here, is that no one is the boss in our house. We make all the decisions together. That's how it's supposed to be.'

'I'm not soft,' I bemoan.

'Oh, Hayden. In business you're the main man, an obstacle is simply a motivator. When it comes to your personal life, you're different. You let Georgina walk all over you and the moment you pushed back and she couldn't get her own way, she walked out. Izzie's much the same: you let her tell you what to do. But that's a cop-out on your part when you're scared you're about to make a mistake. That's life, Hayden. No one can live it for you.'

It's true to say that my ex-wife was pretty scary. 'Living with Georgina taught me a few things, Tricia. I don't intend to make the same mistake again. And Izzie only wants to help but she flits from one relationship to another and none of them have lasted.'

'This is all beginning to sound a little serious.'

'It is. Which is why I'm checking in with you before I go any further.'

Tricia lets out an excited shriek and the sound resonates down the line, making me yank the phone away from my ear. 'Have you finished?'

'Sorry, Hayden. You said you weren't dating this mysterious woman yet but I don't believe you. You've met someone and while you're in the States. At last . . . I was beginning to think this day would never come! Tell me more.'

This could take a while.

* * *

'Your granddad would approve, it's really cosy in here now,' my father says with conviction, as we end the day sitting around a log fire in the library.

With the Christmas lights twinkling on the tree and the bluish-tinged light from a clear night sky filtering in through the window, it's blissful.

Tricia's advice keeps coming back to me in waves. *Be natural, be yourself and don't be afraid to own your feelings.*

'Ria and I had a great time at Santa Town. Didn't we?' I look directly at her but she hesitates.

'Yes, um . . . we did, Hayden. It's a wonderful place to while away a few hours. I was a bit disorientated on the Penguin Spin Out coaster, though. I'm not sure I'd do that again!' She gives a tinkling little laugh. 'I'm not big on rides although the monorail was amazing.'

'Wonderful views,' my mother joins in. 'I remember the first time Mason took me there. It was also the first Christmas I stayed here at the inn.'

'It was, honey! That would have been what, back in the early nineties? Santa Town was a lot smaller then.'

'Hmm. How time flies. It probably brought back a lot of memories for you, Hayden.' My mother turns to look at me, expectantly. Normally this is where I'd brush it off with a bit of a joke and change the subject, but not today.

'It did, actually.' I can feel Ria looking at me, and when our eyes meet, I notice a slight frown. 'It reminded me of Grandma and Granddad, but today was a little different. I was seeing it through Ria's eyes and she didn't stop smiling the whole time we were there.'

And she's smiling now.

'Being up close to a reindeer was an amazing experience. They were so calm and gentle,' Ria reflects. 'When they yawn, they make a curious creaking sound and then they waggle their chins. I always thought they liked carrots, but one of

Santa's helpers told us that it's not a part of their natural diet so it's not something they automatically recognise.'

I do a belly laugh. 'I know, it shocked me, too, many years ago when I asked the same question.'

'You didn't say . . .' Ria gives me an accusing look.

'You didn't ask me, you asked the elf!' I chuckle. 'And the treats are cereal based. It's a supplement because they mostly live on anything green – grasses, leaves, berries and even lichens, heather, and birch in the winter.'

My parents are watching us, slightly amused by the way the conversation is going.

'Anyone fancy a glass of wine? And you guys must be feeling hungry by now. I'll rustle up a quick snack.' My father eases himself out of the chair and my mother goes to stand. 'No, you sit and chat, Evie. I've got this.'

Mum turns to look at Ria.

'This must all feel rather strange to you, working away from home at Christmastime. Your family will be missing you.'

I walk over to the fire, using the poker to rake away some of the ashes before putting on another log, all the while listening.

'It won't be the first time we've celebrated Christmas twice over. My eldest brother is a contracts advisor and often has to fly out to various destinations in Europe and even places like Saudi Arabia. The second one, in my honour this time, will be on New Year's Eve.'

'Ah, that's such a lovely idea, Ria.'

'Mum says it's only Christmas when we're all together. Mind you, when we are it's total bedlam. I'm one of four siblings. My eldest brother has two boys; my other brother got married last August and my sister has a boy and is expecting a little girl next summer.'

'Ria spent ages choosing gifts in the shop at Santa Town, Mum,' I comment as I settle back down in the chair.

'I can imagine! It's all about the kids, isn't it? It's such a fun time for them. Adults don't really need presents, do they? We only give token gifts these days, but I fondly remember the years when, on Christmas Eve, Hayden would be too excited to sleep.'

'Mum!' I groan. 'I'm surprised you can remember that far back.'

'Cheeky. Golden memories, my son. Times I'll never forget.'

'So, after you married Mason all your Christmases were spent here?' Ria asks, sounding surprised.

'Yes. For quite a while, every other year some of my family members would fly out to join us, which was lovely. Those were very special times indeed, but as the younger members of the family reached their teens it happened less and less. Last year, family descended upon us en masse, including two of Mason's cousins. One lives in Texas and the other in California. This year only our niece, Lindy, and her fiancé, Seth, are coming. They live in France and are renovating an old chateau, so I'm looking forward to catching up with them.'

'You also have guests who come back every year, I gather?'

'Yes. People who became friends over time. They book every year. Some are second generation now and have little ones of their own.'

'That's quite something, Evie.'

I look over at my mother and she's deep in thought. 'Hmm, it is.'

After a not-so-light supper and an hour spent listening to music in the library, we all say goodnight.

I stay behind to help my mother carry the glasses and mugs through to the kitchen. It's obvious she wanted to get me on my own when she insisted my father and Ria left us to it.

'You were chatty this evening, Hayden.'

'I'm making an effort to be more sociable, Mum.' I give her a sideways smile as I close the door on the dishwasher and set it going.

221

'It's unusual for you to make small talk, my son.' I can see she's curious.

'I'm practising for the onslaught of visitors. I'm really looking forward to it this year.'

My mother gives a tinkling little laugh. 'I thought maybe you were trying to impress Ria.'

My father pushes open the door. 'We're all locked up. Are you done in here, Evie?'

'Yes, I'm coming.' She leans in to kiss my cheek. 'Have you had a chance to speak to Izzie lately?'

'If I don't get in touch, she's like you – she chases me. Izzie keeps me on the straight and narrow when you're not there to keep an eye out.'

'That's good to hear. It's nice to have people around you who care.'

Something's up as Mum has been a little distant at times throughout the evening.

'Mum, the worst is behind you now, you do realise that? It's why Dad's cheered up.'

She gives me one of her reassuring smiles. 'I know. And the place is already beginning to look lovely, Hayden. That's all down to you, my son. Love you and sleep well!'

'You too.'

As the door to the kitchen closes, I grab a glass and run some cold water, downing it in one. Today felt like a bit of a turning point in more ways than one; hopefully it's all coasting from here on in, I reflect, as I make my way upstairs.

The minute my foot hits the top tread and there's that familiar creak, Ria's bedroom door edges open.

'I was hoping to catch you,' she says, softly, keeping her voice low. 'I just wanted to say it was nice to sit and chat this evening and thanks again for a wonderful day out, Hayden.'

On the floor above there's not a sound to be heard. I take a step forward and so does Ria. Suddenly, she's in my arms and we're kissing each other with an urgency that sends shock waves through me. I pull back a little, staring down into her eyes and we're both conflicted.

'It doesn't feel right, does it?' I check.

'Right time, wrong place. Sorry,' she agrees, reluctantly.

'I know. I sensed you'd feel the same way. I enjoyed showing you around Santa Town. For me it really was like discovering it all over again. I hope you sleep well, Ria.'

'You, too, Hayden. We've a lot to get done tomorrow.'

'I can't wait!'

I messed things up once, and this time around it's going to be different. Tricia told me not to rush things, to simply be myself and let the relationship develop naturally. Given where we are, I guess it isn't going to be that difficult to do. Now if we were back at Frank's cabin, it would be a whole different story!

Ria

19

Passion and Pandemonium

It's the twentieth of December and we can't let up now as it's the final countdown. With the main hallway, the landings and the two largest suites still to tackle, spirits are high. There's a buzz of excitement in the air and a sense of optimism that is growing by the day as the inn is brought back to life.

I'm now simply one-quarter of the workforce and director of operations, I reflect, smiling to myself. We've officially split into two teams. Today, Evie and Mason are going to transform The Balsam Fir Suite. It should keep them occupied all day, as it's also one of the family rooms with an interconnecting door leading into a large twin-bedded room. They're going to have their work cut out, but in forty-eight hours' time the cleaners are due in and time is running out.

Hayden and I are planning a special surprise for the hallway to delight both his parents and their guests, but we're going to need to keep our wits about us.

'I've helped my father carry the last of the boxes through to the main bedroom,' Hayden informs me, his voice low. 'I said as they're working on the top floor and we'll be moving furniture around in the hallway, to shout down if they want anything. I'll keep the coffee and refreshments flowing. Do you think we can get it all set up by lunchtime?'

'It's highly unlikely, Hayden, as it's going to be so fiddly. Let's see how it goes. Right, I'm all kitted up ready to face that arctic wind, are you ready for this?'

Hayden grins at me, his eyes full of fun and mischief as we head outside and make our way over to the barn. The sun is out and the sky is blue, but if you forget and leave a water bottle in the car by mistake, the next morning it's turned to solid ice which will pop the top off. It's the weirdest thing ever and something I'd never seen before.

As Hayden slides back the barn door, I'm excited and he sprints ahead to pull off two large dust sheets. 'Ta-da!'

The unit looks amazing.

Hayden runs his hand over the smooth surface, clearly proud of his efforts. 'What was that colour, again?'

'Almond oyster. But the nice thing is that when we sit it in the alcove, as the wall is the exact same shade, it'll disappear into the background.'

'And that's a good thing?' He glances at me, raising an eyebrow.

'Trust me. It's going to put a huge smile on their faces when they see the display all lit up. I didn't realise this unit came in three separate pieces. How clever.'

'And more manageable for us when it comes to carrying it across to the inn,' he points out. 'I had to take the dowel pegs out, but it's easy enough to hammer them back in once it's in situ.'

While it does make it easier, after two trips back and forth it's hot and heavy work.

'The final piece. How are you holding up?'

I roll my eyes. 'Wishing my arms were longer. It's such a disadvantage. Can we take those dust sheets with us?'

'Sure. Ah . . . great idea. Cover up the evidence at lunchtime and they'll be none the wiser!'

'It does feel a little sneaky, but who doesn't love a surprise?'

'After this, we've probably got a dozen trips to and from Santa's Retreat. I popped over to sort out the boxes before breakfast and stacked them just inside the door.'

'Oh, I do love it when a plan comes together!'

We bend to pick up the carved top moulding section of

what Mason informed me is a Virginia-style step back wall cupboard. It's not that heavy, it's just awkward and we balance the dust sheets over the top of it.

'That mate of Frank's is all set to pop in later?' I check.

'Yes, I said we'd have lunch over and done with by two o'clock. He says wiring in a new socket shouldn't take long.'

Great!

With everything in the hallway stacked in the middle of the floor and covered in dust sheets, I guide Evie and Mason through.

'Mind you don't knock yourselves on anything,' I call over my shoulder. 'We had to do a bit of remedial work on the paint spraying.'

'I know Mason loves that old antique, but it was looking very shabby, wasn't it, darling?'

I push open the door into the kitchen and Hayden is busy at the grill.

'It was indeed,' Mason acknowledges.

'It's in much better shape now,' I assure him.

'Ria was adamant she wanted to use it,' Hayden joins in.

As his parents take a seat at the kitchen table, I switch on the coffee machine before joining them.

'Now they're spoiling us,' Evie says with a little laugh. 'Which probably means that it fell apart when Hayden started work on it and the alcove is going to be repurposed.'

A smile twitches at my lips. 'I'm not saying a word.'

Hayden turns, a loaded platter in his hands as he hurries over to us.

'Never mind all this talk about an old cupboard, you must be hungry, I know I am.' Hayden winks at me.

His mother bursts out laughing. 'It's not the end of the world. Whatever you do is going to look lovely, I'm sure.'

'Tuck in, Ria,' Hayden calls across to me, 'we have red flannel hash cakes, named because they contain red beets – which you and I refer to as beetroot. It's a bit like a patty or a hash brown. And I'm just going to fetch a good old pot of slow cooked bacon and beans. It's a staple food here in the White Mountains.'

'It looks good, my son.' Mason is clearly impressed.

I must admit that it smells wonderful, even if the colour of the patties is a little unusual. 'I can't wait to try it.'

When Hayden takes the lid off the deep casserole dish, I know that I'm going to love the beans, especially when it's teamed with bacon, onions, garlic and tomatoes.

'Now this is the sort of food you need to keep you going on a winter's day like this,' Mason declares.

Having sampled the beans that Hayden kindly ladled into my dish, I help myself to one of the hash cakes.

'This is red beets and potatoes?' I check.

'Yukon Gold potatoes, leeks, thyme and more bacon, but very finely diced. I prefer to put chunks of pork in with the beans. Dad would disagree with me on that one.' Hayden looks across at his father, eager to hear his verdict.

'Everyone has their own version but this is pretty good, Hayden.'

Evie turns to look fondly at her husband. 'We had a great morning, didn't we, Mason?'

'We did. Productive.'

Hayden is eating but tilts his head approvingly.

Mason continues. 'You might have noticed the enormous, bluish-green balsam fir tree back by the fence that the room's named after, Ria. It must be almost eighty-foot tall now and it's a fine specimen.'

'Yes, it's magnificent. Have you hit any snags?'

Mason glances at Evie to give the update. 'We moved the furniture around a bit, but everything is now in place. The beds are fully made up but we still have three Roman blinds to hang. Oh, and a touch of festive decoration, isn't that right, Mason?'

'And that'll take us all afternoon, no doubt.' Although it sounds like he's moaning, he's wearing a smile. 'You haven't forgotten that your mother and I are going out tonight, Hayden, have you? I feel a little guilty leaving you to cook dinner, too.'

Clearly Hayden has forgotten, given the look of surprise on his face, and he certainly didn't mention it to me.

'It just temporarily slipped my mind.'

'We haven't been out socially in a while, have we, Evie? It'll be good to catch up with the old dinner club.'

Evie leans in towards me. 'It's a group of about a dozen of us who get together usually once a month. We take it in turns to host the dinner,' she explains. 'I miss the chatter.'

'Chatter? More like gossip,' Mason mumbles.

I put my head down, smiling to myself at the banter, it's a good sign indeed.

It's gone five o'clock when Mason and Evie call us upstairs to check out The Balsam Fir Suite. I think of all the fabrics I chose this is my absolute favourite.

'What do you think, Ria?' Evie's eyes are shining.

'I love the new layout and what an excellent job you've done of pulling it all together. The muted colours of the Pom-Pom Summer Flower design really suit this room. The salmon pink and the semi-translucent blues of the irises are so pretty but delicate, too. You've taken a couple of items of furniture out of here?'

'Yes,' Mason replies. 'We're getting the hang of that less-is-more thing.' He gives me a bashful grin. 'What do you think of the window seat? Evie got a bit creative there.'

'It's simple, but oh so effective! I don't think I've seen that garland before, it's exquisite.'

Evie looks flushed as I turn to look at her. 'I'm glad you approve. Everything else was a bit too colourful so I um . . . dug out some white silk mop-head flowers. I used to have them in two vases in one of the rooms. They just seemed to complement the pom-poms. It didn't take long to string them together and I know it's not Christmassy, but it does the trick. What do you think, Hayden?'

'I think it's a winner. Maybe you and I should take the next couple of days off, Ria, and leave them to it. They don't need anyone's help anymore. It's time for our reveal, next.' The glint in his eye makes his mother peer back at him suspiciously.

'What have you two been up to?' she asks. 'And who was making all that noise downstairs shortly after lunch? I jokingly said to your father that the whole lot had probably collapsed.'

'I told you,' Hayden labours, 'it was just a friend of Frank's stopped by to do me a bit of a favour. Anyway, come and have a look.'

When we traipse downstairs, Hayden and I hang back a little. I'm about three steps from the bottom when Evie let's out a sharp intake of breath.

'Oh . . . that's absolutely gorgeous!'

As I peer over the banister to look at Mason, he's speechless for a few moments. 'Well, I never! I thought I'd seen the last of the little village. Evie, did you know about this?'

She shakes her head before glancing in my direction, a look of gratitude on her face.

'We usually put the train set here on the large trestle table,' he remarks, his voice barely audible as I walk up to join them. 'Evie was right, it took up too much space and now it's perfect in Santa's Retreat. The village scene, though, was the biggest bane of her life.'

Evie joins in. 'I do adore it but in the right setting. Don't they look delightful now? It's a brilliant way of displaying them!'

Hayden steps forward. 'You'll notice that in the top half behind the glass doors I put the less festive ones, no snow scenes. Even without the lights, they look good so it's an all-year-round display. Now, if you open the two solid doors at the bottom, it's a Christmas fest.'

Mason leans in to get a closer look and the effect of the little dioramas all lit up as he slowly opens the doors is magical.

'It's wired in and there's a new socket just above the skirting board,' Hayden points out.

The small houses are beautiful and so detailed, each one an individual scene set within its own garden. But they're best displayed together. As the cupboard sits inside the alcove, it was the perfect solution.

'We're mightily grateful, Ria and Hayden, aren't we, Evie?'

'Yes, my darling, we are.'

'My dad would be pleased. He bought a new one for my mum every Christmas for what . . . twenty years? It'll put a smile on my face every time I pass by.'

Evie clears her throat. 'It's a part of the tradition here at the inn, isn't it?'

'Some things are too precious to let go,' Mason replies, but he's not looking at the display, he's staring at his wife.

I'm beginning to feel tearful, listening to him and wondering what the inn will be like next year and who, if any of them, will be here. Hayden tilts his head in the direction of the kitchen and the two of us leave them to it. Once we're the other side of the door, I can tell that he's equally as touched as his parents are.

'It was a labour of love for you, wasn't it?'

A gentle sigh escapes his lip. 'Yes and it raked up a lot of old memories. They're good ones, naturally, but it's hard not to wish my grandparents were here to see this.'

It's strange with just the two of us alone here at the inn. Dinner ends up being a joint effort, as I'm assigned to gently grill two plump trout, while Hayden makes a sage butter sauce and fries off some thinly sliced kohlrabi.

I glance across at him as we work side by side. 'You really know what you're doing in the kitchen, Hayden.'

'Anyone growing up in this house ends up having a passion for food. My father learnt from my granddad. At Christmas I'm the unofficial sous chef. Should I do some fries with this?'

'No. This will be just fine as it is.'

'I make a special effort if I'm cooking for someone besides myself, but that rarely happens when I'm in the UK.' He gives me a frank look. 'Most of my friends assume I don't bother much and insist on inviting me over to their houses. It works for me.' He shrugs his shoulders nonchalantly.

'I sort of get the same but then I'm more of an ordering-takeout sort of person. Lazy, really.' I laugh.

'When we've eaten, how about we sit in the library and find a board game? As you've already discovered, I'm very competitive and it's more fun when your opponent also plays to win.'

'I seem to remember that night in Frank's cabin I stole one game from you. You're not the only one who enjoys a challenge.' My laughter is playful.

'I have my doubts that "cento" is a word. If it is, then it's Italian, which is cheating!' I proclaim.

It won't get him many points, but the score is so close it could clinch it given the awful letters I'm left with.

Hayden's face lights up. 'It most definitely is a word. I'll grab a dictionary and prove it to you. Seeing is believing.'

Well, there are a lot of books in here and it takes him a little while. I sit back, basking in the last throws of the heat from the dying flames, amused by his determination to prove he's right.

'It's been quite an emotional day, hasn't it?' Hayden remarks, as he trawls the shelves.

'It certainly has.'

'That was quite something doing the reveal. It's funny . . .' He tails off. 'Ah, I've found it.'

'What's funny?'

I watch as he hurries over to begin leafing through the pages. 'Well, two weeks ago you arrived here as a stranger and now you—' He stabs his finger at the page. 'Cento! "A literary work pieced together from the works of several authors". There you go, see for yourself.'

He passes me the dictionary and I readily admit that I was wrong. Who would have thought? 'My sincere apologies for doubting you.' I give him a half-hearted smile. Darn it! What can I do with letters J, Q and B? I wonder.

'I was going to say that now you feel like a part of the family. You know more about my parents and what makes them tick than most people who are close to me. Admittedly, I'm not sure that does me any favours but at least I've nothing left to hide.' He seems to find that thought amusing.

I show him my letters and concede defeat. The clock on the mantelpiece chimes nine but it feels later, so I start packing up.

'Well, my lot can be a bit overpowering, so I'll warn you now. It's nice to think of Mason and Evie out enjoying themselves this evening, among friends. It's good to get a little normality back into their lives.'

'I think Mum's been going a little stir-crazy so it's probably just what they needed. You look tired, Ria.'

'It's the fire. Maybe I should head upstairs.'

'Can I tempt you to stay down a little longer if I make you a hot chocolate?'

I shake my head. 'It's a kind offer, but I'll take some water up with me, if I may.' I yawn, stretching my arms into the air and arching my back.

Hayden stands, walking over to put the board game back into the sideboard. 'You go on up. I'll just rake out the fire, it's virtually on its last legs anyway and then I'll bring you a bottle of water. Give me a couple of minutes.'

As I stand, I groan a little. 'Thanks,' I reply, stifling another yawn. 'Sorry, I got a little too cosy sitting here.'

Leaving Hayden bent over the fire, I walk out into the hallway, stopping for a moment to admire the village scene in the cabinet. It's not my style and yet it has that feel-good factor, plus it looks so at home here.

I make my way upstairs, leaving the door ajar as I grab my PJs from the drawer. It's a little chilly and I end up standing in front of the radiator beneath the window seat, staring out into the darkness. The sidelight behind me casts a gentle glow as I take in the sheer beauty of the snowy scene with the tall trees and the mountains looming up on the horizon. In miniature it could grace the display downstairs as a backdrop.

Suddenly, there's a movement at my side and it makes me jump. I turn and lock eyes with Hayden.

'I didn't mean to startle you. I'll just put the water here. If you need anything else . . .'

And then it happens again. Before there's time to even consider what's happening, I'm in his arms and what starts off as a gentle kiss, turns into a passionate clinch. Suddenly I'm wide awake and the adrenaline is pumping. We stumble backwards, falling onto the bed, and as we fumble with each other's clothes, I feel carefree. My heart is beating so fast in my chest I'm sure Hayden can hear it, but all I see in his eyes is that haunting look of desire. Passion consumes us both and suddenly it doesn't matter where we are; at this moment we're lost in each other. Nothing else matters.

I'm lying in Hayden's arms feeling happier than I have in a very long time. He plants a kiss on my cheek, then works his way down in increments to my mouth.

'Stop. Your parents could return at any time!'

He bursts out laughing. 'They won't be home until at least midnight. Besides, we aren't exactly teenagers, are we?'

'Don't pretend you don't understand what I mean. If they suspected, you might be OK with brazening it out, but I'm not. This is their home and I'm the interior designer. What will they think? It's not a good idea mixing business and pleasure.'

'But I'm glad you're willing to make an exception in my case. And it was . . . pleasurable?' He smirks, fishing for a compliment he isn't going to get. I reach out to grab a scatter cushion and throw it at him. Hayden flexes his arm, deflecting it as he starts laughing. 'You're not regretting it already, are you?'

'No. And in case you're wondering, the water wasn't a ploy on my behalf to get you into bed.' My tone is deadly serious.

His eyes widen. 'You don't think I—'

I put up my hand to stop him there. 'Whatever you're going to say, the answer is no. The timing was right, obviously, it's only the place that is wrong. We need to keep our hands off each other and pick this up in a more private environment, Hayden.'

He pulls a miserable face. 'Ugh. I know and—'

Bang!

We both recoil, jumping out of bed and suddenly on the alert.

'What was that?' I whisper.

The sound of someone stomping upstairs has Hayden rushing over to shut the bedroom door. His quick thinking saves the day, as I hear his mother's voice shouting out 'You can sleep somewhere else tonight, Mason. I don't want to be disturbed.'

Hayden is frantically pulling on his clothes, looking like an idiot when he gets his foot stuck in his trouser leg and almost keels over. We're both listening for a second lot of footsteps, but there's only the sound of a door slamming overhead and then a few faint noises on the ground floor.

'When you've checked on your father can you let me know if he's all right?' I urge, keeping my voice low.

Hayden blows me a silent kiss before slipping out the door. It's not just my body that is tingling, it's every nerve and emotion within me. Wrong place and now, it seems, the worst timing ever!

20

All Hell is About to Break Loose

While I'm anxiously waiting for Hayden to arrive, I reread the text he sent me late last night.

They've had a big falling out. I'll knock on your door about seven thirty in the morning and fill you in. I think it's best we go down to breakfast together. Sorry, what an awful end to a perfect evening. I'm gutted.

I remember letting out a loud groaning sound as my fingers typed a reply.

Try to get some sleep. I'm sure they'll both feel calmer in the morning. Sleep well.

Seven thirty comes and goes, and I'm about to go in search of Hayden when, finally, there's a soft rap on the door and I rush over to open it. He looks shaken.

'Come on in. Did you get any sleep at all?' I query.

'A little. I went down at around five o'clock this morning to get a hot drink and my father was still sitting at the kitchen table.'

'He was?'

'I made him go to bed. He's in the twin single room, The Black Cherry. He won't surface until late morning at least judging by the way he looked. He's totally wiped out.'

'What happened?'

'Apparently, when they were all bidding each other goodnight, Mum's closest friend – Lori – happened to mention the relaunch party and how she was looking forward to Shelley's buffet.' His expression is grim.

Now I'm confused. 'I thought, from what Shelley said to us the other day, that the deed had been done.'

'That was certainly the way I took it. But my father is the one who plans the menus and Mum simply gave him the final number of attendees, so I couldn't have been more wrong. He said my mother's face visibly paled but she simply hugged Lori back and then turned to walk out. Apparently, when they were in the car he tried to explain, but Mum simply put up her hand and wouldn't let him say a word.'

This is really bad news and I fear that Mason might have undone all the goodwill he's garnered this past week. And by the sound of it, he's aware of that. 'What do you think will happen next?'

'It's anyone's guess. My father said that as things were going so well between them he didn't want anything to spoil it. I mean, talk about burying his head in the sand!'

I let out a sigh of frustration. 'He knew your mother wouldn't kick up a fuss at the party when she realised who did the catering. But it was naive to think she wouldn't be annoyed about it.'

Hayden shrugs his shoulders, dejectedly.

'There's nothing we can do. I suggest we grab a quick cup of coffee and carry on as if nothing untoward has happened. Goodness knows how this is going to play out. Agreed?'

'Agreed.' As we're about to walk out onto the landing, he turns to look at me. 'Oh no . . .'

'What now?'

'Tonight is that drinks thing at Frank's. Someone's coming to pick us all up at eight o'clock. It'll look bad if we don't go. Are you up for it if I express my apologies on behalf of my parents? Everyone will probably assume they're tied up organising the last-minute bits and pieces.'

'That's a great idea, Hayden. The fewer people who know about this, the better.'

'Sorry about the wait! I found it!' I exclaim, holding out the missing item as I step up into the back seat of the sturdy-looking SUV. Hayden is sitting in the front and after Chad waits for me to belt up, we finally set off.

Chad and Lori kindly dropped by to give us a lift to Frank's party and as soon as Hayden spotted them pulling up, he went out to explain it would be just the two of us. I was only a couple of seconds behind him. Hayden was mumbling something about panicking as time is running out and that's when I realised I didn't have my bag with me and had to retrace my steps. Oh, how I wish I'd just let Chad pull away.

Lori is smiling at me as I slide into the back seat. 'Trust me to put my handbag down somewhere and then forget it.'

'It's no bother, Ria. It's nice to meet you in person. Last night Mason and Evie were telling everyone all about what a great job you've done for them at the inn. Mason showed us some photos and I can't wait to see it on Christmas Eve.'

For the moment words fail me as my mind is reeling.

'Our property is nowhere near as big as Mason and Evie's place,' she continues, 'but the layout is awful. I think it's a lost cause and I've been pressing Chad to think about moving. He's stubborn though and says that location is everything. Granted, the views are pretty, but I spend more time indoors, than I do out and I keep reminding him of that.'

I'm trying hard to focus on what Lori is saying as, one by one, she begins to list the faults but my brain is processing what I just heard. When I went back inside the inn it was all quiet, so I'd crept stealthily up the stairs, relieved that the coast was clear.

During the day, Mason had appeared twice, very briefly, but Evie stayed in her room the entire time. Hayden took her up a tray at lunchtime and even Mason didn't eat with us in the kitchen but went off to eat in the library.

As I'd clutched my handbag to me and made my way back downstairs, it was then that I heard loud voices coming from the kitchen and I froze.

'. . . and I felt like a total fool, Mason. A complete and utter fool! We discussed Ralph's Country Kitchen and then you went and set things up with Shelley behind my back?'

I was worried sick, wondering what I'd say if one of them suddenly burst through the kitchen door and saw me hovering.

'Ralph wasn't able to cater for our final number, not on Christmas Eve. Unless you wanted pizza and franks, it was good of Shelley to agree to fit us in. I want the party to be a huge success after the effort we've all put in.'

There was a caustic laugh that didn't sound at all like the Evie I'd come to know. 'Oh, so now you're telling me that you owe Shelley a favour, too, for stepping in at short notice? How convenient for her . . . and maybe for you, too, Mason.'

I was trying so hard not to listen and I wondered if I should just sprint to the door. Instead, I stepped down warily as far to the right of the next tread as possible. In the background the argument was heating up.

'It's a small favour, nothing personal,' Mason replied, angrily. 'I don't understand you sometimes, Evie! You're the one I married. What has that woman ever done to upset you? Nothing.'

There was an ominously loud gasp. 'Nothing? I saw her kiss you last New Year's Eve!'

The silence was deafening until Mason cleared his throat, nervously. 'A peck on the cheek isn't a kiss, Evie. If Shelley and I were meant to be together, when I took the job in the UK she'd have come with me, wouldn't she? We're just old friends. Why can't you accept that?' he'd replied, angrily.

'Because Shelley knew I wasn't aware that you'd asked her to go with you. You didn't mention it to me for a reason.

I bet she was delighted when she saw my reaction because she's still in love with you. The fact that you weren't truthful with me in the first place . . .' Evie went silent and I sucked in a deep breath. 'Be honest with me and yourself, Mason, is the inn the only thing you came back for?'

At that point I was clinging on to the newel post but that was enough to make me bolt. I bravely stepped over the last couple of treads in one go. Then I was out the door, closing it so softly it didn't even click, as a bead of sweat had trickled down my back.

I snap back into the moment, realising that Lori is waiting for a response from me and I look at her, questioningly.

'I know it's an imposition, Ria,' she stresses, assuming that I'm considering whatever question it was that she'd posed. 'I was just wondering whether I could book a consultation with you at the house?'

'Oh, um . . . of course, Lori, although I'm flying back to the UK on the twenty-seventh.'

She looks disappointed. 'Oh, Evie didn't mention that.'

Get a grip, Ria, I tell myself. This is a business opportunity Lori is talking about.

'If I can fit in a visit to your home before I leave, I might be able to pull together a plan for you once I'm back in the UK.'

Lori beams at me. 'Did you hear that, Chad?'

'Hear what, Lori? Hayden is telling me about Frank's little hideaway cabin up on the ridge. What did I miss?'

'Ria's going to try to fit in a visit to our place to see if it's salvageable. I've never worked with an interior designer before. I'm so excited.'

Salvageable? Now I wish I'd let it go. Instead, I give her a pleasant smile.

'If it stops my wife nagging on at me to move, I'll be in your debt forever, Ria.' Chad roars with laughter, nudging Hayden with his elbow.

'Us guys will do anything for a bit of peace and quiet, eh, Hayden?'

'Ria comes highly recommended, Chad,' Hayden replies, no doubt thinking he's doing me a favour.

Right now I'm wishing I was anywhere but here. The last thing I want is a reason to return, as I can't see the situation at the inn ending well.

'Hayden, I'm sure you won't mind me taking Ria off your hands for one dance,' Frank requests, extending his hand to me.

He's such a well-meaning, friendly guy that I can't turn him down. Actually, it's a bit of a relief, too, as I'm having to almost bite my tongue not to tell Hayden about what I overheard earlier on this evening.

I'm not the greatest dancer, but nervously glancing around it's all pretty freestyle. Thankfully, the room is packed anyway so it's not like anyone's in the spotlight.

I lean in, having to shout to be heard. 'This is quite a party, Frank. I'm having a great time, thank you for inviting me.'

'Oh, you're one of us now.' He grins at me.

We're doing a variation of what my mum would call the jive and I'm just going with the flow. Frank is light on his feet and he twirls me around, then pulls me back in and all I do is follow his lead. He's making me look like I know what I'm doing, when that isn't the case at all. He reels me back in and we dance on the spot.

'It's mostly family. I'm the eldest of five. You've met Denny, my youngest brother, of course. He does a bit of work for me around the farm and generally keeps me on the straight and narrow.' Frank extends his arm, raising it and twirling me around twice. 'Cassie has two siblings back home in the Lake District and one of them has two boys,' he continues. 'As you can see, I also have a lot of nephews and nieces who live close by. Cassie's family came to stay last summer and it was good to catch up.'

The youngsters range from about seven, at a guess, through

to their late teens. It's noisy and fun, just what I needed this evening. I was imagining a sort of cocktail party; well, beer and wine, with people standing around and perhaps a little background music. It's that wholesome, family-orientated gathering I've seen in films, with a whole lot of country music thrown in.

'It's great to see everyone enjoying themselves!'

As the music changes, the next one is a slow dance.

'They like to blow off a little steam and it's been a while since I got them all together here at the farm. Thanks for that, Ria, you're incredibly nimble on your feet. Do you fancy filling your lungs with a bit of fresh air?' Frank sounds a tad breathless and I know my face must be glowing from the exertion.

I nod my head enthusiastically. We make our way out through to the back door and next to it there's a shelving unit with a pile of shawls and blankets.

'Here, grab one of these. You'll need it when you cool down.'

Frank helps me to pull the thick, handmade woollen shawl around my shoulders and grabs a jacket off the coat hook before leading me out to the wrap-around veranda. We stand next to an outdoor heater and he's quiet; I can tell that Frank has something on his mind.

'It's beautiful out here in the air. That little boost of heat is a nice bonus though.' I grin at him.

'Yep. Let me know if you'd like another layer. Most of the knitted stuff was made by my mother or my grandmother.'

'How lovely! It's nice out here and rather cosy standing next to the heater. I love the scent of the pine trees, it's more noticeable after dark.'

'Cassie enjoyed coming out here late at night. We'd stand and stare at the stars. I miss that.'

It's funny how it's often easier to talk to a stranger, than it is someone really close to you. 'Does it get any easier?' I throw the question out there, hoping it's the right one. After all, he's brought me out here for a reason.

'Not really, Ria. How do you replace the one true love of your life?'

His words are difficult to hear and my heart goes out to him. 'Having never lost someone I love, Frank, I can't pretend to even imagine what it's like. I've supported a friend who lost her husband in a car accident at a very young age, though, and I saw how she struggled to build a new life.'

'Do you have any tips? It's been three years and all I've been doing is getting through it one day at a time.'

He's not a man looking for pity, he's a lost soul trying to find a way to move forward.

'Loneliness is an awful thing, Frank.' I glance at him and he gives me his signature lopsided grin. 'No one would wish that on someone they cared about. Cassie is irreplaceable to you and the time you had together is something you have forever, no matter what happens next.'

He scuffs the well-worn wooden planks with the toe of his leather boot, as I shuffle closer to the heater.

'There is someone, just a friend, but she's not here tonight. We spend a bit of time together, but I wasn't sure what reaction I'd get if I'd invited her along tonight. Nancy's a widow and has been on her own for eight years. I guess we both know what it's like to have a gaping hole suddenly open up in our lives. Pretending everything is OK when it isn't, sucks the joy out of life sometimes.'

Frank turns to look at me and I can see what he's feeling is guilt and he's not sure how to handle it.

'Maybe it's time to grab whatever happiness you can, Frank. No one will blame you for that. Least of all Cassie. After all, she loved you.'

He bows his head and I avert my eyes, staring up at the vast heavens above. It's so full of stars and, desperate to say something – anything – to lighten the moment, I blurt out 'There's no way we're alone in this galaxy,' and with that both Frank and I start laughing.

'I often think that. It freaks me out.'

'Me, too. I sometimes close my eyes in case I see anything. I don't know how I'd react if I did.'

'I'd go back inside, lock the door and grab another beer.'

I can't help but chuckle at that thought.

The sound of music, laughter and chatter emanating from the farmhouse is comforting but the stillness outside gives a different sort of comfort. A sense of peace seems to envelop us.

'How's Hayden doing?' Frank asks, suddenly.

I look at him questioningly. 'Fine, I think.'

'He never grieved, you know, not when his granddad passed. By the time he arrived in the White Mountains it was too late to say a proper goodbye. He told me it was the biggest regret of his life, not flying over earlier with his parents. That's why he wants to make sure they don't sell up.'

I don't quite know why he's telling me that, or how to respond. It's certainly the last thing I was expecting him to say.

'I had no idea, Frank. Hayden hasn't mentioned anything at all about that period in his life.'

'He wouldn't. Hayden is like that. He keeps things buried. It's time to cut to the chase. Evie's not happy, is she, and I'm guessing her and Mason have had a bust-up. Is that why they're not here tonight?'

This is putting me in a very difficult position now but he's not being nosey, he's concerned. 'I like to think the changes at the inn will make Evie feel more a part of it going forward. It's not just a business it's also their home and—'

'Hey, I wondered where you two had gone. I come bearing gifts.' Hayden suddenly appears at the far end of the veranda. He approaches with a glass of wine in one hand and two beer bottles hanging from between his fingers, on the other.

Frank and I exchange a brief look, tinged with sadness. Who knows what will happen, certainly not either of us. And not Mason, or Hayden, either.

'Thanks, Hayden.' I take the glass gladly, rewarding him with a warm smile.

'Here's to you, bro, and the lovely Ria,' Franks says. The two men chink glass bottles and I air-toast them.

'The relaunch party won't be as wild as this,' Hayden comments. 'Unless you work your magic and get a few up dancing early on.'

Frank chuckles. 'I assumed that was the main reason Mason and Evie invited me. I can't abide a party where everyone stands around politely chatting.'

'Denny said he's doing the music. Dad hadn't mention that to me.'

'Yep. He's the guy when it comes to getting those feet tapping away.'

'The guests will be in for a treat,' I remark, with more positivity than I'm feeling.

I can't even begin to contemplate how awkward it will be if things aren't back to normal between Mason and Evie by then. Twenty-four hours isn't long to forgive and forget a major faux pas on Mason's part, one for which Evie might not forgive him.

As for Frank's comment about Hayden and his granddad's passing, I have no idea what to do with that. But I'd be lying if I didn't admit to myself that I am concerned. Even in the short time I've known Hayden, it's obvious he has issues he hasn't dealt with. It seems to be a family trait none of them are prepared to acknowledge and now they're paying the price.

Hayden

21

Thinking on My Feet

The atmosphere this morning at the inn is dire. My father insisted on cooking breakfast for us all but he hasn't said a single word the whole time. My mother looks drawn and everything is an effort. So much so, she simply gives the occasional weak smile, or nod of her head, as I fill some of the awkward silences with a running dialogue about Frank's party.

Ria joins in when she sees I'm floundering but I don't think either of my parents are listening anyway. They're simply going through the motions because they don't know what else to do. Neither of them has really touched their food. It would have been easier all round if they'd left me and Ria to it.

Without warning, my mother pushes back on her chair and stands. 'If you'll all excuse me, I have a schedule to photocopy ready for when the cleaners arrive. Sorry, Ria. I'll give you a hand a little later, if that's all right.'

'Yes, it's no problem at all, Evie. You take as much time as you need.'

With that, my mother makes a quick exit.

Ria gives me a pointed look, and after about a minute, I can tell she's done with breakfast.

'I'll give Dad a hand to clear up, Ria. Why don't you make a start upstairs? I'll join you in a bit.'

'Thanks, Hayden.'

It's impossible to get a real smile out of anyone this morning and now that leaves just me and my father.

'Do I gather you and Mum have talked and it didn't go well?'

He gives me a deadpan look. 'That about sums it up.'

'For goodness' sake, Dad, I did warn you, several times in fact.'

'I was just waiting for the right moment, Hayden. I'm not making excuses but—' He looks forlorn. 'Look, son, if you don't mind, I need a bit of space this morning. Your mother said a few things in the heat of the moment that I found rather alarming. I need to . . . uh . . . check out Santa's Retreat, you know – see if all the lights are working. I'll take those games over as well, ready for when the kids arrive. I want to make sure there won't be any last-minute hitches.'

'Sure, Dad. Clear your head, but the three of us need to sit down and have a serious chat because this is getting ridiculous. Maybe we can grab a coffee together a little later?'

The edges of his mouth turn down and there isn't a hint of his usual sparkle. 'I'm not sure it'll help but we do need to clear the air. As from tomorrow, there'll be other people around, more or less constantly. Don't forget I'm off to the airport this evening.'

He's not in the mood for me to quiz him but that's puzzling. We don't ferry guests around, as people flying in usually book a hire car. We begin clearing the plates and when, eventually, we walk out into the hallway, I make a passing remark.

'At least there's no heavy snow forecast for the next day or so. If you want me to do the trip to the airport, it's not a problem.'

'No, your mother made a point of asking me, so I'd best not risk upsetting her any more than I have already. Besides, this falling-out of ours puts extra pressure on Ria, I'm afraid. She'll be even more reliant upon you and I'm sorry about that. You can catch up with Izzie tomorrow.'

With that he yanks on his snow gear and seconds later slams the front door on his way out.

Izzie? Why on earth is this the first I'm hearing about it? The moment she sees the way I look at Ria she'll know exactly what's going on and wonder why the heck I haven't mentioned it. Seriously, that's all I need on top of everything else.

'Are you OK?' Ria enquires, her eyes full of concern as they sweep over my face.

'I'm, uh . . .' I pause. Realising now that Ria really is the one for me, the thought of having Izzie quizzing me is the last thing I need. What was Mum thinking? 'I'm trying to engineer getting my parents around the table later this morning. Things are going to get tricky from here on in. If they're not on speaking terms, it's going to be impossible to get everyone, and everything, organised. You and I are going to have our hands full finishing off the bedrooms.'

'Hey, don't worry about the work still to be done. We'll just go with the furniture that's there and your parents can add, or swap out, whatever they want after the holidays. It's not the end of the world, Hayden. What's important is that the beds are made up, and your priority is to step in and act as a peacemaker. I've plenty to keep me busy, so I'll stay upstairs until you give me the all-clear.'

Ria will definitely be better off being well out of earshot when that happens. I'm not sure how it will go and I'm going to tackle my mother about Izzie. Do I tell Ria about that now, or leave it until later? As she smiles back at me, the look is so tender and the empathy so strong, I don't have a choice.

'I've just found out that Izzie's flying in tonight.'

Ria glances at me, frowning. 'Oh, right. You weren't expecting her?'

'No. It was Mum's idea, apparently.'

A momentary hint of concern reflected in Ria's eyes catches me off guard. 'It's too late for me to do anything about it but it's not ideal given the situation, is it?'

'Just do whatever you need to do to keep everyone happy, Hayden.' Ria's response is a little strained.

'I'll try my best.' I sigh, making no attempt at all to hide my annoyance. What's puzzling is why Izzie didn't mention it to me. 'Right, set me to work.'

'If you can put up the new curtain poles, then I can go on steaming the curtains. That would be great.'

The clock is ticking, but the time I'm counting down is leading to what I know is going to be a bit of a showdown in the kitchen at coffee time. In my head I'm already trying to come up with a string of words to launch the conversation. Unfortunately for me, nothing is hanging together.

Two hours later, while Ria has been keeping me busy, I think I've found the right approach to help defuse the situation. What better way, than to reveal a dilemma of my own? Ria hasn't stopped and she simply doesn't have time for a heart-to-heart conversation right now. I'm hoping she'll forgive me when I tell her later on, assuming I at least manage to get my parents to start being civil to each other again. It's the eleventh hour and tomorrow we need to present a united front to the world, no matter what.

'Where's Ria?' my father asks the moment I walk into the kitchen. My mother is already lining up the coffee mugs.

'She's in the middle of something. There's a problem with one of the Roman blinds that requires a needle and thread. I said I'd grab a coffee first, then take one upstairs for her.'

I think they're both a little relieved. It doesn't sit well with them airing a disagreement in front of anyone else – me included, let alone Ria. I can't imagine how badly they feel about that but it goes to show how serious the situation is. It's time to switch the focus.

'I gather Dad's going to the airport tonight?'

My mother glares at my father.

The two of them exchange a meaningful look. 'That was supposed to be a nice surprise for Hayden, Mason!'

My father looks suitably chastised. 'Sorry, Evie. I'm forgetful, you know that.'

'Hmm,' my mother remarks, sharply. 'Too forgetful at times. Or is it, *conveniently* forgetful. I thought you might appreciate the company, Hayden, given your extended stay.'

'I wish you'd mentioned it, Mum. This is unfortunate, very unfortunate and the timing is awful.' Now I have their full attention. 'You see, Ria and I . . . we . . .' I draw to a halt, watching as their eyes widen.

'You and Ria?' My mother half whispers, but Ria is two floors above us and totally unaware of what I'm saying.

I shrug my shoulders, looking dismayed. 'We both feel a little awkward about it. This most definitely wasn't a part of the plan.'

It's obvious that my father is still processing the information, while my mother looks embarrassed.

'Oh, Hayden – Izzie is rather hoping you can spend some time with her. I even wondered whether Frank might lend you the cabin for a night. Izzie was going on and on about never having been to the inn and how envious she is of the snow. I said I was sure we could spare you for a couple of days to show her the sights. I'm so sorry – I had no idea—' Her hand flies up to her mouth.

'I've told Ria that Izzie is a close friend but I haven't said anything to Izzie yet. I thought I'd do that when I get back to the UK. Believe me when I say that this development with Ria is the last thing I expected to happen this Christmas. Izzie will be mad at me for not letting her in on it but Ria and I are . . . well, it's a lot to take in. And Ria feels awkward, given that she's here in a professional capacity. It's embarrassing when we're all working so closely together, too.'

There's a lot of nervous eye contact going on between my parents.

'Ria and I intended to keep it quiet for now but obviously I was rather hoping to spend a fair bit of time with her before she flies back.'

'She's a wonderful young woman, Hayden,' my mother jumps straight in. 'Isn't she, Mason? So talented, hard-working and she has a good heart. I mean, oh! Ria's very graciously put up with us, hasn't she? What on earth are we going to do?'

'Let me handle Izzie.' Finally, my father has something to say. 'On the drive back from the airport I'll casually mention something about you and Ria having unexpectedly hit it off. That way it won't come as a complete surprise. I'm sure she'll understand. Izzie's going to be here for a whole week, so we'll sort something out. However, I will say that I knew it was a bad idea when you first mentioned it, Evie, and I said as much. If Hayden had wanted Izzie here, he'd have invited her over himself.'

Now is not the time for an *I told you so* moment, especially not from my father given the trouble he's in. My mother is in no mood for cross words as my revelation is a big deal and we all know it. What mother doesn't want her son to find the perfect woman, and in her eyes it's obvious that Ria ticks all the boxes. In one way I'm delighted at that, but I hope Ria understands outing us is an act of desperation on my part.

'There's one other teeny, little problem,' my mother begins. 'Your cousin, Patrick, has only just confirmed that he's coming. I'd already reallocated his room to Izzie.'

My father throws his hands up in the air. 'What next?'

'Now calm down, Mason. Rooms aside, Patrick is a lovely guy and he's single.' My father and I make eye contact and he begins to shake his head in dismay. 'All I'm saying is that at least Izzie won't be the only unattached person there if she ends up . . . um, being at a bit of a loose end until Ria flies home.'

When Izzie is upset, you know it. In fairness, I'd understand if that's the case but it wasn't deliberate. If I'd known she was coming, I'd have levelled with her.

'We're still a room short, Evie,' my father points out.

'Lindy and Seth have a family suite and as it's just the two of them, we could lock off the door into the adjoining single and put Patrick in there. He'll have to use the bathroom on the other side of the corridor, but I'm sure he won't mind.' My mother sits back looking pleased with herself. Then she turns her gaze on me. 'You and Ria? I thought you were getting on well but this is so unlike you, Hayden.'

This is the price I have to pay for peace to reign and I can only hope that Ria will forgive me. I, too, wanted to keep our relationship under wraps for now but hey, at least my parents are talking; and united on my behalf. Ria said it was down to me to do whatever I can to keep the peace.

My father saves me from replying. 'I'll have a quiet word with Patrick when he arrives and ask him to look out for Izzie.'

My mother simply looks relieved.

'That's some conversation you're going to have with Izzie, my son, but what about Ria?'

I nod my head. 'I'll take that coffee up to her now, Dad, and explain what's going on.'

It was the best I could come up with. My mother might not be ready to befriend Shelley, but that problem suddenly pales into insignificance compared to my revelation. And my father has stepped in to, hopefully, save the day when it comes to bringing Izzie up to date.

Perhaps it'll make my parents think about their own actions and how it affects other people when you hold things back. To Dad, Shelley is just someone from the past, an old friend. Although I can't say for certain the reverse is true, I do know that Shelley isn't the sort of woman to break up a happy marriage. Well, maybe not quite so happy at the moment. Why Mum is so upset about it is a mystery to me.

Admittedly, my father has handled it badly, but he's not hiding anything untoward and he's never given my mother any reason to suspect otherwise. However, she's a proud woman and I can understand her feeling hurt at what she probably sees as Dad's thoughtlessness.

* * *

'You did what?'

'Look, Ria. I had no choice. My mother thought it would be a nice surprise and I could take a couple of days off to show Izzie around. She meant well.' I sigh, feeling exasperated. 'Izzie will be cross with me because I haven't told her about what's been happening. I mean between you and me.'

Ria places the back of her hand against her forehead, closing her eyes for a few moments. When she opens them again I can see she's reeling a little.

'It's a bit like the Shelley situation, isn't it?'

'Goodness, no,' I reply emphatically. 'With Izzie she'll just be upset she wasn't in the know and then will bend my ear quizzing me about you. In Shelley's case, for her, maybe it is true that you never totally forget your first love. It isn't until you move on that you realise love is way more complex and when you know, *you know*. At least, in my case that's true.'

'I totally understand what you're trying to say.'

I gaze at Ria, my heart pumping in my chest.

'Are you thinking about Will?'

'Yes, and wondering why I ever thought I was in love with him. I never felt like this, Hayden, not even at the beginning.' She lowers her eyes and suddenly I'm feeling elated. I take a giant stride forward to whisk Ria up into my arms.

'I'm so sorry this has been such an awful start to our relationship. I have no idea what you must think, and now the situation has just escalated. You can't imagine how gutted I'm feeling, Ria.'

'But your parents are speaking to each other?' She peers at me, narrowing her eyes.

I nod.

'Then you're forgiven.' Ria stands on tiptoe to plant her lips firmly on mine. The seconds pass until we reluctantly pull away. 'The problem with feelings, Hayden, is that they're difficult to control, even impossible at times.' She's slightly breathless and there's a glow to her that fills my heart with joy.

'Tell me about it. But I am truly sorry, Ria. I would so love to do this discreetly and then reveal it to the world when we're good and ready. I think we both know it's getting harder and harder not to do the things that come naturally. I keep wanting to reach out for your hand and it's a fight not to throw my arm around your waist when I stand next to you.'

Ria looks up at me with a sincerity that takes my breath away. 'My sister warned me not to get myself into trouble because she sensed what was coming. If she saw the difference in me then, next time I call her she'll know what's really going on between us. That's why I've been avoiding her.'

I gaze down into her eyes, wondering what I've done to be so very, very lucky.

'Maybe it's time to give her a call,' I state, firmly. 'From here on in we hide nothing, from anyone.'

'What if it's the magic of being in the White Mountains that is drawing us together, Hayden?'

Ria frowns and I plant a kiss on her forehead to ease it away.

'I don't believe that's the case, Ria. If I did, I wouldn't have mentioned a word to my parents about us.'

'I like the sound of that, Hayden – us – and as for Izzie, it might be a good opportunity for you to open up and talk to her about other things . . .'

'Such as?'

'You've gone to great lengths to rescue your granddad's legacy. Is that in the hope that it will keep your parents together? Or is it because it means much more to you than you're willing to admit? Izzie might be the only person who can help you make sense of that, Hayden, as she was around when you lost your granddad.'

I stare at Ria, perplexed. 'I'm simply trying to take some of the pressure off, so my parents have a real shot at making it work.'

'Are you saying that I'm wrong?' she challenges me.

The realisation that the inn means a whole lot more to me than anyone can know, hits me like a physical blow. Whenever I visit, surely it's only natural to feel as if I'm reconnecting with Granddad. How can I ever forget the time, as a boy, when he told me one day the inn would be mine. His words have never left me. 'And when it does, Hayden, you'll be the fourth generation to own the inn and I'll be a proud man.' I was nine years old, too young to make a promise and yet I did; I can only hope he can forgive me.

'I'm . . . I can't think about that right now, Ria. Things are coming to a head and it all feels like one big, sorry mess.'

It's been a long morning and lunch is running late. But when Ria and I enter the kitchen, my parents are on their best behaviour.

'Just in time,' my father says and I glance at Ria, giving her an encouraging smile. 'Take a seat.'

It all feels a little strained and Ria doesn't really know how to react.

'We've done well upstairs,' I comment to break the ice. Staring across at my mother, I hope she'll pick up the conversation.

'Good. I'm sorry I couldn't join you. We had two big deliveries this morning and I don't know where the time went. I'm free to give a hand in between directing the cleaners,' my mother confirms. 'Mason has done a check of the external lights and Santa's Retreat, and everything is more or less ready for our guests.'

There's a slight pause and Ria clears her throat. 'There are still one and a half suites to go, but it's coming together nicely. I don't know if you guys want to have a quick look at room number three to check that you're happy with it? But it's all made up.'

My father is quick to answer. 'Ah, The White Ash Suite! We'll take a little trip upstairs in a bit, won't we, Evie?'

Oh, this is painful to say the least, and Ria shifts uneasily in her seat.

'I had a phone call from Chad earlier, Ria. Lori is really excited about meeting up with you. Chad said he'll be more than happy to ferry you back and forth for a consultation. They're both free this afternoon if that suits you. What do you think?'

I can see that Ria wasn't expecting that.

'Oh. Of course, Evie. It would be my pleasure.'

'Poor Lori, their house is in a beautiful setting but over the years it's been extended and it just doesn't flow right. Chad loves the place, but Lori is at the end of her tether. You've performed a miracle here. If you could sort out Chad and Lori they'd be over the moon. Money isn't an issue, so you'll probably end up flying out again at some point to supervise the work. Obviously, we'd be delighted to put you up here. Perhaps Hayden could accompany you.'

My mother is trying her hardest to push aside the problems and get things back on an even keel.

'Evie,' my father calls out, 'these plates are ready to go.'

I jump up to give a hand.

'It's chicken pot pie, topped with two buttermilk biscuits. One of my favourites,' I inform Ria, as I place the plate in front of her.

'Hmm . . . it smells delightful! One thing I'm going to miss when I get home is the food.'

I could scoop Ria up in my arms and kiss her because I know that beneath her calm exterior she's nervous and way outside of her comfort zone.

'Then let's hope your next trip is very soon,' my mother replies.

In the interim silence, Ria looks across at my father. 'I always wondered what a pot pie was, Mason.'

I think food is probably the last thing on anyone's mind, as no one knows quite what to say, but it's a welcome distraction.

My father instantly brightens. 'It's leftovers, in this case chicken, with vegetables and gravy. I do a shortcrust base and put a layer of flaky pastry on the top. Rather like a good old-fashioned pie, as they say in the UK.'

'Hmm . . .' she says, taking her first bite. 'It's heartier though, being home-made. It tastes as good as it sounds.'

I give Ria a reassuring smile.

'Mason, after lunch, if you've finished your outside work, maybe you can make a start on flat-packing the boxes and then don't forget to lock off that door upstairs, for Patrick. The clock is ticking,' my mother reminds him. 'Hayden, we can pick up where Ria left off this morning. I'll give Chad a call first.'

'Thank you, Evie. I'll be heading upstairs shortly to do a bit of preparation and get my things together. If you can tell him I'll need about an hour?'

Suddenly it seems that we're back on track, which is – quite frankly – little short of a miracle.

I tap on Ria's door to check how she's doing, as Chad just texted my father to say he's five minutes away.

'I'm almost ready,' she confirms.

On the bed is Ria's familiar-looking briefcase and it makes me smile to myself.

'I'll carry that downstairs for you. Chad will be here shortly.'

I walk over to Ria, reaching out to grab her hand.

'We're almost there and you'll soon be able to stand back and bask in the glory.'

That makes her smile. 'It feels wrong leaving you all to get on with it.'

'No. It's fine. Preparations are in full swing and there's enough of us to cope.'

'It'll probably take me a couple of hours to make notes and take some photos.'

I home in for a kiss and it's good to be up close and hold Ria in my arms again. I wish now that I could cut my stay short and fly back with her, but my parents are going to need all the help they can get.

'I'm moving bedrooms this afternoon. I've been relegated to the spare room.'

'Oh, poor you.' She grins at me.

It's small, accommodating a standard double bed and a wardrobe. It also has the tiniest en-suite ever. It's kept for emergencies and sometimes used to store linen when the landing cupboard is full. On a few occasions it's been used by guests when they were due to check out, but their flights were cancelled in advance because of bad weather.

Ironically, the fact that Patrick replied so late in the day is the only reason Mum could fit Izzie in. There's a saying that everything happens for a reason, but I can't for the life of me figure that one out. I'm sure that when Izzie has had a chance to talk to Ria, she'll know exactly why we're together. And, once Ria flies home, I'll be able to spend some time with Izzie to please not just her, but my mother too. It's going to be full on, that's for sure.

'Anyway, there's no rush. All that's left for tomorrow is to put up a few festive decorations on the landings and it's job done.'

'I don't intend to sit back and do nothing, Hayden; I want to make myself useful. And I'll be keeping an eye out to see how the space is used once there are people milling around, in case we need to make a few adjustments.'

I shake my head at her. 'Don't you ever switch off?'

Her lips twitch as a faint voice shouts up, 'Chad is here!'

'Right, it's time to go. Call me if you have any problems, but it should be pretty straightforward.'

'I keep dreaming about boxes. They're piled high and the stacks are endless.'

Ria starts to giggle as I release her and grab the briefcase off the bed. 'Come on. Your next client is eagerly awaiting you to help them transform their home. At least it should be a lot easier than this job.'

But if someone else had taken it on, I reflect, there's a real chance that our paths might never have crossed. Peter was repaying a pretty big favour I did for him years ago in helping him get started, but he has absolutely no idea he's repaid me a thousand times over. Ria is a catch but I'm the one who is well and truly hooked.

22

The Introductions Begin

Apparently, my father arrived home with Izzie just before midnight last night and she isn't expected to surface for at least another couple of hours. After a cup of hot chocolate she said she was exhausted and went straight to her room. My mother is a little anxious this morning, until the two of them can sit down and catch up. After all, she is Mum's goddaughter and holds a special place in her affections. I'm excited to see her but obviously nervous.

'Ria has a hit list, I see.' My father points at the notepad on the table. 'You'd better give us our orders and get us underway.'

My mother looks keen to make a start. 'Kendall and two of her staff are cleaning the communal areas so it's probably best we keep out of their way. What's top priority this morning, Ria?'

'There are two pairs of full-length curtains still to be steamed in situ to get the creases out. Then the remainder of the boxes need to be stored somewhere, and after that it's on to my wrap-up list of odds and ends.'

'We're a bit short on storage space,' my father points out.

'Then the boxes we haven't used will have to be stacked in the spare bedroom with me. There's not enough of them to warrant shipping them back to the UK.'

'What exactly is left over?' my mother asks.

We all turn to look at Ria.

'It's mainly several sets of bedding with matching curtains, some spare towels and two side lamps we didn't end up using.'

'That's fine. It's good to have a bit of spare stock, and bedding is always handy. I can't get anything else in the linen cupboard though, it's full top to bottom. There's nothing to thin out as it's all new spare bedding. I guess the cosiest room in the house is about to get even cosier. Sorry about that, Hayden.'

Everyone's talking and we're working as a team, so I'm not complaining.

'If we can shift the boxes first and someone can tackle the curtains,' Ria suggests, 'I can start working through my list of finishing touches. That way the rooms will all be ready for the first arrivals later in the day. I'll work around the cleaners. That'll just leave the landings to decorate, and I'll sort that tomorrow morning before I head out to cut some fresh greenery.'

'I'll steam the curtains,' my mother offers.

My father gives me a nod. 'As soon as I've cleared up in here, I'll come and give you a hand with the boxes, Hayden. Right, let's get this show on the road, as they say!'

Ria makes her way upstairs and I follow a pace or two behind. 'You look a little tired this morning.'

'I couldn't sleep, so I started setting everything up for Chad and Lori's new floorplan. It's going to be a big project. They certainly didn't seem fazed by any of my ideas, even though it will mean taking down two walls on the ground floor to make a large open-plan family kitchen/dining room.'

My eyes light up. 'So, you'll be heading back to the White Mountains.'

She gives me one of her cute little smiles, the one that says *maybe*.

As we reach the top step of the first staircase there's a loud creak, which makes us both cringe. Suddenly, the door at the far end swings open and Izzie pops her head out. 'Morning, I thought I heard voices.'

It would be rude of me not to introduce Ria at this point, so we wander down to greet her.

'Izzie! No one was expecting you to be up and about this early. Sorry if we disturbed you, Dad said you were shattered.'

She's in her PJs and her hair tumbles down around her shoulders, but somehow she still manages to look rather chic. She's half Italian, so I guess it's in her blood. I plant a kiss on her cheek as I give her a welcoming hug.

'This is Ria Porter, our interior designer. Ria, this is Izzie Montanari, my fitness guru and childhood friend.'

They shake hands, ever so politely.

'It's lovely to meet you, Izzie.' Ria sports a welcoming smile but I can see she's a little uneasy.

'The same here, Ria. Mason was singing your praises on the way here. I gather that you and Hayden are seeing each other. Perhaps you can find time to give me the tour a bit later so we can get to know each other a little better. You can ask me anything at all about Hayden. I know all his secrets – well, I thought I did.' Izzie's voice is playful but she casts a look of disdain in my direction.

'It all happened so quickly,' I confess. 'Besides, I had no idea you were coming, but it really is wonderful to see you.'

I watch as Izzie's eyes sweep over Ria as if she's measuring her up. Ria shifts uneasily on the spot and it's time to break this up.

'We've got quite a full agenda today, Izzie, so we'd best get started. I'll catch up with you later.'

'OK. I'll get dressed and grab some breakfast, then maybe I can help. The more hands the better, eh, Hayden?'

'Um . . . great.'

Ria and I walk back along the landing and there's a loud click as the door behind us closes. Ria turns to give me a curious look.

'What?'

'You didn't mention how gorgeous and stylish she is.'

'Is she? I hadn't really noticed.'

Ria gives me a knowing look.

'OK, maybe she is, but to me she's a good listener and a really great friend. She'll be fine once she gets to know you.' I reach out to clasp Ria's hand because she's apprehensive. 'We don't have be careful around anyone. It is what it is and I'm not going to hide how I feel about you.'

'As long as you're sure this is what you want, Hayden.' Her eyes search mine, anxiously.

'I'm sure, Ria. Very sure. It's not just a fleeting thing; I've never felt this way about anyone before. It's a big deal for me, more than you probably realise.'

We draw to a halt, turning to face each other.

'I'm just worried that when we slip back into our normal, everyday lives it won't seem quite so exciting.'

'Hey.' I place my hand under her chin, tilting her head backwards so I can stare into her eyes. 'Given the circumstances and how volatile things have been around us, don't you think it's kind of a miracle what's happened?'

'I guess so.'

As I edge even closer that little buzz between us is tangible. When a sound close by registers, we instinctively pull apart and I let out a little groan.

'Oops, it's only me,' my mother warns, giving a little chuckle. 'I'm off to steam curtains so don't let me interrupt you.' She hurries away and I swear she's humming softly to herself as she walks.

I grab a quick kiss and Ria's eyes are now sparkling with amusement. 'Everything is going to be fine, just act naturally.'

'Yes, boss.'

'You're the one in charge, Ria, because this is your project and I respect that. I'm here to do your bidding.' But in my heart I know I'm doing this for all the right reasons. Ria is the interior designer, but when it comes to our life as a couple we're going to be equal partners. Always. 'It's time to move those boxes. In a few hours' time things are going to get lively as our first guests start arriving.'

* * *

Late afternoon I join my father in the kitchen and it's time to get cooking. He's opting for a hot and cold buffet to kick things off. Santa's Retreat has been well received with early arrivals, and I've been constantly on the go. More guests are due at any moment. There's a lot of prep still to do, and as we get on with it, my father is unusually chatty.

'This thing between you and Ria has certainly cheered up your mother. I had a word with Izzie last night. Have the two of you had time to talk?'

'No. I haven't really seen much of Izzie, or Mum. Izzie wanted to give a hand, so Ria had her and Mum checking every room for toiletries, bottled water and glasses. The cleaners also noticed a few side lamps didn't have light bulbs, but I suspect that's on Ria's wrap-up list, anyway. Ria hasn't stopped since lunchtime, she's a woman on a mission. I can't help noticing that things seem a lot easier between you and Mum, or have you just called a truce?'

My father gives a deep sigh. 'There are things we need to talk through, my son, but we'll get there. The trouble is that your mother's a worrier. You know that. And she worries about you, a lot. We both noticed the changes in you, Hayden, we just didn't realise it was all down to Ria. Your mother thought it was stress because you were worried about us.'

I stop chopping carrots to stare at him. 'What sort of changes?'

'Normally, when you're here, you're constantly checking your emails or on the phone. It's always "I'll be with you in a minute" or "Sorry, I must take this call" and we did wonder. I mean, I know you've been hands on here, but it's never stopped your obsession with being available twenty-four/seven before.'

'I'm still in the daily loop but things are going smoothly for a change.' Why on earth do I feel the need to make excuses? Why can't I admit that I enjoy working alongside Ria and, quite frankly, the last thing I've been thinking about is what's happening back at the office. It sort of reminds me of the way my parents used to work together, before they took over the inn.

'That's good to hear. Your mother was concerned that our problems were dragging you down, pulling you away from your life.'

'Really? It wasn't like that. I just want to give you both the best shot and my business brain was telling me it was time to face facts. Putting this latest little upset to one side, now it's all coming together you don't regret going through this process, Dad, do you? Be honest with me.'

My father turns to face me, and the eye contact is direct. 'I think it's true to say that both your mother and I have learnt a few things about ourselves since we moved to the White Mountains. Before we took over the inn, we'd leave the house each morning and go our separate ways. Our work problems were always different and often, when one of us had worries, the other would be in a happier place. It helped to even things out, it allowed us to gain a perspective on life in general. Here, we've been closeted together the whole time and there's no getting away from the business worries when it's also your home.'

'It's all about to get better, Dad, and Mum will forgive you for keeping her out of the loop with Shelley. It's a lesson learnt, that's all.'

He pauses and the wait is agonising. 'I'm not sure, Hayden. Your mother blurted out that she misses having her old friends and family around her. That's not something I can fix.'

My mother said that because she was upset with him. People say things they don't mean when they're angry. We all do it in the heat of the moment and often regret it afterwards.

When I tap on Ria's door to see if she's ready to go downstairs to join the throng, the moment I set eyes on her I get a stab of pain in my chest. It's like I'm seeing her for the first time.

'Wow,' I gasp and she breaks into a smile.

'I thought I'd make a special effort tonight.'

Her hair is piled up on top with little curly bits framing her face. She's wearing make-up and her lips are a bright cherry red.

'You look lovely in that knitted dress; the pale blue matches your eyes. It really suits you.' Having never seen her all dressed up and wearing heels before, it's a bit of a surprise.

I so want to kiss those lips but Ria has spent ages getting ready, I daren't risk messing anything up.

'Why are you looking so surprised?' she questions.

'I'm not. It's just a slightly different version of you. But you do look amazing.' Ria normally wears flat shoes indoors and even our eye level is suddenly different. 'Um . . . before we go downstairs, I was wondering whether you'd feel comfortable if I introduce you to everyone as my girlfriend?'

Ria starts laughing. 'It feels like things are moving so fast, but the truth is that we've spent hours and hours together. It was just all squeezed into a short space of time.'

'It's not that I'm rushing you, Ria, but you're about to endure two days of constant introductions and it doesn't feel right to describe you as simply an awesome, talented interior designer.' She gives me a beaming smile. 'You've captured my heart and I want to tell everyone. I'm really bad at hiding my feelings, I just have trouble expressing them.' Ria can tell from the silly grin on my face that I'm doing my best in my own clumsy way. I'm a happy man and who wouldn't be, with someone as special as Ria standing beside them?

'That's all I wanted to hear, Hayden. I'd have been worried if you were any different. I love you just the way you are. Let's do this. Are you ready?'

'More than ready. And I'm starving, you must be too.'

As I swing open the door and Ria steps out onto the landing, I hear a gaggle of voices and some boisterous laughter.

'Hey, guys! I didn't know you'd arrived,' I call out, grabbing Ria's hand and stepping forward to greet them. 'This is my girlfriend, Ria Porter. Ria, this noisy lot were great friends of my granddad's and are now a part of our extended family. This is Alice, John and their daughters Chloe and Olivia.'

'It's lovely to meet you all,' Ria replies, offering her hand to Alice. 'Have you come far?'

'We've flown in from the UK, but we spent last night at a motel near the airport,' Alice replies.

John steps forward to take Ria's hand rather enthusiastically. 'We've been waiting for the day when Hayden finally turned up with a woman on his arm. It's a real pleasure to meet you, Ria. You'll know by now that he's a hopeless workaholic, of course.'

I roll my eyes at him as Alice gives her husband a nudge in his side. 'It'll fall on deaf ears, John. Ria is the interior designer responsible for updating the inn and Mason told me she never stops.'

John grins at me. 'It sounds like a match made in heaven, Hayden.'

Then I notice Izzie loitering in the background.

'And this is Izzie Montanari, my . . . um . . . my mother's goddaughter,' I explain, as she steps closer. 'Izzie, this is—'

'I caught the names, Hayden. Hello, everyone.'

As they all turn around, I can't help thinking that sounded a little frosty.

'Right, let's head downstairs, I'm sure everyone is ready to eat.'

It's good to see the buffet table all laid up, and with a dozen of us here tonight and Christmas music playing non-stop in the background, I'm beginning to get into the festive mood.

It's brilliant to see my cousin Lindy and her fiancé, Seth, here this year. They recently bought a chateau in the Loire Valley region of France and have just begun renovating it. My father always invites Frank along, naturally, because he knows most of our family and friends anyway. However, tonight he didn't come alone, and her name is Nancy. I said a brief hello, but Ria has been chatting away to her for quite a while and I'm glad. Ria's probably had more than enough of my family by now.

I'm actually scouting around for Izzie, but she seems to have disappeared. I check the hallway, the kitchen and the sitting room, to no avail, so she must be in the library. I open the door slowly, peering around it and she's sitting in front of the fire cradling a large glass of wine. Not wishing to make her jump, I clear my throat.

'There you are! I've been looking for you.'

She turns her head, breaking out into a smile. 'This place is truly wonderful, Hayden. Mum and Dad remember coming here once a couple of years before I was born. They spent several days at the inn and then a week at a skiing lodge in the mountains, with your parents.'

I pull one of the winged chairs closer to the fire, stretching out my hands to feel the blazing heat, even though they aren't cold.

'Are you cross with me for getting myself invited?' Izzie asks.

'No. Of course not. I thought you'd be angry with me because I wasn't totally honest with you.'

Izzie stares down into her glass. 'I had to see for myself. Just to check that you weren't making a mistake.'

'How did you know?'

'I could hear it in your voice whenever you mentioned Ria's name.'

'It just happened, and I remember what you said about Georgina, but this is different.'

'I was being mean; it was unfair of me. You weren't to know it wasn't the real thing, but I did warn you. Georgina had an agenda, she wanted a husband who was going somewhere, and she picked up on that intense determination of yours, at the start. It's obvious to me that Ria is different, but you know what I'm going to say and that's why you didn't tell me.'

Inwardly, I groan. 'Can you forgive me? It's just that with

273

what's been going on here, I wanted to enjoy feeling the way I do and not face a barrage of questions.'

Izzie looks at me with watery eyes. 'Only because I care about you, Hayden. And yes, there's an element of selfishness to it. Who will I call now when I need someone to sob down the phone to?'

'Me, of course! Nothing will change that.'

'I knew that one day you'd suddenly find the one,' she replies, wistfully. 'If that's the case then our relationship will change, Hayden. Like it or not, when you love someone like that, they become your main confidante.'

'Oh, Izzie! Even if that's true, one of these days you'll be introducing me to your Mr Right and I'll be checking him out. You deserve the sort of man who will whisk you off to a meditation retreat in India or take you hiking along the Inca Trail to Machu Picchu! When that guy comes along you'll be off, I know it.' I reach out to place my hand on her arm.

'It would have been much easier if we could have fallen in love with each other, Hayden.'

'We both know it wouldn't have worked. You'd want to change me, Izzie, and you know it, but this is who I am and I'm content with that.'

'I am happy for you, just a bit put out, that's all. And yes, we would have driven each other mad at times, wouldn't we?'

'And some.'

This time I get a wry laugh. 'Does Ria know what she's letting herself in for? All that steely determination, the refusal to give up once your mind is set on something?'

'I think she does, Izzie. I really think she does!'

'Judging by the way the two of you look at each other, whatever happens you'll work it out.'

We're still friends and that's all that matters. Izzie will come around because Ria doesn't have a bad vibe in her body. But I'm not going to let Izzie waste a perfectly good holiday. She's going to love the scenery and the excitement of this winter wonderland and, hopefully, Patrick's company.

Ria

23

Can Santa Work His Magic Tonight?

I wasn't expecting the buzz that suddenly brings the inn, and everyone in it, to life. It's truly wonderful. None of the trivial things matter anymore, it's all about keeping the guests happy.

I'm eager to get feedback and we've already been asked to set up a table somewhere for the smaller children. Possibly in the library, where they can sit quietly and draw, or read together. Parents can sit and talk in front of the fire, well within earshot. I've already assigned that little task to Mason.

This morning has been chaotic. New arrivals are keeping Hayden busy and I'm determined to brighten the landings with some festive cheer. The theme is silver and green, and I'm almost there when Izzie appears.

'I seem to be getting in everyone's way. They all know what they're doing, so I wondered whether I could give you a hand, Ria?'

My stomach churns. I don't think we've been avoiding each other, but our conversations so far have been fleeting. I feel awkward about the situation I find myself in. Izzie dotes on Hayden and I'm not sure she approves of me. As he walks around introducing me as his girlfriend, it's wonderful in one way, but uncomfortable in another. I just wish we could have kept it quiet and had some time together back in the UK without any pressure.

'Oh, um, I was just about to tog up and go foraging for

some natural greenery for the dining room. You're welcome to join me if you like.'

Her eyes light up. 'I could really do with some fresh air.'

'Five minutes and I'll meet you outside on the porch?'

'Thanks, Ria.'

I go in search of Hayden to let him know I'll be disappearing for a while.

'Izzie is coming with me. Are you OK with that?'

'It's kind of you, Ria. She's eager to help but everyone is focused on the task in hand and she feels a bit left out. Are you doing all right?'

'I am.' I grin at him and he leans in to give me a quick kiss.

'This is my last task and then I'm ready to socialise and get to know some of the other members of your family.'

Hayden gives me a bashful look. 'I'm going to be here, there and everywhere. Can you do me a huge favour tonight and if you see Izzie standing around looking lost, could you introduce her to someone? Then just leave her to it.'

'You didn't have to ask, I'd have done that anyway.'

He's feeling guilty and I can understand that. After all, from what I can gather he has two best friends, and one of them happens to be Izzie. I wouldn't be surprised if Izzie will be keeping an eye on me too.

'Wouldn't it be easier to take a short cut? It's hard going trudging through the snow and there's a lot of greenery the other side of the fence,' Izzie points out.

'It's not safe. Underneath that virgin snow is the Androscoggin River. I'm not sure where the bank ends and the actual river begins, so we'd better stick to the path Hayden showed me.'

'Oh, right.'

'So, how long have the two of you known each other?'

This is what I feared, the inquisition. 'I've been a customer of Stylish Homes since I set up my own interior design business, about three years ago. We had a little back and forth by email and phone to set the project up but we didn't meet in person until we were on the plane.'

Izzie is following me, so I can't see her expression but I'm glad of that.

'Right. It's safe for us to go through this gap and follow the trail along under the trees. The snow is a bit compacted in places, so mind you don't slip. But at least we're nowhere near the river.'

'I can hear running water, but it sounds far away,' she comments.

'That's because most of it is frozen. But whether it would take the weight of a person, I have no idea.'

We lapse into silence, walking side by side.

'There's a ledge of rock up ahead that's in the shadow of some tall firs. I think we'll be able to gather what we need there. Do you think you can manage a sack full?'

'Of course.'

'If we can fill one each, then that should be enough.'

'Will you and Hayden be working together again in the future?'

I turn to look at her, thinking it's a bit of an odd question to ask. 'I can't imagine why that would happen. As far as I'm concerned, this is a one-off job. Unless he has property of his own in need of a redesign.'

'You haven't been to Hayden's apartment, or the house?'

My eyes are busy trawling the rocky outcrop to our left. I'm looking for trails of ivy and anything suitable to bring indoors to add a touch of colour, or fragrance. 'No,' I reiterate, 'we met for the first time on the flight over. This looks like a good place to start gathering.' Was that an attempt to trip me up? I've nothing to hide.

I slip off my backpack and hand Izzie a sack and a small pair of pruning shears that Mason kindly lent me.

'You take these and clip whatever you can. I'm going to see what I can lop off the firs. If I can reach a lower branch I can cut it up when we get back to the inn.'

I don't wish to be rude, but Izzie isn't making conversation, she's fishing for information. It's Hayden she should be talking to.

I wander off the path, but most of the branches of the various pines, spruces and firs are beyond my reach. Long-needled varieties are best because they last longer when brought indoors. I gather a few pinecones and put them in the sack with some mountain holly, but when I turn to look at Izzie she's having more luck than I am and her sack is already half full.

Watching where I put my feet, I kick up some of the snow with the toe of my boot, but when I begin to see gravel mixed in with it, I know I'm probably on the edge of the bank.

'No luck?' Izzie calls out.

'No. I'll walk on a little further,' I reply.

It isn't long before I manage to find a low-hanging branch on a sixty-foot-tall white cedar, the flat sprays of tiny, aromatic scale-like leaves and clusters of miniature cones is perfect. Less than ten feet away is a fir with feathery fronds and when I hit off the dusting of snow, there are even some clusters of little cones. However, carrying back the two relatively small, but bulky branches isn't quite as easy as I thought it was going to be.

'That's quite a haul.' Izzie's eyes spring open when she spots me, although there isn't much of me to be seen.

'Let me take that sack off you, Ria, and I'll grab your backpack.'

'Thanks, I'll just keep trudging along before my arms tire of holding these. I'm heading for the barn.'

When Izzie catches up with me, she goes on ahead to slide open the barn door.

'Thanks. Right. You can go on inside if you want and warm up. Just leave the sack on the porch.'

'No, I'm good. I'll steady that branch for you; it'll make the cutting easier. Do you do things like this often?'

'I forage at Christmas, as I like a little natural greenery inside the house. It's the smell that does it for me.'

'Even though Hayden didn't say anything specific, I could tell when I spoke to him after you both arrived here that something was different about him. You hardly know each other, Ria, what if it's just a little fling? He's been hurt before, you know, and he still bears the scars.'

And I haven't been? She doesn't know me, or my past, and this isn't fair.

Having stripped the first one, Izzie snatches the naked branch off the bench as I grab the second one. 'Neither of us was expecting it to happen, Izzie. It's true what they say, you just know.'

'Hayden's vulnerable at the moment, only he doesn't realise it.'

'But I do, believe me.'

We both stop what we're doing.

I sigh. 'Izzie, I'm sorry if you feel it's come between the two of you; but I'm not your enemy unless you decide to make me one. The choice is yours.'

Maybe it's because it's Christmas Eve and it's goodwill to all men . . . and women . . . but I decide that maybe Izzie needs a little time to let that sink in.

I grab the sack of cuttings and start walking back towards the inn. I don't have the heart, or the right words, to talk to her because all I can do is reassure her that I have no intention of hurting Hayden. But would she believe me?

An hour later, the door to the utility room swings open and Izzie walks towards me, her arms around a sack.

'Sorry, Ria. I just want to make sure you understand that Hayden tends to bury emotional stuff if he can't handle it. It's the real reason he hasn't invited me here, because there are some things he still can't talk about.'

When she joins me at the island, I look her straight in the eye. 'He's not ready but, when he is, I hope we can both be there for him, Izzie. One of the things that made me fall in love with Hayden is the fact that family and friends are everything to him. The other is his sensitive side, the one he keeps hidden.'

'It's the start of a new chapter in his life and I am glad for you both, Ria, truly I am. I think he's going to be in safe hands.'

'Thanks, Izzie. You didn't have to say that and it means a lot.'

'What exactly are you doing?' She stares down at the worktop.

'Soaking the cuttings in room temperature water and then spraying them with an anti-desiccant to help them retain the moisture. Do you want to have a go?'

I show Izzie what to do and then I leave her to it. We work in silence but it's companionable, rather than out of a sense of unease.

When Hayden appears, he looks relieved. 'I wondered what you two were doing. You were gone a long time. I see you've been busy.'

He's glances at Izzie rather nervously and then at me.

'Where were you when we needed a pair of long arms?' Izzie complains and Hayden looks apologetic.

'Sorry. You should have said, I would have come with you.'

'You weren't avoiding us then?' Izzie questions.

'No. That looks like a lot of work.' Poor Hayden, he's desperate for something to say knowing full-well that Izzie is intent on giving him a hard time.

I let her explain the process.

'Well, it smells wonderful. Are these for the dining room, Ria?'

Hayden gives me a brief smile and I nod my head to let him know everything is fine. 'Yes, I thought it would look festive along the top of the dresser unit. Well away from little hands, but all the smells of Christmas, and we have some cinnamon sticks and dried orange slices to hang from the garland.'

'Great. Well, the dining room is still a bit of a work in progress. Frank's brother has just arrived and I'm about to help him set up the speaker system.'

'Hayden, Hayden!'

'I'm in the utility room, Mum.'

Evie pops her head around the door. 'Oh, a full house! Could you possibly show the Hendersons up to The Mountain Maple Suite, please? Two lots of guests have arrived at the same time.'

'No problem.' He turns back around. 'I'll . . . um . . . see you both in a bit.'

When the door swings shut, Izzie looks at me. 'At least second time around he chose someone who cares about him and not just his future potential. Georgina knew a catch when she saw one, and I tried to warn him, but he wouldn't listen.'

Goodness, did Izzie wonder whether I might be after Hayden because he owns a company? Or maybe to help my business along? The important thing is that we haven't fallen out because that would spoil the little bubble of happiness Hayden and I are floating on. I've been honest with her and she's been blatantly honest with me, which I really appreciate. It's a start but we both know that trust is a mutual thing and has to be earned over time.

'Happy Christmas Eve, Ria. Wish you were here, lovely, but I'm sure you're having a great time.'

'Thanks, Mum, same back to you all at your end. I'll do a video call tomorrow, to catch up with everyone.'

'Are you excited about the party tonight?' Although I've spoken to my sister Kate several times, I managed to avoid talking about the developments at this end. How could I, when I've totally ignored her advice? Now Mum is fishing because she can sense something is up. It's difficult because they haven't even met Hayden and I need to think carefully about how to break the news to them.

'Yes, but I'm more relieved that everything got done in

time. It's like an end-of-term party feeling for me.' Argh, I'm trying too hard. I need to bring my enthusiasm down a tad.

'You sound happy, elated, even. And you should be, that was quite a job you had there. The photos you sent made us all envious. We've not had a single snowflake here and the forecast for tomorrow is rain! Anyway, everyone sends their love. We're just getting ready to take the kids out to a nativity play at the local dance and drama centre. Let your hair down tonight, Ria, you more than deserve it and we're counting the days until you're back home.'

'Ah, thanks, Mum, and have a great time this evening. Love to you all and we'll speak tomorrow.'

As I do the finishing touches to my hair, there's a tap on the door and it's Hayden.

'Oh . . .' He lets out a deep sigh when he steps inside. 'I've really missed you today. Our paths have hardly crossed.'

'Don't moan, at least everything is ticking over nicely. All the guests got here ahead of the flurry of snow they're forecasting for tonight and your parents have turned into a real powerhouse of activity. They both like to be busy, don't they?'

'Yes. Fingers crossed now that the new photos are up on the website the bookings will come flooding in, because if they're occupied, they can't argue!'

I point my finger at him, accusingly. 'It's time for you to step back now, Hayden. There's nothing more you can do. Just don't . . .' I falter. How can I say this in the spirit in which it's meant?

'Don't get my hopes up?'

'Exactly.'

'It's too late for that. I have a good feeling. I think it's being around you that makes everything look brighter and more positive.'

He's in a playful mood and that's understandable. It's like we've all weathered a storm and the sun is about to come out. Tonight is a celebration of a real team effort and for Hayden and me, personally, our first steps into the unknown – our future together.

Hayden edges a little closer. 'You're looking very elegant again tonight.'

'You can't kiss me – I've just done my lips. Unless you don't mind everyone knowing what you crept up here to do!'

'I don't creep anywhere,' Hayden says, firmly. 'And tonight, if you get lonely, my room is the one with all the boxes stacked up against the wall. It's at the far end of the corridor, next to the linen cupboard.' Hayden winks at me.

'But my room is beautiful and airy,' I reply, pulling a face.

'And mine is out of earshot of anyone,' he retorts. 'Now the inn is full, who knows what people get up to in the middle of the night?'

I bat my eyelashes at him but he just laughs.

'This cocktail dress isn't too much, is it? I'm not a sparkly party-frock type of woman.'

The long-sleeved, silver-grey jersey fabric drapes beautifully, and with a little ruching on the left-hand side at hip level, I feel comfortable in it. It's the sort of dress you can eat whatever you want in as it's very flattering across the middle.

'It's fabulous, just like you.'

I groan. 'You don't need to trot out the chat-up lines; I'm hooked, remember?' I reach out to move a few strands of hair that have fallen over his eyebrow. 'And you're looking extremely handsome this evening.'

He catches my hand as I'm about to move away, spinning me around on the balls of my feet to catch sight of myself in the long vanity mirror. 'There, don't we make the perfect couple? And thank you for spending time with Izzie and making her feel comfortable here. My father had a quiet word with my cousin, Patrick. He was delighted when Dad asked if he could look out for her, you know, make sure she doesn't end up standing on her own with no one to talk to.'

'Is that your father's attempt at matchmaking?'

'Hardly. He's just trying to make sure everyone is happy. I, too, want Izzie to enjoy herself, and Patrick is an interesting guy. He's in charge of the drinks table tonight. Patrick isn't your average nine-to-five sort; I think they'll find they have a few things in common. Now, are you ready to party?'

'Only if everything is under control. What time is the food arriving?'

'Oh, we've got at least another hour, hour and a half. The van called in this morning to drop off the dishes that will need heating up and those are all on trays ready to pop into the oven. The rest will come on platters, so it's a case of the waiting staff carrying them through and taking the coverings off so people can help themselves.' He stops to gaze down into my eyes for a moment.

'What are you thinking about right now, Hayden?'

'How lucky I am. You pulled it all together despite the problems and if we hadn't had the opportunity to spend this time together, what if—'

I put my finger to his lips. 'We did and that's all that matters. Now let's go and mingle.' Despite my warning, I can't resist placing my lips on his as his hands slide down to my hips and he pulls me even closer.

When I stand back, I start laughing. Hayden peers in the mirror behind me, rubbing at his lower lip. 'It's really not my shade,' he replies, a mischievous look on his face. 'And this stuff is hard to get off!'

I grab a tissue to clean him up. What's going through my mind as I do it, is that not only did I get the job, I got the boss as well.

24

Deck the Halls with Wreaths and Greenery

The entire ground floor is filled with people, as Hayden and I make our way through to the kitchen.

'My, look at the two of you.' Hayden grins and his parents turn around. 'Happy Christmas Eve!'

Tonight, Evie is wearing a black dress with tiny silver sparkles running down in a wave over one shoulder, and Mason looks dashing in a white shirt over a pair of black trousers, with a colourful waistcoat sporting tiny reindeers prancing around.

Usually, Mason has an apron on over his sweatshirt and jeans, and Evie is rushing around looking hot and bothered. This evening, the two newest members of The Inn on the River team are busy refilling trays and ferrying them back and forth to the dining room.

'I was just about to come and find you both.' Evie smiles. 'Can we all pop into the utility room for a moment or two?'

As we follow them, Hayden glances at me cagily. However, sitting on the worktop there's a bottle of champagne cooling in a wine bucket and four glasses awaiting us. Mason hands the bottle to Hayden to pop the cork. Evie grabs two glasses and I watch, half expecting a stream of bubbly liquid to shoot up into the air, but while there is a shower and a bit of a puddle on the floor, most of it goes into the glasses.

'Here you go, Ria. The first one is for you,' Evie says,

the sound of contentment in her voice. 'Mason, you can propose the toast.'

We stand huddled together in the small space between the door and the centre island.

'I think we can judge the success by the sounds we can hear. Tonight, the inn is full and I can safely say that we have succeeded in wowing everyone who has crossed the threshold.' He pauses to clear his throat. 'Not only does it bode well for the future, but a gathering like this is what truly brings this place to life. It reminds me of the good old days, which for the past few years were only recreated over the festive period. That says a lot for the loyal customers and friends who kept coming back despite the fact the inn was looking a little past its prime.'

His voice wavers, and he glances at Evie who immediately takes over.

'To our wonderful, thoughtful and generous son, who miraculously found us a Christmas angel – Ria, you deserve all the success that we know is ahead of you and we can't thank you enough for what you've done. But we're beyond thrilled that you've put a huge grin on Hayden's face. That's a little Christmas present we weren't expecting, but it was top of our wish list. Thank you!' She wraps an arm around my shoulders, giving a gentle squeeze.

Now I'm tearful as we all chink glasses.

'Come on, no tears tonight,' Hayden states firmly. He leans in to kiss my cheek and then steps past me to embrace his mother.

Mason comes forward to give me a hug, as I try not to spill my champagne. When he turns to face his son, I notice that Evie's eyes are bright with tears, too. There's so much emotion when Mason hugs his son, it's a powerful thing to watch.

'Right.' Evie draws in a deep breath, easing back her shoulders. 'It's time to circulate and have fun. The Inn on the River is back in business!'

* * *

Denny's playlist is back-to-back dance songs that seem to be getting almost everyone tapping their feet. Hayden and Frank are determined to get people up dancing ahead of the buffet and it's working.

With the furniture in the sitting room pushed back against the walls, there's a sizeable dance area. Most people are standing around in small groups, gravitating towards the lower end of the dining room and through into the delightfully festive hallway.

The fresh greenery wound between the spindles on the staircase was the perfect finishing touch. With the alcove aglow with the tiny lights from the village scene and a row of candles high up on a shelf running halfway along the entire length of the hallway, the flickering light adds a lovely touch to the ambience.

The general hubbub is quite loud, so Hayden tilts his head close to my ear. 'Frank and I are going to get the children up first, then encourage a few adults to join in. I'll see you in a bit.' When he pulls away he catches my hand, putting it up to his lips and planting a gentle kiss on my fingertips before he lets go.

I watch the two men walk away, then turn to look at Nancy. 'Shall we grab a drink?'

I'm not sure if Nancy knows anyone here, as she lives about an hour's drive away. I'd hate to get pulled into conversation with someone and have her standing around on her own. We make our way over to the refreshments table, which is being manned by Patrick, whom I spoke to briefly at breakfast. To my surprise, Izzie is helping him.

'Hi, Ria. What can we get you?' Patrick is a good-looking guy. He has that rugged, outdoorsy vibe, and that's a natural tan he's sporting so he's been somewhere hot.

'I'll go for a glass of white wine, please. How about you, Nancy? This is Patrick, Hayden's cousin and Izzie—'

As Patrick shakes Nancy's hand, Izzie interrupts my introduction.

'I'm a friend of the family and Evie's goddaughter.' She gives me a fleeting smile.

'I'm . . . um . . . with Frank,' Nancy replies, extending her hand to Izzie.

Patrick holds up the bottle and Nancy nods her head. 'That would be great, thanks.'

'I have no idea what the inn looked like before, Ria, but people are gobsmacked. You deserve a huge pat on the back by the sound of it.' Patrick seems impressed.

'I had a great team, although I won't let on to my crew back in the UK,' I joke.

Izzie passes us our drinks and we head off to stand by one of the windows in the sitting room. 'Is there anyone you know aside from Frank?' I ask.

There are only a dozen people in here and after a quick glance around, Nancy's eyes focus back on the people she can see through the open double doors leading back into the dining room.

'Oh, there's Chad and Lori. They live quite close to my parents' house.'

'We'll head that way, but first we can stop and I'll introduce you to Hayden's cousin Lindy and her fiancé, Seth. I spoke to them briefly this afternoon; they flew in from France yesterday.'

It's a joy to feel the buzz in the air and Frank and Hayden have already succeeded in getting four of the younger children up dancing. Frank is now trying to persuade Alice and John to join them. Frank puts his all into his dancing, although Hayden is a little more restrained, but even I intend to join in later.

After I introduce Nancy to Lindy and Seth, she says France is a place she's always longed to visit and before long they're telling us all about their renovation project. I mean, who isn't enthralled with a tale about the joys of renovating a chateau?

The kitchen door opens and closes several times in quick succession. The waitresses are busy ferrying food across to the buffet table. Then, to my horror, I spot Shelley rearranging the platters. Excusing myself, I go in search of Hayden and find him deep in conversation with Lori.

'Sorry to interrupt. Hayden, I think they need a hand in the kitchen putting out the buffet?'

'Oh, right. I'll catch you in a bit, Lori.'

As we begin to thread our way through the crowded dining room, I put my hand on his arm and he stops to look at me. 'Shelley is here. Maybe you'd better check everything is OK in the kitchen?'

His look is one of disbelief. 'I'm on it.'

I hover, gravitating over to the drinks table to place my empty glass down. Patrick is now managing on his own and several people are hovering around, waiting to be served.

'Do you need a hand?'

'Please. Izzie's gone to collect some more clean glasses.'

It's not easy serving and keeping an eye out for Hayden, but as the minutes tick by, every time the swing door to the kitchen opens, someone else walks through it.

'Patrick,' I half whisper, as I grab a bottle of red wine from behind me. 'Have you seen Evie?'

'She went upstairs about ten minutes ago. Mason wasn't far behind her. I suspect they're taking a moment to catch their breath.'

Suddenly, Hayden appears and heads in my direction, his face grave. He indicates with his hand for me to follow him.

'The rush seems to be over, Patrick. I'd better go and check if Hayden needs any help.'

'Thanks, Ria. Izzie should be back shortly.'

Hayden is already in the hallway and he disappears into the downstairs cloakroom. As I approach the door, I tap on it lightly and he swings it open, grabbing my hand and pulling me inside.

'What's going on? Patrick said your mum went upstairs a little while ago and your father wasn't far behind her.'

Hayden looks shell-shocked. 'I'm in deep trouble.' Hayden

stares at me, looking distraught. 'I asked Shelley when Dad invited her and she said he didn't. I did.'

'You did?' I'm startled by that revelation. What was Hayden thinking?

'You were there, apparently. That day we ate in the bar and grill on our way back from Santa Town.'

I cast my mind back. 'I'm pretty sure you didn't, Hayden.'

He breathes a huge sigh of relief. 'You'll back me up on that?'

Then I twig what the problem is and he's not going to like it. 'You said something about Shelley won't believe how good the inn is looking when she sees it.'

His jaw drops. 'Oh . . . and she smiled at me and said . . . she couldn't wait . . .'

'It wasn't an invitation, Hayden, it was a misunderstanding.' I reach out to squeeze his arm to get him to look at me. 'When you asked her how the catering arrangements were coming along, she said it was all fine and they'd agreed the menu.'

'I took that to mean it was agreed by both of my parents,' he replies, sounding mortified. I can see that's he's angry with himself.

'The two of you were simply talking at cross purposes. It's . . . unfortunate.'

'What should I do?'

This is a major problem, given what I overheard that day when his parents were rowing. Even if Evie is misinterpreting a friendly, Happy New Year peck on the cheek between Mason and Shelley, it's obvious she believes there's still a spark between them. Mason had no idea he'd end up coming back here permanently, so it's not as if he engineered his return. But I know only too well that unexpected feelings can catch you off guard. If that's the case, how do you deal with it?

'As difficult as it's going to be, I think you need to go upstairs right now and explain what happened.'

He blinks in rapid succession; I've never seen him this

nervous before and I don't blame him. 'Oh, Ria. What have I done? Wish me luck.'

And with that, he's gone. I'm left trembling at the thought of the conversation ahead of him.

It seems like hours later, but in reality it's probably no more than twenty minutes until Hayden reappears, his father a couple of paces behind him. Hayden makes a beeline for me as Mason heads over to Patrick to get a drink.

'Are you OK?' I question, trying to ascertain his mood, but I can't read his expression. I think it's more shock, than anything else.

'That was tough but thank goodness I arrived when I did. Mum has now calmed down, but her make-up is a mess. She asked if you'd be kind enough to go up and give her a hand. She can't stay up there all evening, but she's a little shaken.'

'Of course.' I give Hayden a hug and, boy, does he need it. Over his shoulder, I glimpse Mason, who is now talking to Chad and he's as far away from the kitchen as he can get. 'What about Shelley?'

'She has no idea there's a problem. Mum stormed out the minute she saw her. It would be embarrassing all round to ask Shelley to leave now.'

I give him a quick kiss on the cheek and make my way upstairs. Before I knock on the bedroom door, I take a second to steel myself. Evie hasn't just reached out for my help to make herself look presentable. Even if Hayden doesn't realise that, I do.

I tap softly and the door slowly opens.

'Oh, Ria! Thank you for coming up. What an absolute nightmare of a situation.' She blows her nose, her eyes a little puffy from the tears she's shed. 'Tonight is the worst possible night for Mason and me to do this, but I just snapped!'

There's no point pretending I'm not in the loop, so all I can do is add a little weight to what Hayden has said.

'That's understandable, Evie, but I was sitting there at the table that day, so I heard every word. It wasn't an invitation, it really wasn't. But when I think back over what was said, I can see how Shelley might have taken it that way. I really don't think she would have turned up unless she believed she was welcome, Evie.'

I'm feeling tense as I try to gauge her reaction to what I'm saying. She stoops to sit on the padded stool in front of the dressing table, staring into the distance.

'It's not really about Shelley, Ria. That's not why I'm crying.'

'It isn't?' That stops me in my tracks.

'I'll admit that when I clapped eyes on Shelley tonight I did fly off the handle, thinking that Mason had invited her. If he had, though, it would be to force the two of us to make peace.' She gives a half-hearted little chuckle. 'He still has a soft spot for her, that's obvious to me and, yes, I will admit that it makes me very protective of him. Mason is oblivious to the fact that Shelley would have him back in her life in a heartbeat. Not just because she's lonely, but I think she regrets her decision not to follow him to the UK all those years ago.'

I wonder where this is going.

'Please, Ria, take a seat. Oh, how the timing of your coming into Hayden's life is the very thing I've been praying for.'

Oh dear. I swallow hard.

'I've had time to think it through. Mason has proven by the sacrifices he made for me at the inn during the past couple of months that I'm the only love of his life. What I'm going to tell you now is for your ears only, because I know I can trust you. You love Hayden as much as he loves you. I don't know why I didn't see how close the two of you were growing as the days passed. Unfortunately, my head was somewhere else entirely.'

'You've made your decision?'

'Yes. Mason and I talked frankly to each other. I told him that I want the old Mason back, the man who wasn't bogged down by the past but lived for today. His father wouldn't have wanted that either. This was only ever meant to be a place we came for holidays and Christmas to have a fabulous break before getting back to normality. When I challenged him about how he felt, he admitted that running the inn was too much for him, too. This isn't the life for me, or – if the truth be known – for us. I'll fly back to the UK in the spring and, unless he has a change of heart, he said he'll join me shortly afterwards.'

I'm gutted because I know how hard it's going to hit Hayden.

'You will promise not to breathe a word of this to Hayden, won't you, Ria? He'll think I've forgiven Mason and I'll make a show of making up with Shelley. It's not her fault and I'll admit I've been a little jealous knowing someone else is waiting for Mason in the wings. But the past is the past and he really is the one who got away. The irony is that my little fit of pique proved to him just how much he means to me and that changed everything. Anyway, I can't help thinking that even though you succeeded in making the inn beautiful to keep me here, you're not surprised.' Evie is telling me this because she knows I'm the one who is going to be supporting her son through the reality of what's to come.

'You have my word, Evie, and you're right. A part of me hoped it would be enough to keep you here but deep down I sensed that longing in you to go home wasn't going to evaporate.' I heave a weary sigh.

'Ah, my dear! What a treasure you are. Hayden is a lucky man and I like to think you feel that you, too, are a lucky woman. He'll love and cherish you, but he has a stubborn streak, which can throw up surprises. Just look at Mason – the apple doesn't fall far from the tree. My decision is as much about rescuing a truly wonderful man, as it is slipping back into the life we both loved. He was forced into making an impossible choice and I tried hard to support him by coming here. But it was the wrong decision and it's time for us to face the truth because true love can survive anything.'

* * *

I don't know whether to laugh, or cry, but when I return to the party it's in full swing and life goes on.

Shelley and the two waitresses carry through trays of her infamous lobster rolls and there's a little round of applause. As the nearest eatery to the inn, I suspect that a lot of the people here will have eaten at Shelley's Bar and Grill.

Standing in a sea of smiling faces, Hayden suddenly edges up close to me.

'Is everything OK? You were able to sort Mum out?' He looks at me in earnest.

'She's fine. She'll be down shortly. She understands that it was just a case of talking at cross purposes and nothing at all to do with your father.'

Hayden closes his eyes, his chin sinking into his chest as he lets out a huge sigh of relief. 'We came so close to disaster tonight, all because of me. Thank you, Ria, for coming to my rescue.'

My heart feels like it's being squeezed and I can't bear it. I do a half-turn, almost throwing myself into his arms.

'Everything is going to be just fine, Ria,' Hayden whispers into my ear.

Am I having a crisis of conscience right now? Of course I am! That's what his mother wants him to believe and I won't break my promise to her. Evie loves Mason and her son with all her heart and knowing that it hurts *her* deeply to hurt them means it would be wrong of me to interfere. She isn't ready and neither are they, and the timing is in her hands entirely. When the time comes, I'll be there for Hayden every step of the way. For Mason, it was yet another impossible choice – The Inn on the River, or his wife. It looks like he chose Evie and, in my heart, I believe if he carries through on that, he's made the right decision. But this is real life and, as we all know, anything can happen.

Hayden

25

Peace on Earth, Goodwill to All

I'm lying here in bed physically tired, but wide awake. Everyone else is asleep and the silence around me is comforting, I feel a sense of peace and tranquillity. It's been quite an evening and my emotions have gone from elation to rock bottom and back again, as I watched my father witnessing Shelley and my mother exchange a few civilised words.

There's something about Christmas that encourages us to be, perhaps, a little more forgiving. Maybe it's because the holidays give us time to sit back and count our blessings. With my mother and Shelley deciding to put the past behind them, it bodes well for the future.

When, ever so quietly, my door slowly opens, my heart leaps in my chest. The nervous waiting is over.

'If it's not Santa, you have the wrong room,' I whisper in the gloom.

Ria lets out a soft 'Shh!' quickly stepping inside and shutting the door noiselessly behind her.

'It's fine. No one can hear us. We're at the end of the corridor, the suite opposite is at least five feet away on the other side of the landing and the linen cupboard is the other side of us. What took you so long?'

I pull back the duvet and Ria slips into bed next to me.

'It feels a little odd, all this creeping around,' she admits. 'You're right, it does feel a little more private and it is cosy.'

'You mean with the small double bed and the restricted space because of that stack of boxes against the wall?'

Ria gives a chuckle as she eases herself closer. She shivers and I wrap my arms around her, snuggling down under the duvet.

'It's just nice to be together and to feel relaxed about it. Did you think I wasn't coming?'

'I knew you wouldn't be able to resist,' I say under my breath and Ria gives me a playful poke in the ribs. 'What a day we've had, eh?'

'Yes, and some.'

I couldn't help noticing how quiet Ria was after the incident mid-evening, but the events leading up to it were a bit of a roller coaster. Even I'm still reeling from it. I can't believe it ended on a positive note and my father was simply relieved, as I'm sure he was fearing the worst. Family, friends and guests had no idea what was going on and the party was, thankfully, a huge success. There was a lot riding on tonight and a full-blown argument over a simple misunderstanding would have spoilt the evening for everyone.

'This time next year we'll have the perfect Christmas, Ria, I promise you. It might involve more than one celebration to make sure we spend time with both families, but no drama and no creeping around.' Ria wriggles even closer. 'And you know me well enough by now to understand that when I make a promise, I keep it.'

Even so, there's a hint of sadness emanating out of her and I realise that she's missing her family. My mind begins to formulate the plan. It would be awesome for us all to gather here for the festive holidays next year but that's too much to hope for. However, we'll sort something out. Two Christmases mean double the enjoyment.

I reach under my pillow and pull out a little box wrapped with a bow.

'It's well past midnight, so I think you're allowed to open this now. Merry Christmas, Ria.'

I push up on my elbow, grabbing my phone to shine a light so Ria can see what she's doing. The surprise on her face makes my heart flutter. 'But I didn't bring any presents with me,' she bemoans. 'This is unfair.'

'You don't give to receive. At least, that's what my mother always says. Open it.'

Ria eases herself up the bed a little. I don't think she'll be cross with me when she sees what I've bought her.

As she unties the bow then lifts off the lid, her breath catches in her throat. 'Oh, Hayden. A bracelet. It's beautiful.'

'I know you like natural things and there's a very talented young woman in town who makes bespoke jewellery. It's silver, which she said brings balance back into your life, and the stone is citrine. That's supposed to promote and manifest success. I can't think of anyone more deserving of it than you.'

Ria holds the bracelet in her hand, closing her fingers around it before throwing her arms around my shoulders.

'I love you, Hayden. And I'm here for you, always.'

I really didn't mean to make her cry but I meant what I said. Next year will be the best Christmas ever!

'Merry Christmas, everyone! I hope you're all having a great time,' Ria says with great enthusiasm. I'm doing my best to make sure I'm not in view in case she changes her mind about the big reveal.

It's daunting watching her, as even from this angle the screen is just a sea of faces staring excitedly at her.

'You missed the nativity play, Aunty Ria!' a little lad calls out.

'I know and I'm sorry, Ben. I'll be home soon, I promise, and we'll have some family time together.'

'Yes, it's going to be a wonderful New Year's Eve celebration and we're kicking it off with a second Christmas lunch in Ria's honour.'

I'm guessing that's her mum. Ria reaches out, yanking on my arm.

'I can't wait. I also have a little news. I think it's time I introduced you to Hayden, a . . . friend of mine.'

I lean in, putting up my hand in acknowledgement and feeling decidedly awkward. There's no reaction. I told her this wasn't a good idea.

'Hi, Ria's family.' Ria's family? That's the best I could come up with? I sound pathetic.

'Is Hayden your boyfriend?' an older boy pipes up. He's, I don't know . . . seven, or eight maybe? From what Ria has told me, I'm guessing he's probably one of Ria's eldest brother's sons.

'Yes, Harry. And he loves playing board games.'

'Can he come to the New Year's Eve party, Aunty Ria?'

'Sadly, no. Hayden will still be here in the White Mountains. But when he does fly back in January, we'll have a special party as he can't wait to meet you all.'

I plaster on a smile to mask my nerves. Ria turns her head, giving me an encouraging wink, but I can see a look of general bewilderment on some of the adults' faces.

'Oh . . . that's wonderful news, lovely!' Her mum fills the silence. 'And how did the relaunch party go at the inn last night, um . . . Hayden?'

I draw in a deep breath before I answer. 'It was a huge success and everyone had a great time. The new-look interior blew them all away.'

'That's heartening to hear.' Ria's mother – Viv – replies, looking a tad bewildered.

The silence is deafening.

'And guess what, kids?' Ria continues.

There's an ominous hush.

'It's snowing here. Do you want to see?'

Ria hands me her phone and I take it over to the window.

'Can you see the flakes, they're quite big. In the background is a huge mountain range. And if I tilt the screen downwards, somewhere beneath that wide expanse of white snow there's a river.'

There are a few 'oohs' and 'ahhs' which is more reassuring.

'How big is the inn?' The children are really getting into this now.

'It's pretty big. It has eleven bedrooms, most of which are suites.'

I eagerly hand the phone back to Ria.

'It's a hotel?'

'Sort of, Ben. It's called The Inn on the River.'

Ben must be Harry's younger brother. I'm starting to put names to faces now. I think.

'I wish we had snow,' Harry declares.

'Ah, wait and see what January brings. Anyway, it's just after nine in the morning here so if I add on five hours, I'm guessing that things need stirring in the kitchen. You'll be sitting down to eat shortly. Have a wonderful Christmas lunch and we're sending love to you all!'

Ria kicks me with her foot as my attention has wandered.

'Merry Christmas!' we say in tandem.

We're met with a whole chorus of different greetings in return and this time I wrap my arm around Ria's shoulders and give a confident wave. When the screen finally goes blank, I let out an agonising 'Uhh.'

'You did just fine,' Ria confirms, rewarding me with a kiss. 'I know it was difficult, but believe me, if I hadn't said something soon, I'd have faced a myriad of questions anyway. I think my sister Kate has already sussed out the reason I've been avoiding talking to her.'

'Did you talk to her about me?'

Ria looks at me rather guiltily. 'I didn't say much but I went against her advice to keep this strictly business.'

'Oh, I see. It wasn't quite as simple as that, though, was it? Your phone is pinging . . . and again . . . and again.'

'I know.' She waves her hand in the air dismissively. 'It'll be my siblings demanding to know more, but it's Christmas Day and Mum will be eager to get them seated

around the table, so it can wait. The deed has been done.'
She sounds pleased with herself and that's good enough
for me.

'It's time to lend a hand downstairs. If you can help my
mother to set out the buffet breakfast, my father and I can
crack on with prepping Christmas dinner in between flipping
pancakes and waffles.'

The sound of children laughing, as they run along the
landing, indicates there's already some movement.

'Frank – I mean, Santa – will be here in a bit but he'll go
straight to Santa's Retreat with Nancy in tow. They'll get the
fire going to warm it up and I'll carry the sacks of presents
over in a bit. Alice and John collected them from the various
parents yesterday and Mum always wraps up a few things
for each child.'

Ria gives a soft, 'Aah.'

'Frank and Nancy also offered to do the nature walk
afterwards for those who want to take part. It'll no doubt
end up with a snowball fight. Things are really beginning
to fall into place quite nicely, aren't they?'

I grasp Ria's hand and her eyes are drawn to her bracelet.
'I love it, Hayden, I really do. And the thought you put into
it, makes it even more special.'

'Time was short, but I just wanted to give you a little
something to mark our first Christmas together. I love you,
Ria, and this is just the start for us. Even though your family
didn't seem too impressed when my face appeared on the
screen.'

She reaches out to touch my cheek. 'Only my dad will give
you a hard time, the others will be a pushover.'

Great. Now she tells me. That's a challenge for the new
year, then.

The awesome thing about Christmas Day at The Inn on
the River is that no one around the table is a stranger.
Even the surprise newcomer to the inn, Izzie, is already

at home and making plans with Patrick to head off for a couple of days' skiing.

What time Ria and I have left together is going to be filled with fun and laughter. I reach out to straighten her party hat. It's cosy with twenty-three adults and eight children to seat, but we managed it.

Ria rolls her eyes. 'I obviously wasn't destined to wear a crown,' she laughs. 'It's a pity Frank and Nancy couldn't stay.'

'I know, but his middle brother is cooking for them all this year and it's the first time they've met Nancy. Naturally, he's anxious about it, even though I assured him it'll be fine. You know what Frank's like, he doesn't say a lot. Oh, he's the life and soul of a party, and he'll happily joke around, but that's about it.'

'I don't think anyone will replace Cassie in Frank's heart,' Ria remarks, 'but that doesn't stop him from having a deep and meaningful relationship with someone else, does it?'

I notice a fleeting hint of concern in her eyes.

'No, and to be honest, Cassie would hate the thought of him spending so much time on his own. Frank is good at making excuses because he can't bear being fussed over. He likes to be doing things for other people, it's just the way he is.'

'I think they'll be good company for each other, even if they don't end up living under the same roof.'

It's funny, but Ria's thoughts mirror my own. 'Who knows what might develop. If I hadn't spent time under the same roof as you, we might never have . . . scratch that, we would have, for sure.'

That makes her laugh and she looks around hesitantly, hoping no one will notice how flushed she's suddenly looking. 'Right time, right place, even though I didn't think so at first.'

I guess last night sealed the deal. It's the best Christmas present anyone has ever given me.

Ria gives me a pointed look. 'Why are you chuckling to yourself?'

'I was just thinking about how generous Santa is, even when his presents aren't gift-wrapped.'

She shakes her head at me, as my father starts singing 'Good King Wenceslas' and before long virtually everyone joins in, even if they don't know all the words.

Boxing Day isn't a holiday in its own right in the States, but a lot of people spend it recovering from the excesses of Christmas Day. At the inn it's a day of activities and once breakfast is over my parents, too, hang up their aprons. There's the option of a couple of hours spent snowshoeing, with an experienced guide who knows most of the trails like the back of his hand. Then there's birdwatching, which is fun for the kids and adults alike, the additional benefit being it's easier on the leg muscles as it's more of a meander than a hike.

'Right, the minibuses are here, everyone,' I call out, and people come at me from all directions. 'The red bus is for the snowshoeing trek and the blue one for birdwatching at the reservoir. We're due to meet back at the inn by five at the latest. That gives us two hours before the mini coach arrives to take us all to Ralph's Country Kitchen for dinner. Have fun!'

As everyone streams out through the door, my father calls out, 'Enjoy yourselves.'

Ria hurries over to me. 'I'm ready to go.'

'Will you lock up, Dad?'

'Yep. I'll just grab my gloves. Evie's already outside. I won't be a minute.'

As Ria and I saunter over to the blue bus, she pulls a face. 'It's my last day. In one way it feels like I've been here for such a long time, and yet in another, I don't quite know where the time went.'

'I'm not surprised, it's been pretty hectic. And emotional.

I wish I was flying back with you, but I'm needed here. I'll be counting the days until I can hold you in my arms again, Ria.'

'Me, too, Hayden. Me, too.'

It's our last night together. After being around each other anywhere up to fourteen hours a day for the last twenty-two consecutive days, it's going to be hard to say goodbye to Ria at the airport tomorrow.

'Don't frown,' she says, snuggling into me.

'Your room isn't just bigger and better than mine,' I complain, 'but this bed is so comfortable that my muscles aren't even complaining.'

'It's your fault for leaving the others to it at the reservoir and getting adventurous. It was fun in among the trees though, just hard on the calf muscles.'

I start laughing. 'Coming down was a bit easier in places.'

'That's so mean of you!' Ria points out.

'Hey, you slid, that's all. For all I know you did it on purpose. I was quite impressed when you landed on your feet.'

'The problem is that it wasn't planned and it definitely wasn't the most elegant way to tackle quite a steep slope.'

'If it weren't for the high-pitched scream, I probably wouldn't have twigged. You are OK, though, aren't you?'

'I bounce well.' Then she sighs. 'I've had an amazing time, Hayden, you know that, don't you? I'm not just talking about what happened between us, but being made to feel a part of everything.'

'The inn seems to have that effect on people, for some reason.'

'It's a sprawling house, but it also feels homely when you step inside. You can feel it's been loved and a lot of . . .' She stops for a moment to yawn and I can hear the tiredness in her voice now. 'A lot of happy memories have been made here. I like the thought of that.'

As we wriggle down the bed, my arms are still wrapped around her. Every second feels so precious now and it's hard to envisage being here without her by my side.

'Tomorrow night this bed will be all yours,' she murmurs, her eyes beginning to close.

'But I'd rather you were in it with me,' I whisper, softly into her hair.

This Christmas has changed my life forever and I didn't even see it coming.

Thursday, 2nd February

26

The Final Chapter

Ria has her back to me; she's gazing out over the rooftops at the Oxfordshire countryside stretching far into the distance. Christmas and New Year seem like an eternity ago but, oh, how I wish I could turn back the clock.

'This view is amazing,' she mutters. 'You seem a little preoccupied. There's nothing wrong, is there?'

'Come and sit down, I've poured us both a glass of wine.' My tone reflects my mood as it's time to break the news. I'm in total shock and my emotions are in free fall to the extent that I'm feeling numb.

'It's a bit early, isn't it?' Ria glances at the clock. It's only just after four in the afternoon.

When I rang and asked her to drop everything and come straight over, I tried to sound upbeat, as if I was simply missing her – as I do, all the time when we're not together. But as I'm still trying to assimilate what is a devastating blow, repeating it means it's real and it's going to sting.

'I think you'll be glad of it when you hear what I have to say.'

Ria's face is expressionless as she sinks down onto the sofa next to me.

'My parents are planning on returning to the UK for good.'

Her face visibly pales. 'Together?'

She looks like she's holding her breath as I nod my head. 'I think we both knew everything was in the balance, even though it was looking so promising. I'd hoped . . . well, hope is one thing, reality another.'

Ria chews her lip. 'It's good news in one way, Hayden. At least they're not going their separate ways.' She reaches out to grab the glass in front of her, taking a hefty swig.

Even the words of encouragement that roll off her tongue sound as empty and forlorn as her expression. We're both gutted.

'They rang about an hour ago. Mum asked if I was sitting down and I thought she was joking. I could tell by their faces something was up, but not this.'

She puts the glass down on the coffee table and moves closer, reaching out to clasp my hand.

'It's hard to take in, Hayden.' The anguish in her voice is real because she knows how tough this is for us all. 'What about the inn?'

'A realtor is going in tomorrow to talk through the process of putting the inn up for sale.'

'How do you feel about that?'

'Truthfully?'

She gives me a look of encouragement.

'Angry with my mother for what she's doing.'

Ria clutches my hand a little tighter. 'Which is?'

I turn to look at her, surprised she's even asking that question. 'Forcing my father to choose. It'll end up breaking his heart, I know it. How can she say she loves him when she's given him an ultimatum?'

Ria looks flustered. 'What if . . .' She pauses, her eyes searching mine. 'Have you considered that running the inn is simply too much for them?'

'Yes, but with the bookings slowly but surely coming in since the website was updated, they'll be able to employ all the extra help they need. I thought that was the whole point. My mother will just restart her business again when she gets back to the UK, but what will my father do? And their house is rented out, so they'll have to find somewhere to stay until the lease is up. It's going to be such an upheaval.' I realise I'm venting and that's unfair of me. Ria, too, must be reeling.

We lie back, snuggling up on the sofa for comfort until the light fades. Eventually, I ease myself up to turn on the sidelights.

'What hurts the most, Hayden?'

'It's not just a business, Ria, the inn has always played an integral role in our lives. How can they let it go just like that? I don't understand.' I turn to stare blindly out the window.

'Please hear me out, Hayden, even though I know this is difficult to talk about. I understand your anger and the huge sense of loss that's hitting you right now. What's important is that your parents are happy and, clearly, they're both on board with the decision that's been made. So this is about *you*, not them – can't you see that?' She draws in a deep breath, before slowly expelling it. 'When your granddad died you didn't have a chance to say goodbye. Not properly. When we were there I don't know if you were even aware of what you said to me one day, but it almost broke my heart.'

I look back at her questioningly.

'You said that you felt he was still there. To you he wasn't . . . gone. That means you haven't grieved; you haven't been through the process of saying goodbye. And that's what you're having to face now that your parents are going to sell the inn, isn't it?'

Granddad is there with Grandma, he'll always . . . I feel choked, unable to find my voice and Ria walks over to throw her arms around me. It's the end of an era, the end of a way of life that I hold dear and always will. It's like someone has plunged a dagger into my heart at a time when I've finally found the woman I was meant to be with. Life certainly gives but it also takes away.

Friday, 3rd March

27

Life Is All About the Choices We Make

In hindsight, the wake-up call was when I realised that, as the days passed, Ria was wearing a frown more often than she was wearing a smile. Admittedly, February was a tough month all round and she kept telling me that things would get better. Problems seemed to be coming at me from all angles and it was taking a toll. I felt haggard and helpless. So much so, that two days ago I gave in and told Liam I was taking a couple of days off work, thinking I had some sort of flu.

Ria was in London at the time, attending a trade show and I did my best to hide how I was feeling from her as she wasn't due back until tomorrow. However, yesterday morning the doorbell rang and when I swung the door open she was standing there, a suitcase in her hand. It was an epic moment.

'Don't worry, Hayden,' she'd said as she stepped into my arms. 'It's time to clear our heads and decide what's important. In my case, that's you.'

'This feels wonderfully decadent, even though I'm supposed to be combing through the latest trends in fabrics.' Ria grins at me. She picks another strawberry off the plate she has perilously balanced on her knees. 'Now this is exactly how life decisions should be made, Hayden. You once said that taking a duvet day was defeatist and I disagreed with you. I still do.'

In our case it's two days, but who's counting. My eyes take in her bed-hair and the baggy cotton T-shirt with *sleepyhead* emblazoned across it, as she leans back against the headboard.

315

'You're right. But it would be better if one of us could be bothered to get up and make some pancakes,' I hint.

'Maybe later. I think we should continue with the brainstorming, or do you think we've already identified the salient points?'

I slide the notepad closer to her, then reach out for a couple of strawberries while she studies it.

'Well, your parents do need help and I know it's affecting us all. Having made their decision, your father is dragging his feet getting things moving. I notice that he's suspended all bookings on the website.'

'He has? That's madness if he wants to sell it as a going concern. I need to get them both on a call and find out what's happening. Continue.'

'And, yes—' she gives me an apologetic smile '—we do need to arrange an engagement party to celebrate you getting down on one knee and giving me this beautiful ring.' Ria flashes her bejewelled finger at me. 'But we're not exactly in a position to get everyone together, are we? I've been so busy and you've not been quite yourself. However, Chad and Lori's construction work is about to start and you know what that means. Lori is anxious as she wants everything to go smoothly.'

We look at each other and Ria pulls a face.

'You'll be flying off to the White Mountains?'

She nods her head. 'Sorry, I know the timing is awful. I'll try to convince Lori I can manage this with daily video updates, but if she asks me to drop everything, I will. I really don't want to leave you on your own, though, not right now. You're not sick, you're mentally and physically exhausted, Hayden.'

'At least if you stay at the inn you can be my eyes and ears. I only know what my parents are prepared to tell me; I can't gauge the mood between them.'

I put my head back, closing my eyes for a second, hoping to put a halt to the thoughts whirling around inside my head. I guess the last day or so has driven me to breaking point.

'You know, Ria, I did a lot of thinking yesterday. When I flew back to the UK, all I could think about was meeting your family and planning our future. I was excited and optimistic. We made a good start and since then it's been all work, worry and stress, hasn't it?'

I can see the frustration etched on Ria's face but she's trying hard to hide it for my sake. 'Spring is just around the corner, Hayden. Everything will seem brighter once we get the next couple of weeks out the way.'

It's a concern when even Ria is struggling for something positive to say to lift my spirits.

'Radical change is the result of courageous actions,' I mutter. 'Either I'm having an epiphany, or I might have read that somewhere a long, long time ago.'

Ria licks her fingertips, putting the empty plate down on the bedside table.

'Tell me what you're really thinking, Hayden.' She plumps up the pillows, adjusting her position so we're making direct eye contact.

Something inside of me lights up. 'Do you ever feel that life is controlling us, Ria, when it should be the other way around?'

I'm on the cusp of something . . . I just don't know what. Going crazy? Or maybe trying to talk Ria into taking a month off work, so I can whisk her away to some exotic place to escape the stark reality of life.

I will admit that my thoughts are a little irrational at the moment.

Ria is staring at me; I'm scaring her and I give an apologetic smile. I'm about to suggest she ignores me, when her expression changes.

'If we let it, life is always going to be like this, Hayden. There's one reason after another to delay the things we want to do, simply to get through the trials each new day presents us with.'

'Yes,' I sigh, wearily. 'I couldn't have put it better myself.'

'Are you feeling brave?' she asks. I can see it's a serious question.

'With you by my side, Ria, as brave as I need to be.'

'Then let's be honest with each other about what really matters. I'll go first.'

She isn't taking this lightly and I wait a few moments, my eyes taking in every little detail of the face I often see in my dreams. When I am able to get to sleep, that is.

'*Us*, we're the top of my list. I want us to be happy, Hayden, and make that a priority. It doesn't matter where we live as long as we're together. After that, doing something I enjoy that also allows me to fit in time with my family and friends.'

That brings me up with a sharp jolt. 'What about your aim to grow your team?'

I watch as she catches her bottom lip between her teeth, a sure sign she's anxious.

'If it helps to make our life easier, I'll consider working for Peter. It would be less pressure, a guaranteed income every month and better hours than I work now. I could do worse.'

'You'd give up your dream for me, I mean – *us*?'

She blinks, seemingly surprised. 'Of course I would. Now it's your turn and be brutally honest, Hayden.'

'Why wouldn't I be honest?'

Ria looks down at her hands, her eyelashes dark against her pale cheeks. 'Maybe a full-blown relationship isn't easy to accommodate right now, given everything else going on around you.'

Within moments, I'm up on my knees, half lifting her off the bed to clasp her to me.

'You mean everything to me, Ria. Everything. It's time to think outside the box and create the sort of life that will put a beaming smile back on that beautiful face of yours!'

Thursday, 1st June

28

The End Signals a New Beginning

'Welcome home, it's so good to see you both. This calls for a group hug!' My mother walks toward us and we huddle together in the hallway of The Inn on the River. 'Mason, they're here.'

'Come on through to the kitchen. What a landmark day!'

You know the old saying *Be careful what you wish for*? Well, I thought I got my wish – a successful business with huge potential. But after spending time at the inn, working side by side with Ria last Christmas, I didn't have the same enthusiasm about anything when I returned home. Only a sense of disappointment for the time we were spending apart. And then when my parents said they were selling up, it seemed that nothing in my life made sense anymore.

The day I had my epiphany was the day I realised I wanted something different out of life. The dream has changed. And the greatest wonder of all was when Ria said nothing mattered to her, as long as we were together.

After that, everything slotted into place. And now, here we are.

My father comes barrelling through the door, a huge smile on his face. 'At last! It's so good to see you both and, my, don't you look well!'

He gives Ria a lingering hug and then turns to me. 'And you look happy, my son.' His hug is emotional, as I pat him firmly on the back.

'Did you sleep well?' my mother asks, as she begins filling the coffee mugs she had lined up and ready to go.

'We were both shattered when we got off the plane,' I admit. 'I don't think I would have been safe driving, as the past few days have been totally exhausting. We were asleep by nine. Still, we awoke refreshed and we were up early to get to Chad and Lori's in time.'

'How did it go?' My parents both turn to look at Ria.

'Very well indeed. The open-plan layout is amazing, isn't it, Hayden?'

'Yes. They're delighted with it.'

Ria is in her element. 'The fitted kitchen is almost finished and the next step is to source the furniture.'

My father takes the tray from my mother, to carry it over to the table. The eye contact between them warms my heart. It's like turning back the clock and it's clear to see that a huge weight has been lifted from their shoulders.

'Are you guys all packed and ready to go?' Ria checks.

'We are. Our tenants moved out of the old house last week and we'll be doing a bit of painting and decorating before we get our things out of storage, won't we, honey?'

My mother gives him a beaming smile.

'It'll be a mini makeover, Evie. Thankfully, a more manageable project than the inn, but at least we'll know what we're doing the second time around.' He laughs. 'And with Ria's plan for the colour scheme and furnishings all in hand, by the time we fly back to the inn on the first of September, everything at home will be exactly as we want it.'

When it came down to it, none of us had the heart to walk away from the inn and that included Mum and Ria. Together we came up with a way of keeping Granddad's dream alive while also ensuring we all get quality time here with family and friends. Life isn't solely about work, and Izzie was right about that. Ironically, she'll be backpacking with Patrick and they might not make it here this Christmas. But, for the Reynolds family, one single decision changed our lives going forward for the better.

My father opens his new laptop, bringing up the scheduler and turning it around so we can all see the programme running through to the end of November.

'That's looking pretty healthy, Dad. You and Nancy have been busy.' I glance at Ria and the look we exchange is one of relief.

None of us really knew if our crazy idea was going to work, and it involved my parents finding a capable manager. When Frank suggested Nancy, it was the perfect solution.

'You guys are here for the next three months.' He stabs his finger at the coloured boxes on the screen. 'There are six week-long bookings in total. Three are corporate hirings, then there's the business course Hayden is running and two Interior Design 101 workshops Ria will be holding. All three are fully subscribed and we now have a waiting list of interested people ready for next year.'

Ria looks across at me nervously, but we're going to be just fine.

My father turns to my mother to take over. 'Nancy has the housekeeping team under control and will make herself available while the attendees are here,' she confirms. 'Then you'll hand back to us for September and October. Izzie and I are running three wellness retreats and there are four corporate hires. Then we fly back to the UK for a month and will return on the first of December ready to prep for the biggest Christmas celebration ever!'

I notice my mother and Ria beaming at each other because I'm confident that the preparations are already well advanced.

'Well done pulling all that together, that's amazing in such a short space of time. I bet the two . . . sorry, three of you, now that Nancy is on board, haven't stopped.'

Ironically, neither of my parents look at all stressed.

'We've had a lot of help. Aside from the business contacts you gave us, Hayden, Lori has gone out of her way to advertise the new venture to everyone she knows,' my mother explains.

'Which is why Ria's workshops were oversubscribed. Then Lori roped in Chad and he gave us some great leads that turned into bookings. Two team-building events and an in-house training seminar.'

'Did any of my contacts come up trumps?'

'Yes, two of them. One next month, through a Mr Eddie Kaminsky, and another in October.'

'Ah, I thought Eddie might go for it. He's in manufacturing. It's a networking meet-up for their overseas agents. Just a bit of a jolly really, but he said it usually sparks a nice little uptick in sales.'

'Who's covering November?' Ria checks. 'It looks like there are a couple of things already booked in.'

'Yes, two one-week courses making Christmas decorations and festive candles. Frank and Nancy have offered to provide cover. His brother Denny will stay at the farmhouse while they're here.'

'I see that you managed to get the new cabin erected in good time. It looks great nestled among the trees,' I remark.

'It's going to be a fabulous conference-cum-workshop space. It'll come alive once the two of you get it kitted out,' my mother emphasises. 'Mason has some paperwork and a list of delivery dates for the furniture Ria selected.'

We all sit back contentedly, just gazing around at each other as the reality of what we've managed to achieve finally kicks in.

'We did it, guys,' my father states, proudly, raising his coffee cup in the air and we all follow his example. 'Here's to us! When they say you can't have your cake and eat it, our extended team are about to prove that old adage wrong.'

'The White Pine Suite is my favourite. I love this view,' Ria reflects, as she stands gazing out the window. 'And it's so good to be back, Hayden. I can't wait to rediscover the White Mountains without the snow. It was lovely, but it must be at least seventy degrees out there today. The scenery is beautiful in a totally different way.'

I saunter up to place my arms around her.

'None of this would have been possible if you and Mum hadn't put your heads together. She could see that my father was going to be miserable if he left the inn and miserable if he stayed on here all alone.'

Ria turns on the balls of her feet to face me. 'And it would have broken your heart, too, Hayden. Now, look at us! I know I'll be spending some time at Lori's. And we'll both be busy preparing to wow our respective attendees when we stand in front of them, but what are we going to do with all that downtime?' She grins up at me and her eyes shine so brightly I'm simply dazzled.

'Walk, talk, visit Shelley's. Just generally enjoy life until we go back to the UK for a short while. And then, before we know it, the Christmas holidays will be on the horizon and this year it's going to be wild!'

Ria puts a hand up to her face, her eyes opening wide. 'I know . . . is it sheer madness, planning a Christmas wedding here at the inn? But it makes up for the fact that we ended up missing out on an engagement party. Now I'm imagining my noisy lot adding to the general hubbub of your family and friends at the inn. How will we fit them all in? I mean, some of Jackson's regulars book a whole year in advance, so that's three rooms taken.'

'It's not a problem,' I state firmly, planting a kiss on the tip of her nose. 'Frank has that big old farmhouse and Nancy is already sowing the seed about using some of the bedrooms.'

'You've been colluding with Nancy behind everyone's back?'

'This is just between you and me, Ria. She's been calling me now and then to let me know how my parents are doing, that's all. It's one thing to come up with a radical idea, another to put it into practice. One thing Nancy did point out is that Frank's place is badly in need of a makeover.'

Ria rolls her eyes. 'I guess I won't have quite so much time on my hands as I thought, then.'

I chuckle. 'Maybe not. Oh, and it looks like Nancy and my father are keen to work out everyone's availability for next year so he can begin taking bookings. You and I had better synch our diaries.'

'Is that a problem for you? I thought Liam was happy having a deputy to ease his workload on your extended trips to the White Mountains.'

'Oh, he's more than happy to spread his wings. He says he could easily run the place without me and I'd say that's a pretty fair statement. I trained him well.'

'Gosh, how you've changed! It's really not a problem for me now that I'm back to taking on one project at a time while I develop the model for my new interior design workshops.'

'Hmm . . . the thing is, what if something unexpected crops up?'

'Like what?' Ria shrugs her shoulders.

'Starting a family?'

Ria breaks out into a huge smile. 'Oh. Right. Goodness, I'm not sure I'm ready. You sound like you are. This is all Kate's fault, walking around glowing as the big day approaches.'

'I just wanted to put it out there, even though I appreciate that planning a wedding is a job in itself.'

Ria turns back around to take in her favourite view. As she leans into me, I place my arms around her waist, lightly resting my chin on top of her head.

I let out a sigh of complete and utter satisfaction as I murmur, 'There you go, Grandma and Granddad. All of this is only possible because of you. And now Ria and I are so happy to think of the inn as our home from home.'

Suddenly, I feel a slight pressure on my left shoulder and I instinctively turn my head but, of course, there's no one there. It's simply my imagination, but just in case it isn't, I raise a grateful smile. I'm blessed to have a life I could never even have dreamt of and if it's taught me one thing, it's that with the right person by your side anything is possible.

Acknowledgements

A virtual hug to my wonderful editorial team on this project and special thanks go to editorial director Cara Chimirri, for taking the story to the next level. And thanks to managing editor Anna Perkins, for keeping me on track.

Not forgetting the other incredible driving forces behind the Embla team – because our lives are built on stories, and each book does matter! It's a thrill to be a part of it.

Grateful thanks also go to my wonderful agent, Sara Keane, for her sterling advice, support and all those long phone calls putting the world to rights. It's been an amazing journey since the day we first met, and your friendship means so much to me.

To my wonderful husband, Lawrence – always there for me and the other half of team Lucy – you truly are my rock! It was a memorable holiday in the White Mountains that inspired this story and the people we met, the places we visited, are memories we will never forget.

There are so many family members and long-term friends who understand that my passion to write is all-consuming. They forgive me for the long silences and when we next catch up, it's as if I haven't been absent at all.

Publishing a new book means that there is an even longer list of people to thank for publicising it. The amazing kindness of my lovely author friends, readers and reviewers is truly humbling. You continue to delight, amaze and astound me with your generosity and support.

Without your kindness in spreading the word about my latest release and your wonderful reviews to entice people to click and download, I wouldn't be able to indulge myself in my guilty pleasure – writing.

Wishing everyone peace, love and happiness.
Lucy x

Lucy Coleman

Lucy Coleman always knew that one day she would write, but first life took her on a wonderful journey of self-discovery for which she is very grateful.

Family life and two very diverse careers later, she now spends most days glued to a keyboard, which she refers to as her personal quality time.

'It's only when you know who you are that you truly understand what makes you happy! Writing about love, life and relationships – set in wonderful locations – makes me leap out of bed every morning!'

About Embla Books

Embla Books is a digital-first publisher of standout commercial adult fiction. Passionate about storytelling, the team at Embla publish books that will make you 'laugh, love, look over your shoulder and lose sleep'. Launched by Bonnier Books UK in 2021, the imprint is named after the first woman from the creation myth in Norse mythology, who was carved by the gods from a tree trunk found on the seashore – an image of the kind of creative work and crafting that writers do, and a symbol of how stories shape our lives.

Find out about some of our other books and stay in touch:

Twitter, Facebook, Instagram: @emblabooks
Newsletter: https://bit.ly/emblanewsletter